RIFT

WHY READERS LOVE RIFT

Wow! The world building, the magic, the banter, the suspense! This book had everything I wanted. I devoured this story so quickly! I absolutely loved this story so much!

— @BOOKSCOFFEELOVER

If you crave romantasy with lush worldbuilding, found family for days, sisters who'd die for each other, and a love interest who ruins you in the best way, Rift needs to be your next read.

— @TALESWITHATTICUS

I've finally come to the conclusion that there is no review that I could write that would give this book the credit that it deserves.

— @FOSTERINGWANDER

RIFT
THE COURTS BETWEEN
BOOK ONE

CB WOODS

*To the daughters who burn
the bridges their mothers built*

*To the mothers who watch
the flames in reverent silence*

May the embers keep you both warm

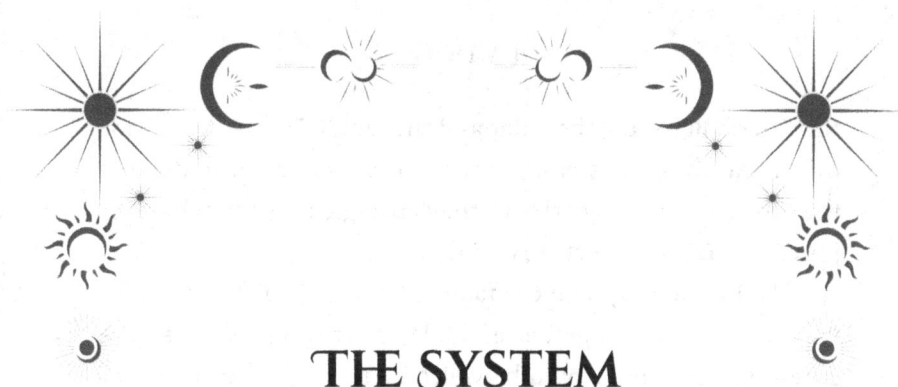

THE SYSTEM

The System falls into three realms.

The Divine Courts, the Court Above and the Court Below, welcome those who leave their mortal timelines. While all manner of creature Descends to the Court Below, only the Souls willing to embrace their Shadows can unify themselves and Ascend to the Court Above.

The Living Courts are home to nine celestial courts, each with their own unique cultures, species, monarchies, and mythology. They devote themselves to their namesakes, the Old Gods in the Court Above.

The Inner Courts are comprised of the Mercurian, Venusian, Earthen, and Maritan Courts.

The Outer Courts include the Jovian, Saturnian, Neptunian, Urasian, and Plutonian Courts.

For now.

There are rumors the Outer Courts are considering removing Pluto from their alliance in light of recent struggles with their resources.

Resting in the mist between the Divine and the Living are

the Courts Between, the Solar and the Lunar Courts. At war for millennia, these mysterious courts of demigods have divided the Living Courts' loyalties as they struggle to grasp whatever power the Divine Courts toss at their feet.

The Rift, a cosmic river made of light and colored threads, weaves the courts together and allows for travel between the gates–whether one would be welcome through that gate is at each monarch's discretion.

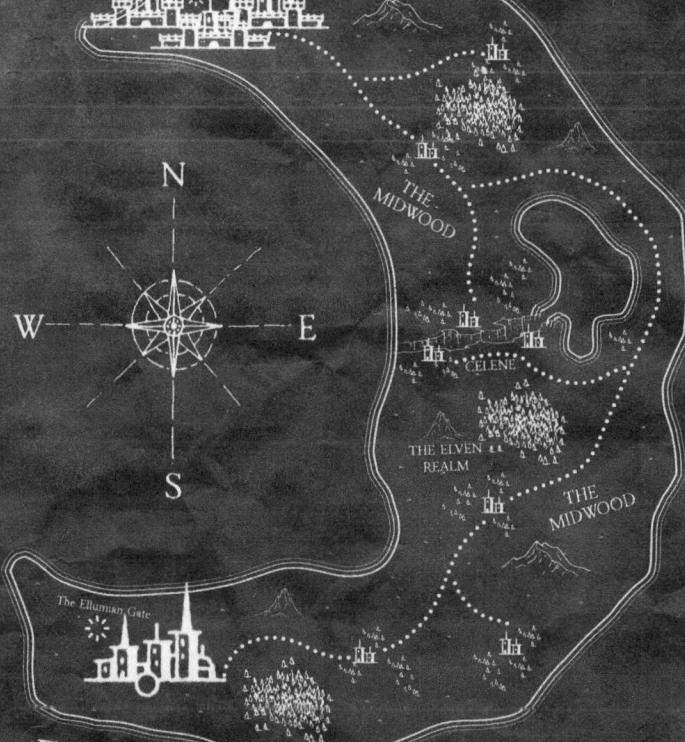

LUNARIA

The Lunar Gate

N

W   E

S

THE MIDWOOD

CELENE

THE ELVEN REALM

THE MIDWOOD

The Elluman Gate

ELLUME

THE
LUNAR
COURT

ONE

The clearing of a throat pulled Astra out of a spiraling thought.

"Sorry," she mumbled, her hands folding the book in her lap. She smoothed the silk of her skirt over her long legs, attempting to shake the mounting heat sizzling in her veins. The weight of something strange—unfamiliar—had pressed down on her shoulders a moment before, a shift in the air she wasn't sure what to make of.

Perhaps she'd merely felt the interruption in her morning gate duty coming.

She did not have to look up to identify who begged her attention. The cool greens and blues of Cam's inner world spilled over her, an energy she could pick out of a crowd of hundreds. The tranquility she'd come to expect of her friend faded quickly, overtaken by something hot, something grating.

There, nestled between blood and bone, a bright spot of crimson worry on behalf of Astra.

Cam's midnight-black hair floated on the breeze in a

serene contradiction to her mood, spiraling deeper into uncertain reds by the second.

Astra rose from her well-worn spot in the grass, bracing herself as her eyes dropped to the roll of parchment clutched in Cam's tan fingers.

"This came for you," Cameren said. The nervous red swirled into angsty maroon within her lungs, unsettling Astra as she caught the royal seal along the scroll's edge.

Ah. Of course.

Astra took her time gathering the half-drained mug of tea she'd perched on a gnarled root, buying time to work through her friend's emotions before they became her own.

When she surfaced, she took a long, slow breath hoping it would cool the fire brewing in her soul instead of stoking the vicious flames.

Cam's focused sapphire eyes widened as Astra pinched the bridge of her nose. She could never fully understand the burden of Astra's sensitivity, but she'd witnessed the chaos Astra reined when it consumed her. The women of Celene *tried* to conceal their emotions for Astra's benefit, or at the very least mute them, but Cameren's concern about the note's contents overrode the hold she had on her feelings.

Astra reached for the parchment, tucking her book against her chest and balancing the mug on the edge of the spine. Cameren plucked them both from her hands as they strolled across the humble village, alive with the early-morning bustling of women tending to their duties.

Astra weighed the paper in her palm, pursing her lips as it settled. "Hmm," she sighed. "Feels like something I'm going to regret opening. Who brought it?"

"Someone new."

"I suppose she wouldn't chance sending someone with an affinity for me," Astra laughed. "You can relax. I dreamed of a hatchling clawing my eyes out a few nights ago. Should have expected something from her Royal Highness soon."

She attempted a laugh, but the sound was too dark. Too heavy. Cameren didn't need Astra's heightened intuition to see the anxious tug at her sleeve as they passed through the village and down a set of steps carved into the cliffside before coming to a wooden platform.

Cam reached forward and gently tugged on a fraying rope, ringing a bell at the city's gate below.

"What do you think it is?" she asked.

"All the intuitive gifts in the world couldn't tell me," Astra muttered.

Both women leaned over the platform, watching the pulley cart ascend the cliffs. Astra held the gate open for Cam, following her onto the small cart and steeling herself against the railing as the ropes began moving, lowering them into the city.

As they descended through the morning mist, the open-air moonstone towers of Celene emerged, overlooking the Somnia River racing out to sea. The unfiltered feelings of a thousand women permeated the air as Astra drew in a slow breath, readjusting her tolerance from the dozens of women in the village to the busy city streets.

Cam chewed her bottom lip as she hopped off the cart. "Perhaps a birthday note?"

Astra cast a heated glare. "How many birthdays have passed without so much as a whisper?"

Cam nodded, weaving a trail from the pulley landing to the crystalline bridge over the river, sparkling in the half-Moon glow above. As Astra slipped her finger beneath the wax seal, a flock of young girls rushed them.

"Astra!" One of the smallest girls chirped as they fell in a dense circle around the women. "Alura said you survived The Flare!"

Both Cam and Astra flinched, unprepared for such a heavy hit so early in the morning. Astra tucked the scroll back under her arm, searching for the words—they were only children. They knew just enough to be dangerous to their elders. She glanced across their faces, each round with the benefits of full plates and uninterrupted sleep—they did not know the exhaustion of war or how their questions poked at ancient bruises.

"*Who* said that?" Astra asked calmly, maintaining a soft smile to soothe herself more than the girls at her feet. They shuffled, pushing one of the older girls to the front, her face lit with silver freckles and curious amethyst eyes. She could not have been older than ten or eleven, an infant practically.

"Alura," Astra repeated her name, a blush crawling over the girl's face. The muscles in her back tightened as she exchanged a look with Cam. "Well. I do not think it's fair to the brave people who lost their lives in The Flare to say I survived it. I was still in my mother's womb, unaware of the Solar King's cruel attack or the pain those who did survive endure, even to this day."

She blinked a vision away of the burn scars across her mother's chest, always obscured by robes and high-necked gowns, but they were a presence in her life from even her earliest memories. Though, Astra knew the physical scars were nothing compared to the emotional damage inflicted on her mother—not that she'd ever allow either to show.

She took another breath, digging deep within herself to be the leader she strived to be, despite wishing she could dissolve into the air and escape this topic entirely.

"What other questions can I answer? Get them out now, ladies."

Another tiny voice spoke up. "Is that why your hair is red?"

Cam barked a laugh beside her. The innocence of the question hit the release valve they desperately needed. Astra laid a gentle hand on the girl's shoulder.

"I'll tell you the truth—I'm not certain. Bloodlines can be finicky things, girls." She winked at them, grateful they could leave this conversation on a lighter note.

Cam pushed her shoulders back into an intimidating stance. "Now, if I go check the gardens right now, will today's chores be done?" A chorus of nervous giggles sent the girls running toward the temple beyond the bridge, moving in one fluid mass of pastel braids and silver robes.

Astra raised her eyebrows at Cam, who exhaled with a soft chuckle. They continued their trek into the city, the weight of the scroll in Astra's arms growing with each step. Cam bumped her hip into Astra's.

"I heard your hair is red because you fucked Mars in a past life."

Astra's jaw dropped as she snorted and shoved her shoulder. "The gossip in this city is a rapidly spreading blight! You should do something about that, you know."

"Ah! She does not deny it!"

Astra pursed her lips, a wicked smirk unfolding. "You act like you'd pass if the God of War propositioned you."

"*A man*? Please," Cam scoffed. "Venus, however..."

They entered the tower at the very edge of the city, pale moonstone floors bouncing light back at them. Cam set Astra's things on the abandoned desk at the front of the small library they frequented in the mornings. She knew Astra preferred to stay tucked away into the corner of her tower over the busy three-story collection of books in Celene's center—here she could breathe easier, away from the constant waves of vivid color that plagued her strange senses with each fleeting feeling in her vicinity.

"Why do you think they were talking about The Flare?" Astra asked as Cam sank behind a table she'd worked at late into the night, an aged map of a Neptunian city sprawled across the polished oak. She shifted one of the quartz markers she used to plot the city's ports—a hobby she'd inherited from her mother's fascination with the Outer Courts.

"Same reason you *aren't* talking about it," Cam said, glancing up between crystals. "Next week is the gauntlet for you—isn't it?"

Astra laughed at her phrasing, but as always, Cam was spot on. The Summer Solstice used to be a time of celebration, with week-long festivals and tributes to gods of the Court Above. Things were more somber now, thirty years after the Solar King killed the Lunar Queen and attacked the Inner Courts with a lethal light. The Flare left deep scars on the Lunar Court and her allied human courts, claiming thousands of lives.

Now, the Summer Solstice was a solemn reminder of the bloodshed, marked by temple ceremonies and memorials.

"You know what I never understood?" Astra said, tossing the scroll onto the table. "Why was my mother even in the Solar Court at all that day? She was living in the Earthen Court by then."

"You... could ask her?" Cam eyed the scroll, treading lightly into the territory of Astra's complex relationship with her mother. The arch of Astra's brow was all the answer she needed. "I think you've avoided opening it long enough."

Her shoulders collapsed. Cam was right once again. She plopped into one of the plush armchairs and unfurled the note.

It was simple. No flowery prose or birthday felicitations. Just a single line.

I need to speak with you.

A looped "O" punctuated the note, filling Astra with a heat she rarely allowed herself to feel. No ignoring it then.

"The queen herself, hmm?" Cam leaned over her, scanning the note before Astra could tame the smoke rising to her lungs. "Should I have Riverion readied?"

"I suppose." Astra folded the note and slipped it between the leather cover of her book and its fading pages. "But take your time. I'm in no rush." Cam leaned out of the library door, catching someone's attention.

What Astra wished she could say was take all night—*all week*—but how long would the queen wait? She brushed her hands against the pale lavender silk of her robes, desperate for something to incinerate.

How long had it been? She chewed on her thumb as she thought back to the last holiday she'd celebrated within the pristine walls of the palace. Was it the Winter Solstice ball she'd been thrown out of? Or was that an Equinox feast?

She'd been wearing a red dress. She remembered that much. Autumnal, most likely.

That was what? The two-thousandth and eighty-third Harvest Moon? Next week's Summer Solstice would be the two-thousandth and eighty-sixth Strawberry Moon.

Nearly three years.

The math was right, but it sounded impossible.

She turned to Cam as she stared at her map. "You'll send word if anything happens?"

"Of course," Cam murmured, skimming over rivers and forests. "You know, Celene got along just fine for decades, perhaps even centuries, before you showed up." A smirk played at Cam's curved lips, her jewel-toned gaze ungluing from the map and meeting Astra's.

"Is that so?" Astra crossed one leg over the other, tossing the scroll back onto the table.

Cam shrugged. "We weren't as well-funded."

"Is that all I am to you? A financier?"

She wiggled her brows at her friend. "Certainly made taking in someone with your reputation easier."

Astra sat up straighter. "I haven't set anyone on fire in nearly two years and you know it. Just admit you'll miss me!"

"Dearly," Cam assured. "Aren't you even a little excited to see your family?"

Astra's heart stuttered. She so rarely allowed herself to think of the things she'd left behind in Lunaria, and even then, she avoided any faces entirely. Her sister's silver eyes and brazen white hair flared in her memory before she could will the image away. Everything about Lunelle's bright and frigid complexion contrasted Astra's warmth—the girls were fire and ice from the moments they entered this world, crafted by the Mother herself to orbit one another.

She unclenched her jaw. "Excited doesn't feel like the right sentiment."

"Lunelle must miss you terribly?"

"I know she does," Astra mumbled. A stack of letters bleeding with Lunelle's elegant prose sat unanswered on her desk. Astra wrote when she could, but she'd neglected their correspondence over the last few months. "At least *one* person will be happy to see me."

Cam sighed. "Please, your father thinks you hung the Moon."

Astra waved her fingers between their faces, glowing with a faint lick of fire, fueled by her anxiety. "The flames hear you, but they don't believe you."

Cam nodded, knowing her friend far too well to attempt to

soothe her nerves. She marked another mountain range with an azure crystal, one she always saved for her favorite spaces.

"The thirtieth anniversary of The Flare, your birthday, and the Solstice all at once... can't imagine why the queen would want to speak with you," Cam chuckled to herself.

Astra's lips dropped into a frown, out of reasons to delay her departure. "She'll want me to stay at least through the Solstice. I'm sure of it."

"That's not that long." Cam set another marker near one of Neptune's moons. "You'll be back here before you know it. Besides, who wouldn't want the royal treatment on such a significant birthday?"

Astra rolled her eyes. "Yes, I'm sure there will be many moonshine fountains in my honor. A parade, at the very least." Astra reached across the table for a piece of obsidian, sliding it along the edge of Neptune's capital city. "The southern side is more vulnerable." She rose, smoothing her dress. "I'll be home as soon as I can."

"Bring that Ameera of yours back with you," Cam muttered, tapping her finger against the obsidian. The corner of her mouth ticked up into a sorrowful smile Astra ignored for both their sakes.

"I mean it, Cam. Even a whisper of something wrong and I can be back here in three hours. Two and some change if Riv is in a good mood."

Cam nodded, she understood the urgency Astra felt.

"Go then, before moonfall."

Riverion's roost, a tall, skeletal tower, loomed over the Somnia.

Astra skipped across the rickety bridge, noting she should send for the builder in the villages that helped construct the pulley system last Summer as soon as she landed in Lunaria.

The fifteenth step to the roost buckled under her weight. She added that to her endless mental list. The builder over-charged, but her fee was better than broken ankles.

"He's fed, saddled, and pissed you took so long," Sephone said, handing Astra a satchel filled with pastries she wouldn't need for the short flight. "Promise to come back. We might not have the amenities of a big city like Lunaria, but we make up for it in charm."

Astra frowned. "Lunaria's amenities come at the cost of my sanity. Trust me, I'll be back."

A steamy sigh rolled over Astra.

Riverion, beast that he was, huffed as he perched on the ledge of his roost, desperate to stretch his wings. As his faithful rider rounded the corner of his pen, he lowered his massive head for a pat. His gleaming emerald scales pulled silver where beams of moonlight poured in through the windows. Summer storms had swept in and done their best to keep them both grounded, and he was restless.

"Hi, old man," Astra whispered, stroking her fingers over his warm snout. It would take but one quick shake to toss her over the ledge to her death, but he was too good for that, despite his ruffled demeanor. "We're heading home, Riv."

She flinched at the word. *Home.* Was Lunaria still home? What made one place home and another simply where you came from?

Another violet tide rose in her, but she shoved it down into the cellar where she locked all the complex colors and emotions she'd rather not untangle away. In one swift movement, she hooked one boot into the saddle and hiked her skirts up, settling into the leather seat Riverion hated, but it had been ages since they'd flown more than twenty minutes at a time and she wanted to be comfortable for the trek back. The worn grooves in the saddle gripped her thighs and a breeze struck up as if the gods that hid behind the mountains blessed their journey.

How irritating of them to finally notice her.

Astra flung the satchel around the horn of the saddle and took a breath before nudging Riverion with her heel. He dove headfirst off the ledge, plunging toward the temple pillars below in a graceful arc, his mammoth wings stretching and breathing against the winds to find their rhythm. She held on as he banked left and then right between two towers, eliciting gasps from the girls in the gardens.

"Easy, asshole," she muttered as she leaned into the steep curve upward, her stomach dropping as he spun higher and back again in a series of twists. He cleaved the air around them in two as they cut a path over the cliffs and into the forest beyond Celene's gates. As they sailed away, the violet worry faded into a scarlet guilt climbing the column of her spine.

They'd protected themselves for decades without me, she reminded herself.

It took but ten beats of Riv's wings to clear the Midwood, the dense amethyst forest dividing the crescent-shaped island of the Lunar Court. Purples and pinks and blues slipped by in the haunted forest, all quiet, save for a few small villages perched along the Somnia as it cut inland.

The tips of the southern city, Ellume, sparkled beyond the Midwood, barely visible through the mist and trees. The crystal architecture caught the endless moonlight and refracted it across the realm in metallic waves.

Riverion coasted for a moment, his claws clipping the tops of the pines playfully. Astra felt the tension coil in his muscles and saw a flare of vicious scarlet in his chest. She leaned forward, draping herself over his neck.

"Please, don't do it—"

Pleading was no use. Once Riverion was within sight of the Rift, he was insatiable. He spiraled upward, too fast and too close to the edge of the misty aurora stretching over the entire realm. Astra hissed as she gripped the reins around his snout, though her frantic yanking did nothing to distract him from his target.

"You're going to get my ass thrown in prison if the queen finds out!" Astra glanced up at the rainbow road above, pulling back once again as Riv's wing scraped the edge, sending shimmering dust flying as the pastel threads that made up the Rift's strange current shivered at the disturbance.

Riverion let out a smokey sigh as he dipped back down, the torture of his rider complete.

"It's not *funny*, Riv!" She smacked at the back of his neck, her nerves on fire as they put enough distance between them and the band of lights she'd been forbidden to enter her entire life. The Rift carved a path from one end of the court to another, touching the edge of the Lunar Palace before it swept back up and into the ether. Astra squinted as they drifted away. When the Moon was full and bright, one could see the silhouettes of passing travelers on their way to other courts. Two dark frames shot by, their hands outstretched to grasp their destination's designated thread.

Or so Astra had heard.

A spot of emerald envy flared in her chest. She'd only dreamed of the freedom the travelers experienced—of all the demigoddesses in the Lunar Court, she was one of two banned from its use.

She closed her eyes for a moment and tried to imagine it—the Rift on that Summer Solstice three decades ago. It had been teeming with passengers, both the demigods of the Courts Between and the humans of the Living Courts traveling between cities to celebrate. She wondered if those on the ground heard the screams as The Flare's light consumed them.

Riverion plummeted, flinging Astra over the saddle and snorting a flamed warning. "Fine, fine, gods, I'll pay more atten —*shit!*"

The dragon lurched backward, smoke ruffling around them as he roared and pushed away from the treeline.

"Mother above, Riverion, what are you *doing*?"

They jolted sideways, the sharp sound of something whizzing past Astra's ear. She whipped her head around, trying to find the object. Beneath them, an arrow fell back toward the forest and disappeared into the canopy.

"Ah!" A second arrow grazed her arm, severing the silk of her sleeve. Wine-red blood soaked into the pale lavender. Astra wrapped one hand around the horn of the saddle and tightened the grip of her knees, trying to sense what might lurk below them. Red fury; orange self-righteousness. No energy she recognized.

Riv righted himself before soaring higher, pushing his wings with burgundy determination. A third arrow sliced through the air, just barely missing Astra's face.

"Who in the Court Below—"

Another twist cut her curse short as Riverion slipped into a current and drifted over the stone walls of Lunaria. Glowing streets unfurled below like satin ribbons peppered by low-lit lanterns.

Riverion's route was pure muscle memory from there, giving both of them a chance to catch their breaths as he wove around the city gates and into the towering roost above the amethyst palace. The roost housed dozens of dragons much smaller than him, but his space still sat empty as he crashed into the wooden nest. His claws hardly brushed the hay before quick steps rumbled up the steps and through the door, bouncing yellow energy, preceding a voice Astra had missed every second of every day she'd been gone.

"As!" Ameera's lungs puffed as she shoved her way through the royal roost's endless stalls. She must have sprinted from whatever library she spent her morning in when she spotted Riv. "You're home!"

Her lips broke into a wide smile, a soft point of relief in her golden, angular face. Astra slid off her dragon, pushing at the split silk on her arm. She held up the scrap of parchment that brought her here.

"I had little choice, and I *barely* made it!" Astra wiped at the blood still weeping from the wound. "Gods dammit, I liked this dress."

Ameera brushed her fingers over the sleeve, examining the cut. "Who did you piss off?" Her musical laugh lit something inside Astra as she wrapped her in a desperate hug. Her warm honey scent soothed the sting in Astra's arm.

"That's how you greet royalty now? I leave for a few years and everyone's manners go to shit?"

"Oh, my apologies, Princess," Ameera muttered as she bowed comically low, rolling her eyes.

"Better. And I didn't get a feel for who they were. No one I recognized. Whoever it was had damned good shot. We were mid-flight over the forest." Astra tossed one more glance out of the roost as if she could spot the offender through the stone walls.

"Does it hurt? It could be poisoned! There are rumors of rebels in the woods. The queen should have sent someone to escort you," Ameera grumbled, fussing with Astra's satchel.

Astra winced. "Please, we both know I wouldn't have taken kindly to a babysitter. Besides, if she forbade *you* from visiting Celene all this time, there's no way she would have sent someone even less tolerant of my... quirks. What do you mean, rebels?"

Ameera's smile tightened, an expression Astra knew well from years of prodding at whatever it concealed. She'd worn it many times over the nearly two decades she'd served as Astra's Head Maiden. "It's a long story. We can fill you in later. Your mother is waiting for you in the Celestial Hall."

Astra's shoulders fell—she wouldn't even get a moment to let Lunaria's salty sea breeze rehydrate her lungs before facing the court.

"I'll alert Archera about the arrows. She'll want to send out the sentry." Ameera eyed Astra's soiled sleeve. "Change first. The council is assembled."

A whirl of amber anxiety flickered through Ameera's lungs. Astra tried not to flinch. Not three minutes back in Lunaria and she was already causing Ameera heartburn. As if the guilt of leaving Celene wasn't enough, now she'd have to face what sent her there without a second to adjust to court life.

Astra followed Ameera down the stairs. "I presume you kept my council robes? Or did the queen burn them in effigy after shipping me to Celene?"

Ameera snorted. "Don't be ridiculous. She let the stable maidens use them to keep the hatchlings warm in the Winter."

Astra let out a laugh, but they both knew that her mother at least considered it.

She muttered, "So good to be home."

THREE

Nothing about the palace had changed in her absence.

The same dark halls glittered with clusters of opal and amethyst under the glass ports in the arched ceilings. The same metallic threads wove tales of goddesses and wars in the same tapestries lining the walls. The same ancient busts of queens with full lips and proud eyes watched as she darted across the courtyard to the wing of the palace she shared with her sister.

The same palace maidens shuffled from room to room in their silver robes, carrying out their daily tasks with wide eyes as Astra zipped between them.

Some of them smiled and some of them pretended not to notice her altogether. Both reactions seemed fair.

Ameera left Astra in her dressing room with her council robes already laid out in a strange silence. In Celene, the quietest it ever got was in the dead of night—and even then, the patrol units giggled together over stories from their home courts. Their tinkling laughter would float into the open windows of her tower apartment. Astra searched for any evidence that her space had been deemed off-limits, but no dust settled on the shelves. No cobwebs caught the moonlight.

Her council robes tied at her waist, complementing her curved hips and soft belly. Gold always flattered her more, but one can't help being the first flame in a thousand years of ice queens.

Second, she reminded herself. Her Autumnal hues perfectly mirrored her late Aunt Leona's, the very reason she'd ended up second in line to the throne. Perhaps the resemblance to her ill-fated sister was the reason Astra's mother struggled to meet her eye without a pained grimace.

Astra poked her head into the hallway, catching a maiden as she rushed from one chore to another.

"Sorry," she interrupted. "Could I trouble you for some help? I need a bandage."

The maiden—her soft, tan face untouched by time—jumped at the unexpected voice. Her eyes landed on Astra's bleeding cut, widening as she pieced together who was speaking to her.

"It's not that bad!" Astra assured her, unsuccessfully disarming her with a smile. "Shouldn't require much."

The maiden backed away slowly, her eyes fixing on Astra's fingers as bright red fear bubbled to life in her chest.

Ah, Astra thought. She should have realized her reputation preceded her. "I'll just take care of it myself," she whispered as the maiden scurried away, leaving her alone as a maroon shame washed over her.

At least there were no witnesses this time.

She stepped back into the dressing room and flung open the wardrobe, flicking through dress after dress. She yanked a simple linen frock off its hanger and pulled at the hem, tearing a thin strip to use as a bandage. Astra wrapped it around her bicep and tied it off, letting the long sleeve of the robes fall over it so no one would see.

She swept her hair back into a long braid, the scarlet strands so out of place in a world of cool blues, purples, and greens. Setting her shoulders back, she filled her lungs with air as one final stalling tactic and stepped into the hall, ready to face the maidens and courtiers watching her every move.

Their chests exploded in critical rainbows as they held their tongues—scarlet fear, violet intrigue, amber disdain, emerald envy. She appreciated the last one, for what it was worth, though if they only knew the weight of the Lunar Court, they might turn their ambition elsewhere.

She reached the Celestial Hall, her mother's preferred assembly space, and stopped outside of the ornately carved stone doors flanked on either side by maidens with amethyst circlets hovering over their foreheads.

She didn't recognize either of them—they must be new.

Well, newer, she corrected herself.

One averted her gaze as the princess approached, the other smiled curtly and pulled back the door, allowing a sea breeze to roll into the hallway.

The hall overlooked the Empyrean Sea's rolling black waves. Foam curled and spun as it crashed against the gray rock below, spraying the sides of the palace with sparkling mist. The walls rose into a high dome peaking in the center in a glass moonlight, filtering the bright glow of the cosmos above into an opal haze. A ring of constellations and goddesses reached for one another in an intertwined circle, watching as Astra crossed the floor, her shoes tapping rhythmically as she maintained an even pace.

Inside the center of the domed hall sat a circular table cut from a smoky shadow diamond, reflecting a dozen faces as they turned in unison toward her.

Twenty-four eyes seared into her chest at once, but only one gaze held hers.

Queen Oestera stood at the side of the table, her pointed chin held high as she let her silver eyes drag over her daughter's estranged face. Her hair, the same sharp metallic as her eyes, fell into several woven braids at her hips, wide with the curves of a woman who brought two souls into the realm. Her robes matched Astras in all ways but one. Where her sleeves draped to the floor in plain waves of silver silk, the queen's bore dozens of gilded stars commemorating the skies each of her daughters were born beneath.

She blinked, moving on from Astra's face quickly, almost as if she'd seen her just a few hours ago at breakfast. She gestured with a long arm toward a seat that had remained empty for three years and Astra took her place quietly, unsure of what greeting she'd expected.

She settled in next to a slender frame, nearly identical to the queen's long lines, who didn't break her carefully constructed mask as her heart flared in shades of bright pink and yellow.

Where Oestera's mouth creased with impatience, Lunelle's folded into a gentle smile.

You came home. Lunelle's soprano voice rang in her sister's mind so clearly Astra's shoulders jerked back with the shock. It had been three years since she'd heard a voice bounce off the walls of her inner world. She'd nearly forgotten it was possible.

Astra's lips twitched as she shook off the rust around her mind. *What can I say? Autonomy got boring.*

I don't care how irritated you are. I'm so happy to see you! You don't write anymore.

Astra winced as her mother spoke in low tones to her commander, Archera. *I'm sorry, Lu. I've been busy.*

Before Lunelle could argue, Oestera stepped forward, resting a cloth-covered object on the table.

"This isn't the first time we've found an object like this in the court," she began, nodding toward the mysterious item.

Archera reached forward, pulling the cloth away, revealing a glittering golden orb that hurt to look at, rays of light bouncing in all directions. They blinded Astra but begged her eyes to stay at the same time.

She could only hold the object's gaze for a moment before her eyes watered. Archera threw the cloth back over it, each councilwoman's shoulders relaxing when the light disappeared.

"Is it Solarian?" A priestess asked.

Oestera shrugged as much as she ever allowed herself to reveal she didn't know the answer to a question. "I had hoped Astra could help us identify it."

There it was. Scarlet pain wrapped its fingers around Astra's throat. She was forever a tool in her mother's clutches, called upon when a matter stumped the rest of the council.

"Have the divination laws changed in my time away?" She smirked, knowing her disingenuous question would not be well received. She knew as well as any of the other women gathered around the table that the rules banning the use of intuitive magic didn't matter when the queen's mission was at stake.

Oestera's brows knit together. "Astra." A warning. The only one she'd get.

"Don't touch it," Lunelle whispered, leaning away from the object as Astra stretched forward and pulled at the cloth's edge beneath the orb, dragging it closer to her.

Oestera stared as her daughter observed the object's weight in her mind, holding it as best she could to understand it. Though Oestera would never display the vermillion concern building in her chest, Astra appreciated she still felt it at all.

The warmth radiating from the object repelled and intrigued Astra in ways she did not quite understand. The heat was offensive as it crashed against her cold Lunarian skin. Even with the flames that ran through her blood, she found it too foreign—too *other*.

A buzzing wave radiated from its center, rolling over itself again and again. As she let it reach out and stroke her cheek, she realized it wasn't just a vibrating sound, but a distant melody, garbled through gods only knew how many dimensions. The echo of the strange muted music climbed the hall's domed interior as the rhythm slowed to a hypnotic lull.

Who are you? She asked it as if it would answer. It might. It certainly wouldn't have been the first time.

Images flickered across Astra's mind. A man's hands, deep bronze with thick, leather bands around his wrists, cupped the orb in the cover of night—the same obsidian sky they sat under now. He peered into the orb, his face warped around the curvature of the glass, and he asked it a question in a language she'd never heard—the musical lilt did something strange to her chest.

She couldn't understand the string of words, but she felt their request as the innards of the crystal ball swirled and twisted through space and time, stopping within the gates of a village she knew all too well.

A village perched just outside of Celene, alive with morning chores and activity. Women laughed in the center of the town, balancing baskets of fruit on their heads and hanging laundry.

It was a facade, a carefully curated one to protect the real Celene carved into the cliffs below. If anyone went searching for the long-forgotten city, they'd see the crumbling village and assume that's all it offered.

And there, under a gnarled oak in the Midwood, sat Astra in a black morning dress, tucked gently around her knees as she read from a poetry anthology just this morning, surely no more than an hour or two before the queen sent for her.

Astra's heart lurched as she realized the ball had been used to locate something—not just something, *her*. She pushed the object away, glancing from her sister's concerned expressions to her mother's waiting eyes.

Her mother tilted forward. "What is it?"

"Are you okay?" Lunelle asked.

"I can't be certain," Astra mumbled. She worked to keep her voice even. "It's some sort of divination tool that locates things—people. The user stared at it and said something in a language I didn't recognize. It swirled and showed him what he asked for."

"What did it show?" Archera studied Astra's face as she stilled her mind again, unsure if she should be honest. She searched her body, begging her muscles to tell her what the consequences might be if she were honest. What they'd be if she weren't.

"The Midwood," she said hesitantly. The wound she'd earned on her way in ached as she crossed her arms over her chest. *Had a Solarian fired that arrow?* "A village not far into the woods, near the Somnia's bank."

Oestera asked, "Did you see who wielded it?"

Astra turned toward her. "No, his face was warped in the reflection. But his skin glowed a golden bronze. He had cuffs around his wrists."

"Solarian," Archera said, looking at her second-in-command beside her.

Oestera's eyes snapped to her. "This is exactly what I was worried about after Ellume's little stunt at the Equinox. I should have sent you down to check on the wards in person.

We can't trust their High Priestess. I want every corner of the Midwood searched. We're either looking at a leak in the Rift or a traitor in the court. Neither is acceptable."

"Yes, Your Highness," Archera mumbled, scooting her chair back from the table. "Can you draw me a map of the village, Princess?"

"I could go with you—"

"You're needed here," Oestera cut her daughter off.

"Ameera can guide you. She knows it," Astra muttered, a red anger crawling up her throat.

"Excellent." Oestera moved on. "If this is connected to the rumors we've heard of rebels in the woods, we'll need to be careful with the girls." Archera nodded as Astra shrank in her seat.

A normal day in the court was restrictive enough, but with heightened anxiety around her safety?

Misery.

"Rebels?" She asked.

Oestera's chest flickered briefly to life in Astra's mind's eye, a rare slip of color allowing her to glimpse the turmoil within.

"Much has changed since your departure, Astra. Rebel activity has bubbled up within the cities across the courts. We believe they're in service to the Solar King."

"But why would they be here? Doesn't he have bigger problems in the Outer Courts?"

"It only benefits him if the Inner Courts and Lunar Court are focused on suppressing civil matters and not on preparing for whatever plans he's laying in the Outer Courts. If our armies are tangled in war here, we can't attack him, much less defend ourselves."

An ache pulled at Astra's attention in her bones. Something wasn't quite right with her mother's theories, but she couldn't see a clear reason to continue pushing.

"I see," she settled.

"It's time we talked about strengthening our alliances within the Inner Courts," Oestera announced, her eyes scanning the other councilors. "We know they won't stand against us. We've maintained healthy enough relationships with their leaders, but many of them have turned over to their heirs. We should re-engage them."

Astra's mind fell into the sea below, the icy water churning her thoughts as she considered what she'd heard here in tandem with the stinging wound on her shoulder.

"There's much to consider," Archera said, nodding. "We'll brief you this evening with what we discover in the Midwood."

"Thank you," Oestera replied, a chill in her tone serving as a dismissal for everyone else at the table. The women stood and shuffled, leaving only Astra, Lunelle, and a silent observer resting at the back of the hall that Astra had failed to clock when she entered. Her father ambled over, hesitant to disrupt the meeting, and laid a hand on Astra's shoulder, squeezing as he dropped a kiss on the top of her head.

"Welcome home," Oestera said as she joined them, in what she was sure was a warm enough tone, though the sentiment didn't quite translate to her daughter, despite her sensibilities.

"Did you need anything else from me?" Astra asked as she gestured to the orb, sitting dormant beneath the cloth. "Or was that all you sent for?"

Oestera sank into a chair across from her daughters, leaning forward with perfectly poised shoulders. "We think it's time you returned home. For good."

She swallowed the panic erupting in her chest, the faces of dozens of women back in Celene flashing to her mind. "I don't think that's an option for me," she mumbled.

Oestera sighed. "I'm happy to hear you've found yourself

useful in Celene, but the Solstice is days away. Wouldn't you like to spend your birthday with your family?"

Astra flinched. "You didn't seem too concerned about who I spent the last three birthdays with, Mother."

"Things were still too fresh, darling. We've spent enough time apart. I can't stand to see your seat remain empty. At least stay with us through the Solstice and let us celebrate you. A Lunar Princess leaving her first cycle behind is a huge accomplishment."

Astra considered this. She remembered the fanfare of Lunelle's thirtieth birthday, the last party she'd attended at the palace before her exile. Perhaps if she allowed the firestorm brewing in her fingertips to slip out, nothing too destructive, maybe just a bust in the hall, would that be enough to get her shipped back to Celene permanently?

Lunelle's voice slipped into her mind again. *Please stay, As. I miss you so badly.*

Why? So I can parade around as if I'm still a part of this family for a night before she gets angry and sends me home again? I may be leaving my maiden cycle behind, but I'm still me, Lu.

Lunelle glanced at her sister, their parents exchanging an exasperated look they hadn't shared in three years—Oestera had forgotten about this particularly annoying feature of her second-born's strange magic. *I need my sister,* Lunelle pleaded. *This is our last few months together before I take the throne. Let's enjoy it, hmm?*

She could never tell Lunelle no. Astra's lips twisted into an irritated pout. "I will stay for my birthday... if you promise to hear me out on some changes I think you should consider," she said, turning her amber gaze onto her mother.

"I think there's enough changing right now," Oestera said,

her eyebrows arching in a way that did not invite more discussion.

"Of course," Astra relented. Oestera was already up and crossing the room, on to the next.

"Come Lunelle," she said as she waved her hand. "We have lunch with the treasury."

Astra watched as they made their exit, both swaying in the same pattern.

"Gods, it's good to see you at the table, my love," her father said, a wide grin breaking over his olive skin as he plopped into the chair Lunelle vacated. His deep brown eyes filled with the same sadness Astra recognized from the night she was cast out of the court, the regret and pain still living just under the surface.

"What's the point of coming to the table if I'll never be heard?" She asked.

Her father's shoulders softened. "You have a brilliant mind, Astra, and a heart that seeks so much good. You always have, but you've seen so very little of this world. Your mother has seen too much."

"Oh," Astra snorted. "And what has she seen lately? When was the last time she visited Ellume? Or Celene? The Middle Villages? She hasn't met with anyone since I've been old enough to protest. Her court is dissolving outside of this city. She's out of touch."

Her father took this in, always careful to weigh every word that left his lips—one of the few traits his daughter hadn't inherited from him, for better or worse.

"Things are not always as they appear, Astra. Your mother is beholden to thousands of lives. That's not a responsibility many could bear."

"And yet she will not allow any of us to take up any of the weight."

"Perhaps you both could spend some time reacquainting yourselves with one another. You've both constructed stories that aren't necessarily true." Nayson rose, kissing her one more time, lest she escape from the hall and never come back, and smiled warmly, despite the prickling in both their chests. "Come and find me when you've settled in. I've missed our afternoon teas."

His footsteps faded, leaving Astra alone to listen to the crash of the sea below. The only thing louder than the waves breaking against the cliffs was the all-consuming hum of the orb before her, begging her to touch it as she stared.

Perhaps many of the narratives she'd been taught her entire life needed to be pulled apart at the seams.

FOUR

I t was simply irresponsible of the queen to leave the object on the table.

At least, that's what Astra told herself as she smuggled it under her robes and tossed it into a sack, the weight of it dragging against the black cloak she wrapped around her shoulders.

It only took a few gold coins to convince the stable maidens to let her take a midnight-black mare into the Midwood, breaking away from the watchful eyes of the palace courtiers. Her shimmering silver mane slipped through Astra's fingers like silk as they edged their way into a clearing where she knew every fallen log, every babbling stream.

She paused at the treeline, the wound on her shoulder still *very* apparent as she gripped the reins of her mount. The expanse of gnarled oaks and twisted birch hid plenty of creatures, both mystical and terrible, but now she wondered who else lurked in the shadows.

She closed her eyes, sinking beneath flesh and muscle, letting her bones have their say—would they push her into the darkness, or back into the stoic halls of the palace? The orb at her back whirred, answering before anything within her could.

She took that as enough of a sign.

Though off-putting in its tangled appearance, the Midwood had always called to her, even as a small child. Hundreds of Lunar Queens upheld a bargain—the Midwood would act as a protective barrier to the palace as long as its inhabitants were not bound to the same strict laws around practicing magic as Lunarians were.

Anything that happened within her dark woods belonged to the Midwood's stewards, the Lunar Elves, and their ancient queen, Ehlaria.

She had neither beginning nor ending, she always was and always would be—some stories passed down claimed she was the mother of all life in the Lunar Court, but she denied it. Ehlaria had been through centuries of Lunar queens and seen them each through their struggles, though the last few generations had a more tenuous relationship than previous rulers.

The magic that ruled over Astra's veins was not always a forbidden practice in the court. It had once been commonplace —any of the women born within the court could access the flow of mystic power from their souls. They all had the blood of their Mother Goddess pumping in their hearts. Astra would not have been an outlier a few short centuries ago before everything crumbled.

The Lunar and Solar courts had always been enemies, really, but they'd at least been dignified about it in decades past. It was when a Lunar queen was murdered by a Solar king while traveling her inner astral realm that things got murky. It had never happened before—the women of the Lunar Court had always felt safe exploring their deepest selves, but her death toppled centuries of tradition and ritual in favor of strict regulations and the rise of the priestesses of the court who banned any use of magic as a protective measure.

Temporarily, of course. To keep them safe, of course. That it resulted in a complete shift of power from the people to the priestesses and the royal family was merely a strange coincidence.

Of course.

Before she ventured too far into the Midwood's marred depths, Astra reached into her cloak and pulled a small velvet pouch from her pocket. She tossed a few gold coins onto a smooth stump she'd left dozens of trinkets on over the years.

"I seek nothing but a blind eye," she said to whatever forest spirits might be listening. A soft whoosh and clink of coins whispered through the trees, followed by silence.

She didn't have to make it far into the woods for her safe space—though it felt less so this afternoon. She aimed for a small meadow just far enough away from the city that she'd be unlikely to get caught practicing illegal magic, and far enough from the elusive village of the Lunar Elves that she wouldn't be a disturbance. She could buy the forest's peace for a moment with her gold.

She tied up her mare, slipping off the saddle and gripping her pack as she settled into the middle of the meadow, tucking her feet beneath her. Overturning the bag, she watched as the orb rolled away from her, still singing its inaccessible song into the fluffy ryegrass. The moonlight above bounced off the crystal, amplifying the unbearable ethereal glow.

Before the bans, powers ranging from divination to elemental practices were honored as a gift, not shamed into compliance. She'd never been able to silence her strange alchemy of flames and intuition, despite many attempts made by her mother and the councilors.

She had no way of accessing information about her capabilities; the texts had long since gone missing, but if Astra trusted anything, it was her gut.

An onyx river opened within her chest as she mourned the knowledge she'd never have. Breathing in to still her heart, she let the song of the night larks above her lull her into an easy state.

She peered into the orb, the light warming her face.

Show me your user, she imagined herself saying, closing her eyes and letting the humming music swirl over her skin, pulling her under its spell.

Those same hands from earlier appeared again, this time more clear, without the pressure of an audience. Foreign runes and markings crawled over his cuffs, invisible earlier, but she could make them out in the stillness. She reached for her pack, finding a piece of charcoal and her notebook so she could sketch the lines for Ameera to research later.

Where are you? Lunelle's voice disrupted her, the hands flickering away. She tossed the cloth back over the orb and opened her eyes, a searing warmth still prickling at her back even as she pushed it into her bag.

The woods, what's wrong?

Mother is looking for you, Lunelle sent back.

Buy me fifteen minutes, she beamed, something in her stomach turning as the heat refused to break. She glanced at the edge of the meadow, suspicious that she wasn't as alone as she'd hoped.

There. Across the meadow, a scarlet flare in someone's chest as they raced between trees.

"Shit," she muttered, springing to her feet. She flung the bag over her shoulder and bolted for the mare, shoving her boot into the stirrup and hauling herself over her saddle in record time. "*Shit*," she whispered again, realizing she was still tethered to the tree. Against her better judgment, she let the panic push a rush of flame to her fingers, allowing the sparks to burnish against the leather of the lead and sever the tie as she dug her heels into the horse's side.

She'd deal with any witnesses later if need be.

That damned heat was still there, though the scarlet mist was no longer traceable to her alert intuition. Every gallop back allowed her to catch her breath, the sear fading as she put space between whoever had been watching. Nervous energy jolted through her in plumes of orange, red, and yellow. Whether it originated in her chest or the chest she'd nearly spotted in the Midwood, she wasn't sure.

Ameera stood waiting for her in the gardens as she dismounted, shoving what was left of the crisped lead into Ameera's hands. Her eyes creased, unhappy with the state of Astra's attire and demeanor as she rushed to right herself.

"Your mother—"

"Yes, yes, I've already been informed," Astra tapped her forehead, rolling her eyes.

"I forgot how hard managing you was," Ameera huffed.

Astra laughed darkly. "I'd be happy to relieve you of your duty, but alas. I'm staying."

"Why is this so heavy?" Ameera asked as she picked up Astra's pack. "Gods above, Astra, if there's a severed head in here—"

"If there was, wouldn't you be at least a little proud?"

"As!"

Astra ran her fingers through her hair, loosening her curls from the braid she'd kept it in. She needed to feel less restricted if she was going to face her mother again so soon.

"It's the orb from earlier. My notebook is in there as well. I traced some runes from the owner's cuffs. They're completely unfamiliar to me, but perhaps you might recognize them?"

Ameera nodded, absorbing what she said and cataloging

everything in her library of a mind. "Your mother is in her study."

Astra squeezed her eyes shut, preparing herself for another round of Astra versus Oestera. The last time they'd faced off, it ended in Celene. But this time, she was older, a more seasoned leader. She'd cut her teeth in the city and she'd learned so much more restraint than she'd had three Summers ago.

She burned her way out of her maidenhood the moment she'd seen Celene's neglected shores and the dilapidated villages across the court. Her mother may not make time for them, but she'd spent every moment of her exile listening and learning about their needs, and solving their problems alongside them. Her mother may not see it right away, but she wasn't the girl who left Lunaria.

An amber sense of power bubbled to life in her chest as she wove her way through the halls. Surely, Oestera would see her growth and hear her out.

She had to.

"PRINCESS," a maiden outside of Oestera's personal study nodded as Astra approached under the crystal arch framing her parents' wing of the palace. Her gleaming eyes fell to Astra's fingers, still warm from her escape in the Midwood.

The shame was violent as it crashed over Astra.

She set her shoulders back and flashed a saccharine smile as she wiggled her fingers between them.

"No theatrics. Promise." A ripple of yellow uncertainty flared in the maiden's ribs as her gaze dropped to the floor beside them, landing on a metallic cistern at her feet.

Astra scoffed. "Misty Mother above," she muttered. "Is that... is that in case I set something on fire?"

The maiden's eyes searched frantically for a better answer, but it was too late. The scattered colors in her lungs gave her away. Astra pushed past her, determined to keep her composure, but she couldn't resist kicking the cistern over as she entered her mother's study.

Oestera sat behind a quartz desk. Her robes and jewels from this morning retired in favor of a simple Summer dress. Her silver hair twisted atop her head and balanced in place with the help of a crescent-shaped pin. She did not look up as Astra slipped into the space, her nose buried in some sort of correspondence.

This was the version of her mother Astra held tight to when disappointment inevitably clutched at Oestera's jaw. She sank into the plush armchair across from her desk and crossed one leg over the other.

Their eyes both landed on the mud clinging to Astra's hem.

"I won't pain either of us with that line of questioning," Oestera murmured as she shuffled her parchment into a neat stack. It was a peace offering Astra didn't expect, easing the tension in her spine slightly as she folded her hands over her knee. "I would like to hear of your time in Celene. Your father tells me you have much to discuss."

"I won't bore you for Father's sake," Astra mumbled.

"Come now," Oestera sighed, leaning back in her chair and setting her pen on the desk. "I'm not trying to offend you."

Astra reset her jaw, willing away the childish impulse to roll her eyes. "Celene is thriving, if you really care to know."

"My sources tell me you funded a rather large building project last Winter."

"The city, like many of your villages, was in disrepair. Someone had to do something."

"The city," Oestera clicked her tongue. "Was never meant

to be inhabited again after their little uprising. But here we are."

Celene had rebelled under Oestera's mother, Selenia. The women who maintained the city, Cam's mother amongst them, refused to pay their annual tithe after seeing no benefits from the crown, earning them Selenia's endless stamp of disapproval. Selenia's unforgiving glare settled in Oestera's eyes.

Trees and their apples, as it goes.

Astra breathed the rage away, tamping down anything that might give way to sparks to be dealt with later.

"You cannot ignore people into submission, Mother. It only gives them time to plot."

"I suppose Cameren is thrilled to have your ear." Oestera's careful veil slipped, a strange mix of emotions bubbling within her Astra couldn't quite make out, colors she so rarely picked up on others.

"She has a vision and the support of a thousand women. That's no small feat. You'd be a wise leader to entertain her thoughts."

Oestera shook her head. "You know so much, but learn so little, Astra." She rose, pacing behind her desk, the books behind her illuminating softly by the glow of her pale complexion as she moved. "Cameren is just one of many, many women who have tried to change the tides of this court under the guise of equity without ever considering the impact on every other realm beyond us. The Lunar Court is a small piece of a very large, consequential puzzle, and you all seem to forget that."

Oestera tapped her fingers against her arms, crossed in a slow-moving fury. "We are not just spoiled monarchs, getting fat off the backs of our people, Astra. I know you may perceive things that way, but everything we do here is in the best interests of people across the realms, not just ourselves. We are the stewards of the Living Court's sentiments, the keepers of all things intrinsic, and guardians of dreams and whims. It is our sacred *duty*, the very reason the Court Above blessed us with our station in the Courts Between, to uphold the traditions that allow the rest of the courts to function without disruption. Your field of vision may be too narrow to understand the weight of that responsibility, but everything that happens here has a ripple effect on the hearts of courts from here to Pluto."

Oestera sat again, leaning toward her daughter. "You hold the dreams of millions in your palms, Astra Leona. Your passions and delusions of a better world have disastrous consequences when you lose focus."

Astra swallowed the crimson desire to spit on the polished desk. "I believe those dreams rest in the palms of my sister, as you are so keen to remind me."

"And I will also remind you that those palms are a mere heartbeat away from being yours," Oestera hissed. Her eyes glazed over with distant memories of her own mother sharing a similar reality check as news of Leona's assassination spread across the court. "Act accordingly."

Astra frowned. "So you'll never change your mind. Never even consider seeing how things function when power is evenly distributed?"

"The traditions are traditions for a reason, Astra. Because they work. They keep everything in balance and protect us from losing control. We lose control, we risk opening ourselves up to an attack from Solaris, and then what?"

"Fine," Astra scoffed, out of energy to argue. "Aside from the success in Celene you aren't interested in, what else may I illuminate Her Majesty the Queen's mind with?"

Oestera graciously did them both the favor of ignoring her attitude, desperate for Astra to stay calm.

"To solidify our alliances in the Living Courts, we're going to host dignitaries from each Inner Court for the Solstice holidays. Thirty years is more than enough time to mourn, I think it's time we celebrated again. I need you on your absolute best behavior for the week. We cannot afford to look anything but perfectly aligned as we prepare for whatever Solan has in store."

Astra nodded. "No fire, no fury, no fun. Got it."

"Lunelle will befriend the new Mother Nature. She's fresh on the throne and green, but if Lunelle sucks up to her for advice on how to take over a court, I'm sure they'll be fast friends. I want you to speak to Ameera about keeping the High Regent of Venus engaged. They know each other from her family's service to the Venusian Court and should have much to talk about. And then Mars..." Oestera pushed a breath through her teeth. Her own tattered history with their king seared her lungs. Once betrothed, it had not gone over well when she broke off the engagement to elope with a lowly Earthen soldier, shocking the entirety of the courts.

But what was she to do? She hadn't expected to Tether to Nayson just days after accepting her Fate as the Martian queen.

"Mars will be a tough sell, as you know. The king declined my invitation but offered to send his son, Prince Omnir, which is generous considering. I'd like you to turn your attention to him and try to evaluate their feelings. He's young and inexperienced. He could use someone of your prowess to guide him."

Astra's lips ticked up into a wicked grin. "Careful now, that's almost a compliment, Mother."

"Almost," Oestera agreed.

"What of the Mercurians?" Astra asked, curious if they were attending. Their proximity to the Solar Court was always a spot of fear when it came to allegiances, but it had worked against Solan during The Flare. His outburst hit them hardest.

"Ah, yes. The Mercurian king will be here. He took over the crown a few years ago after his father Descended. I'm not sure if he'll be much of a strategic alliance, what with the size of their armies still so depleted, but leave him to your father. The king served in the Intercourt Army at the Earthen camps for years after his schooling. They'll have plenty to talk about."

"Well, then," Astra huffed, clapping her hands together to stand. "You have it all figured out as always, Mother."

"We have to move quickly and quietly, Astra. Before things take a turn."

"When do they arrive?"

"They'll trickle in as early as this evening. We'll hold a birthday ball in your honor on the Solstice. I've arranged for a new wardrobe for your approval. Ameera mentioned you arrived with nothing from Celene."

"I hadn't planned on staying," Astra reminded her. "I know you think my coming home for good is the right thing to do, but I've built a home in Celene. A community. I would like to return after this alliance business is settled."

Oestera studied her daughter, eyes scanning the face she'd known in many lifetimes. When she was quietly raging the way Astra was now, she looked so much like her ill-fated sister, it was hard to breathe.

"If war breaks out... *when* war breaks out, I can't risk having you in Celene. You're safer here. If someone were to get their hands on you—"

"Ah," Astra snorted. "Of course. It's not about my safety, but your ability to leverage me."

"That's not what I mean," Oestera insisted. "You are a target, Astra. That's all."

The worry in her tone unsettled something inside of Astra

as she turned to leave, catching her off guard. She's always been set aside in her mother's eyes, meant as a conduit to whatever ends Oestera saw fit, but rarely had she expressed a fear for her well-being.

"Best behavior," Oestera repeated.

"Would I ever disappoint you, Mother?" Astra asked, notes dripping in bruised anger.

Oestera did not reply, for both their benefit.

T he Empyrean Sea inhaled, held her breath, and then sighed as Astra stared across her shadowy waves.

Pale crests shimmered under a full Moon. Salt stuck to her lips and hair, transforming her gentle curls into a wild tangle of fire. Surely she wasn't the first Lunar princess to sulk on these crystalline shores, wondering what the fuck was even the point of trying to change the minds of those that came before her.

"I think this is the longest you've ever gone in my presence without speaking," Lunelle laughed, lying beside her sister in the sand, her hair floating in celestial streaks on the breeze.

"Sorry," Astra mumbled. "It's been a long time since I had to go up against the queen."

"Not even a full day back and you've already given up on her, then?" Lunelle picked at her nail beds, unwilling to risk a glance at her sister and see the pain in her eyes. The way her lips pursed reminded Astra of many of the paintings in the halls of great rulers in their lineage.

"That's not fair," she protested.

Lunelle chewed on her lip, weighing her loyalties. "I know it's hard for you to be back here after... well, after everything. But she's not a monster, As. She just has to prioritize in ways we don't understand."

"Sure," Astra scoffed. "She could at least pretend to care about the world outside of these walls. Celene is not the only city crumbling under her neglect. There are entire villages falling apart, or *gone* now. The optics have always mattered more to her."

"She cares," Lunelle insisted. "She sees a bigger picture than we do, As."

"I appreciate that she's trained you well," Astra returned. She said no more on the matter, plagued by her uncertainty about what was true. Perhaps it all was. Her mother hadn't led a charmed life in the palace by any means. She grew up under the heavy stare of a woman even less tolerant than she was. When Leona died, she was plucked from her peaceful life in hiding in the Earthen Court and forced onto a throne she'd all but sworn off. She never even got a chance to mourn her dear sister before she was shoved into her dresses and jewels.

Astra could understand that, couldn't she?

Wonders struck her as she traced half-moons in the sand. Did Oestera sit on these very shores, a Martian ruby pinning her hand to the ground, misery her only companion as she considered abandoning everything she'd ever known for a man she'd just stumbled into in the garden? Did her lungs ache from screaming into the void, her mother turning away from her pain over and over again? Did her palms sweat from violent anxiety that shredded her from the inside out as she packed her bags to disappear into the Rift?

Did she ever resent the outlet her sister found in the fire in her veins, the violence she was allowed to get away with simply by being born different?

The very same fire she now resented in her daughter.

Perhaps centuries of women came to the same conclusion Astra arrived to as she sat up, brushing sand away from her drenched skirts. Sometimes, there was nothing to do but endure.

Duty would come clawing for her anyway, so why fight it now, when so much was at stake?

She could let the Solstice slip by, make nice with the courtiers, smile, nod like the perfect princess she'd never be. She could play nice, mind her manners, and maybe even manage to make her mother proud.

Then, she could escape back to Celene. If war was imminent, there was no way she'd leave them defenseless.

Courtiers are arriving, Ameera's voice echoed. She relayed the information to her sister, who drew in a sharp breath.

"Here we go," Lunelle laughed, nervous for her sister. While Astra maintained an easy charm about her, Lunelle knew that she was bound to struggle back in court life after such a peaceful three years. It was hard enough for her to deal with their own courtiers, but hundreds of strangers, each with their own unique cultures and customs, most completely unaware that the Lunar princess could see every flare of emotion in their chests?

Torture.

I'm going back to my room before the collective excitement of half the courts makes me throw up, Astra beamed, already feeling the rise in opinions even from here as they poured in through the Rift's Lunar gate. Lunelle rested a hand on Astra's shoulder, smiling in the way she had their entire lives. It took Astra nearly two decades to develop even a shred of control over the way her abilities left her vulnerable. Lunelle had seen her through a thousand meltdowns, her soft nature forever serving as a tie to reality.

The demigods and goddesses of the Lunar Court had some understanding of what Astra was up against, either through speculation or witnessing her younger years, and they mostly made an effort to suppress their stronger feelings. But the humans of the Living Courts? They tended to have much less restraint.

Astra envied them. Emerald tendrils wrapped around her chest as she climbed up the dunes below the palace gardens. It must be so freeing, to let your emotions run rampant without the weight of multiple courts on your shoulders. The monarchs of the Living Courts bore plenty of responsibility, of course, but they would never quite understand the pressure on a Lunar heir, their well-being resting in their palms.

If the Lunar Court thrived, the Living Courts thrived. If they didn't, well, the Living Courts would be sure to make their displeasure known.

Gathering her soaked skirts, Astra jogged across the sandy line between well-manicured hedges and wild, unkempt beach, careful to avoid the Lunar gate. The last thing she needed was someone spotting her barefoot and half-drenched. Her mother would have her sacrificed before she could make it through her maidenhood transition.

Astra crept along the back of the gardens and palace, skimming by windows and pillars open to the ocean breeze. Silk curtains brushed her shoulders, sending goosebumps down her arms. Maidens flitted in and out of rooms as courtiers flooded the gate, settling them in their wings.

The Venusian Court arrived in a slow lull, dozens of dreamy eyes set against gleaming golden complexions glanced along the paintings and busts as they floated to their arrangements. Astra watched their waifish features, reflected in Ameera's bone structure, her lineage carved into the hollows of her cheeks and a curious arch in her brow.

"It's rude to stare," a deep voice interrupted her observations, causing her to lurch forward.

Had she been paying attention to her surroundings and not just the ethereal Venusians, she would have felt him sneak up behind her well before he was within speaking distance. Astra spun, dropping her wet dress to cover her bare feet. She met a jade gaze, so bright his eyes were practically glowing, green as the first hints of Spring on the orchards beyond the city. The contrast between his eyes and deep complexion was captivating.

She watched in horror as those eyes slipped over her hips and down to her sopping skirts.

"Are you well?" He asked, concern and curiosity wrestling each other in tumbles of red and blues within his broad chest. They fought for dominance beneath a pale green tunic with a metallic insignia woven into the fabric, a lion roaring.

Mercurian, then.

Astra grinned, slipping away into the shadows of the hall. "You never saw me!"

"I'm not sure it matters if I did!" He called out after her, a divine smile spreading over his full lips. "What would I tell people? A half-drowned goddess is on the loose in the palace? Who would believe me?"

Astra stepped back toward him. "Not only would they believe you, but they'd know exactly who you were speaking of." She glanced over her shoulder, measuring the distance between the stranger and one of the hidden doors in the halls the maidens used to traverse unseen.

His eyes sparked with a gilded amusement. "Ah, you have a reputation for this sort of thing, then."

Astra sighed. "No. I fear my reputation is far worse. Good evening!" She bowed her head, unsure if his station demanded it, but felt it was better to be safe just in case.

"You as well." The man tucked his hands behind his back and tilted his head, the red concern in his chest losing out to the blue curiosity, a victory that delighted something in Astra's soul as she skipped back toward the door. A sudden craving to shed her title and engage with the rest of the universe as just a girl overwhelmed her.

"Wait!"

Astra stopped, her fingers slithering along the wall looking for the seam she knew was there but couldn't seem to grasp.

"Yes?"

He pulled at a chain in his pocket, producing a glittering timepiece. His eyes flickered from the face of the small trinket to Astra's.

"Happy birthday, Princess."

She smiled, trying to hide her disappointment that she hadn't been as anonymous as she'd briefly let herself believe. Her fingers found the crack in the wall she'd been searching for and pried it open.

She tossed one last smile to the stranger before disappearing into the moonstone door.

SHE'D BEEN *asleep for a few hours when she spiraled into a current, a hazy awareness that she was dreaming kept her from panicking as her head slipped under an icy black wave.*

The ocean pulled at her curls, whipping them around her as she bobbed in the water and another wave crashed over her. The air left her lungs, bubbling upward as she swatted at the water, sinking deeper with every attempt to break the surface.

The edges of her vision faded as she fell below the crush, whatever air left within her floating away into the ether.

For a moment, there was a peace she didn't expect.

And then, there was a blazing heat.

Flames licked at her skin as someone looped an arm around her waist and jerked her back through the surf. She slammed against the shore, the sand clinging to her wet body as she rolled and choked on seawater.

She woke up coughing, a lingering heat still soaking into her skin.

Ameera raised an eyebrow as the maiden held out her hands, a velvet garment bag suspended in the air between them.

"Who is it from?"

The maiden only shrugged, handing a pale green card over before disappearing. Ameera hung the bag on the edge of Astra's wardrobe, unsure what to make of the gift.

"What's that?"

"Birthday present?" Ameera suggested. She went back to adjusting the diadem over Astra's perfectly pinned curls so the stars would halo her head like the goddess she was. Astra fidgeted in her seat as she waited with every ounce of patience she possessed, which amounted to very little.

"Go," Ameera sighed. "I'll fix it after you're dressed."

Astra leaped from her perch at her vanity and unfastened the jade ribbons at the top of the bag, revealing a green spectacle of a gown. In a second bag were several clusters of aventurine jewels—a set of earrings, a bracelet, and a necklace.

Ameera gasped. "Who in all thirteen courts—"

"There was a card, yes?" She searched the vanity for the brief note that accompanied the gift.

In case everything you own is wet.
—M.

Ameera arched her brow. "Is that the Mercurian seal? What do they mean by wet?"

"You don't want to be an accomplice," Astra muttered, fighting a smile as it begged to break on her lips. "Mother won't be too disappointed if I wear this over her selection, right? To secure an alliance?"

"Are you kidding? She'll arrange the engagement by the end of the evening."

Astra's blood rushed to her cheeks. "That's not—no. She has to know that's not going to happen."

Ameera's forehead wrinkled. "You're no longer in your maiden cycle. She needs allies. What did you think tonight was about, As?"

"I can't think about that right now," she hissed, forcing the well of anxiety that opened within her closed. "I need to focus on getting down those stairs."

Ameera snorted, returning to the dress to loosen the laces. She helped Astra slide it over her curved hips, tightening the ribbons to highlight the long lines of her tall frame. Astra battled back all the swirling fears in her chest—her mother wanted allies, but surely she would focus on Lunelle first. Her upcoming coronation trial would require several champions to be selected. There was no reason to waste one on Astra now. No, she needn't spend any more energy on that.

As the laces around her waist pulled, last night's dream raced forward in her mind. That heat... the same heat from the

53

Midwood before. Her eyes glanced at the reflection in the mirror, falling to the pale wound on her upper arm.

That orb did not materialize in the court by accident.

If Solarians were infiltrating through the wards meant to stop them, there could be any number of them lurking in the realm. Perhaps they were waiting for an event such as this evening's ball to strike.

"Ameera," Astra said, breaking her friend's concentration as she fluffed layers of tulle and silk.

"Hmm?"

"What do you know about Solarians?"

Ameera stopped her movements, rising to meet Astra's gaze. "Less than you, I'm sure."

"In the woods yesterday, when I was trying to source more information from the orb... I felt something in the trees. Something very, very warm."

Ameera immediately shifted into solutions mode. "Anyone not from the Lunar Court feels warm to you, no?"

"You do," she admitted. Ameera's Venusian heritage certainly read as warmer to her than her own cool Lunar skin. "But not like this. Not so extreme."

"When you meet with the Mercurians this evening, pay attention. They're even closer to the Solar Court than we are. Perhaps you ran into one of their courtiers in the woods, they could have arrived earlier to explore?"

"Perhaps," Astra conceded. It was true that she would know more about her Solarian counterparts than Ameera, but even that knowledge was quite limited. It was somewhat taboo to discuss openly, given how many courtiers were impacted by Solan's last attack. She knew that their warmth was a warning—a siren song to the humans of the Living Courts, but a death rattle to Lunarians. A constant reminder of what they'd lost. What they still stood to lose.

But it was more than their physical repulsions.

Stoicism was a shared value amongst the monarchs of each court, but beneath the robes and crowns, the two couldn't be more different. The rigid natures rooted in proven logic and facts of Solarians often butted up against the softer, more intuitive minds of the Lunar Court. Political differences aside, the chasm between their ethos on just about any other facet of life would drive them apart at best, to madness at worst.

"You look lovely," Ameera sighed, smoothing the last ruffle on Astra's gown.

"Thank you."

"Are you ready for your debut?"

"Don't call it that," Astra muttered.

"Question stands." Ameera folded her arms over her chest.

Astra inhaled, letting the air cool the burning fears in her spine, fighting the urge to escape from a window and run off into the Rift, despite her lack of knowledge about how to traverse it.

"Born ready," she laughed, hearing the wobble in her false confidence.

"ONE LAST TOUCH," Ameera said, fussing with Astra's hair outside of the Celestial Hall's mezzanine.

The crowd below buzzed and hummed with dozens of feelings so intensely Astra could see the colors from outside the room. Her family waited at the bottom of the staircase, she could sense their unique signatures on their feelings—or in her mother's case, the lack thereof.

She'd practiced this entrance all morning with Ameera, but they'd planned on a slinky silk dress, not a bejeweled ballgown with dozens of layers. The weight was staggering.

"Just a little something so you truly shine," Ameera whispered, puffing a fine mist over Astra's collarbones.

"That's fun," Astra murmured, marveling at the way her skin lit up.

"Archera and I found it in the village market last Summer."

"Tell me everything. Spare no detail—even if it takes all night!" Astra begged. Ameera rolled her eyes, backing away.

"She's ready," she directed to the maidens guarding the mezzanine door. They pulled the heavy stone doors back, a rush of whirling sound and color flooding over the marble floor and clutching Astra's hem. The wave hushed as the High Priestess motioned Astra forward.

"Astra Leona Aurellis, born on her mother's thirty-seventh Strawberry Moon, princess of the Lunar Court. May the Mother bless her within and without," the priestess announced.

"Damn," Ameera muttered behind her. "She forgot Fire Queen."

Astra's fingers twitched at the moniker, the twin nickname she shared with her sister: the Fire and Ice Queens. As the strings below struck up a simmering melody, she stepped forward. A collective breath from the mezzanine below knocked her back as she scanned the crowd. For a moment, she could have sworn she'd felt a tinge of that same merciless heat from before, but she must have been anxious. It faded quickly, replaced with a cold sweat dripping down her spine as she took in that first step.

When they'd rehearsed it earlier, the distance between the mezzanine and the ballroom floor seemed relatively short, but they hadn't accounted for the dizzying potion of the lowered lighting and hundreds of sets of emotions.

Sizing her up.

She took the top two steps easily enough.

Comparing her to Lunelle.

The next few weren't as gentle. The heft of the train on her dress dragged her backward.

Wondering where she'd been.

Twenty-four steps to go.

Did the music need to be so loud?

Astra watched a soft hand rise as her mother stepped forward to meet her, the only anchor point she had in this world as she descended the final steps. Impossibly fine threads wrapped her arms as if woven by the Moon herself. Her skirt ruffled out in great swaths of pale tulle, reflecting the candle-light in the room. The dome above scrolled back, baring the room to the Moon above, her gentle light bathing everything in a Summer shimmer.

Gossamer curtains fluttered around each arched opening, dancing on a breeze sweetened by the wisteria and roses in the garden.

Oestera pulled her daughter gently into her side and led her across the floor as courtiers backed into a wide circle. Their eyes locked on the two women as they stood facing each other, two ends of a spectrum. Oestera's chin nodded nearly imperceptibly, sending the orchestra into a flurry of high notes as Astra sucked in a breath.

It caught between her ribs as the melody stroked her cheek, a familiar trill she had not prepared for. The image materialized in her mind at once, Oestera's silver hair piled on top of her head, rocking her slowly under a full Moon, humming the melody as she drifted to sleep.

The memory could not survive the anxiety that gripped her as Oestera stepped back, starting a series of complicated twists and turns she'd rehearsed in her younger years. The dreamy low candlelight, the music she'd grown to, the slip of their gowns as they spun in a wide circle all came together in a mystic spell that transformed Oestera's face. Her cold, restrained countenance fell away, melting into something relaxed.

Relief, Astra realized.

After a few days of her best behavior, perhaps Oestera saw the potential within her daughter's abilities and not just the devastation.

Astra set her face and shoved the pathetic hope down where she kept plenty of other weak thoughts locked away, so they never got the best of her.

Oestera raised her arm and Astra followed, setting her hand atop her mother's. They caught the downbeat and twirled again, twin leaves circling one another in the night air, falling to the polished stone floor in a decadent arc. Their skirts traced intricate patterns around the ballroom, brushing against the shiny boots of the courtiers as they looked on.

The courtiers.

This was Astra's one chance to take in the room before everyone was in motion. She mimicked her mother's movements perfectly, noticing the signature scarlets of the Martian Court just over her shoulder. Their juvenile prince could not have been more than twenty, twenty-one—an infant by Lunarian standards.

Oestera twisted them back in the other direction, her braid whipping behind them. Astra had missed a step, forcing her mother to take up the lead. Astra's ribs flared at the mistake, but her mother's jaw unclenched in a silent apology.

"That's a new dress," Oestera remarked as they turned.

"A birthday gift," Astra confessed. "From the Mercurian Court." Something sparked in Oestera's eyes, something Astra wasn't sure what to make of. "I have a question," Astra said, choosing not to investigate. She threaded herself below her mother's arm and held her shoulders steady as she looked toward the crowd and dipped below her arm again. "If I behave myself this week, make nice with the courtiers, ensure our alliances are in good shape... would you consider appointing me as the High Priestess of Celene?"

Oestera's lips twisted, her hold on her emotions slipping momentarily. She twirled Astra away from her, a crushing navy tidal wave cresting over her lungs. Astra knew her answer before she spoke it.

"You will not be returning to Celene, Astra. In any capacity. Your duty is elsewhere."

"You have Lunelle!" Astra cried, stumbling as she clung to the rhythm. "You have no need of me, Mother. Celene does. Desperately!"

"I have plans for you, Astra. I'm asking you to please trust me," Oestera whispered, a harsh warning not to make a scene.

"What if I have bigger plans?"

Oestera did not immediately respond, the tension in her silence underscored by a run of low notes from the orchestra pit as the lullaby drew nearer to its end.

"Your duty is more important than your will, Astra. The sooner you learn that, the better. You're not a child anymore, you've left that cycle behind. Tonight, you enter into your Mother years, and it is your sacred responsibility to care for your people, *all* of them. Not just Celene."

There it was, in the way her brows tucked together. Final decision. No room for appeal.

A scarlet rage burned against Astra's chest. She inhaled, cooling the hurt, no one here needed to watch her fall apart. It would only make all of this more impossible.

She turned to the courtiers, choosing to distract herself with her audience. The music swelled for one final refrain as her eyes landed on a woman across the room, wrapped in sky-blue silks and feathers. She shuffled toward the edge of the dance floor. Her clay-colored hair was tucked into three neat buns down the back of her head, the sides shaved down to reveal two rows of ruddy tattoos flowing down her neck. The runes were Earthen. She recognized them as the same insignia from her father's old uniforms.

She was stunning, simply put. Everything about her implied power and confidence, one leg darting out of the seam of her dress, daring any of the men behind her to cross it.

Astra watched the stars above bounce off her tan skin, wondering briefly what they might feel like beneath her fingertips.

Mother Nature, Lunelle's voice surprised her as it slipped into her mind, chasing away the rather pleasant vision she'd concocted to distract herself. *She's as mean as she is pretty. You two would either be the best of friends or mortal enemies. A romance is out of the question.*

Sounds exactly like my type, Astra snorted. *Way more fun than the Martian infant.*

A familiar smile snagged Astra's attention as she twisted in her mother's arms. The tunic matched her gown perfectly. A clever maneuver. His smile was entrancing on its own, but his eyes held her captive beyond any of his other notable features. The Mercurian nodded his head, a soft curve of his lips sending a curious rush over Astra's spine.

Oestera twisted them again, noticing Astra's lack of focus. A vermillion irritation boiled over her guard before she followed Astra's gaze, the angry orange fading into a docile amber as she seized the opportunity.

She dropped her daughter's hand as the crowd applauded and pulled it forward through the dense crowd, ushering Astra directly to the Mercurian.

"King Mirquios," Oestera hummed, utter delight pouring off her shoulders. He was easily the most beautiful man Astra had ever seen. The king folded his head before her, tucking his strong jaw to his chest before smiling broadly and lifting the queen's hands to his lips.

Are you... drooling? Over a man? Lunelle mocked her sister. Astra attempted to close her jaw, realizing too late that it was hanging open.

She rolled her eyes as her sister's giggles bounced off the inside of her skull, recovering her face quickly as Mirquios dropped her mother's hand and reached for hers. It was damn near painful to hold such an intense gaze—but then again, when was the last time Astra had truly looked someone in the eyes?

"Astra Leona," he said as he bowed, his voice as low and enticing as it was the night before. "Happy birthday, Princess."

Astra managed a nod, but no sound came to her lips as her mother stared at her. Ever the social mastermind, she chirped, "I believe the next dance is starting!" And nudged her daughter forward.

The king's hand slipped into Astra's as she stepped back toward the floor. This time, thank the gods, other couples happily joined, taking some eyes of the room off her as chatter and laughter rose over the orchestra.

Though, who would want to look at anything other than him? She found herself thinking.

As the music strummed up, she stepped back in time with the strings and he easily followed, a hand landing on the small of her back as he held the other up, waiting for Astra to guide him across the floor.

"You've studied our customs," Astra said with a smile, surprised. She'd had plenty of dignitaries over the years struggle to keep up without turning the dance into a power struggle.

The king laughed, a rumbling trio of notes. "Please. Do you

know how nice it is to be led for a change?" His lilting accent ran over Astra's shoulders like liquid starlight.

"So you like being told what to do, then?" Astra arched a brow, reveling in the burgundy flush that climbed his neck as they spun under the moonlight. "I'll be sure to keep that in mind."

"I thought Fire Queen was just a nickname, but here I am, burning in your presence."

Astra's lips tilted into a dark smile as she spun him away from her and pulled him back in. "Thank you for the birthday gifts."

The king's eyes passed from the delicate cluster of jewels around her neck to her hips as he leaned in closer. "It was a tad selfish on my part, if I'm honest. To see such a beauty in Mercurian colors... that's a true gift."

Astra twirled under his arm and wrapped herself up in him before stepping away and linking her hand with his, facing the opposite direction of his bright gaze.

"Now, now. I'm sure you say that to all the Lunarian princesses."

"You caught me," he laughed, stepping around her in a ring. "I've said that to every Lunarian princess I've met tonight."

"I knew it," Astra said. "Scandalous."

"I've been called much worse, Princess." The king slid his hand behind her back as the orchestra worked up to a crescendo, brilliant notes suspended in the air between them.

"Astra," she said, her breath tight. "I hate being called Princess." She spun one more time as the music crawled to a soft finish, a final high note ringing out as the dancers stalled.

The king stared a hole right through her, that same cerulean curiosity from the night before welling up in his chest. "I wonder how you would feel about being called 'Queen'?"

Astra raised a brow, completely unprepared for such a forward question. He bowed as a rush of strange colors pooled in her stomach. She considered following him as he wove his way back into the crowd, but her mother was already cutting across the floor, her hand attached to yet another dignitary.

"Kahlia Artemi," she announced, slipping a golden hand into hers. "High Regent of Venus." Astra barely looked at the figure as she pulled them out onto the dance floor, shaking off the thrill of his question as the music started again, this time a spirited group dance. A hazy rose glow settled around them as they stepped in time with the strings. Kahlia was tall, with a thin, ethereal structure to their frame. Gleaming gold braids rained over their shoulders, their cheekbones jutted out with the same sharpness she recognized in Ameera's countenance. Golden freckles bedazzled the smooth planes of their face, a lovely mark left by their time in the Sun.

"So lovely to finally meet you, Princess," they cooed as they dipped their head toward the floor, ducking beneath the arms of other courtiers. That sweet rose color carried into an aroma that flooded Astra's senses, drowning any logical line of thinking she might have been able to hold on to in such a crowded space.

Unlike the king, who Astra imagined had been quite calculated in what he allowed her to ascertain of his emotions, Kahlia took full advantage of her abilities to perceive feeling. Her head felt light as they turned, meeting in the middle of two lines to wrap up in each other's arms before breaking again.

She'd studied the Inner Courts in depth. Naturally, she'd gravitated toward Venus, intrigued by Ameera's home court. Devoted to the Goddess of Love, she knew Venusians held a potent ability to seduce and attract, but she'd not taken it seriously. Reading about it was one thing, but experiencing it was another entirely.

Her eyes snapped upward as she heard her mother's laugh from the edge of the ballroom, gesturing toward her as she spoke with the Martian prince.

Kahlia was not just charming her, Mirquios wasn't flirting.

They were courting her.

All of them.

Ameera had been right, as usual. This wasn't a solstice ball or a birthday celebration—it was an auction.

The sharp knot of betrayal in her gut tightened, a violet flood pushing the air from her lungs. Kahlia whisked her from one end of the floor to another as she played back her conversation with her mother in her mind.

Who had she told her to focus on? Omnir?

Kahlia leaned closer, the rose haze making it hard to breathe.

You need air! Lunelle's voice pulled Astra from under the rosy tide. Gods, she was right. She could barely get her head above Kahlia's spell.

"Thank you for the dance," she gasped. They bowed to her and before Oestera could push her into the arms of Mother Nature or Prince Omnir, she darted into the crowd in search of her sister.

"She's marrying me off!" Astra hissed when she found Lunelle. Her sister did not respond. Instead, she pulled her hands toward the edge of the ballroom.

The courtiers buzzed, the colors and textures of their thoughts and opinions ringing in Astra's ears as she lost control over her perception. Their emotions became hers—excitement, curiosity, and judgment bubbling to life in her lungs.

She should have spent more time mentally preparing for

court life. She hadn't considered how difficult it would be in a crowd. She should have read between her mother's lines the other day, should have known that this would be her plan. Her intuition should have screamed at her the moment the note pulled her away from Celene.

Maybe it had. Maybe she'd ignored it. *Fuck.*

"You need to breathe, As," Lunelle called out over the crowd. "I'll cover for you, get out of the chaos."

Astra could try to fight the rising bile in her throat, muscle through the fire igniting in her veins. Or she could slip beyond the arch and into the cool night air and shake off the pain in her fingertips.

"I'll be back," she huffed.

If she stayed, she risked showing everyone just how brightly the Fire Queen could burn.

SEVEN

Moonblossoms dripped from ancient terraces, releasing a sweet perfume that stuck to her skin.

It only took a few moments roaming the lush gardens to get the fire under control, though her panic was still roaring against her bones.

In the inner courtyard, she was blessedly alone, able to hear her own breath for the first time since she'd descended the stairs inside. She perched along the edge of a fountain, letting the water cool her fingertips as she sorted through the tangled mess in her mind.

In the privacy of the flora, she let the panic devolve into rage.

Not only at her mother's strategic betrayal but at herself for playing right into it.

The pretty dresses, the dreamy music, all of it a con to get her in front of as many dignitaries as possible. Had she pushed her toward the Martian prince as a way to make up for her forsaken engagement all those years ago? Was her plan to marry her off to correct a diplomatic misstep?

She buried the thought, desperate to get on top of the all-consuming buzz inside her chest before it melted her bones and boiled her blood. The boning in her bodice tightened with each shallow breath.

Between her gasps, shocks of fluorescent green ire speckled her vision, and it struck her.

She could outmaneuver the queen.

The rush of King Mirquios's hands along her waist washed over her again. The queen had asked her to all but ignore him and focus on Mars to smooth things over with their wounded king, but why shouldn't she have a say in her Fate?

Who could blame her for falling in love with a handsome king?

She shook her head. It was a ridiculous thought. And a cruel one. She didn't need to tangle up an innocent monarch in her mess. And besides, no one who knew her well would buy it... unless—

The air in her lungs disappeared in a sudden heave. A whirlwind of torment swept through the garden, inky black and moving at a rapid clip along the hedges beside her.

She flinched as she held her chest, the midnight-black pain overwhelming her entire body. Her eyes searched the hedgerow for the intrusion, but just as quickly as it crashed over the cobblestones, it was gone.

"Hello?" she called out, rising and pushing her skirt behind her, ready to make a run for it. She could feel something—someone—running at an unholy heat on the other side of the hedges, though the initial downpour of feelings dissipated into silence. She edged toward the wall of foliage, letting the flames in her blood bubble toward her fingers.

She'd be damned if she let a Solarian get the jump on her this close after that nonsense on her way into the city.

Astra stilled her body and closed her eyes, trying to hold

the space across the leaves in her mind, searching for any hint of them. It was impossible to sift through so many blurry emotions and spirits, the crowd just a few yards away interfering with her vision.

She called again, "Is someone there?"

The only thing beyond the gardens was the Midwood. Any courtier looking to visit either had plans she didn't want involved in or was just plain stupid.

There. The heat concentrated into a tight ball, a faint smoke rising from the other side of the hedges.

"I can feel you," she whispered. The last dregs of darkness she'd felt before drained away, leaving only that intolerable warmth. It wasn't uncommon for folks to block her from their feelings, but it was eerie to feel absolutely nothing but that terrifying heat—whoever it was had an intrusive understanding of how her power worked.

The notion sent a shiver up her spine. She backed away from the wall, just in case.

"Fine," she relented. "Stay hidden, but it's my obligation to warn you that the Midwood will not take kindly to trespassers. It wouldn't be surprising if the Lunar elves decided they could use a meal. Especially one so warm," she said, sinking into her stance.

"Oh, please," the warmth rumbled back. The leaves rustled as they shifted. "Everyone knows the price of a Lunar elf is but a handful of gold coins."

Astra rolled her eyes. "For the average citizen, perhaps. But you..."

The voice barked a laugh. "What of me, Princess?"

She couldn't bring herself to lob the accusation. It felt too serious, if she wasn't certain, though the sweat rolling down her back seemed to confirm her suspicion.

"Take your chances then. Between the elves and my army,

you'll find yourself in quite a predicament." Astra crossed her arms. "Or, you could surrender yourself now. I'd be happy to deliver you into the queen's hands myself."

"As much fun as that sounds, I have somewhere to be."

"Who are you?" She demanded.

"No one you need to worry about," he replied.

"Surely, that's not true. Who are you here with?"

A dark chuckle wove through the leaves. "I have somewhere I have to be."

"Suit yourself!" She called as the flames retreated, moving toward the Midwood. Everything ravaged her nerves. The noise, the shoulders brushing past her as she stepped back into the ballroom, the heat of him that seemed to cling to her skin like the seawater below. It was all too much.

She shook her head, searching for Ameera in the crowd. She should have fired first and asked questions second—no one that warm could have anything but ill intentions for her.

"Princess!" A set of hands, warmer than hers but nothing like the ghost in the garden, gripped her shoulders. "Everything all right?"

"Your Highness," she sputtered, glancing frantically around the ballroom.

"You know, I think I'd prefer you to call me Mirquios," he said with a grin that she was sure should calm her nerves, but only tore a larger hole in her chest.

She needed to find Ameera and Archera.

"Very well," she muttered, searching through blues and reds and greens and pinks, looking for the glittering honey of Ameera's soul.

"I hope it wouldn't be inappropriate to ask you for a second dance?"

"I'm sorry," Astra sighed. "I would love to, but I need to find my Head Maiden."

"I'll accompany you."

Astra nodded, pushing through the dense crowd to the other side of the ballroom. Ameera was nowhere to be seen, though Astra swore she felt a flicker of her near the door.

Where are you? Astra beamed, hoping it would land in Ameera's ears. Mirquios trailed behind her dutifully as she exited the ballroom and slipped out into the hallway, intending to head for her wing of the palace. Ameera was even less enthused about these things than Astra, perhaps she'd retired for the night.

"Is this okay?" The king asked as she led them down an empty hall.

"What?" She couldn't be bothered to turn toward him, determined to follow the faint wisp of Ameera's signature she'd caught.

"The two of us alone?"

Astra stopped and turned, a slight laugh escaping her. "Oh. I'm afraid I'm no expert in Mercurian societal boundaries, but Lunarians are far less... concerned with things of that nature."

"Ah," he said, nodding as she slipped into her private study.

Mirquios pulled the door shut behind him, the colors in his chest shifting from guarded oranges and reds to a gentle ocean of blues and greens. "That's one of the many mysteries of the Lunar Court solved, then."

"Are we that mysterious?" Astra asked over her shoulder, plopping into the plush chair behind her desk. From this distance, all the energy of the Celestial Hall couldn't touch her. The heat of the Solarian dissipated. She could concentrate.

"The rumors range from terrifying to... tempting," Mirquios said, sitting across from her, crossing a foot over his knee.

"I'm happy to confirm or deny any rumors you've heard, Your—Mirquios."

70

He leaned back in the chair, examining her carefully. "Can you really read minds?"

She snorted. "Is that what they say about me?"

"Oh, they say a great deal about you, Fire Queen."

"I can't read yours," she offered. "But I can communicate telepathically with a select few women, yes. It depends on the relationship."

"Your sister?"

Astra smiled at the mention of Lunelle. "Yes. And my Head Maiden, Ameera. But it requires a two-way push and pull. It's not a free-for-all."

"Can I admit I'm disappointed, but also thoroughly relieved?"

"That makes two of us," Astra mumbled. The constant onslaught of everyone's emotional state was bad enough, but attaching their exact words to it? A nightmare. As Mirquios watched her face, a slow heat burned over her chest, so different from the one in the garden. There was no alarm in this warmth, no warning.

The only threatening thing about it was the sickening thought that she just might enjoy the way he looked at her. The spiraling line of thinking from the garden drummed up again.

What if... what if?

"So you can't read my mind, but do you see my aura or...?"

"I don't see auras," she answered him, shaking her head. "I see colors I've learned to tie to specific emotions. Well, I don't physically see them. It's more like I just know them, in here," she said, tapping her forehead.

"Can I test you?" His eyes held onto hers, a wicked grin breaking across his deep skin, sending a shiver over hers.

"Of course."

"So just... think of a feeling?"

"A memory. Something that made you feel strongly." She leaned over her desk as he conjured the memory, the cool tones in his chest swirling to a hazy gray with tendrils of lavender woven between midnight blues and icy teals. The colors gave way to the emotions in her mind. Trepidation, worry, clouded by something stronger, more resolute.

Duty.

"I know this one well," she said softly. "The complexity of obligation and honor. Resentment for choices made on your behalf. The strange blend of pride and moral decay beneath your skin. Hope that you aren't letting your court down."

"Incredible," he murmured. "Another one."

The smokey cloud rolled into something warmer, gilded. Glowing yellows and whites with a streak of ruby flame overtook him. Anticipation waltzed with nerves, a blush of relief, the whisper of something sparkling across a dance floor.

She dropped her eyes—gods be damned—was she blushing?

"This is certainly the most intriguing way someone has ever flirted with me."

"I think it would be much less exposing if you could read minds over feelings," Mirquios whispered, his eyes turning toward the paintings behind her.

"Most people around me have learned tricks to keep their feelings quiet. I try not to pry unless invited, but in a large crowd, it gets difficult to breathe. Most strangers have no idea what they willingly give away to me. It's exhausting."

"Hence the hiding," he said, gesturing to the study.

"Hence the hiding," she repeated.

"How long do we have until someone notices and insists you return?"

"Hard to say," she sighed, running a hand over her wild waves. "Lunelle would alert me if Mother were searching." She tapped her forehead to reinforce her point. "Although it's entirely possible Father has already dragged her back to their quarters. He's not one for parties."

"That's another rumor I'd like to get to the bottom of," Mirquios said, leaning on his knees. "Your parents. The legends are fascinating—are they truly Tethered? A Lunar demigoddess and a common human soldier?"

Astra's lips parted in a wide smile. "Unusual, to be sure," she explained. "But the gods weave souls together for a reason. If you observe them, watch the way they move together as one spirit, the way they orbit one another... you'd understand why they couldn't escape one another."

Mirquios took this in and tapped his fingers against the desk. "I don't know that I've ever witnessed it."

"Never? Are Tethers not common in Mercury?"

"I'm sure they are outside of the palace. But to my knowledge, none of the pairings I grew up with were anything more than carefully arranged legal documents."

"Ah yes, that first feeling you showed me. Duty."

"Does your mother expect you to marry without it, even with her own experience? Life Untethered?"

Astra thought about this for a moment. She'd never really considered it either way—it wasn't unlikely she had a Tether roaming the realms. Most did, but her mother's case was the exception, not the rule in the upper echelons of society. Matches were made through strategy, not stars.

Some courts didn't recognize Tethers at all, merely viewing them as a fairytale. Others, like the Venusian Court, thrived on them.

Her mother suffered greatly when she chose to honor the Tether—though she hadn't intended to be queen when she did it. No, the girls grew up understanding they were destined for alignment and alliances, not star-crossed love affairs.

"That second feeling you shared..."

"Seeing you slipping your way into the palace the other night," Mirquios whispered.

"That feeling. That could be enough, couldn't it? Our lives are so carefully curated on our behalf, but there's comfort in knowing that people can still catch us off guard, even without Fate pulling the strings. I almost think it might be preferable to stay Untethered. There's no distraction. No loyalties to consider except to my people. It's liberating if you think about it."

A quiet smile unfolded across his face. "You almost sound like you believe yourself."

"Almost," she admitted.

"Princess?" Three soft knocks against the door jolted Astra out of her chair.

"Come in," she said, Ameera's honey-gold energy rolling into the study. *Took you long enough,* she beamed to her maiden. "Mirquios, King of Mercury. Meet Ameera, my Head Maiden and best friend."

Ameera bowed, tucking one ankle behind the other. "Your Highness."

"Pleasure to meet you," Mirquios said. "I'll see you two back out there?"

Astra nodded as Ameera studied her, searching for what might have caused her panic. Mirquios slipped out of the study and surely wasn't even out of earshot when Astra turned and hissed at her best friend.

"We have a *major* problem, Ameera!"

"What? You might actually be enjoying yourself?"

Astra rolled her eyes. "Beyond that, though, add it to the list. There was someone out in the garden. I couldn't see him. He was on the other side of the hedges. He was scorching hot, Ameera. It was unbearable, just like in the

Midwood the other day. I'm concerned there's a Solarian spy in the court."

Ameera's eyes widened. "The Midwood?"

"Sorry," Astra muttered. "I forgot to tell you about that."

"Are you *sure*, Astra? The wards in the Rift wouldn't let anyone with Solarian blood through."

"That Solarian orb didn't just fall into the court, Ameera."

Ameera sighed. She had a point.

"I felt this storm of awful dread, but it was like when he spotted me, he shoved it all away. Completely untraceable. I could hardly read a whiff of him, which means he knows how I work, and he knows how to defend himself. He *must* be Solarian."

"Shh," Ameera hissed, all too aware there were always maidens in the walls. She pointed to her temple, switching to a silent conversation. *Tomorrow we'll speak with Archera. Surely the sentry can locate him.*

Astra nodded. That was really all they could do, she supposed.

Perhaps we should consider telling your mot—

No. If I'm wrong, if he's not Solarian, it'll look like I'm trying to get out of whatever plot she has for my hand. A dark cloud of violets and navy blues settled over Astra's chest.

Ameera frowned. *What do you mean?*

She's clearly trying to marry me off to Mars to atone for her broken engagement. I had to cling to the Mercurian all night just to stay out of the infant's path!

Certainly not the worst Fate, Ameera giggled.

Astra closed her eyes, leaning her head against the armchair. If there was one Solarian in the court, there could be any number of enemies lurking.

If they could get this close to the palace, they could get to her sister.

They could all be in terrible danger.

"Tomorrow," she said aloud. "Tomorrow, you'll speak with Archera and tell her everything you know. But please instruct her not to alert my mother until we have something to show for it."

Ameera nodded, chewing on her nail. "Whatever you say, Fire Queen."

EIGHT

"Good morning, future Queen of Mercury!"

A white blur bounced up and down at the foot of Astra's bed, much too enthusiastic for the early hour.

"What *time* is it?" Astra groaned.

"I brought you breakfast," Lunelle chirped, flopping a tray piled high with pastries near her feet. "Figured you'd rather fight a dragon than deal with last night's regrets by the hundreds in the dining hall."

"Goddess bless you," Astra mumbled, smoothing her hair. She was thrilled to avoid the heavy hangovers of the nobles—wait. "What did you call me?"

Lunelle giggled, tossing her sister a knowing glance. "Like you didn't spend nearly all of last night on the arm of that king, or tucked away in your study with him."

"That doesn't signify—"

Lunelle's amused gaze flashed. "Please. Since when are you so modest with me? He looked at you like you were the Mother herself. You can pretend all you want, As, I know what I saw."

77

Astra didn't respond as Lunelle fussed with a croissant, pushing a cup of coffee in her direction. She'd much rather her sister assume she had feelings for the king than poke at the fear coiling in her chest. She sipped the hot liquid slowly, letting it soothe the ache in her uncertain bones. Her sister watched her with playful eyes, a smirk tugging at the corner of her lips.

She took three long, measured sips before setting the mug down, Lunelle's eyes still watching her. *Oh, fine.* It wouldn't be a bad idea to plant seeds in case she *did* have to go with the plan swirling around her mind. "He was not terrible," she admitted.

"Oh, I knew it!" Lunelle sprang up, spinning in a circle. "The mighty, infallible Fire Queen has a crush on a *king,* of all people!"

"It doesn't matter," Astra muttered into her coffee cup. "I have much more important matters to worry about. I have to figure out how to get Mother to release me back to Celene."

Lunelle pulled one of Astra's hands into hers. "Mother is not keeping you here to punish you. Things are getting more tense by the minute across the courts. We need you here."

Astra dismissed her, choosing instead to focus on the buttery pastry and berry jam before her. "Tell me how your night went."

"You know me, I prefer to observe," Lunelle said. "Not nearly as exciting as your night."

"You could do with some excitement," Astra mumbled around a bite of pastry.

Lunelle glared as she plucked a strawberry from the tray. "I have plenty of excitement coming my way in Winter. I've been in training misery for my coronation trial. Last month, I caught Mother lining up portraits of eligible nobles to nominate as champions."

Astra frowned. It may be frustrating that her mother was actively trying to auction her off, but at least she didn't have to endure a coronation trial.

"Anyone interesting?"

Lunelle shook her head, her lips falling into a pale line. "How should I know? I've been locked in Lunaria for thirty-two years. You're my only friend," she laughed, squeezing Astra's hand. "Allow me to use this week as a distraction and live vicariously through you."

"While you're *observing*, can you keep an eye out for anything strange?" She made every effort to keep her voice even as if asking about the weather or tomorrow's dinner menu, but her chest broke into a cherry-red alarm.

"Did something happen?"

"No," she answered much too quickly. "I just have a feeling, Lu. Something is off."

Lunelle nodded, never one to second guess her sister's premonitions. "I should go. I have meetings all day with these courtiers. Whoever scheduled Mars and Venus back to back should be hanged."

Astra laughed. "Perhaps your meeting with Venus will go long and run into the Martian prince's nap time."

Lunelle's lips curled into a smile, a soft giggle flowing over her shoulders as she left. "I'll see you at the beach this evening?"

"With bells on!"

ASTRA REACHED for her fourth glass of moonshine under the linen tent, staked into the soft sand of the Empyrean shore.

"Perhaps you should slow down," Ameera whispered.

Astra's eyes focused on the roses dripping from the center

of the lavish tent. Well, they made an *attempt* to focus. Ameera may have had a point. She sighed and set the glass back down, gladly accepting the water her maiden offered instead.

Beyond the tent, courtiers played their hands at a spirited round of Star Cross. They gripped wooden mallets and batted glowing orbs down the beach toward silk nets, whooping and hollering as they went.

At the tables, older courtiers played dice games and cards. Astra plopped into an empty seat and Ameera sat across from her as she shuffled a deck of divination cards. Their slick, painted faces made a satisfying clicking sound as they slipped over one another.

"What will it be?"

Ameera sighed. "If it's another bad omen, please don't tell me. I've had enough."

Astra smirked, flopping out three cards from the top of the deck and turning them over in quick succession.

"All coins," she muttered. "You best go put some money down on Lunelle's team," she said as she waved her hand toward the Star Cross court. Ameera did not hesitate to take her advice.

For better or worse, Astra's intuition was rarely wrong.

"How much for a reading?" A low voice hummed as Mirquios slipped into the seat across from her.

"First one's free," she chuckled, sliding Ameera's cards back into the pile.

"I've never had my cards read before," he confessed.

Astra shuffled the deck, letting her fingers move on their own accord, reluctant to twist Fate any more than she was already conspiring to. "They only mean what they mean," she advised. "There is no magic within their colors or names. Whatever they stir within you is exactly what's meant to be."

Mirquios nodded, leaning back as he sipped his drink, watching her with heavy eyes.

He *was* handsome, she allowed herself to admit as she set the deck on the table.

She closed her eyes, waving her hands over the deck and listening to the whispers in the wind for numbers. They rushed forth all at once. Thirteen, forty-one, nine, twenty-six.

"Gods above," she murmured, opening her eyes and counting through the stack as the numbers arrived. She laid each card out in a diamond configuration.

"The Lovers," Mirquios said, grinning as he reached forward and ran his fingertips over the card closest to him. "Well, then."

"Don't get ahead of yourself," Astra warned. "You have to consider it all within the context of each other. You don't get to pick and choose." She studied the cards, letting the story before her fall into place.

"The Lovers are reversed to you, signaling something may be out of balance, or blocking you from receiving the kind of wholeness you could have. And The Tether is also reversed."

"That doesn't bode well."

"It doesn't bode anything, Mirquios. Only what you want it to." She pursed her lips, running her fingers over the brightly painted colors of the other two cards. The Nether Queen and The Rift stared back at her. "Fascinating," she whispered. "There's so much in transit here, a grand weaving together of threads—"

"The Nether Queen is suspicious."

Astra's lips curled. "She's not nearly as scary as one would think. We often associate her with Descending, with death, but she really represents change—acceptance of your flaws so you can be your most authentic self."

"Huh." Mirquios nodded, unsure what to make of that information.

"It only means what it means," she repeated.

"I hate that," Mirquios said, laughing as he drained his drink. His eyes flickered to the edge of the tent where a large group of Venusian and Earthen courtiers entered, the volume escalating rapidly. "Would you like to go for a walk?"

Astra nodded, stacking her cards neatly and placing them back in their wooden box as she rose. Her skirt dragged behind them as they carved a path down the beach, away from the raucous crowd. The stars glittered above, punctuating their comfortable silence as Astra tiptoed at the edge of the water.

Mirquios watched her from the grass line, delighted in the way she glided into the surf. He stepped forward, drawing in a deep breath. "May I be forward with you, Astra?"

She stopped skipping over the rolling waves and turned, her silk skirt folding in the tide around her ankles. "Of course." Her blood twisted like the currents below as he spoke, eyes fixed on the shoreline.

"We've heard rumors in Mercury that a certain Fire Queen has a much more progressive outlook on the world than her contemporaries."

Astra chuckled, folding her arms around herself. "That's a kind way to say it. My mother thinks me a foolish dreamer."

"The powers that be always do. I think we might have similar dreams, Astra." Mirquios stopped pacing. "I heard about a restoration project you helped fund. Celene?"

Her eyes widened. "You've heard of Celene?" The confusion tangled in her throat. They'd done so much work to keep Celene quiet and protect its fragile ecosystem, if the Mercurians knew about it, who else did?

"Only whispers," he assured her. "I believe there is a

woman there who left a Mercurian village to seek refuge from her husband. Alana—"

"I know her," Astra said quickly, the young woman's face so clear in her mind. She'd arrived half-starved, with deep purple bruises around her neck.

"She sent word back to her sisters, one of whom is friendly with a member of my court. When she heard of the project, she told me. We've been discussing Mercury's future for a long time, and the court system. When we heard a Lunar princess was proving the concept... even without your mother's invitation, I would have sought you out for your advice."

Astra shook her head, hardly hearing him. "Do your courtiers know what you're considering?"

"Only a select few. As you can imagine, there would be outrage and counter-movements. The establishment will not distribute power easily."

"Of course," she rolled her eyes. She'd seen her own mother's resistance time and time again. "Gods forbid they get placed in the same category as someone whose hands aren't pristine."

"They'd revolt. This will be a bloody business. It's a delicate matter that requires careful planning, but Celene is proof that community living can work. Perhaps you could take me to visit—"

"No." She sucked a breath in through her teeth, her bones screaming to protect her family. "I'm so sorry. It's not personal. Most of the women in Celene are survivors of unspeakable atrocities at the hands of men. You understand?"

"Of course," he sighed. "I should have realized."

Astra bit her lip, willing the scarlet urge to defend them into submission. He was not an enemy. He was curious.

"Some of the leadership would be willing to speak with

you, we could perhaps meet in Ellume or one of the Middle Villages."

"That would be incredible. I'm sure I don't even need to say this, but please, keep this between us. If the Mercurian courtiers caught wind..." Mirquios shivered, unwilling to even imagine the consequences.

"Understood," Astra agreed. A roar of screams rose over the beach, Lunelle's silhouette hoisting a mallet over her head. She was but a blur of silver from this distance, but Astra knew what a Lunelle victory sounded like.

"Your sister..."

"My sister?"

"She'll be taking the throne in the Winter. Is she of a similar mind to ours?"

Astra twisted her fingers into her skirt. "I'm not certain. I think so. I want to believe so. But my mother has been molding her mind for three and a half decades. It's hard to say."

"Perhaps we could bring her into the fold eventually, too."

"Maybe," she whispered. "Don't laugh, but before we head back, I need to make my offering to the sea."

Mirquios tilted his head to the side. "Why would I laugh?" He reached into his pocket and produced a thin gold chain. "I find it a charming notion. What's the protocol here? Do we just throw them? Is there an incantation?"

Astra giggled, fishing around in her pocket for the small velvet offering bag she'd filled with aventurine stones from the gown he'd gifted her. Somewhere between breakfast with Lunelle and dinner, she'd felt a longing within her she knew meant she needed to at least consider her plan for the king, and all this talk of transferring power was only making the yearning worse.

It wasn't perfect, it wasn't Fate, but it was appealing.

"You make your plea to the sea goddesses in your mind, and then toss it into the ocean as far as you can."

"Ladies first, then," he said, turning toward the vast expanse of the Empyrean Sea, stars slipping under the horizon as the night drifted on. Astra stepped forward, the layers of her dress swirling around her ankles like a silk jellyfish. She closed her eyes and drew in a salty breath. The loose thoughts in the back of her mind crystallized into a vision she could no longer ignore. Mirquios was kind, he understood her vision, and he certainly wasn't difficult to look at.

If she cemented herself to him, she could shed her mother's meddling. Oestera would have to accept a king over a prince, wouldn't she? She wanted allies, and this was a powerful one.

Astra's big visions for the future were not out of grasp with a king at her side.

They were not two cosmic lovers, predestined by the gods to fall into one another—rather, they were two kindred spirits leaning on each other to change the unchangeable course of their bloodlines, and that had to count for something.

Right?

Give me the king, she thought as she reared her arm back, flinging the bag into the black waters.

Mirquios waited until she returned to his side to make his plea. He did not hide the rush of feelings within him—nerves and nostalgia, a longing for something, a release. He wound his hand back and skipped forward as he hurled the chain through the air and watched it sail across the night sky, landing with a satisfying splash.

"Now what?" He asked.

"Now, we wait," she said, shrugging. "We'll check the beach at moonrise. If we've chosen the right path, our offerings will return to us."

"Are you going to tell me what you wished for?" He asked softly, eyes finally releasing from the spot where his offering submerged and landing on Astra's face.

"Never."

"You could sense mine, couldn't you?"

Astra's nose scrunched. "Only how you felt about it."

"So unfair," he murmured, stepping a tad closer to her. She felt it then, the magnetic pull between hands that concluded they *would* touch, but weren't sure how or when.

Astra drifted her fingers into the charged space between them, lingering just near enough a strong breeze could seal the deal.

Perhaps he moved first, perhaps she did—their hands entangled all the same. A comforting warmth rolled off the king. Just enough to intrigue her, but not enough to set her instincts ablaze. There was something within his touch that felt familiar.

Easy.

He watched their skin dance together under the Moon, those feelings he showed Astra in the study rushing forward again, this time louder, with more intense hues.

Mirquios inhaled, his breath laden with the fear of a man about to put himself at the mercy of a woman. "Is it crazy to think that sometimes the gods mistake the whole Tether thing? Surely a few souls slip through the cracks?"

Astra shook her head, ruby curls bouncing against her shoulders. She tried to fight the smile that broke over her lips, but her lungs filled with those vibrant colors of his, making it hard to resist the urge. "I've heard crazier things."

"Astra," he whispered, but she did not let him finish whatever the thought might have been.

She didn't care. If she *was* going to attach herself to someone, it might as well be as beneficial to her body as it was to her soul.

She pitched forward, slipping herself under the surface of him, waves crashing around their ankles as she pressed her lips into his. His hand sat at her waist, gently squeezing his long fingers into the hazy silk of her dress as they moved closer still.

As his lips waltzed against hers, she waited for the fire in her veins to spark—the way it had in past encounters—for a flourish of gilded desire to explode in his chest. She waited for her back to arch involuntarily, for the blood to rush to her cheeks.

She waited for her fingers to desperately curl against his strong arms, unable to fathom letting go.

She waited to feel, well, *anything*.

Astra pulled away from him, the clouds within her head now decidedly tainted with something new.

"Oh," he said, surprised.

"Huh." Her eyebrows crashed together. "Perhaps we put too much pressure on it?"

This relieved him. "Yes! The first kiss can be so daunting!"

"Right," she agreed. "Well, then. Um—"

"Princess?" Ameera's voice cut between them, an interruption they were both silently grateful for.

"Ameera!" Mirquios boomed, a little too enthusiastically. He reached for the back of his neck, the relief visible as the colors within him straightened out. "I should get back," he muttered, pointing toward the tent.

"Of course," Astra replied, eyes cast at the water below them. Ameera's eyes flickered between them, unsure how to proceed.

"Your Highness," she bowed as Mirquios darted back toward the beach.

"Good evening!" He called over his shoulder.

"Oh!" Ameera cried, stepping on something in the shallows. She stooped and snagged a thin gold chain from the water. "Is this either of yours?"

A twist of ruby alarm gripped the king's chest. "Yes," he hesitated to say. "Yes, that is... mine. I suppose I'm on the right path, then?" He looked at Astra and gestured toward it. "You know what, why don't you keep it, Princess? A gift."

"Oh, um, yes, thank you," Astra said, pulling at the bodice of her dress. Mirquios trotted through the surf, disappearing up the shore.

That was the worst kiss I've ever seen. Ameera snorted, the amusement tickling her lungs.

Astra gasped, "Ameera!"

"You have better chemistry with Riverion."

"Mother smite me, Ameera, that's *foul*," Astra hissed. But she couldn't help herself. The harsh sound faded into a giggle.

Ameera rested a hand on her forearm. "There's always the Martian child. In five, maybe ten years he just might know where to find—"

"Absolutely *not*!" Astra choked. "I left education in my maidenhood, *thank you*."

Ameera shrugged beside Astra as she drowned in midnight blue misery. It *was* the worst kiss she'd ever had, and she'd had some weak starts.

She spent the next thirty minutes searching the shallows for her offering, dreading that it might show up.

Dreading that it wouldn't.

It did not reappear before she finally gave in to her exhaustion and fell into bed.

"Princess," a deep voice thundered over Astra's shoulder. "What are you looking for?"

She twisted, a sudden heat sending a sheet of sweat rolling down her back. The sand on her astral plane sparkled like crushed diamonds instead of the grainy beige she shook from her dress before bed. She dragged a finger through the coarse glitter, leaving a trail as warm waves lapped at her feet.

"I thought I knew," she whispered. "But the gods don't seem to agree."

The voice scoffed. "You didn't strike me as someone who gave a single shit about what the gods desire."

Astra woke with a start, a lingering heat in her skin, drowning her throughout breakfast.

CHAPTER

NINE

You're being weird.

Lunelle's voice broke Astra's staring contest with her coffee cup—and she was so close to winning.

"I'm sorry," Astra answered aloud, unable to muster the energy for anything else. She barely slept after last night's events. Her heart was too tangled up in seawater and conflicted feelings. That, and she'd gotten up just before moonrise to search the expanse of the sandy Empyrean shore for a small velvet bag that neglected to make its way back to her.

She shook the thought from her head. Perhaps she hadn't been clear enough—too afraid to really demand what she wanted. Perhaps the Court Above simply couldn't watch her suffer a lifetime of sterile, passionless kissing.

The gods had not been particularly merciful to her so far, but maybe this was their way of making it up to her.

"What's going on?" Lunelle asked, eyeing the golden chain around Astra's wrist. "Another gift?"

She sighed. "Sort of."

"I never thought I'd see you so lovelorn," Lunelle said wistfully, reaching for a bowl of fruit. "I hardly recognize you. You're all flustered. It's *quite* unsettling."

She brushed her glimmering hair over one shoulder, the last light of the waning Moon washing her in pale beams as the dining hall filled in with courtiers. The sea breeze crept over the tables, tickling their collarbones, though Astra did not shiver. A heat crawled up her neck as she weighed telling her sister what had transpired between her and the king.

Or rather, what *hadn't*.

Gods, she would love to be flustered. Flustered would be wonderful. She'd even take thoroughly ruffled—Mother above, she'd trade all the coins in her pocket to replace the strange dread in her bones with something new.

"Astra!" Her mother's voice snapped her from her spiraling thoughts as she crossed the dining hall. A slender form trailed her, wrapped in the scarlets of Mars.

Oh, shit, she sent to her sister, who snorted into her tea cup. Astra held her breath. An angry purple flared in her chest as her sister stifled a giggle with her sleeve.

"Prince Omnir was hoping to go for a ride on this lovely morning," Oestera chirped.

"Ah, well, unfortunately, I don't believe we have any saddles that fit me, Mother," Astra mumbled, the queen's eyes flaring with irritation. She sighed and straightened her shoulders. "I'd caution you against the Silvershifts. Perhaps one of the smaller wyverns would be more enjoyable. Have so much fun!"

Oestera hissed through clenched teeth, "You're one of our best riders. The prince has competed in dozens of inter-court races. Surely, you two would enjoy some spirited competition."

"Competed in... but not won?" She glared at the princeling

who shifted in his boots, avoiding eye contact. His face flushed as he glanced toward Oestera.

Help me, Astra begged her sister.

"Enough, you will join Omnir—"

"She cannot!" Lunelle perked up, her delicate brows arching in surprise at the sharpness of her tone. Oestera rolled her eyes. It had been quite some time since she'd found herself embroiled in a two-on-one match with her daughters—she was out of practice and they knew it.

"And why is that, Lunelle?"

"She..." Lunelle pursed her lips, glancing at Astra as if she had the magic solution. Her eyes darted across the dining hall and Astra watched a pale daffodil yellow unfurl in her chest. "She's already promised to take the Mercurian king..." Lunelle tapped her fingers against her glass as she thought. "On a tour of the distillery. Yes. She's giving the king a tour. Look, there he is now!"

Astra's eyes followed her sister's gesture across the table, wondering if Prince Omnir might have been the better Fate.

She caught Mirquios's eyes widening in recognition.

"Oh," Oestera said, taken aback. "Is she now?" The pleasure her mother derived from this revelation should have been a point of caution for Astra, but she was too busy drowning in the blood rushing to her ears. "Well, I won't interfere with your plans, then."

"Thank you, Mother?" Astra couldn't help but tilt her voice up at the end, unsure she'd ever left a conversation with Oestera on a positive note. She hopped to her feet and crossed the dining hall, dozens of courtiers watching as she wove through the tables. They judged her in shades of orange and red, blue and violet.

But no one drowned in violet apprehension quite like Astra.

The king gauged her path immediately, bracing himself as a carnelian panic rose in his lungs. She watched the cloud dissipate as he drew in a measured breath.

"Princess," he said, leaning back against the table his court occupied.

"Good morrow," Astra ventured, attempting to sound breezy, though her tone settled between them with a thud.

"Indeed," he replied, a smirk pulling at his lips. He'd been nervous about this interaction, but something about the way she rocked on her heels amused him.

"I believe I promised you a tour of our moonshine distillery this morning."

Mirquios tilted his head as she narrowed her eyes. "I... sure?" Astra's lips twitched. "Yes. You did. I was just going to grab some breakfast—"

Astra released a breath, grabbing a pastry from a basket at the center of the table and shoving it into his hand. "Make it to go, Your Highness!"

"You're quite famous for your moonshine, you know," Mirquios mused after three and a half miserable hallways of silence.

"Mmm."

"There's a Lunar stall in the Mercurian Bazaar that sells it. They have the most splendid little bottles, with crystals on the corks!"

"Sure." Astra shoved a thick moonstone door open with her hip, revealing a damp staircase. "Down we go."

The king's eyes flickered between her face and the stairs. "After you, my lady."

Astra huffed, happy to escape to the cooler underground of

the palace. She took the steps two at a time, sweeping her black skirts behind her. Mirquios missed the final step, lurching forward, his hands landing on her hips to steady himself. He attempted to yank them away, but a finger caught in the delicate chain around her waist, between a metallic star and Moon charm. She yelped as the weight of him pushed the sharp tip of the star into her flesh.

"Sorry," he sighed.

Astra spun and faced him, eye to eye with his surprised stare. The cellar air chilled her bones, the heat from his chest suddenly much more appealing. He *was* handsome, by all accounts. She'd done much more interesting things with much less interesting people.

Perhaps it *had* been a case of the first kiss jitters.

Her silk slippers ground against the frigid stone floor as she pushed onto her toes. His arms closed around her waist in a halo of warmth, pulling her against him. Their lips brushed tentatively, both afraid to repeat last night's failure.

His fingers wrapped around the side of her neck, applying pressure just below her ear. Her hand wandered the vast plane of his chest, pressing into his shoulder, searching for something to hold on to.

A subtle flicker of rosy pink, so slight she almost missed it, came to life between them but disappeared. Astra gave up.

"What is *wrong* with us?" she cried, clasping her hands together in frustration.

"Oh, thank the gods," Mirquios gasped, backing away from her. "I was so worried it was just me."

"Certainly not," Astra muttered.

"I did not mean—"

"I know! I know," she said, waving her hands to silence them both. She leaned against the clammy wall, letting the cold stone soothe her temper. "Mother above, I really thought it was just a one-off."

"Listen, I was doing some of my best work just now. Women usually love the neck thing!"

"I believe you! Fuck," she hissed, the expletive catching him off guard. "This really ruins my plan."

"Plan?"

Astra shook her head. "Um. No plan."

"Princess—"

"Mother, spare me. This is so humbling." She slinked around the corner, the narrow passage opening into a massive cellar filled with barrels upon barrels of moonshine. Mirquios followed, propping himself up on one of them. She let her body fall to the floor in a heap against the wall. "My mother is trying to marry me off."

"Yes," Mirquios said, confused by *her* confusion.

"To the Martian prince," she sighed.

His lips twisted. "The boy? Would he know the first thing to do with you?"

She glared, the implication that *he* had any more luck with her irritating.

"That's why I've basically thrown myself at you." She blushed as she confessed to him. "I thought that if you and I could make a good match, if we saw the world the same way... well. There are worse Fates, surely."

The king straightened his back, his lips twitching into a smile as he laughed. "Is that a proposal, Princess?"

Astra rolled her eyes. "My mother will never allow me to go back to Celene and I can't do enough from here to further the cause. But she knows war is coming and she needs alliances. I think that's why she's so set on Omnir."

Mirquios considered that for a moment, his bright eyes

sweeping over her. "Mars is no place for a mind like yours, Astra."

"*I* know that. What you said last night, about Celene, about building a similar community—I thought maybe that was a sign to pursue it. But then we kissed and..." She released another sigh, letting her hand fall to her side.

"And... it wasn't an instant success," he suggested. "But sometimes things like this aren't. We just met." He stood, pacing. "I came here hoping I could learn how Celene functioned, to emulate it for my own court. I won't pretend that I hadn't thought about the potential. Romance is not really a priority for me, Astra, but if the rumors were true, I thought perhaps I could learn from you. My mission is to my people, not a queen. But, if that's not a concern..." He trailed off, standing before her, his eyes sparkling with something like hope.

She tapped her knee. Romance *had* been her first plan, but only because it was the easiest path. It wasn't the only one. She'd experienced her fair share of flings, but she always knew that she'd end up shackled to a noble at some point.

She'd accepted it long ago.

Omnir's sullen face popped into her mind, void of any experience in those deep-set eyes. She shuddered. Her options were limited, and Mirquios was the best-case scenario.

"And you mean it, about disbanding your court and distributing your power?"

"I can show you the plans, Astra. In fact, I *need* you to see them as an advisor. This could work." He held out a hand, lifting her to her feet. "These inter-court arrangements have always been so hollow. But, we'd have a common mission, and shared passions. That's a bond that most would kill for. And perhaps the rest of it comes someday?"

"Perhaps," she whispered, a rush of warm adrenaline tickling her bones.

"Do you think your mother would bless a union? Or is she set on Mars? I understand there's a complicated history."

Astra's ears buzzed as he spoke. There certainly *was* a history that complicated things.

"That's exactly it," she gasped, turning on her heel and pulling him through the hallway and up the stairs. "Genius! This will work just fine," she laughed, the king desperately trying to keep up with her.

"Where are we going?"

"We have an announcement to make," Astra answered, shoving the door open. "You'll need to look utterly besotted, my king."

"Say it one more time?"

Nayson shook his head, his amber eyes darting between his daughter's face and the young king she'd flung into the chair across from him, interrupting a rather peaceful tea. "I don't think I heard you correctly."

Oestera clapped her hands together, glowing with excitement. "She *said* they've Tethered, Nayson!"

The Lunar king leaned back in his chair, rubbing his hands over his chin. Gods bless him, he tried to hide the utter disbelief on his face, but Astra saw every vivid color flare and retract as he sorted through his feelings.

Oestera squeezed her husband's shoulder. "It's wonderful news, Astra. We've always valued our relationship with Mercury, and now we'll be family!" Her lips broke into a wide grin, the closest she'd ever gotten to pride flickering to life beneath her scarred flesh.

Astra had prepped for a battle the whole way across the palace, certain her mother would disapprove, but she was damn near delighted.

"It just seems rather sudden," Nayson mumbled, unsure if anyone was even listening to him.

"I believe you have us beat," Astra replied, her brows knitting together in frustration. Mirquios stiffened next to her, out of his depth with the complex emotions of her family dynamic.

"Well, yes, but—"

"I couldn't have arranged a better match myself," Oestera declared, ending any more discussion. "The gods have blessed you both. We of all people wouldn't dream of standing in the way of something so sacred, would we, Nayson?"

"Of course not," he said, shrugging, his chest still alight with a million opposing emotions. "At least there's no inter-court scandal attached to it."

"Exactly," Oestera chirped. "Ameera! Could you send for some moonshine? We should celebrate!"

Ameera moved quickly for the first time since Astra pulled her into the queen's private wing. She'd hardly believed the words coming out of Astra's mouth as she spoke, but she'd had very little time to process. She darted to the maidens in the hall, requesting a celebratory bottle immediately.

"Make it two," she instructed, glancing at the deepening reds of Nayson's cheeks. Astra smiled at Mirquios, doing her best to appear ever the doting fiancée.

"I hope I did not circumvent any Lunar customs by asking Astra directly to be my queen. With the... the Tether, we got a bit swept away. I didn't think she would appreciate being left out of the discussion."

"Perhaps you know her just fine, then," Nayson scoffed.

"No offenses here," Oestera beamed. "Tethers are impossible to predict. We're much less formal than some other courts when it comes to these things. Of course, we'll have to discuss the marital contract, but we don't need to get into all of those details now."

"Where is Lunelle?" Nayson asked, interrupting Oestera.

"I would like to tell her privately," Astra said. She pursed her lips, the one thing she hadn't been able to solve for was how she was to leave the sister she'd only just gotten back to.

"Of course," Oestera said. "Our girls are very close."

"I've gathered I come second to Lunelle," Mirquios said. "I hope to earn her trust and affections, as well."

"You say that now," Nayson sighed. "Wait until they have their silent conversations about you at the dinner table."

"Father!" Astra protested.

"I'll adjust," the king replied.

Nayson nodded, reaching for the bottle of moonshine as Ameera reappeared at the end of the table.

He poured heavy.

⁓⊃⁊ᴄ

"COME IN!"

Lunelle sat behind her reading desk, the very portrait of a Lunar queen as Astra took in her ethereal sister from the doorway.

"I was just looking over a report from Ellume—it seemed to put Mother on edge earlier." She moved to hand her sister a stack of parchment but paused when her eyes caught Astra's. "Oh gods, what's happened?"

"Well," she said, sounding rather stupid as she edged into the room. She'd thought about how to tell Lunelle all afternoon, but the words just never seemed to capture the exact weight of her feelings.

Lunelle knew her sister far too well to belabor it. "Just tell me, whatever it is. Has that king of yours proposed?" She laughed as she tucked her stationary into a drawer, sitting back in her chair. "Oh," she sighed, catching Astra's solemn stare as she sank into the chair across the desk.

From birth, Astra knew their girlhood would end this way. That was the job description—they'd never grow old together. She'd always imagined Oestera would drag her kicking and screaming down the aisle to marry some distant cousin as a last resort, and they could both blame their mother for their inevitable separation.

She'd never thought she'd be the one holding the knife.

"Lu," her voice trembled. "I'm sorry."

"Sorry!" Lunelle pushed away from her desk, rising. "Do not be sorry, Astra." She rounded the desk, perching on the smooth surface beside her sister. Her eyes dropped to Astra's left hand, a lovely cluster of aventurine and diamonds settled on her skin.

"We Tethered," she lied. "Otherwise I wouldn't have agreed so suddenly—"

"Yes, you're known for your careful, deliberate planning," Lunelle chuckled. "Mother above, As. This is wonderful," she mumbled, tears welling at the back of her throat.

"I genuinely believed it would never happen for someone like me, but... but it did."

"A Tether," Lunelle sighed, rubbing the bridge of her nose. "Who could fight that?" Her eyes hardened as she grazed her sister's face, pushing the rush of emotions into a neatly contained ball.

The way a queen would.

"I think he and I could do good together, Lu. We see the world the same way. We want the same things. He's funny enough, smart."

"And handsome."

"A noted perk."

"Mercury is far away," Lunelle whispered.

"The Rift makes it a quick trip," Astra insisted. "Mother can't ban me if I'm no longer her loyal subject."

"You forget that come Winter I'll be on the throne. Your ban would be lifted either way."

"He's a good man," Astra repeated. "I feel it in my bones, Lu."

"But a man nonetheless," Lunelle hummed. "Be careful, As." Astra swallowed, the sorrow in her chest easing into a melancholy gray, tinged with little flashes of yellow happiness. "You know, I've yet to even introduce myself to him. He's been so obsessed with you."

"I think you'll find him quite charming," Astra insisted, resting her hand over her sister's and releasing the breath she'd held since the moment the idea formed at the base of her skull.

"Sure, except for the whole stealing my sister away to a far-off land thing."

Astra chuckled. "You will have to look past that part, yes."

"I'll do my best, As."

Lunelle waited until Astra was surely across the palace and out of view of her emotions before she allowed her tears to flow across her delicate cheeks.

S leep eluded Astra that night.

She'd wrestled with her sheets for hours when she finally slipped under the current, only to land in a long, dark hallway, billowing at the edges as her subconscious mind tried to patch together a message. She stepped forward, the darkness whispering to her.

Each step dragged her deeper into herself, the hollow sounds of her steps echoing off ribs and marrow. As she came to the end of the hall, the walls fell away, revealing another world entirely. Everything was stark white marble, walls and steps falling into place as she moved through the dream. She turned her face upward, the walls stretching into oblivion.

White towers sprouted to life, looming over her, topped with puffy opal clouds. When she turned her eyes back to the room before her, two thrones sat in the middle. They were carved from crystal, clear facets refracting a strange orange glow, something like fire rising behind them.

The light seemed to ignite the thrones from within, sparkling as it slipped higher over the backs, chasing the moonlight from above.

She glanced downward, a row of runes carved into the marble flooring running through the middle of the thrones.

She recognized the shapes—they'd been emblazoned into the cuffs of the Solarian in the orb.

Sit, a voice whispered, not from behind her, but from further within her. She stared at both thrones, overwhelmed by their brilliance.

She searched her bones for some sort of guidance, but nothing came. She was alone.

Tsk, tsk. Where is your intuition, Fire Queen? Have you forgotten who you are?

Astra spun, sure the voice was in the room with her. The ghost chuckled as she fixed her gaze back on the thrones. Refocusing her eyes, she narrowed them to make out more detail.

There, on the arch of the throne to her right, a Lunar etching.

The sigil was the Aurellis family crest, but dripping with a metallic liquid. She drew nearer, a humming reverberating off the thrones that called to her. It was the same as the orb—a song that fell apart through space and time. As she climbed three shallow steps she felt a pull behind her, a heavy train dragging her back.

She twisted to see where she was caught and a dreadful realization settled into her stomach. The robes were not just fancy wrappings—they were the very same coronation robes being stitched together now by the maidens for her sister's trial.

The shock hit her in the chest, pushing her from the dream and back into her bed.

⟡

"Astra?" Ameera asked, slipping into her bedroom the next morning.

She must have drifted back to sleep eventually, though it took some doing.

"Are you feeling all right?"

"Fine," she lied.

"The council is assembling in the Celestial Hall. There's news from the Outer Courts." Astra jumped from her bed, catching her council robes as Ameera flung them across the room. Ameera swept her hair into a somewhat presentable braid before stepping into the hall, doing everything she could think of to shake the strange feeling after her dream.

It was all the celebratory moonshine, she told herself.

Something was gravely wrong in the Celestial Hall. She felt the shift as she passed through the moonstone doors, no less than twenty concerned clouds, dark grays, and purples spinning above the heads of the council. Mirquios and his court lined up near the back of the hall.

She nodded as he smiled at her, heading straight for her mother.

"What's happened?"

Oestera sorted through notes and a letter with a broken seal, Pluto's navy blue wax cracked across the opening. Oestera dropped her notes and looked at her daughter.

"Sit, Astra. We'll wait for the rest of the courts."

Astra sank into her seat at the council table, watching Lunelle's face.

I don't know either, she beamed.

Nayson patted Astra on the shoulder, seeing the tension rise in her spine.

He whispered, "All will be well, darling. Try to block them out."

Oestera waited as the room filled with Venusian, Earthen, and Martian rulers and advisors. When the buzzing in the hall slowed, Oestera rose and stepped to the center.

"Pluto has been removed from the Outer Courts."

Hundreds of whispers ran around the room, rising in plumes of teal and orange.

"Solan has moved his armies into the Jovian Court's rings according to the intel Pluto's prince, Arcas, shared with me this morning." Oestera waved the parchment in the air as Astra realized Mirquios, Kahlia, Mother Nature, and Omnir held similar missives. "We've been invited as the leaders of the Inner Courts to a summit to discuss Pluto's plea to join our alliance against Solan. If they're sincere in their description of events, Solan is moving quickly and furiously."

"Why would they remove Pluto? Wouldn't they want to keep Arcas and his court?" Astra asked.

"No," Mirquios said, stepping toward the table. "Pluto has been a weight on the Outer Courts' resources for some time. They've struggled to stamp out rebel activity and their prince is in debt beyond calculations."

"If you have spies in the Jovian Court, you'd best call them home," Oestera said to the crowds gathered. "If you're departing to Pluto from the Lunar Court, please don't hesitate to let us know what you need. We will leave tomorrow morning, but tonight," Oestera turned toward her daughters. "We have great news to celebrate. The Mercurian Court will have our very own Astra as their queen."

Astra's stomach flipped once again, a feeling she probably needed to get used to. She glanced at Mirquios, grinning as nearby dignitaries congratulated him.

"Make whatever arrangements necessary. The Lunar Court is here to help. But, move swiftly. We will see you this evening."

The room tilted, spinning in a flurry of anxious oranges as Astra tried to get her head about her. Oestera stopped between her daughters.

"Lunelle, you will leave with me in the morning for Pluto.

War is never a good time for the transfer of power. It makes the courts nervous. The more we can get your face in front of them, the better."

"And who will lead Lunaria?" Astra asked, her fingers clenched as the tenor of the room reached a fever pitch. Eyes watched her curiously, concerned.

"Tula will," Oestera said as if it were obvious. "She is the High Priestess. We've been preparing for this possibility for years, Astra."

"I could help—"

"This is not personal, Astra. The brink of war is no time for make-believe," Oestera snapped, her eyes falling toward Astra's fingertips.

Ah, but it *was* personal.

She didn't trust the Fire Queen.

The flames within her sprang to life, bubbling against her skin, pressure mounting within the valleys of her fingerprints. She battled it back, absorbing the sting, but the way her mother looked at her only stoked the flames.

"Your fear is written all over your face. You've hardly been home a fortnight, Astra. Tula is far more prepared than you are to lead this court. I cannot leave the Fate of our people in your burning hands."

"I need some air," Astra gasped, rising from her seat. Of course, her mother saw the flames, but not the ocean's tide of restraint she employed to keep them at bay. And she was only proving her point as she cut a path through the hall.

Ameera moved in tandem, trailing her into the courtyard. Astra let a few sparks escape, just enough to take the pressure off, but it did little to settle her.

Ameera reached for her, but pulled back at the rush of heat beneath her skin.

"Astra," Mirquios called.

106

She spun, tucking away as much of the pain as she could as he crossed to her.

"Your Highness," Ameera said, bowing.

Astra forced herself to make eye contact, hoping he hadn't heard her mother as the courtiers shuffled inside. "I'm sorry that we'll be separated so soon."

"It is unfortunate," she replied.

"But this could be beneficial for us. Pluto is in a tough position. It will be good to have someone on the Outer Courts in our corner."

"Of course," she mumbled.

"At least we'll have tonight?" He offered, his eyes softening as he laid a hand on her crossed arms. If he felt the flicker of fire beneath her skin, he played it well.

She nodded.

"I'm excited to introduce you to more of my courtiers this evening. They're all beyond thrilled to hear of the engagement."

Astra smiled. "I look forward to it."

"I'll see you this evening," he said as he leaned in and placed a quick kiss on her cheek. As he disappeared, she felt her shoulders loosen, but the heat did not dissipate. Instead, it only grew harsher, licking at her spine and whispering danger.

"Ameera," Astra whispered, moving closer to her. "I can feel it again."

"Feel what?"

The heat, the Solarian, she beamed, afraid to be overheard. Her skin prickled and she spun, searching for someone out of place. The courtyard was mostly quiet, save for a few maidens darting back and forth to prepare for that evening's festivities.

I'll tell Archera. You only feel it here? Or in the hall?

Just out here.

Ameera nodded, silently ushering Astra out of the open courtyard and down the hallway to her chambers.

"I'll speak to Archera right away, but with Pluto's announcement, your mother has every sentry available on the palace grounds. If someone is here, they'll know, Astra."

"Tell her to triple up on Lunelle's guards. She has to be their target."

Ameera arched an eyebrow. "Please don't get yourself into trouble, Princess."

"Who? Me?" Astra forced a smile, feeling her body finally release the emotions of the hall.

"This is a good thing, you know," Ameera sighed. "Your mother leaving. You'll be free from her strict rules. You won't have to worry about Lunelle's divided loyalties. You won't have a fiancée to impress with your ladylike charms. We could have some fun."

Astra leaned her head against the wall. "You're right."

"We could visit Ellume?"

This perked her up. "Excellent point."

"Relax a little. I'll bring lunch to your room. You don't need to be in the midst of so much chaos before your betrothal ball."

Ameera closed the door gently, leaving her to sit at the desk alone, absorbing that tonight would be all eyes on her once again.

Perhaps for the last time, if things didn't go well in Pluto.

She shuddered to think of it.

HER BACK WOULD NOT FORGIVE her when she came to, slumped over her desk as she thought about the worn path in the Midwood between the palace and the Lunar Elven village.

She wasn't sure what drew her hazy thoughts in that direction, but it was irresistible. A siren song she followed through misty layers of memory and emotion.

Draining her deep within herself, she spiraled through her mind and into the Midwood until she landed in her favorite clearing.

"Princess," a silken voice cooed from the treeline. The woods sparkled in this version of the dark woods. Deep amethysts and emeralds hid the unimaginable creatures as they lurked.

Astra turned, her gaze landing on a tall, lithe form, dripping in jewels of all colors. Her lavender-hued skin glistened under the moonlight, and her snow-white hair fell in sheets of thin braids. Golden beads and crystals tangled with the woven threads.

But it was Ehlaria's startling blue gaze that stood out against all her adornments. She stepped from the trees into the clearing, floating on the breeze as she kneeled before Astra.

"How long has it been, Astra?"

"Too long," she returned, happy to know that even on this astral plane, the Lunar elf queen smelled of tea leaves and honey.

"We saw that beast of yours last week. I assumed you'd seek me out immediately."

Astra frowned. "It's been a busy few days, Ehlaria."

"Oh, yes. I know." She sat back on her heels, her dazzling robes pouring over her legs like liquid silver. "The man you met on your birthday—what an interesting little turn of events."

Astra smiled, the gods may have abandoned her plea, but sometimes she thought Ehlaria was wiser than any ancient god anyway. "The king of Mercury."

"He did have quite the regal posture in my vision," Ehlaria nodded. "Very handsome. And kind."

Astra held up her hand but realized a moment too late that, here, she wore no ring.

"You're new to astral traveling. The details take many decades of practice," Ehlaria laughed, tossing her pointed ears and sending a dozen earrings into a jingling hymn.

"Why *am* I here? Not that I mind the company, of course."

"Your soul called to me," Ehlaria said. "I heard it all morning."

Astra inhaled, holding all the strange fear from the morning in her lungs. She released it, finding the queen's gentle gaze.

"Pluto has been removed from the Outer Courts. I think war is coming, Ehlaria."

The queen snorted a rather inelegant sound for all her languid gestures. "When you live long enough, Princess, you realize war is always coming and going."

"Well, it's my first time, so be gentle," Astra huffed, drawing a laugh from the mystical queen.

"We believe you're right. We've felt the rumblings from the Solar King for a while now. Something is off. The air sits heavier in our bones lately."

"Yes," Astra breathed. "I think something is wrong with the Rift."

Ehlaria's brows tucked toward one another. "What sort of something?"

"I keep running into this insufferable heat in the Midwood. I fear the wards have faltered and Solarians have infiltrated."

Ehlaria's eyes glazed over into a milky white, a transition Astra had seen before. "The man you met, the Mercurian. He is the key to your explorations, Astra. It's hazy, but something you discover together will help you. Help all of us."

Astra pursed her lips, hesitant to even ask lest she admit

her skepticism in her own plan. "The king... is he a good man? Am I stupid to chain myself to him?"

Ehlaria's eyes stayed locked to another dimension, seeing what Astra could not.

"The gods do not make mistakes, Astra. Be comforted in that." Her cheeks heated. She'd half-expected Ehlaria to know the Tether was only a ruse, but maybe her all-seeing eyes weren't flawless. "I have something for you, a book. It contains the origin story of the Rift. It was not always there, you know."

"What?"

"Our worlds used to exist completely independently from one another." Ehlaria held a small, black book. The binding was cracked on one end. She handed it over, but here, in whatever space between they sat, the weight of it didn't quite settle into Astra's hands. "Start with the Rift. You need to understand how we got here before you set it all ablaze, Fire Queen."

"Thank you," Astra whispered, running her fingers over the soft velvet cover. When she looked up, Ehlaria was gone, all her splendor disappearing in a blink.

Astra stood, careful to rise slowly and methodically, curious to explore the strange numbness of the dream. As she edged closer to the forest, she heard footsteps cracking over skeletal twigs and decaying leaves.

She felt it then—so much softer on this plane. A warmth, damn near pleasant through the rippled wavelengths of the dream's distortion. She tucked herself behind a thick tree trunk, the bark peeling off in dead strips, listening.

"You shouldn't be here," a voice hissed from the other side of the tree, sending a shock through her ribs. She reached for the pin in her hair, a crescent Moon with two fine points that wrapped around her fist. She could still hear footsteps, several sets, voices low as two men discussed something in a tongue she didn't understand.

They must have been twenty, maybe thirty paces into the trees.

"Wake up, Princess," the voice pleaded.

She squeezed her knuckles around the cool metal of her pin, her curls slipping freely over her shoulders as she leaned around the tree, the warmth growing more insistent.

"You," she whispered through clenched teeth, spinning from her stance to shove an arm beneath the voice's chin, pinning him against the decrepit bark.

He hadn't anticipated she'd be bold enough to move on him.

Astra leaned into her stance, applying brutal pressure to the man before her, the heat of his skin intensifying with each passing second as he reached for the sharp pin in her hand. She pushed it harder against the soft flesh beneath his ear, digging the tip under the hood covering half his face.

The exposed skin she could see was a deep bronze, buzzing beneath her touch in a way that repelled her, that told her he was absolutely a threat. He glared down at her with an amber gaze that mirrored her own.

Thick, dark brows knitted together in irritation.

"Get your breathing under control or they'll hear you," he whispered harshly, holding his hands up in surrender. His eyes darted from her clenched jaw to the treeline.

The point of her blade carved a sizzling line beneath his ear as he moved, a mark that would surely hurt more when she released him from this strange dream state.

"And for gods' sakes if you're going to pin a man against a tree, at least anchor into your back foot so he can't do this," he muttered, shoving Astra backward and catching her hands in his fists. He was only slightly taller than her, but he was broad in ways with which she could not contend, and clearly experienced in hand-to-hand combat. He squeezed her fingers together, the pain jarring—she'd expected the strange, dull haze that suggested pain, but everything about the sear in her knuckles was real.

Her pin dropped to the brush between them as he released her hands without warning.

Astra tumbled to the forest floor and snagged the blade as the man attempted to run. She swung her boot out and caught his foot, kicking it out from under him. His heavy form slammed to the ground beside her. She scrambled after him, climbing over his flattened body and regaining her position as she slid the curvature of her blade against his throat, pushing him into the undergrowth of the Midwood. He wriggled beneath her, shoving his knee into her back and sending her forward but she regained her position quickly.

She could taste the anger on his breath, the misery in his sweat.

"Who the *fuck* are you?" she demanded, his flailing stopping as the voices grew nearer.

"It doesn't matter who *I* am! What matters is two Solarian sentries are about to step into this clearing and they won't hesitate to kill us both! You. Must. Wake. Up."

Astra stared down at him, adrenaline flooding her lungs. She could not read a single whiff of emotion within him, neither intrinsic nor in the panicked expression falling over her face. Another log shattered beyond the trees, they were closing in. She squeezed her eyes shut, desperate to rouse herself, but she wasn't sure what brought her here, let alone what might send her back.

"Come on, Fire Queen," he growled against her blade. "Either wake up, or finish the godsdamned job. I'd rather die by your blade than theirs."

Astra thought about it for a split second—she need only reposition her weight. A mere tilt forward and she'd sever the artery pulsing with the sizzling blood of the men who never once thought to spare her ancestors.

His knee rammed against her back again. "Make a *choice*, Princess!"

Her bones resisted as she made to lean forward, every flickering muscle in her back refusing to comply. She tilted her head, the panic in his eyes reflected in hers.

"Who are you?" she asked once more, her fingers loosening their grip on her pin. The man shoved her away from him, the sudden sting against her shoulder shaking the flames begging to spring free from her fingers loose. They leaped from her fingertips before she could gain control of the fury.

"Ah, fuck!"

He screamed and thrashed as he gripped his shoulder. She hadn't meant to hurt him, though perhaps she should have, but she was too panicked to concentrate. He froze as she tried again, eyes wide as he took in the scarlet fire in her palms.

"So the nickname isn't just because of the hair, then?" He smirked as Astra closed her eyes, letting everything within her burn her way out of the astral plane.

She heard two sets of boots sprint as the men yelled, the body beside her twisting and shuffling as she felt her grip on the forest fade.

She opened her eyes in her study, sweat rolling down her spine, an ache within her chest where bruises were surely already taking shape.

"There you are," Ameera said, rubbing her back. "You were having some sort of nightmare. I couldn't wake you!"

"Oh," Astra mumbled, the haze of smoke and heat still drowning her senses.

"What's that?"

Astra followed her inquiring gaze to a small black book resting beneath her clenched palms.

"Just a novel," Astra said, unsure if she should burden her friend with the strange encounter she'd just had. Ameera seemed to accept this, though her demeanor noticeably shifted as she helped Astra prep for that evening's events.

There *were* Solarians in her court.

She was about to be the only Lunar royal to come after— and when she'd had one's life at the edge of her blade, she'd let him go.

She would not make the same mistake twice.

"Don't you look lovely," Oestera said quietly as Astra passed her.

Her hair twisted and twirled beneath a tiara of sparkling emeralds. An iridescent opal silk gown flowed over her hips and pooled at her ankles.

"It is a *fantastic* dress."

"You picked it, did you not?" Lunelle asked from beside her mother.

"I have excellent taste," Oestera laughed to herself. It was as pleasant of an interaction as Astra could ask for. She plucked a flute of moonshine from a passing maiden's tray, throwing it back before the strange blend of revelry and anxiety in the room drowned her.

"Are you nervous?" Nayson asked, turning from his conversation with one of the Earthen courtiers.

"Everyone is," Astra muttered. "It's hard to tell where my worries end and theirs begin."

"Try to have a little fun tonight, darling. And then tomorrow, once this lot clears out, we'll have our run of the palace," her father said through a playful smile.

"I suppose I should find my betrothed," Astra sighed, searching the crowded garden for Mirquios's tall frame.

"Should be simple," Nayson said, a brow arched. "Just follow the Tether."

Astra nodded, her cheeks flushing. Ameera trailed behind her as she stepped forward, thankful for the king's height. A worried yellow flare rose over Ameera's shoulders.

Are you sure you're all right? She beamed as they crossed the lush moonlit terrace.

Earlier, when you found me sleeping, I wasn't dreaming, Ameera. I was... I was somewhere else.

She felt Ameera searching through her neatly catalogued thoughts. *Astral traveling?*

I believe so, Astra thought. She'd come close a time or two in her youth when she practiced her forbidden magic much more freely, before she truly understood the consequences— before so many eyes watched for a chance to expose her.

The Solarian was there, Ameera. Not just him. Several of them.

You saw him? Ameera stopped beside her, stunned into stillness. Her worry shifted to a crimson fear, thrumming against her chest as Astra slipped back toward the edge of the crowd.

I didn't just see him, I... I touched him.

Ameera's eyes widened. *Do you have a death wish, Princess?*

I didn't mean to. I attacked him, but I don't think he was trying to hurt me. He was... he was watching two other Solarians in the Midwood. He knew I wasn't really there. It was all very confusing. Astra glanced over her shoulder as Mirquios's calming presence entered the garden at the far end.

This is not good, Astra.

She nodded as she reached for another glass of moonshine. *Ehlaria met me there. She said I called out to her. She said they've been suspicious of the Rift as well, that they feel the rumblings of war. She gave me that book.*

Ameera sighed. *We can talk about this later, but Archera needs to be notified.*

Of course, let her know. They were near that clearing we like in the Midwood.

"Good evening, ladies," Mirquios grinned, kissing the top of Astra's hand. There was no spark at his touch, but there was something like comfort in his easy warmth after she'd suffocated in the Solarian's grasp. "Might I borrow my fiancée for a dance?"

Astra nodded, hoping to silence the panic clawing at her throat. She let the king lead her to the center of the garden, a soft melody striking up as they took their place. The garden quieted, all eyes falling on the couple beneath the soft glow of lanterns and stars, twirling softly in the Summer breeze.

"You're quiet this evening," Mirquios said, leading Astra this time, for which she was grateful.

"Am I?" she asked, forcing a smile. She could tell it didn't do enough to soothe him. She'd missed the first course of dinner, distracted by her own spiraling thoughts, something her mother was quick to point out. Astra spent most of the dessert course pushing something decadent around her plate for fear anything she ate might make a quick return. Before she knew it, she was stepping into the palace gardens, unsettled as she wove through courtiers on edge about tomorrow's departure.

She could not get her mind off what she let go of in the woods. Who was now roaming freely in her court.

She'd left him in the Midwood as the footsteps closed in.

They came from the east, and if they'd circled any further back in that direction, they surely would have encountered Ehlaria's sentry. The Lunar elves weren't known for their mercy on anyone, let alone sworn enemies of the court.

They may have continued west, where the Rift briefly touches the Somnia. Maybe they weren't using the Lunar Gate at all, but infiltrating through the Midwood, though Archera had a number of her army stationed at any touch point that might survive a drop from the Rift's mist.

She shivered—she should have asked more questions. She should have been more focused.

Mirquios dragged Astra back from the dance floor and into a circle of courtiers. He made brief introductions to his closest advisors, who Astra couldn't help but notice were exceptionally hard to read—though not impossible.

Mirquios must have trained them on her.

For a moment she was irritated, but it quickly faded to gratitude as she sipped a drink in the closest semblance to peace she'd get all night. Mirquios was in the midst of a charming tale of a battle gone wrong with his commander, waving his hands as he spoke. He chuckled softly at something Astra didn't quite catch, a question Ameera lobbed.

"We met when we were just boys. He's a Flare refugee, actually, though I should note he doesn't enjoy speaking of it. I imagine our relationships are quite similar," Mirquios said, gesturing between Ameera and Astra.

"Ah," Ameera grinned. "So he's the king's babysitter."

Mirquios barked a laugh as Astra glared, though she was distracted by the map she traced in her mind. If they'd run toward the Rift from where she left them, they would have passed the fork in the forest that led to Celene.

What if they had gotten curious?

"Something like that," Mirquios continued. "He came to

Mercury well before I finished school. We were stationed in the Earthen Court for our Inner Court military service. We spent a few years there during their civil conflict—he made quite the name for himself. He's an excellent soldier and probably would have been content to stay there for the rest of his life if I hadn't forced him home with me two years ago. When my father Descended, I turned over quite a few advisory seats to younger, fresher eyes."

Astra was hardly listening to them, nodding where it felt appropriate. A buzzing had started at the back of her mind, she was losing herself to the anxiety. A bead of sweat ran down her back, drawing her hand to adjust the scooped silk neck of her betrothal gown.

The room's temperature rose.

The mix of celebration and uncertainty created a strange haze as the courtiers slipped into discussions of Pluto—she felt her grip on herself fading fast, but could not release the threads tangling in her mind.

Shit, if the Solarians *had* taken a wrong turn in their panic and ended up at Celene's gates, would they have been prepared? The city below was well-warded and camouflaged, but Solarians were only a threat in concept.

They didn't actually know much about Solarian tactics. None of the women in Celene were old enough to have faced one.

Perhaps she could sneak away after the ball and make a quick turnaround trip with Riverion, just to be sure. Gods, her head was swimming, drowning in the tenor of the room and the fear creeping up her legs. She needed to get back into the gardens, where she could breathe in the evening air.

But even the gardens weren't safe.

Mirquios continued beside her as she questioned if she

would faint. "Luxuros was an obvious choice for my commander. I've never met someone so disciplined or loyal."

"You forgot devilishly handsome," a rich voice returned from over her shoulder, cutting into the conversation.

A voice she recognized.

A voice she'd held on the other end of her blade just a few hours ago.

The air tightened into a suffocatingly warm wall between Astra and the commander in question as he edged into the circle. She gasped for a breath, unable to keep her face from faltering as she searched for Ameera's eyes.

"How nice of you to finally join us!" Mirquios called, clapping his hand over the commander's shoulder as he pulled him into an embrace. He was wrapped in a clean set of leathers—no evidence of a Lunar princess pinning him against trees or brush.

His hair fell in dark waves, wrapped around his neck.

A neck she knew bore a shallow red line where she'd failed to protect her court.

We have a big fucking problem, Ameera, Astra shot out across the circle, watching as Ameera's eyes took in the two men laughing at something together.

Mirquios was oblivious to Astra's distress. "Lux, meet your future queen. Astra Leona."

Astra could not breathe. No, worse, she was breathing all too quickly, inhaling the smoke rolling off his shoulders.

Ameera shifted toward her slowly, so as not to draw attention to them, weaving behind the Mercurian advisors as she stopped to touch Astra's hand gently.

What? The commander?

His massive frame smothered Astra in flames as he turned toward her, meeting her eyes with the same fiery gaze she'd seen in her dream.

So much more intense in reality.

A flash within them dared her to say anything here, in front of his court. In front of his king. In front of *her* king.

His chest was still a blank space, completely inaccessible to her intuition.

The commander, and the Solarian, Astra beamed, squeezing Ameera's hand as she released her grip and stepped toward Luxuros, conscious that dozens of eyes were on them.

Oh, gods, Ameera slowly backed away, searching the crowd around them for Archera.

"The Fire Queen herself," Luxuros mused, bowing before her, unbothered in a way Astra envied. "I've heard so much about you, Princess."

Everyone is watching, As, pull it together. I'll find Archera.

Do not leave me, she begged. Ameera slid around the circle, staying in Astra's field of vision. Her hand rested near her hip, ready to pull the blade tucked into her skirt should she need it.

"Good of you to join us, Commander," Astra forced, her voice betraying her fear.

Luxuros turned to Mirquios. "Apologies for my late arrival."

"Did you have somewhere better to be?" Astra sneered before she could stop herself. Ameera's head snapped from looking for Archera to Astra's face, set in a glare.

The commander's eyes locked on Astra's, reigniting the crushing fever in her veins. "I was in the infirmary," he explained.

"Are you well, brother?" Mirquios asked.

"Fine, fine," he laughed lightly. "I found myself on the business end of a torch in the hall. Left a nasty burn." His head tilted back toward Astra as he spoke. She'd burned him—

badly. If she folded his collar down right now, there would be a shallow mark under his ear proving it was all real.

She'd actually traveled the astral plane. She'd gone within, despite the cautionary tales on which she'd been raised.

"Spatial awareness seems like an important skill for a commander, no?" Astra stepped toward him, sweating under his warmth, but emboldened by the way his eyes widened at her question.

One side of his full lips flicked upward in a smirk. "I was off duty."

Astra sipped her drink, folding her arms over her chest. "Hmm," she mused, shaking her head. "Seems the king's go-to man should always be ready for anything. My Head Maiden, for example, stands behind you with her hand on her weapon, ready to act should anyone step out of line."

The commander did not flinch as Mirquios stepped between them. "I believe I mentioned she's a fiery one."

"Indeed," Luxuros replied, a spark of something within his eyes Astra didn't recognize. They dropped to her fingertips, an implication that enraged her.

Not here, Ameera beamed as a flicker of light against her palms died. *Just get through this evening, Astra. I'm right here. Every sentry in the palace is here. He can't very well attack anyone within these walls. He'd be a fool.*

Where is Lunelle? Astra asked as she sank back into her hip, tilting her chin. *We can't let him out of our sight.*

I'll keep my eyes on her, you keep your eyes on him. The second this is over we'll get a plan together.

Astra pressed her shoulders back. "Do you dance, Commander?"

"Not of my own volition, no."

"Make an exception for your future queen?" Astra held her glass out to Mirquios who eyed her skeptically, a shimmer of vivid green hope within his chest. He wanted them to get along. She could see the desperation for the commander's approval embedded deep within the king's ribs.

Luxuros sighed, his eyes sliding toward Mirquios who nodded enthusiastically, a feeling the commander would not mirror.

His hand reached into the space between them, hovering, despite his reluctance. Astra stared at his bronze fingers, scarred with years—perhaps even decades—of battle and gods knew what else.

She'd touched him in her dream and did not burn for it. It was uncomfortable, but not lethal. Surely, the rumors of the Solarians' deadly touch had been greatly exaggerated, but the fear imprinted on her bones screamed at her as she stepped forward. Her eyes traced the leather lines from his wrist to his shoulders, over his stubbled jaw and molten gaze that threatened her with thousands of thoughts.

She placed her hand in his, the space between their palms catching fire—it was nearly intolerable. The commander pulled her away from the Mercurian courtiers and onto the dance floor, peppered with a dozen other couples as a new melody struck up.

When he did not fall into a rhythm Astra sighed. "Well?"

"Well, what?" Luxuros asked. "Aren't you supposed to lead here? Or do you not know your own customs, Princess?"

Astra rolled her eyes, yanking him forward and placing her other hand on his shoulder. The commander winced and dipped, forcing her hand away from the flesh she'd singed. She fought the urge to apologize as she caught the downbeat, rotating them toward the center of the floor.

"I know *my* customs," Astra muttered. "But *yours* are quite the mystery."

"You should have somewhat of an idea given you're marrying Mercury's king—"

"*Not* Mercury," Astra hissed, pulling the commander into her and then pushing him away. Their heads turned in opposite directions. His posture stiffened beneath her palms, slick with sweat. She'd clearly poked at a bruise.

"I am Mercurian, Princess. I do not claim any other lineage and I resent the implication—"

"Tell that to my bones, Commander! I can feel it—I can feel the traitorous blood that runs through your veins—"

His hand tightened at her back, crashing her into the sweltering mass of him as he growled beneath orchestral notes, "You do not know what you speak of and I'd appreciate it if you waited to accuse me in private, and not in a room littered with gods know how many courtiers who would hold their questions until after my head hit the floor."

Astra twisted from his grasp as he clenched his jaw against the pain in his burned flesh. She spun herself out and then into him, her back pressed against his chest. Her shoulder checked him in the sternum as she turned her head, his breath brushing her cheek.

"Tell me one thing. Are you here to harm my sister?"

Luxuros held her gaze, frozen in the center of the floor. She missed the next step, unable to move until she knew Lunelle was safe. He lowered his gaze, bitter poison laced in his reply.

"Who attacked *whom* in the Midwood, Princess?"

Astra caught her breath, the heat from him hard to think through. "I do not know what to make of you."

"Make nothing of me. It's better for both of us," he spat, dropping her hand.

He marched off the floor, leaving her alone in the midst of the other dancers, a scarlet rage rushing to fill the void he left as he took his flames with him.

Astra stared at a pile of divination cards, her mind finally cooling from the evening's chaos.

She'd pulled cards for dozens of the king's courtiers all evening, perched at a table where she could watch Lunelle and the commander orbit around one another. Most of the courtiers had retired for the evening, knowing tomorrow would bring its own set of exhausting tasks.

The night air whispered soothing secrets against her bare shoulders, her heart still unsure if it was free to breathe.

It wasn't, she decided, as a lick of heat disrupted her pensive state.

"I think we're calling it a night," Mirquios said to her, dropping a hand onto her shoulder. Ameera sat upright as the commander approached, a trill of vermillion worry sparkling in her stomach.

"I believe I'll stay for one more drink," Astra said, resting a hand over his. "But get some rest for your travels." Mirquios leaned forward and placed a soft kiss on her hair and headed into the palace.

Trail them, please. I want to be sure they go straight to their chambers, Astra sent to Ameera.

Ameera slowly rose, taking the outer perimeter of the garden as she stayed a few steps behind. When she was completely alone, Astra finally let out the breath she'd held for hours.

"Shit," she whispered to herself, reaching for the nearly drained moonshine bottle at the center of the table. Every muscle in her body strained against the knowledge that a Solarian wasn't just here, he was in her palace, attached to the king.

The complications were dizzying.

She threw the rest of her drink back and gathered her divination cards, slipping them into a silk bag. Astra took her time meandering through the palace to the wing she shared with her sister, careful to sense for anything amiss down every hall.

Just in case.

She bumped her hip against her study door, gasping at the heat that rolled forward through the opening.

"Princess," Luxuros said, an irritation in his voice from his perch on her writing desk. She thought back to her dream from earlier—had she left anything sensitive out? Her eyes dropped to the black book resting against the smooth marble of the desk, untouched.

"Commander," she huffed, pulling the door shut behind her. She tucked the bag of cards into an opening on the bookshelf, her blood racing beneath her skin. "If you're going to kill me, can you at least do me the mercy of making it quick? I'm quite tired."

Luxuros snorted and uncrossed his arms. "You nearly got us both killed this afternoon, so perhaps you can drop the attitude, Princess."

"I didn't plan on running into any Solarians in the woods! I fell asleep one minute, and the next I was in the clearing!"

"You're undisciplined," Luxuros said, pushing away from the desk and pacing as he spoke. "Dangerously so."

"I—"

"Don't deny it, Princess. If you had a lick of training, you wouldn't be boiling right now, on the verge of passing out because you're in the same room as someone with a few drops of Solarian blood!"

"What?"

Luxuros sighed, landing on the sofa against the wall. "The heat you feel, it isn't real. It's how your sensibilities interpret the threat of me, but no one else feels it. Your mind is trying to warn you, but you've no finesse, no understanding of what it's telling you."

"So you are Solarian!"

He flinched. "Part. We weren't sure how sensitive you'd truly be. I think we'd hoped it was so slight you might not notice."

"Not a chance," she snorted. "I felt you a mile away on my birthday. And in the woods before today, I'm sure that was you, too."

Luxuros frowned, rubbing at an ache in his chest. "Don't be so sure, Princess."

Astra moved closer but thought better of it as her skin prickled. "How did you get through the wards?"

"What wards?"

Astra sighed, her suspicions confirmed once again. "They must be down. Fuck." She fussed with the bag of cards on the bookshelf, unable to look at the commander as she thought back to that arrow on her way into Lunaria. Her fingers drifted toward the scar on her arm, healed over now but still visible against her lighter skin.

"When you say 'we' thought I wouldn't notice... the king knows about your lineage?"

Luxuros nodded. "I am loyal to my king and court, Princess. I am a Mercurian above anything else." His face fell as he recalled something painful, something she'd expect to have a flare of bruised purples or reds associated, but there was nothing. "I have no memories from before The Flare. I was just a child."

"I'm sorry," Astra said, knowing how deeply embedded the trauma of The Flare was in anyone who survived it. "Your chest," she continued, pointing to the black box beneath his leather. "How are you so tightly guarded from me?"

He tilted his head sideways, a slow smirk crawling across his lips. "You Lunarian women are so addicted to your intuition, you hate having to use your human sides."

"I'm not complaining. I've no interest in your emotions, Commander. Merely curious how you manage it."

"Decades of practice. Lunarians don't have a monopoly on magic. I've been in and out of all nine Living Courts. I've had to protect myself."

Astra's heart squeezed at the thought that she wasn't alone in this world, that perhaps there were others suffering with her same affliction. She'd always assumed she was singular in her curse. She turned toward him, forcing herself to stare at his face despite the heat's irritation to her eyes.

"You have to get your head above the heat or you'll never be able to stand me."

"Can my will also supersede your personality?" She muttered.

This drew a surprised laugh from the commander, his shoulders shrugging with the sudden force of it. He winced and reached for the injury she'd caused.

"How bad is it?"

"The wound to my shoulder or my pride?" Luxuros stretched, grimacing against the pain.

"I don't much care about your pride."

"It's not good," he said. "I was unaware of the... the flames." He wiggled his fingers between them.

"I have something that will help," she mumbled as she slipped through the door to the right of her bookshelves, directly attached to her bed chambers. She darted across the darkened room and into the vanity, searching through the drawers for the salve Ameera made.

When the fire first started, she was just a child, unable to maintain her control of the embers. They'd often scorch her fingertips or thighs as she sat in lessons. She took in a gulp of cool air, unaffected by the commander's heritage through the wall.

"Ah," she exclaimed as her hand found the cool jar at the back of the drawer. She moved quickly back into the study, where Luxuros had abandoned his perch, and moved closer to the painting above her desk, examining it.

"My father's work," Astra said quietly as she unscrewed the lid from the jar.

"It's incredible."

Astra glanced up, used to Nayson's talent, but always thrilled to hear someone else acknowledge it. The commander touched his chin, taking in the ruddy canyon as a brilliant sunrise popped over the horizon. "It's an Earthen canyon?"

"Yes, my father's home village."

"What's in the—oh! Is that a dragon?"

Astra smirked as she scooped a generous amount of the salve onto her fingers, steeling herself as she approached him.

"*My* dragon."

"You ride?"

"Not as often as I'd like."

"How many princesses ride dragons?"

Astra shrugged, gesturing for him to sit down in her chair. "Plenty, I'm sure. They just aren't allowed to brag about it."

The commander leaned away from her outstretched fingers. "You don't have to do that—"

"Don't get too excited, Commander. I'm mostly curious about what the damage looks like. I typically only burn myself."

Luxuros stared at her, unsure if he was willing to be that vulnerable with the person who caused the injury in the first place. He straightened his back, setting his mouth in a hard line. "Typically?"

Her lips fell into a frown. "Typically."

He straightened his shoulders but made no move to let her get closer. Astra was out of patience at so late an hour. She scraped the salve from her fingers back into the jar and tightened the lid, shoving it into his hands.

"Morning and night. If it starts to look worse, let a maiden know. You'll need a healer quickly."

"You'll destroy our court," Luxuros said, tucking the salve into a pocket. "If you don't get it under control."

A ruby rage flooded her lungs. "Seems a little unfair to gauge my level of restraint from an unexpected attack by someone who, for all I knew, was my sworn enemy. The fact I didn't kill you should tell you everything you need to know about my restraint, Commander."

"And it would, if that's all I was speaking of. There are rumors about you, Fire Queen. You're reckless."

"You don't know anything about me, Commander."

"I know you didn't spend three years in Celene out of the goodness of your heart—"

"Do not speak of them. I may not have left here on my own accord but that city is home to me and you'll watch your tongue." The rage simmered into a boiling ache as she willed it back down. "You may leave."

Luxuros stood, the heat in the room rising. "You have to get your head above it, Princess, or we're all fucked."

"Good evening," she forced as his hand hit the door handle. His arrogance was bad enough, but his flippant willingness to throw around Celene had her steaming. "And Commander?"

His head snapped left, one eye peering over his shoulder at her.

"If you find yourself on the edge of my blade again, know that I will not hesitate a second time."

His lips twisted into something like a grin, an unbelievable coolness to his stare, considering his sweltering presence.

"If you had any grit to your fighting stance, I might just take you seriously."

He closed the door quietly behind him, leaving her to seethe for the better part of the night.

"Don't get excited, Commander. I only want to see the damage."

Astra's study was much less suffocating on this plane. The walls rippled as she approached the commander. The salve against her palm was cooling but not nearly as effective as it was in reality.

Luxuros held her stare once again, but here, in the dream version of him, there were fewer reservations.

He sat at her desk, untying the laces of his leathers and letting his chest piece fall away to the floor, revealing a soft linen shirt stained with whatever concoction he'd gotten from the infirmary. He pulled the collar of his shirt to the side, revealing a fist-sized wound at the top of his shoulder, tangled with golden ink that ran under his shirt and disappeared.

He hissed as she reached for it, pulling away. "Those hands cooled off?"

Astra rolled her eyes, pushing a leather cord around his neck to the side to make sure she fully covered the wound. He flinched as she worked, the faint heat between them popping and sizzling.

She touched the edges of the golden tattoo, tracing one of the lines. "Chains?"

"Don't touch them," he said softly. "They'll only trap you."

Astra woke sweating, her fingers tingling with the heat of his blood.

T he feel of his flesh lingered the next morning, even through the muted maze of her dream.

It was worse when he passed her table at breakfast, laughing with a Mercurian advisor, the heat so staggering it lit up her nervous system anew.

"How did you sleep?" Mirquios asked from across the table, his eyes fixed far away. The energy in the room was stifling to Astra. They'd make their departures soon, either back to their home courts or to Pluto, and the anxious oranges clouded her vision.

"Fine enough," she said quietly. "And you?"

"Quite well, considering. Though I don't think Lux can say the same. That burn kept him up half the night."

Her eyes flashed across the terrace, Lux's dark hair loose and wild around his shoulders this morning. "It'll heal," she insisted.

Come pack with me, Lunelle beamed, her voice tight from her room.

Be right there. Astra looked to the king, who sipped his morning tea gently. "My sister is searching for me. I'll see you at the Lunar Gate?"

He smiled, but she could tell his mind was drifting toward Pluto already. She knew that gurgling gray inside of him well. She was no stranger to the distraction of a court's weight.

Lunelle was much less pensive, much more frantic as Astra entered her room. Maidens flitted about, stuffing gowns and jewels into trunks while she tucked journals into her bag.

"I'm sure everything will be fine," Lunelle said softly, mostly to herself.

"Of course," Astra said, nodding. She stretched out over Lunelle's luxurious bed, giving Lunelle's tension places to hide within her limbs.

"I've been training my whole life for this," Lunelle chirped, a shaky red rolling over her gut.

"And you'll have Mother, for better or worse."

"Right."

"Right," Astra assured her.

Lunelle stopped moving, her eyes welling. "Mother above, Astra. This is it, isn't it? This will be the start of the next inter-court war. It will define my entire reign and I'm not even on the throne yet!"

"Lu." Astra rolled off the bed and crossed the room, wrapping her hands around Lunelle's shoulders. Her panic was so palpable it drained both of them into a tornado of violet fear and white-hot frayed nerves.

"Mother does not want a war. Mirquios does not want a war. Pluto *certainly* doesn't want a war. The majority of the courts are on our side and will want to settle things peacefully. This is an exercise in diplomacy, nothing more."

Hot tears danced at Lunelle's lashes. "Do you really believe that?"

"Absolutely," Astra lied. "Solaris has been silent for thirty years! Mother has spent my entire life preparing for her chance to shut Solan down."

"You're right," Lunelle conceded. "Thank you."

"You'll return home to me in a week or two and we can forget this whole awful mess."

Lunelle sighed. "Just in time to marry you off."

Astra's eye twitched. "Let's take this hour by hour, shall we?"

Lunelle nodded, pulling from her sister's grip and reaching for a few books from the nightstand to add to her bag. "I suppose you should go say your goodbyes to your betrothed."

"I suppose I should," Astra sighed. "I had Ameera slip a few satchels of tea into your bags, just in case Pluto is a desolate wasteland."

Lunelle only gave a clipped giggle in response, her eyes tracing the lines of her sister's back as she left her room, committing to memory the way she moved so confidently.

Astra dodged frantic maidens in the halls, wandering her way through the Andromeda wing where Mercurians dashed in and out of rooms.

She reconsidered saying goodbye now, the panicked plumes of reds, oranges, and violets pushing her back down the hallway.

Instead, she climbed the tower to the roost, reveling in the open air—thin and brisk at this elevation. Riverion sensed her right away. He poked his massive head up and over the stone wall separating him from the next dragon, snorting a smokey greeting laden with irritation.

"Hush, you," Astra grumbled. "I know you've been well taken care of. I saw you circling for hours yesterday."

Riverion ruffled a disagreement, but he still pushed his head into her hands. Astra slid into his pen, taking a seat against the stone and gliding her fingers over his cool scales.

Emerald and blue hues poured over one another into an oceanic coat, hypnotizing under the faint slip of the waxing crescent in the early morning sky.

"With Mother away, we can take to the skies again, hmm?"

Riverion seemed pleased with this, releasing a long sigh as he looked toward the city below. She never dared to leave the palace when she was in Lunaria. It was far too much work to get her mother on board, but she enjoyed watching the citizens below bustle about their morning chores. She envied their blissful ignorance of what lurked outside their gates.

A heatwave billowed behind her and she craned her neck, searching for which of Riv's juvenile stablemates was getting too bold.

"Oh," she sighed. "You."

The commander leaned against the roost's far wall, arms crossed in what seemed to be his default stance. "If you were better trained, you'd have sensed me tracking you from the Andromeda wing."

"If you were less of an asshole, I might take your advice into consideration. Alas." She tossed him a bitter smile, rising from her spot on the floor. Riverion's head perked up, taking in the stranger.

"Hornsby?"

Astra muttered, "Look closer." People always did that. They saw a big, powerful dragon and assumed he must be a coveted pureblood Hornsby. They never considered a more common mutt like Riverion could be so well-raised.

"Will he burn me if I get too close? Or is that just his rider?" Luxuros sounded as if he was joking, but Astra saw it in his eyes—his uncertainty.

"Perhaps he could even you out," Astra said.

Silence and spite were all she got back. The commander's large frame slipped over the stable walls. He leaned closer to

Riv, still maintaining enough space between them to get behind the wall should he lunge. Riverion turned and glanced out of the roost, twisting his neck skyward to show off the way his scales lit up when the Moon hit him.

Luxuros gasped. "A Silvershift! Of that size?"

"Half," Astra offered. "Half Silvershift, half Firestarter."

"Remarkable," the commander breathed. "Where did you find him?"

"I didn't. I inherited him." Astra drew in a tight breath. "He was my aunt's."

Luxuros hung his head for a moment. "Ah." He stepped forward, extending his hand toward Riverion's snout.

"Wouldn't do that," Astra mumbled. "He doesn't like men."

Riverion swung his head around and threw Astra a glare that she could interpret as *fuck you* as he nuzzled the commander's waiting fingertips.

"Traitor!"

"Good boy," Luxuros chuckled, patting him gently. "Half-flame recognizes half-flame, I suppose." The commander winked, drawing a content chortle from Riverion.

"Gods smite me," Astra cursed, wiping her brow as the heat of him settled against her.

"Mirquios is leaving," Luxuros said. "I came to find you so you can bid him farewell."

"Great," she chirped. "I'm glad to be rid of your insufferable temper." She hopped over the stable wall and Luxuros trailed her, laughing darkly.

"Oh, I'm not going with him. He requested I stay back." He stepped over the gate with little effort and crossed his arms, a sickening smirk on his lips. "Babysit."

Astra's head started shaking before he got the final syllable out. "No. Absolutely *not*," she growled, a red tide crashing against her lungs. The commander backed away, his eyes flashing to her fingertips. "I'm not a fucking *monster*, Commander. I thought you were attacking me!"

"Can't be too careful," he said, shrugging.

"This isn't happening." Astra took the steps two at a time, the cool air streaming into the roost eaten up by Luxuros at her back. She darted across the courtyard and through the Celestial Hall, Luxuros never more than a pace behind her. As she burst into the palace gardens and through the cobblestone paths to the Lunar Gate, her father's eyes widened, recognizing the flame burning within hers.

"Astra!" Mirquios broke from his conversation with Nayson, turning with arms out for his bride, but by the time he registered her ire, it was too late.

"I do not need your commander here to babysit me. I am a grown woman," she barked, dodging his hands. The king's eyes swept from Astra's to Nayson's, who found himself particularly interested in something in the trees above. "I can manage perfectly fine on my own!"

The king held his hands up in surrender. "I meant no offense."

She snarled, "I am not offended."

"You certainly *sound* offended," Luxuros groused behind her.

"Commander," Mirquios warned, turning toward her. "We have *no* idea how long we might be gone. What if Solaris uses this as an opportunity to mount an attack here? You can hold your own, but can you hold an entire city?"

"I don't know," she pouted. "I've never tried."

"Lux has decades of experience in these things. He is a resource to you," Mirquios insisted. "If you're to be the queen of Mercury, you have many, *many* things to learn about the inner workings of our court. Lux has spent his entire life navigating it. He can teach you."

Astra sighed. She hated a fair point. She unfolded her arms and nodded reluctantly, settling into this unfortunate truth. "Very well."

"We'll start with manners," Luxuros whispered. Astra glared at him over her shoulder, debating if anyone would really blame her if she fired another spark at his arrogant ass. Nayson's lips twitched into a smile, only fueling the fire within his daughter.

"Is every man in this godsforsaken court determined to insult me?"

"I'm sorry, darling," her father hummed, pulling her to his side. "But the king here makes a solid argument."

"And I conceded!"

"Tell that to your face," Luxuros snarled, gesturing at the glare firmly settled across her lips.

Mirquios put up a valiant attempt to suppress the laugh in his throat, but he was unsuccessful.

"You know, I don't believe the queen has signed any contracts yet," Astra huffed.

"That's true," Mirquios smirked, reaching for her hand. "I've heard the Plutonian princess is quite beautiful. Decisions, decisions," he mused. Astra softened at this, but her father stood taller, eyeing them as he spoke.

"Good luck with that," Nayson scoffed. "Do you two know what denying a Tether does to one's mind?"

Astra blushed. The same rush of heat raced to the king's face. It had been easy to forget the lie their entire betrothal was predicated on. She frowned, swaying closer to him, mimicking the gravity she'd watched her parents cope with their entire lives. "You'll watch out for my sister?"

"Of course," he said, pressing his lips into the back of her hand. "Lunelle is family now."

Astra nodded, grateful her sister would have someone of

the same mindset in the foreign court. "Come back in one piece," she whispered, placing a soft kiss on his cheek.

"Don't destroy each other, please," he begged, gesturing between Astra and the commander. Mirquios gave her one last smile before fading into the whirring mist of the Rift, dozens of courtiers following.

Luxuros leaned toward her. "Princess—"

Astra held up a hand as she passed him, unwilling to entertain another word from him this morning.

"As!" Lunelle skipped toward her sister, throwing her arms around her neck. "I'll write to you," she insisted.

"You better," Astra laughed. "I feel I'll perish of boredom without you here." Lunelle squeezed her tightly and then bounded off to Nayson, leaving Astra to contend with a cool gaze as Oestera's eyes settled over her.

"I know you won't stay out of trouble," she said with a slight smile on her lips Astra wondered if she imagined. "So I won't ask you to."

"And I appreciate that," Astra returned.

"But do try not to do anything that opens us up to a two-front war, hmm?"

Astra grinned. This was something she could adhere to. "I think I can manage that."

Then her mother shocked her by pulling her into a hug so brief, so strange, that she was almost unsure it happened. She released Astra just as quickly, her breath caught in her lungs.

As Astra turned to leave, a strange devastation pooled in her chest, catching her completely off guard. She glanced around the gardens, sure something horrible was happening, but her eyes landed on a clash of color at the gate, plumes of peony pink longing and screaming violet fear.

Oestera and Nayson faced each other, their eyes locked, the buzzing feelings between so sincere Astra felt she needed to turn away as they prepared to say goodbye for perhaps the first time since they'd crossed paths nearly four decades prior, at that very gate.

Astra hardly made it back to her room before she fell onto her bed in a heap, the aching within her parents' chests driving her to tears.

THIRTEEN

A quiet knock on the study door that evening ripped her from the book Ehlaria had left her. It was written in an Elvish dialect she didn't quite understand.

She spoke modern Lunar Elvish fluently, but this one was strange. Her translation was murky at best. She'd thought about sending it to Cameren in Celene for help, but was nervous to let it out of her sight.

"Come in," Astra said, resting the book on her desk.

"I brought you some dinner," Ameera said, setting a tray before her. "Figured it was easier than eating with everyone else. Emotions are still running quite high."

"Thank you. Did you eat?"

She nodded, sitting on the sofa against the far wall and tucking her feet beneath her. "Are you okay?"

"Fine," she huffed.

"Even with the Tether?"

Astra smiled tightly. Of course, she should be in utter disorder. The glaring flaw in her plan with the king was that neither of them had the first clue about what a Tether felt like.

"It strains, I suppose." She rested her hand on her chest, breathing deeply. "Very irritating, but not nearly as irritating as his commander's opinion on it."

Ameera nodded, watching Astra's face carefully. "Speaking of the commander—"

Astra groaned, focusing on her plate. "Ah, yes, Luxuros. He's only part Solarian, as it turns out. Doesn't remember anything from before The Flare and swears he isn't here to harm anyone. Pledges his loyalty to Mirquios, and thinks I'm a disastrous half-wit who will destroy the Mercurian court with my reckless curse... to sum it up."

"I never said you were a half-wit," a deep voice thundered from the hallway. Astra's eyes whipped upward, her cheeks turning a deep shade of pink. The commander leaned in the doorway, far enough away that she hadn't realized the faint prickling against her arms was due to his approach. As he stepped into the room, the smoke of him filled the space, fogging her mind even more than the embarrassment.

"The commander *is here*," Ameera mumbled, finishing the sentence Astra had cut short.

Astra groaned with embarrassment, clenching her teeth. "Thank you, Ameera. Might I help you, Commander?"

"I have a note for you." Luxuros held up a tightly wound scroll. "Came just a bit ago. Seems everyone has arrived and settled into the Plutonian Court."

"You may leave it with Ameera," Astra said, casting her eyes back to her plate. Ameera stood, caught off-guard at her sudden involvement. She reached for the missive, but Luxuros flicked his hand upward from her grasp, stepping forward to leave it on Astra's desk. She glared at him before sliding it into a pile of communications she'd been meaning to get back to.

"Is that all?"

"That's all, Princess."

"Goodnight," Astra said as Luxuros gave a brief two-finger salute and backed out of the doorway, his leather boots squeaking against the mirrored obsidian tile. Astra rose and slammed the door behind him, turning toward Ameera.

"Really, Ameera?"

"I tried to tell you!"

"Gods, he is irritating," Astra hissed. "I have *got* to figure out a way to function around him."

Ameera rolled her eyes. "You *are* aware that you're to be his queen, not the other way around, yes?"

"If he doesn't talk Mirquios out of the whole thing!"

"I only mean that you're letting him intimidate you because, what? He thinks you're undisciplined? Half the council, and your own mother for that matter, have said as much and you'd never *dare* let them make you feel small."

"He doesn't make me feel small," Astra sighed, sinking into her chair. "He makes me..." She closed her eyes, unsure she could say it out loud. The thought had been rolling around in her mind for days, and the shame was almost too much to bear. "He makes me believe they're all right about me. It's different. My mother has had thirty years of questionable decisions and behavior to shape her opinions. I understand why it's hard for her to see me as anything other than reckless."

Astra stood, unable to stop herself from fidgeting anxiously in her seat. "The council doesn't concern me. They share one mind between the lot of them. But the commander has known me for all of three days and already sees me for exactly who I fear I am."

Ameera absorbed this, quietly organizing her thoughts in a way Astra always envied. "I know he's riled you. But *you* know that you've worked hard over the last few years to get control over yourself. You could have killed him in the woods, and you only left him with a little scrape. What he thinks is his business, not yours."

Astra nodded. She knew Ameera was right, but her bones still ached at the worry the commander might fuck her entire world up with one word to the king.

"If you're worried about his influence over Mirquios, perhaps you use the next few weeks to befriend him. You can be quite charming when you want to be."

Astra returned to her desk and stabbed a fork through something vegetal, thinking about Ameera's suggestion. "I suppose I *am* delightful when I don't have the pressure of impending war and marriage on my shoulders."

"Exactly," Ameera chirped. "You can do this."

"I'll try," she relented, taking another bite. "While I'm tackling that problem, do you mind taking on this one?" Astra held Ehlaria's book up between them. "I can't translate this dialect. I think we'll need to find an expert, but I don't want anyone in the court to have it. Can you take it to the city this week?"

Ameera nodded and took the book with her as Astra returned to her dinner. It took an inordinate amount of energy to finish her plate before finally falling into bed.

ASTRA HAD HOPED to spend the next day tucked away in her room, but when Ameera did not appear with a breakfast tray or to usher her to whatever plans had been made on her behalf, she knew she'd have to brave the palace on her own.

She couldn't very well hide until Lunelle returned, as appealing as the notion was.

She slipped into a pale green set of pants and a sleeveless top, something her mother would have frowned upon, but with half the courtiers in Pluto she didn't much care for fussing with anything else. She ran a comb through her unruly curls and watched as they sprang back up, wild in a way that wasn't fit for a princess, but a perfect fit for her.

Astra tried sensing Ameera in the halls, but it was clear by the time she got to the courtyard Ameera was gone.

"Astra!" Nayson jogged across the garden, a warm cascade of greens and blues enveloping her as she threaded her arm through his.

"Good morning, Father," she said, relaxing slightly with his kind eyes fixed on her.

"Ameera told me to inform you she was running an errand in the city this morning. She said you'd know what she meant."

"I do," she said, smiling. "Thank you."

"Do *I* want to know what she meant?"

Astra shook her head. "I don't think you do."

"Good enough for me!" He guided her across the gardens, their early morning blooms still turned to the sky above. As they approached the dining hall, he banked left, confusing Astra.

"Are we not heading to breakfast?"

"I am tired of entertaining the court," Nayson breathed. "I don't know how your mother does it day in and day out. I thought we could have a more exclusive meal this morning."

They rounded the hedges of the palace gardens, the gently bubbling fountain tickling her ears in the morning breeze. She took a long, slow breath, pleased at how much easier it seemed to be now that only a skeleton crew remained in the palace.

They approached a small table, set with crisp linens and an array of teas and coffees. Two bowls exploded with berries and pastries.

Nayson gestured to the head of the table. "Give it a try, queen-to-be."

"Oh gods," Astra said, her cheeks heating. "I'm going to hate the queen thing so much more than 'princess.'"

"I wondered how you felt about such a lofty title. A nickname is one thing, but a true crown..." Nayson watched his daughter's face carefully, looking for any hint of regret. He winced and took the chair to her left, seeing the uncertainty in her eyes, but knowing a Tether made any notion of undoing impossible in her heart.

He'd fought that battle himself, and if anyone could handle it, it was Astra.

She scanned the spread before them, trying to decide between a lemon berry tea or something stronger when her eyes landed on a third place setting.

Before she could even ask, she felt a wave of warmth wash over her.

"Luxuros!" Her father exclaimed, his warm gaze flaring as the commander sat. "You got my invitation."

"Good morning, Nayson," the commander said, scooting his chair into the table. "Princess."

"Nayson?" Astra asked, surprised at the lack of formality between them.

"You come by your aversion to titles honestly, my dear," her father said, piling his plate high with more cured meats than he would have if his wife were present. "Your commander here was stationed just outside of the village I grew up in."

Ameera's voice echoed in Astra's mind. She *could* be charming, even affable if she tried. Cordiality was the first stepping stone to charming someone, right?

"Is that so, Commander?"

Luxuros nodded, reaching for the coffee press at the center of the table just as Astra's fingers landed on the curved handle. In the interest of civility, Astra jerked her hand back, nodding toward the commander to go ahead. He lifted the press and filled her cup first as he spoke.

"I spent a few years there. It's a beautiful place. It's what inspired your painting in the princess's study, yes?"

Nayson's eyes lit up, a spark within him catching and running along his smile. "Indeed! I've tried many times to describe the way the Sun washes over the red rocks of the Earthen deserts for Astra, but I'm afraid it's impossible to explain to someone who has only ever known moonlight."

"You've never seen the Sun?" Luxuros turned to Astra, setting a carafe of cream between them. She shook her head, pushing it back toward the center of the table.

"Only in my father's artwork."

"You're talented, Nayson, to be sure. But I'm afraid it doesn't compare to the real thing."

"Certainly not!" Nayson waved him off. "You know, as much as I hate to see you go, Astra, I delight in knowing you'll get your eyes on the Sun firsthand."

"I worry I'll burst into flames."

Both men chuckled at this, though she wasn't sure she was joking. The commander seemed to read the trepidation on her face.

"We'll make sure you're properly protected, Princess."

"Astra," she sighed.

"Pardon?"

"Call me Astra," she said. "I *hate* Princess. It just feels... silly."

Luxuros leaned back in his chair, bringing his coffee cup to his lips. "Silly?" he asked after a long sip.

"It's not like I earned the title. You're a commander. You've battled in wars and led armies. I was born into the right bloodline. Hardly an accomplishment."

His lips twisted into something like a smile. "I can't tell if that's refreshingly self-aware or very irritating."

"Not the first nor last time you'll wonder that of me, Commander." Astra sipped her coffee, watching him decide if he wanted to spar.

He was much easier to take out here in the open air, though she felt every bit of space close between them as he leaned forward. He took a long drag of his coffee, closing his eyes and enjoying the spiced roast.

"Gods, it's been a long time since I've had such a good cup of coffee. We have a market in Mercury open to all the courts, but I rarely have time to make it down to the Earthen stall. Do you import it to the palace?"

Astra could bow out of this conversation for the next two hours and they'd still be going when she came back. Her father could talk about the nuances of coffee for days.

"I was raised by coffee farmers," Nayson said. "I'm the first in seven generations to leave the farm. I had every intention of returning after the Earthen civil war, but a certain Lunar princess changed my plans." A wide grin broke across his face at the mention of Oestera.

Luxuros scoffed. "If I had a silver for every time I heard that lately." His eyes briefly landed on the ring on Astra's hand, a scarlet blush rising over her neck. She listened as they discussed the Earthen traditions they missed most, the best views of the sunrise, foods they hadn't had in years, but she struggled to focus on both what they said and keeping her head about the commander's heat.

"Astra?"

"Sorry," she mumbled. "I missed what you said."

"Lux asked if you had a note for the king he could add to his package to Pluto this morning."

"Oh!" She flushed again, realizing she had completely

forgotten about Mirquios's letter. "Yes," she responded confidently. "I'll get that to you as soon as possible."

"I'm on my way to the post station next. I don't want to miss the morning drop. I can stop by your study on my way?"

"I'll have to catch tomorrow's send," Astra admitted. "I haven't quite finished my response."

Nayson's head tilted. "How *is* the king finding Pluto?"

"Uh, fine, I suppose," she said.

The commander's brows slipped toward each other. "Is that what he told you?"

Astra set her face into a hardened mask she learned from her own mother. "I prefer to keep our conversations private, thank you."

"Of course," Luxuros said, returning to his breakfast. "Apologies."

If she had looked at either of the men, she would have caught a curious glance between them, so quick she would have thought she misread it.

But she did not.

She was too busy composing a letter to the king in her mind, stuck on what to say other than she hoped his travels were smooth.

It took nearly two weeks of tense dinners and late nights holed up in Astra's study before Ameera's contact in the city could translate Ehlaria's book.

Astra spent most of her mornings drifting around the palace in wide circles with Riverion, more tempted by the day to burst into the Rift and get out of the court. Most afternoons were spent with Ameera, leafing through old texts about the Rift, should they find anything relevant to their suspicions. In the evenings, she managed her correspondence with Cameren. Celene had suffered a flood after a late Summer storm. Astra sent a list of repairs to her builder in the villages and a hefty bag of coins.

Any spare moment she had went to the commander and his lessons on Mercurian history and customs.

They'd settled into somewhat of a routine. She half-listened to his lengthy lectures on whatever war reshaped Mercury's economic policies two hundred years prior, inevitably he'd notice her attention waning and say something sharp that pushed against her bruises. She'd seethe for a few hours before they glared at one another over dinner.

It was in the middle of yet another drawn-out complaint about her lack of discipline that Ameera appeared in the library with a stack of pages wrapped in parchment paper.

Is that the translation? Astra beamed as she hovered behind the commander, on his fourth point of why Astra's inability to rise above his heat was going to be what eventually got them both killed.

She'd heard it enough times now that she knew she had about two minutes left before his exasperation gave way to hunger and he quit their lessons for dinner.

Freshly delivered. As soon as Lux leaves, we can dive in. The translator said it was an unfamiliar dialect to anyone in her circle, but with enough patience, she was able to get us ninety percent of the way there.

"Could you at least pretend to listen to me?" Luxuros sighed, leaning against the white marble tables of the Lunarian Royal Library.

"I'm listening," Astra insisted, her eyes unable to tear away from the package in Ameera's hands.

They both concluded the same thing at the same time. Astra leaped from her seat and reached for Ameera, but Luxuros was much closer.

"Hand it over," he growled.

Ameera's eyes widened, unsure what to do as she ducked below his outstretched arm and shoved the parcel into Astra's hands.

Astra jumped up and down. "Yes! Ha."

Lux huffed. "You're thirty, Astra. Have some pride."

"Don't be a sore loser," she snapped, unwrapping the pages. The original text was tucked into the folds, falling to the floor with a loud thump. Before Astra could stoop to grab it, the commander snagged it.

He turned to Astra, imitating her. "Ha. What in the Nether is this?" He cracked the spine open, flipping through a few pages.

Astra thought quickly. "Ameera wrote a novel. She wanted me to read it."

Luxuros's brows arched as he read a page somewhere in the middle. He turned to Ameera, who blushed. "What's it about?"

"You wouldn't like it," Astra yelped. "It's a romance."

His nose scrunched. "And?"

"And... you're not exactly... the romantic type?" Astra reached for the book, but he pulled it away.

"And how could you possibly know that?" Luxuros leaned in closer, singing the hair on her arms with his heat.

"Intuition, remember?" Astra tapped her temple, smirking.

Luxuros laughed, a deep, thunderous sound she rarely heard. "You and I both know your intuition doesn't work for shit around me. You're too preoccupied with not melting because your stubborn ass refuses to ask for help." Astra huffed a sigh as he read another line. "Do you speak Solar Elvish?" He asked Ameera.

"Do *you?*" she threw back.

"Of course." Luxuros shrugged as if everyone should. "This is a very old dialect. Where in the worlds did you learn it?"

Ameera glanced at Astra, a wave of vermillion panic drowning her.

"Did you say *Solar* Elvish?" Astra asked.

"Yes. The Solar elf king and his clan have lived in the Solar Court for thousands of years. Why do you Lunarians always think you're so unique? The Solar Court is your counterpart in just about every way, Princess."

"Don't call me that," Astra warned, turning to Ameera. "Why would Ehlaria have a book from the Solar elves?"

The commander's eyes narrowed. "Why do *you* have a book from the Lunar elf queen?"

Ameera slipped into Astra's mind. *Just tell him. Maybe he can help? If he's fluent in the language...*

"Please stop thinking about me like I'm not here," Luxuros muttered as he glanced between the women.

"Fine," Astra grumbled in defeat. "Ameera and I are investigating some strange occurrences in the Rift. Solarians are getting through it," she said, gesturing at him. "Who knows what else is wrong? That afternoon we met in the woods, I was speaking to Ehlaria in the clearing and she gave me this book. She confirmed that whatever is happening in the Rift isn't right."

"What are your theories?"

She shook her head, her loose curls bouncing off her shoulders. "We don't have any yet. This book was hopefully going to help spark something."

"We've been trying to find more information about the Rift's origins," Ameera cut in. "Every court seems to have a different story."

Luxuros squeezed his eyes closed, searching his memory. "The Mercurian Court and the Solar Courts have differing legends. In Mercury, they learn that one of the demigods of the Solar Court fell in love with a human queen in Mercury in a dream and tore a hole through space and time to get to her."

Ameera nodded. "That's similar to the Venusian mythology. A golden goddess in the Court Above falls in love with a shadow goddess in the Court Below and their love forms the Rift through the realms to connect them."

Astra frowned. She'd never heard any such story. "We don't learn about it at all here. It just is. Like Spring or rain."

"There was a story when I was a child," Luxuros ventured, but quickly struggled to hold on to the thought. It was like grasping for wind. "Something about a Divine Queen. I cannot remember the details—"

"That's okay. We've already concluded that none of the courts know the truth, but the common theme seems to be that the Rift appears as a mechanism to connect two lovers. We were hoping Ehlaria's book could clarify."

"The Space Between," Luxuros read aloud, running his hand over the tattered pages. "It's fiction. A romance after all," he chuckled quietly as he skimmed a particularly intriguing passage.

"Appears that way," Astra mumbled, leafing through the translated pages. "I'll have to spend some time this week reading."

We should consider going to Ellume, Ameera suggested silently.

Ellume?

The High Priestess requested a similar translation a few months ago from my connection. She turned her down at the time because her books were full.

Ivonne is always up to some shit, Astra beamed.

"You two are relentless," the commander groaned. "I'll go so you can stop your ridiculous silent conversations."

"See you at dinner," Astra laughed.

"I'm taking this," Luxuros muttered, holding up the book. "I love a good romance." He winked at the women, disappearing between two shelves.

Astra couldn't help but shiver in the sudden chill of his absence.

"I THINK it's time we moved on from history," Luxuros rumbled in the palace gardens over lunch. He set down the letter he'd received that morning from Mirquios, ingesting the latest discussions between courts. His fingers drifted toward his chest, rubbing at a sore spot in his muscles. "I can't watch you suffer anymore, and I know you're never going to admit you need my help, so why don't we just skip the part where we argue for days and I show you how to mute my heat?"

Astra looked up from her tea, dropping the silver spoon against the crystal cup. She'd been several chapters into Ehlaria's novel, though she hadn't read a thing that made any connections to the Rift. She folded the pages into their package and rested her hands on the wrinkled brown paper.

"I'm getting used to it," she insisted.

Luxuros leaned forward, a tidal wave of heat crashing over her as she leaned away. "Name four cities in the Mercurian Court."

Her head swam, the bastard had been holding back for her benefit, she realized. "Cereulia, Jestine, and, um, fuck," she murmured, closing her eyes against him.

The commander leaned away, taking his boiling temperature with him. "You hear half of what I say on a good day, Astra."

"That's because you're boring," she teased.

"My *gods,* you are stubborn!"

She straightened her shoulders. "I prefer 'dedicated to my craft.'"

Luxuros gripped the bridge of his nose. "Have you considered that whatever you call it, it's extremely off-putting?"

"Have *you* considered, Commander, that I'm not trying to be *on*-putting?"

"Fine," he sighed, rising from the small garden table. "Let

me put this in a way I think you'll appreciate. You need to get over me, or we're fucked, Fire Queen."

It stung, the disappointment in his eyes. The expression was so similar to the way her mother would look at her.

"Okay," she whispered, stuffing the scarlet shame back into the box she kept all her self-loathing. "Impart your wisdom on me, oh wise one."

"Do you meditate?"

"Not frequently," she confessed. She knew she should. It always helped when she did. But shaking off the thoughts and feelings of dozens of other courtiers, let alone her own, was daunting at best.

"Why not?"

"My mind is not one that thrives on silence."

"That's because you're undisciplined," he said, shrugging. "It's a cyclical problem. You don't meditate because you can't stand to be alone with your thoughts. And you can't stand to be alone with your thoughts because you don't know how to observe them or parse them out from the surrounding ones."

"So, what? I meditate, and then boom, I stop spitting fire when you piss me off?"

"That's another thing entirely, I'm afraid." His eyes dropped to her fingers. "I've known many people with intuitive abilities similar to yours, but I've never seen that."

Astra frowned. "My mother was pregnant with me during The Flare. We think it's a weird side effect."

The commander's eyes widened. "She was there?"

"If the rumors are to be believed," Astra said. "She doesn't speak of it."

"I can understand that," Luxuros said, his lips twisted into a pained knot. He paused for a moment to resettle himself. "Sit on the ground. Really root yourself to it and try to clear your mind. The goal isn't to think *nothing*; it's acknowledging what you *do* think without dwelling on it."

"Got it," she said, sinking to the ground and arranging her linen skirts over her knees. She laid her hands over her thighs, straightening her back. The warmth of him stung her lungs as he brushed by, walking around her in a circle.

"Still your thoughts. Breathe in deeply, hold it for a few seconds, and then out again." He swirled around her like smoke, her eyes squinting at the burn. "Anything you see in your mind you can manipulate, Astra. You're unbound within yourself, but the physics are totally different. You need to think symbolically. Picture me, how do I appear?"

"Scowling," Astra quipped. Luxuros snorted but did not engage further, determined to keep her on track.

The commander in her mind was entirely different from the Luxuros she saw in the real world, or even the one she dreamed of. Flames rolled off his limbs in wicked oranges and reds. Tendrils of yellow licked at the fountain behind him.

"Oh," she breathed.

Luxuros stopped before her, smoldering her in the fire in his veins. "It doesn't matter *how* you do it, but you need to extinguish me in your mind."

"How—"

"Don't question it. Whatever comes to you is what your mind needs to feel safe in my presence."

Astra watched him burning in the garden, searching for an answer. It bubbled up quickly, moving over her shoulders and into her mind in a swift force. She ran at him, leaning into the momentum until she caught his torso in her arms, pushing him backward and into the bubbling fountain. He landed with a splash and she crashed into the water with him, a shocked expression on his face.

A giggle escaped her lips, the flames of Inner Luxuros fading quickly.

Outer Luxuros sighed, "You shoved me into the fountain, didn't you?"

She shrugged. "You said whatever came to mind."

"Did it work?"

Her eyes fluttered open, the commander's warm gaze hovering unbearably close to hers. The surprise drew a gasp from her, no heat radiating against her skin. For the first time since meeting him, she could think clearly—she could observe him without feeling like she was staring into the soul of a fire. She could smell the real scent of him, not just burning embers, but a warm blend of leather and spices.

She cleared her throat. "Seems like it."

He stood, his hands tucked behind his back. "Can't promise it will last. You may have to do something of that nature daily for all I know, but it should make being around me less painful."

"So which fountain do I need to push you in to drown your shitty attitude?"

"Another cyclical problem," Luxuros explained. "You fix yours, I'll fix mine."

She left him with a glare and a gesture her mother would have slapped her for.

THE EMPYREAN SEA *glowed an iridescent purple within her dream, sparkling under a full Moon. Her cool waves were lighter here, less like vials of ink swirling against Lunaria's cliffs, more like a reflection of the Rift above.*

"Does your fire work in water?"

Astra twirled against the waves, enjoying the cold rush over her shoulders as she swam. The edges of the beach rippled, the sand glittered as the edges stretched and bent to fit this plane.

"I've never tried," she laughed, spinning as Luxuros submerged himself under the water. He broke the surface, flinging his dark hair over his shoulders.

"What's stopping you?"

Astra considered his question as she let a wave roll over her head, sending her scarlet hair flying in all directions. She pushed herself below the surface, outstretching her pale fingers into the black currents, cold against her rapidly warming fingertips.

She didn't expect it to work, but a flash of light from beneath illuminated the surrounding water. She pushed herself upward, through the surf.

"Huh," Luxuros breathed, his brows arching. "What else have you never tried?"

The chill of the water couldn't stop the blush that ran over her skin.

"I've tried plenty, thank you," she argued. "Not that it's any of your business."

The commander splashed her playfully, a smirk playing at his lips. "I meant with your magic, Astra."

His grin only broke wider as she groaned, falling back beneath the waves, desperate for something to wash the heat clinging to her skin away.

FIFTEEN

"Gods be damned," Astra cursed under her breath as she tightened Riverion's tack.

"What?" Ameera asked, slinging a satchel over her wyvern's saddle. Astra groaned and pointed at the door to the roost as it flung open.

She might not drown in his heat any longer, but she knew the sound of the commander's boots as they stomped down the palace halls and the strange tightening in the air in any room he entered.

"Good afternoon, Commander," Astra said cheerily, stepping in front of Riverion as though she could hide the saddle and tack she'd just finished fastening. "I thought you were staying in Mercury for the day?"

Luxuros folded his arms. "I had the strangest feeling that I shouldn't leave you two unsupervised for so long. Can't imagine why."

"We're visiting Ellume for a poetry reading," Astra said, the same lie she'd fed to Nayson an hour earlier.

"I don't suppose you're any better at lying?" Luxuros asked as he turned to Ameera.

"How—"

Luxuros tapped his temple, glaring. "Call it intuition."

"You can't come with us," she declared, folding her arms. Luxuros stepped closer, staring at her over the bridge of his knotted nose.

"I'm not going to let my king's fiancée traipse around a city with gods know how many Solarians in the court—"

Astra stomped her foot. "You can't forbid me from going!"

"If you would let me finish—"

She threw out the only shred of control she could think of. "I am to be your queen, Commander, therefore *you* answer to *me*—"

"Oh!" Luxuros laughed, a dark, murky thing. "That's hilarious. Oh my gods," he reached for the stable wall, bracing himself as Astra turned red with irritation.

"Please," she huffed, rolling her eyes. "Let me know when you're done."

"My queen," Luxuros dropped his head, kneeling before her, chuckling between breaths. "My queen, please, bestow upon your humble servant—"

She'd had enough. "Commander."

"Grant me this, Your Merciful Highness, Goddess Divine—"

"Commander!"

A tear formed at the corner of his eye. "Would that I be fortunate enough to receive just a drop of your kindness—"

"Luxuros!" Astra stomped her foot as she hissed his name, well and truly furious with him. "You've made your point!"

He rose from his stance, standing entirely too close to her as he reined in his laughter. "If you had let me finish, Princess, I am not trying to forbid you from going—"

"Great! Thank you." Astra turned to fling her leg over Riv's saddle but a thick hand caught her belt, yanking her backward.

"But I am coming with you."

"You'll do no such thing!"

"As long as you have that ring on your finger, I'm responsible for your well-being, Astra!"

She held her hand between them, smirking as he saw it bore no such jewel. "Looks like you've got a free night, Commander."

Luxuros groaned, throwing his head back in frustration. "And what am I supposed to tell Mirquios when some Ellumian criminal sells his fiancée off for parts? Do you have any idea what the head of a Lunarian dignitary is worth in Solaris?"

"Tell him to light a candle for my Ascent."

Luxuros growled, "You are unbearably stubborn!"

Astra opened her mouth to protest but Ameera stepped between them. "It's not the worst idea, As."

Her eyes sliced through her friend, shocked at the betrayal.

"Ellume is not the same city it was the last time you visited, Astra. There are entire neighborhoods that would skin you alive just for your last name. It wouldn't hurt to have some muscle on our side."

Astra's bones rattled with something like a premonition— a knowing that Ameera was right.

"I don't want to hear a single complaint about our plans."

Luxuros folded his arms, satisfied with his victory.

"Done."

"I DON'T THINK it's fair that Ameera got her own dragon."

Astra sighed. She'd enjoyed nearly a full hour in silence,

drifting through the Midwood, when Luxuros stopped pouting and finally said something from behind her.

"You're too heavy for a wyvern and we don't have the supplies for a second dragon. Didn't I say no complaining? Besides, I thought you liked Riverion." Ameera zipped ahead of them on her smaller creature, her scarlet wings carving elegant curves in the skyline.

The commander rubbed at an ache in his chest as he leaned away from her. "He's fine. It's just a little crowded."

"No one said you had to be up my ass, Commander. Scoot back."

Luxuros didn't move, grateful that Astra couldn't sense anything within his chest, especially the discomfort he battled as Riv dropped again, jolting him closer to her.

"No fighting!" Ameera called out as she dropped below them. "I can't listen to you bicker all day. We still have four hours before we're in Ellume."

"Fine," they both sighed.

"What *is* the plan for Ellume?" Luxuros asked.

Ameera's eyes flickered to Astra's face, unsure what she should divulge to the commander.

"That's none of your business," Astra said. "You're basically a stranger, Commander."

He snorted. "Aren't you the woman who accepted a marriage proposal after forty-eight hours?"

Astra gasped, a silver ribbon of furious shame tightening in her spine. "It was seventy-two, first of all. And second, I wouldn't expect someone like you to understand the nuances of a Tether."

He bristled. "Someone like me?"

Astra tapped Riverion on the back of the neck, letting him know she was leaving him in charge. She twisted in the saddle, swinging a leg over the commander's lap as she turned to face him. She tucked her brows together and lowered her stare, carving a frown to mimic the pained scowl he so often wore.

"You're right, Luxuros. You're the portrait of someone looking to weave the threads of his very soul into another's."

Luxuros leaned forward, letting the soft heat of him sink into her skin as a wicked grin slipped over his lips.

"You're doing it all wrong. I do not *scowl*, I stare angrily into space as I pray to every god I've ever heard of that your stubborn ass will finally listen to something I say." He stroked the worn leather over his chest, his face falling into the exact expression Astra imitated. He sensed it immediately, huffing a sigh before he reset his face into a neutral mask.

"I know I annoy you," she said, a rare moment of vulnerability softening her eyes. "And I know that we're stuck together whether we like it or not. But you could at least *try* to be less miserable around me."

He let this sit in the air between them for a moment, absorbing the foreign sincerity in her words. "It would make me more comfortable if I knew what we were in for," he finally said.

Astra appreciated the effort and opted to reward him. "Ellume's High Priestess, Ivonne Bloodmoon, is a known contrarian. She and my mother have a contentious relationship. Ellume has always been a sore spot for my mother's control and if Solarians are in the court, I have a hunch they're coming in through Ivonne's gates. At the very least, she's hunting for the same information we are. Ameera's translator reported that she requested a translation of the same novel just a few weeks ago."

"Do you think she'll talk to you? What's your strategy?"

"I'll request a meeting with her and feel her out," Astra said, shrugging.

"That's it?" the commander asked.

"What do you mean?"

His eyes narrowed. "What if she refuses to speak with you?"

"She doesn't need to," Astra said. "I just need to ask her a few questions and read how she reacts."

His thick brows arched, and his head tilted. "Read?"

"Her emotions."

"Oh, the things that change with the wind? The things that you can't access in anyone who's had a lick of training against you?"

"Even your Mercurians, who you've clearly trained well, are still readable to me, Luxuros. You're the only person I've ever met that I can't get a single trace on. It's infuriating, frankly."

"It's meant to be! You think I'm going to give a volatile demigoddess unfettered access to my inner world? Are you mad?"

Astra shrugged. "I'm a tad disappointed that it's merely self-control. My working theories were born with a stone for a heart or cursed by some sort of witch."

Luxuros snorted. "Not nearly as mysterious."

"On the contrary, Commander. Willfully blocking me is *much* more intriguing than any mystic magic could ever be. The secrets you must keep."

He held her gaze, two fires burning against the night sky. Astra turned back around, draping herself over Riverion's neck, enjoying the whirl of the emerald oaks beneath them as they sailed across the island.

"What's that?" Luxuros asked, gesturing to a stone gate at the edge of the Midwood, the icy blue Somnia curling around it.

"Celene," Astra said, unwilling to elaborate.

"Ah," he nodded, sensing not to push her.

They glided over the rest of the Midwood, the trees breaking against mountain chains and azure lakes before the gleaming crystals of Ellume rose through the clouds. The rainbow river of the Rift poured over their heads as it fell toward the Ellumian Gate at the center of the city.

"We shouldn't land in the roost!" Astra called out to Ameera. "It's getting late—we won't be able to get to the temple until tomorrow. I'd like to catch Ivonne by surpr—"

"*Fuck!*" Luxuros hissed behind her, an arrow sailing between them. Riverion reared backward, a steamy snort blinding Astra as she reached for the reins and the commander's arms, wrapping them around her waist as she pulled back.

"Hold on!" She called, searching below for Ameera. Another arrow sliced through the air. The commander held onto Astra with one arm and reached for the arrow with another as it arched back toward the ground. He held it between them, examining the markings in the shaft.

"Up, up, up," he called into her ear. "Shit's Solarian, As!"

Astra leaned forward, tapping Riv's neck as he bolted straight up into the sky.

She searched for Ameera's energy. **Where are you?**

Above you. I'm fine!

Get to the roost, I'll find you!

"The higher you are, the harder it is for them to spot us," Luxuros said, the calm demeanor of a man who has faced much larger threats than an arrow. Another *thwip* at her ear forced her head down, her heart slamming against her ribs. Riverion pulled upward, sending them over the clouds and toward the Rift.

"You ever ridden a dragon through the Rift?" He yelled at her as he dodged a third arrow, the tip just nicking his shoulder, the scarred flesh still sensitive.

Astra glanced up, her stomach plummeting at the thought.

"You want me to lie to you, Commander?" She called over her shoulder as she braced herself for whatever lay on the other side of the mysterious river. Her fingers curled around the leather reins, white-knuckled as they spiraled.

"Yes!" Luxuros screamed, reaching for his forearm as another arrow sliced through his bronze flesh. Astra closed her eyes as Riverion's mouth breached the colorful barrier, unsure if she would feel the transition at all.

It was nothing like she imagined it would be.

The Rift swirled around them in a magnificent spiral of hundreds of colored threads. They whispered as they ran past her, glittering against the night sky. They felt weightless as they crashed through the wall and floated into the current, silhouettes slipping by as Riverion's massive wings tucked into his side.

Luxuros squeezed his knees against Riverion's saddle, rising to wrap his hands around a gleaming silver thread. They jolted forward, barreling toward a crystal gate Astra recognized in the center of Ellume's bustling city.

"Oh, Mother Above," she whispered to herself as she watched Ameera and her wyvern fall through the portal. How in the Nether was she going to explain this to her mother?

She squeezed her eyes shut as Luxuros released the thread, pushing them through the gate. Several horrified shouts greeted them as they crashed onto the platform.

Astra righted herself quickly, attempting to set her face in the way a Lunarian princess was trained to do from birth. But as she looked at Ameera, she knew something was very wrong.

The last time she'd been in Ellume, the city's center was a bustling park that stretched for miles through the middle of crystalline skyscrapers. It was lush and calming, built to frame

Ellume's heart-stopping temple at one end and a set of a dozen piers at the other.

But that sparkling amethyst and emerald park was no more.

Her eyes fixed on the dozens of boots before her as guards in mismatched leathers surrounded them. They carried various blades and one wrapped their hands around a bow that had seen better days. Each of their rib cages filled with orange anxiety as they took in the sight before them.

"Princess?" a voice called out, the attention of a dozen other guards in the trees catching and turning toward them.

"Oh, *this* is excellent," another voice murmured as the guards closed in.

"Who are you?" Astra called out. "What do you want?"

"Easy now," the first voice assured her, holding her hands up as she got within spitting distance. "We won't hurt you, Princess."

Astra sighed, bored with their theatrics. The nerves within their chests gave them away. Not one of them was confident in how to handle this situation.

"Get on with it then," Astra said, waving her arms in exasperation.

"We won't hurt you as long as you cooperate."

"Who is '*we?*'" Astra asked. "Have any of you ever accosted a dignitary before?"

The second man sank into his hip. "It's not every day that one falls at our feet."

"Well, lesson one. You're wasting both of our time with the tough guy act. Just tell me what you want," she growled.

"For gods' sakes, Astra," a feminine voice huffed. The lilt of the voice did something to Astra's stomach she didn't quite understand until a tall, tanned woman broke through the line of guards, her opal hair gleaming from the lamplights above.

A full head taller than the rest of the leather-clad warriors, Daria's shoulders were broad and packed with muscle that Astra hadn't had the fortune of running her hands over in their past encounters. No wonder she hadn't recognized her immediately.

Ameera's fiery panic wafted over Astra as she took in the figure approaching them.

"Daria?" Astra asked, her voice dripping with irritation—if only to mask the nostalgic blue blossoming in her chest. "What are you doing here?"

"What am *I* doing here? You royals really are out of touch, aren't you?" Daria stopped just a breath away from Astra's face, their proud chins tilting upward toward one another. Her leather nearly covered her golden skin, but a few exposed patches at her chest and wrists revealed colorful tattoos Astra hadn't seen before, either.

And she was pretty certain she'd seen every stretch of Daria several times over.

"You should get back to your palace, Princess."

Astra watched a slow curl of peony pink rise in Daria's chest, stroking her sternum in an attempt to self-soothe.

"What have you gotten yourself into, Dar?" Astra crossed her arms over her chest, trying not to get lost in the sweet chamomile scent of Daria's skin.

A sly smile played across Daria's lips. "It's a long story. We won't hurt you, As, but I can't just let you walk freely, either. Send Riv back to Cam in Celene. You don't want him in the city roost, it's overrun with criminals."

"And... you... aren't one of them?" Ameera asked.

Daria rolled her eyes. "Nice to see you, too, Ameera."

"Sure," she muttered as Astra threw her a glance.

"What do you want with me, Daria?"

Daria glanced over both shoulders toward the guards

behind her. "Just a moment with the people's princess. Surely you can spare a conversation with me?" Something in her deep brown eyes pleaded with Astra.

I promise, you're in good hands. You have my word, Daria beamed, her voice inside Astra's mind a searing shock to her nervous system.

Your word never meant much to me, Daria.

Daria's lips curled at the corners and Astra tried not to think about the way they'd felt against her neck two Summers ago.

"You heard her," Astra said, turning toward Riverion and patting him on the nose. "Find Cam, she'll take care of you. Take the little guy, too." Riverion looked to the commander, a move that sent Astra's blood boiling again. Lux gave him a soft nod. "Go!"

Riverion shuffled backward, disappearing into the mist, followed by Ameera's wyvern.

"Well?" Astra asked Daria.

Look captive, Daria beamed as she curled a finger over her shoulder and toward a set of steps carved into the park grass, flanked on either side by two guards.

Astra looked to the commander and Ameera, nodding as she headed for the steps, Daria hot on her heels.

"You look good, Blastra."

"Fuck off, Bloodmoon," Astra hissed, plunging into the damp darkness below the grass.

CHAPTER
SIXTEEN

What are we doing, Astra? Ameera cried from behind her, the stone steps creaking below their boots as they followed Daria down a long, dark hallway.

We're doing whatever we have to, so Daria and her weird gang don't murder us? Astra thought back.

She led them around a corner and stopped at a stone door. Pushing inward, she revealed a makeshift study of sorts. A desk in the middle held dozens of documents, tattered maps speckled the dim walls. She gestured to the two empty seats in front of her. Astra took one and Ameera sank into the other as the commander scanned the maps.

"I'll be right back. I need to grab something," Daria muttered, searching through the pile of documents nearest her. "There are guards outside the door. Don't fuck around, Astra."

Daria shut the rickety door behind her.

"I, too, would like to be involved in the argument," Luxuros whispered as he spun on his heels, glaring at Astra.

"Everyone, breathe!" Astra whispered sharply.

"This is insane," Ameera said. "You *know* she can't be trusted!"

Astra huffed. "She probably tells her friends the same thing about *me*, Ameera."

"Who is this 'Bloodmoon?'" the commander asked.

"Old friend," Astra answered as Luxuros read *very* far between the lines.

"Ah. I see."

"You don't see," Ameera said. "Daria Bloodmoon is a fucking baby who ran off to Ellume when—"

"Enough, Ameera!" Astra held out a hand. "It's not important. Daria and I have our issues, but there's no reason not to hear her out. We're all adults here."

Luxuros scoffed as Daria returned, a scroll in her tattooed hands. She sank into the seat behind her desk, setting the parchment between them.

Astra watched Daria's face as she rifled through feeling after feeling to categorize them and give them places to hide before she could turn her steel gaze onto the princess's face.

Astra could only see a girl she once knew, who told her every secret, every passing thought. One who knew how to unfasten a column of linen-covered buttons in record time—

"Well," Astra said, sucking in a cooling breath through her clenched teeth. "You have me. What do you want with me?'

"I need your help," Daria admitted. "Much as it pains me to say it."

Astra sighed. "Gods, what—"

"I need you to not freak out, As."

"I'm not called the Calm Queen!" She gestured to the room around them for dramatic effect. "Just tell me where the fuck we are."

"You," Daria said, inhaling deeply. "Are sitting in the barracks of the Lunar chapter of the Nova Rebels."

Astra's head spun, unsure what to make of the words coming out of Daria's mouth. She knew them all individually, but strung together in that order she was at a loss. Fortunately, she didn't have to say a thing, because the commander did the talking for her.

"*Li elomhi eontu?*" he asked, his Mercurian accent slipping away into something unknown.

Daria's eyes sparkled. "*Eontu neu.*" She returned, stretching her arm across the table to grip his in a quick shake. Astra looked between them, shock settling into the hollows of her cheeks.

"Seems you might already know quite a bit then," Daria said.

"No," Luxuros replied, shaking his head. "She knows nothing about the rebellion." His shoulders relaxed as he turned his attention back to the maps behind Daria.

"I'm a quick study," Astra protested.

"I remember," Daria whispered, her eyes fixed on Astra's face as a twist of something dark, like sweet wine, crawled her neck. "The Nova Rebels are a network of activists working to dismantle the oppressive monarchies that do nothing but take from their courts."

"Amazing," Astra whispered, glancing toward the commander. "That's fantastic!"

"You're, uh, kind of part of those monarchies, As," Daria murmured.

"Only by blood," Astra insisted. "You know me, Daria. You've seen what we're capable of in Celene."

"Of course," Daria said. "There are plenty of monarchs who understand our mission. You're one of them, I presume," Daria looked toward Luxuros who nodded.

"Not quite. Luxuros, Commander to the King of Mercury."

"Mirquios is a good man," Daria chirped. "I've met him a few times now. I heard a rumor that he was engaged to the Lunar princess—does that mean Lunelle is sympathetic to our cause?"

Astra laughed darkly, a violet wave tickling her back. "He's not engaged to Lunelle," she said, leaning across the desk. "He's engaged to me."

Daria was silent for a beat too long. "*You?*"

"Me!" She mocked. "Is that really so surprising?"

"Yes," Daria insisted. "It is. Besides the obvious, I assumed your mother would keep you chained to the Lunar Court all your days."

"What do you mean?"

Daria turned to Luxuros. "She really doesn't know anything, does she?"

"By design," the commander scoffed.

"You're an incredibly powerful weapon. Your mother knows that. The moment she lets another court get their hands on you, she loses all control, and we just didn't think she'd ever do it. Especially to someone like Mirquios. Mars, maybe."

"She tried that," Astra cut in. "But the king and I Tethered. She couldn't fight it." Daria held Astra's eyes, a ruby streak of resentment painting the walls of her ribs. Whatever she wanted to say, she kept to herself.

Luxuros let a deep sigh sink between them, squinting as he revealed more information than he felt comfortable with, but they were in too deep now. Astra needed to know.

"The Mercurian rebels believe the queen is trying to get Astra out of the Lunar Court to protect her from Solan. If she was married and settled in another court, Solan would have to engage in yet another war in order to attack her. Mars would be an obvious choice for her—they were good enough to trust a Lunarian princess once, so why not a second time?"

Daria tucked her chin as she processed this. "That can't have gone over well with Mars. There's no trouble between your courts now, is there?"

Luxuros shrugged. "It's not the first time a Lunar princess has Tethered her way out of a Martian engagement."

"I'm sure Omnir is pissed. He's young, his temper is nothing short of volatile."

Luxuros waved his hand. "The child has been dealt with."

"What does *that* mean?" Astra growled.

"It means the Mercurian treasury looked quite a bit lighter the morning after your engagement, Fire Queen," Luxuros muttered. Astra's cheeks warmed. She hated the idea of a bunch of men sitting around a table striking deals against her hand. "Mirquios believes you to be a worthy investment, though sometimes I'm not sure," he said, a hollow grin on his lips.

"I don't understand—"

"The last Lunar princess with your... spark..." Daria began, a wicked smile pulling at her berry-stained lips. "...bled out on the Solar Court's gilded tiles for a reason, Astra. Leona was a dangerous threat to them and they knew it. You've barely scratched the surface of what you're capable of. Your little reading ability? Party trick."

"Thank you!" The commander sighed. "I've been trying to tell her this. With a little training and, gods forbid, some structure, she could unleash gods know how many talents. She doesn't listen."

"That's your first mistake," Daria laughed, leaning back in her chair. "You can't tell Astra Leona what to do. You have to let her come around to it on her own."

"Time wasn't on my side," Luxuros laughed.

Astra's head swirled, a thousand different thoughts dying on her tongue as she tried to process. "I believe you wanted my help with something," she said.

Daria focused. "Yes. You saw that Ellume's Gate is no longer under Ivonne's control. The rebels have claimed it as a port for other rebels to use. We've taken half the city at this point. But Ivonne is still High Priestess and making our lives miserable. She's conceded what we've taken, but her side of the city has fallen into ruin as she rakes in her tithes. It's bad, As."

"How long has this been going on?"

"We took over the gate near Spring Equinox."

Astra winced. It had been half a year without a whisper of something so dire—her mother was even more out of touch than she feared.

Daria continued. "The Ellumian Council is doing anything they can to stamp out the rebels. Our ranks have grown to hundreds now, but we don't have the funding or the sentry. They routinely sweep our barracks and imprison us, if not worse. Two weeks ago they arrested our Nova Captain, Lumas. We've been unsuccessful in locating him... but *you* could waltz into the temple council chambers and no one would bat an eye. We only need to know where they're keeping him—I won't ask you to risk your neck for a stranger."

Astra tilted her head. "Does your mother know about your affiliation?"

"Does *your* mother know about your affiliation?" Daria returned, glancing toward Luxuros. "Ivonne suspects, but she would fling herself off the Ellumian cliffs before she'd let the council find out her own daughter is poised to gut her city once and for all."

Astra flushed, her nerves flaring in her fingertips. "Understood." Her lips twisted into a concerned knot. "I'll help you. I have business with your mother. I'll seek her out first thing in the morning."

"Mother?" Luxuros asked, his brow arched.

Daria dropped her gaze, chuckling under her breath. "Astra is not the only Lunarian with mommy issues."

Ameera clarified for him. "Daria Bloodmoon, daughter of Ivonne Bloodmoon, High Priestess of Ellume. Though you hardly get either of them to admit it."

"At your service," Daria quipped, saluting the commander. "I'll escort you home. It's dangerous in the streets, but we've built underground paths all over the city. The Crescent Manor still falls under Ivonne's territory, but she hardly leaves the temple these days. She certainly doesn't know her own daughter is raising an army against her," Daria said, winking. She rose from her desk, tugging on the leather hem of her chest piece.

"Do me a favor and look a little distressed if we pass anyone. A Lunarian princess is a good get, and I'm aiming for second-in-command."

SEVENTEEN

They walked through endless hallways, dimly lit by flickering torches as they passed under the city streets.

Strange doors peppered the walls, made from a myriad of materials, each stationed with guards who nodded dutifully as Daria passed with her captives.

Astra mentally cataloged questions for Luxuros as they approached the Aurellis family home on the far edge of the city, backing into the Empyrean Sea. Daria poked her head out of a creaking wooden door, looking both ways before she stepped aside and let them through. The street was silent save for a few cats that scattered at the sounds of their boots against the pale lavender cobblestone.

Daria pulled her black hood over her face, casting a dark shadow across her eyes.

The Crescent Manor's stone walls ran along the last street in Ellume, bits of quartz and crystal sparkling under fading lamplights. A guardhouse glowed from within at the center of the wall. Two maidens perched on chairs inside passed a bottle of moonshine back and forth.

When one spotted Astra, her eyes widened, but she waved them off quickly as they crossed the street.

"Princess! We were not expecting the family." Her heart exploded into a flurry of violet shame.

"It's okay! We didn't send notice. It's just us. No need to make a fuss," Astra assured her.

The group pulled back the stone and crystal gate, allowing them passage onto a long curved driveway with an end that disappeared into a lush garden of trees teeming with Summer blossoms. They tracked up the path as the crystal manor rose above them, shining against the velvet sky.

"While they visit the council, perhaps you could stop by the barracks, Commander," Daria offered as they approached the glittering amethyst front door. "I wouldn't mind getting your eyes on some things we're working on. I imagine you have much more experience than I do with these things."

Luxuros only nodded, his signature pensive stare crumbling as his eyes took in the bizarre array of flora on the manor's porch.

"Eileen manages the house," Astra said, noticing his fascination with the colorful spray of petals and leaves. "She's got quite the green thumb."

"Speaking of," Ameera said, her eyes flickering to the glass door at the top of the steps.

Four maidens poured out of the door to greet their mistress. On the tail end stood a woman wrapped in iridescent threads, her robes slipping over the quartz tile of the porch. Her seasoned eyes quickly assessed who she was dealing with, a sigh of relief drawing a cerulean wave within her chest.

"Astra Leona!" The Head Maiden lifted her skirts and stomped across the porch.

RIFT

"I promise that we have zero expectations, Eileen!"

"Have you forgotten how to write, Princess?"

Astra blushed. She had lapsed in many of her communications, but Eileen had perhaps been her biggest victim. "I am so sorry, Eileen. I promise you, it's just for a night or two and I don't care if we're sleeping on the floor."

She scoffed, arching an ancient brow.

"Put me to work," Ameera said, taking Eileen's hands in hers and disappearing into the house, leaving Astra, Luxuros, and Daria to stand in a tense silence.

The commander spoke first. "Where should we meet you tomorrow?"

"There's a tavern across the street from the temple, The Waning Wren. Ask the barkeep for the Vega Special. She'll get you to me."

"Goodnight then," Luxuros said, heading for the door. He left it cracked open slightly, unsure whether Astra would follow.

"We trust this guy?" Daria said, leaning against the railing of the porch, her opal hair tucked behind her ear.

"You're the one shaking hands and speaking in foreign languages."

"Vetting," Daria said, flashing a grin.

A wave of burgundies and dusty roses wafted from the floors above them as maidens zipped room to room to prepare for house guests. Astra tried to tune them out, focusing instead on the rhythmic crashing of the waves against the beaches beyond the gardens.

"So you're marrying a Mercurian king, then?"

Astra leaned her back against the banister, cradling her arms as she spoke. "I have to."

"You don't—"

The heat in Astra's eyes silenced her protest. "I do, Daria.

Mirquios has a vision that I believe in and marrying him gets me out from under my mother's thumb. He wants to dismantle the Mercurian Court in favor of something like Celene."

Daria nodded, pulling on the end of a ruby curl that sprang free from the knot at the back of Astra's neck. She dropped her gaze, the heat of it sizzling against Astra's lips.

"But a man?"

Astra laughed—a full, round thing that she so rarely felt reverberated in her chest. "I was surprised, too. But the will of the gods..."

"Spare me the details, Princess. You broke my heart once. That was more than sufficient for this lifetime. I don't need to hear about the wonder and awe of a Tether." Daria winced, an emerald flicker wrapping her throat.

Astra squeezed her eyes shut, letting her fingertips brush Daria's forearm before turning to head inside. "Goodnight, Bloodmoon."

"Until morning, Blastra."

Luxuros stood trapped on the second-floor landing of the manor, Eileen listing every possible amenity he could need.

Astra caught her at the end of her monologue.

"And please, whatever you do, do not believe a word this one says about where to find things. She has never once put something back in the proper place." Eileen pointed an ancient finger at her.

She fluttered her lashes. "And here I thought you liked our little games, Eileen." Astra leaned over the banister and placed a quick kiss on the maiden's cheek.

"You're my favorite job security. Don't tell your sister," she laughed. "I turned down the queen's quarters for you—"

"Oh! No, Eileen, that won't be necessary." Astra waved her hands, small sparks dancing against the stair railing.

"It's already done. Beggars can't be choosers, as they say." Eileen sank into her hip. "And besides, it's not like your mother is using it anytime soon."

"Fine," Astra conceded. "Where did you put the commander?"

"Your father's room. Best book collection in the house. You look like you read, Commander." Eileen's eyes slid over Luxuros, a spike of heat warming his bronze cheeks.

"Thank you," he murmured, the deep tenor of his voice sending a thrill through Eileen's heart. Astra made a note to use this as leverage for teasing her in the morning.

"I'll show you. Goodnight, Eileen." Astra passed him on the staircase, climbing a third set of steps to the top floor of the manor. She led him through a narrow hallway that ended in two ornate moonstone doors, the Lunar cycle carved over the entries.

"That's you," she said, and before she got the final sound out Luxuros was through the door. "Goodnight!" She called out as the door clicked shut.

She twisted the crystal handle on her mother's quarters, holding her breath as she entered. She much preferred the soft, amber glow of the smaller room here than in the cavernous chambers at the palace. The luxurious bed tempted her, singing a sweet song, but she *had* to get out of her riding pants before she allowed the duvet to cradle her.

She yanked off her pants and vest, tossing them toward the bed. They slipped into a heap on the floor, but that was a problem for tomorrow. She flipped through the dozens of silk nightgowns in her mother's wardrobe. Pale pinks, purples, and blues slid from one end to the other until she landed on a deep emerald green, a color she'd always been drawn to. The silk poured over her curves, caressing her sore muscles as she stretched.

She reached up to her hair, sliding her crescent pin from the knot at her neck and resting it on the onyx table beside her bed.

Something cracked against the floor in the next room over, shattering against the aged stone.

"Ah, shit," Luxuros muttered through the wall.

Astra darted across the hall, bursting into her father's room. The commander stooped over a pile of amethyst shards.

"Are you okay?" she asked.

"I'm so sorry." Luxuros rose, cradling the pieces in his hands. He set the larger pieces on the desk beside him, where she realized a painting used to live. "I knocked over the frame," he explained.

Astra crossed the room, kneeling beside him, only now aware of the cropped length of her nightgown. She reached for the slip of canvas lying on the floor as he gently swept the remaining pieces into a pile on the edge of the desk.

"Baby Astra?" He asked, gesturing to the canvas in her hand.

Astra held it up, an image of her mother's face, though several decades younger, peering back at them from her throne. To her left stood a white-blonde princess in all her glory at five, maybe six years old.

On the floor sat her fiery counterpart, chubby legs jutting out from under a golden dress, a wild spray of red curls already unfurling from her head.

"Baby Astra," she confirmed. Luxuros glanced around at the other paintings on the wall. Dozens of women with pale skin, ice in their veins, and snowy silver hair watched them.

There were but two smoldering flames amongst them, standing out in a sea of cool masks.

Astra, and her aunt, Leona.

Her aunt's portrait sat behind the desk, painted shortly after she took the Lunar throne. Her burning hair coiled in a glorious crown, woven into a thick braid beneath a starry diadem. Her amber eyes glowed with an inviting warmth.

"What do you think changed in your family line with Leona? Thousands of years of silver queens, and then one generation everything changes. It doesn't make sense," the commander mused, strolling along the wall and taking in the portraits.

Astra shrugged, the hem of her nightgown crawling up her thighs with the movement, something she quickly remedied.

"We don't talk much about her. But Lunaria's High Priestess once told me Leona was born with cooler features, but they warmed over time. Some say it was a divine fire gifted to her by the god Mars as part of the arrangement for my mother's hand."

Luxuros snorted, his hand drifting to his bare chest. In the low light, she could just make out the stretched pink skin over his shoulder, tangled with golden ink.

"That whole ordeal can't have been easy on your father," he snorted.

"It was a disaster," Astra said. "Even now, forty years later, there's still a lingering tension. But it wasn't like my mother did it on purpose. She was perfectly content to accept her duty and marry the Martian king. They got on well, from what I've heard. But one night she bumped into an Earthen soldier and everything changed."

Luxuros took that in. His lips pulled into a slight smile as he found a portrait of Oestera, painted with the same love and care as the Earthen canyon in Astra's study. She sat on the edge of the Lunarian garden fountain, her chin tilted just so that she looked rather like her daughter after she'd won an argument.

"Nayson must have been shocked, too."

"Just imagine it," Astra laughed. "You're on your way to a foreign court as a security guard, and you stumble onto the throne. Selenia was enraged—"

"Selenia?"

Astra scanned the wall before them.

"There," she said, pointing to a large painting of a particularly sharp-featured woman with Oestera's icy gaze, but something else, something chilling to the bone in the cut of her jaw.

"My mother's mother. Ascended Lunar Goddess Selenia Aurellis, may she bless us all," Astra muttered, reflexively. "She was horrified by the Tether. My poor father wasn't even supposed to be there. Another guard had gotten injured the week prior, and he agreed to sub in before his leave at the last moment. Leona was trying to prevent war with Mars, Selenia was trying to prevent a riot with the council. You have to understand, most Tethers in our lineage have fallen between nobles, if at all. A princess and a soldier? It was unheard of."

Luxuros nodded. "And then Leona died—"

"Her death was a shock to my mother's entire world. They'd eloped and set up a home in the Earthen Court to avoid Selenia's wrath. Mother hadn't been near the court in years. Selenia dragged her back kicking and screaming."

Astra's eyes fell to the commander's fingers, twisting into a leather cord around his neck that held a moonstone pendant. She turned her gaze back toward Leona's portrait.

"I would give anything for just five minutes with her. To understand what really happened in Solaris. To learn how to avoid the same Fate."

"You will," Luxuros said, as if it was that simple.

"And yet here I am," Astra giggled, gesturing toward him. "Putting myself at the mercy of a Solarian after all. You know, we're raised to believe that one touch from you is lethal."

"You've touched me and no one went up in flames," Luxuros mumbled. "Well, I suppose not *no one*." He grinned, but the point stung. She lost her grip on the heat of him in her embarrassment, the smoke rising in her throat quickly. She tried to change the subject, to shift her focus.

"Earlier, you spoke another language to Daria. What was that?"

"*Li elomhi eontu* and *eontu neu*," Luxuros said, the notes flowing like music off his tongue. "It's a Jovian phrase their Nova Captain started using years ago to identify ourselves. It's a question and answer. 'For crown and court?' 'For court.'"

Astra nodded, repeating it to herself a few times. "Common, Solar Elvish, Mercurian, Jovian... how many other languages do you speak, Commander?"

"I think that's the list. Well, and Earthen, of course."

"See? You don't like my silent conversations with Ameera, but you could easily speak about me with my father and I'd have no idea."

"And I have," Luxuros laughed.

She frowned but quickly realized her own hypocrisy. "One's own medicine is always quite bitter, isn't it?"

Luxuros sank onto the bench along the foot of his bed, the other end piled with a perfectly neat stack of his clothes. He ran a hand through his hair, a single gray tendril popping out from his temple Astra hadn't noticed before. It shimmered in the low light.

"How old are you, Luxuros?"

He frowned as his eyes narrowed. "Are you judging my streak?"

Astra giggled, embarrassed that she'd been so blatant. "Perhaps."

He groaned, stretching his neck. "Well, I've aged about a decade since meeting you."

"Oh, come on now, Commander, we were getting along for once!"

He turned his amber gaze to hers, a solemn stillness settling between them she wasn't sure how to interpret. "I don't know exactly how old I am, Astra," he said.

"Ah," she whispered. "Of course. I'm so sorry—"

"I'm not quite forty, I don't think. But not far from it if my back is any indication."

"A man of many mysteries."

Luxuros shrugged. "Yes, well. Good evening, Astra."

"Goodnight," she said, backing out of the doorway, too self-conscious to turn around and walk out.

༄ ༄

THE PAINTINGS *on the walls watched them, rippling at their edges as she waded through the dream version of her father's room.*

"I wish you'd tell me a secret," Astra said, crossing the room as he stood from the bench.

"Trust me," he scoffed, folding his arms over his chest, closing her off from him. "You don't."

"Just one?"

Luxuros shook his head, the low torchlight reflecting off that pale streak.

"And you say I'm stubborn."

"Please," he laughed. "Between the two of us, it's no competition."

"Sure, sure," she mused, circling him. Here, without her control over it, he was warmer, though much less unpleasant than before. "Keep your secrets."

"I will," he huffed as she stopped in front of him. She couldn't help it. Her hand reached up of its own accord, drifting toward the silvery slip of hair behind his ear.

"I'm so sorry," she gasped as he pulled away. "I just—I wondered—"

Luxuros glared. "If it was cooler than the rest of me?"

"Yes!" It felt so childish to admit. "It sounds stupid out loud."

"Well," the commander backed another step away. "Was it?"

"I didn't get to compare."

Luxuros sighed, softening his stance. "Go on, then."

Astra debated if she should, if this was over the line of appropriate for him, but she found herself drifting forward with both hands, one tangling into the dark curls on the left side of his face, another into the lighter spiral on the right. She dragged her fingers through the silken strands, brushing them away from his irritated glare. It was harder to sense here, where everything felt a little like being underwater, but her right hand did, indeed, feel colder.

"I've always had it," he whispered as if reading her mind.

"Fascinating," she mumbled.

EIGHTEEN

Ellume's temple was only a short jaunt from the Crescent Manor, but Daria insisted they take the underground tunnels.

Just in case.

Ameera and Astra left Luxuros with the Nova Rebels, climbing a rickety staircase to the surface of the city. They stood at the entrance to the temple's thick gardens, wondering what the Nether they thought they were doing.

Ameera released a slow breath. "You still feel good about the plan?"

"No," Astra laughed, a tangle of scarlet nerves tightening in her chest. "But let's do it."

The lavender temple pillars loomed over the desolate street. A decade ago, the park surrounding it teemed with colorful blossoms and gurgling fountains in the Summer. Today, it was quiet. Tangled branches hooked around dormant springs, like skeletal fingers desperately searching for something to hold onto.

"Where is everyone?" Astra asked.

"I'd heard rumors of Ellume's decline, but never imagined this."

"Ivonne's gotten too comfortable here. My mother's absence has allowed her to bleed the city dry."

Ameera and Astra approached the temple steps, breaking through the trees and landing at a long hallway, open to the sea breeze. Carved goddesses watched as they quickly walked through the ivy-coated pillars, a few maidens strewn about performing their morning prayers. No one seemed to notice the princess and her maiden as they scooted through a large altar that hadn't been swept clean in some time.

Labradorite lamps remained unlit along the halls, a few sparking to life as they entered the center of the temple. An oblong table cut from iridescent quartz jutted out at all angles in the middle of the room, punctuated with altars to several Lunar Goddesses. Astra approached the altar and Ameera reflexively reached for the small bag of rosy pink stones she carried. She offered one to Astra who took it and left it at the base of a worn statue of her grandmother, her shoulders sloped in the same heavy disappointment her mother carried.

"May the mothers who came before bless us," Astra mumbled.

"Within and without," Ameera answered.

"Princess?" A shocked voice bounced around the table from the hall as a temple maiden approached, her soft slippers swishing against the shiny floors.

"Good morning," Astra called, seeing the rise of crimson panic in her chest. "Don't be alarmed! I know this is a surprise."

"Oh!" The maiden sighed. "I was worried I'd missed a crucial communication." Her nerves twisted into bundles of flickering reds and oranges as she stood before them, her deep complexion reflecting the rainbows of the quartz, citrine, and flourite pieces on the table.

"What is your name?" Astra asked gently.

"Helena."

"Helena," she repeated, making sure to drip the last syllable with a honey sweetness. "So lovely to meet you. Can you do me a favor and let Ivonne know I require an audience with the council?"

Helena's dark eyes widened. "Of—of course, Princess." She disappeared into the hallway she came from, her tangled nerves tightening.

I'll buy you whatever time I can, Astra beamed to Ameera, who slipped away and down the opposite hall, aiming for the temple's library.

Helena returned with two glasses of water, setting them on the table as she glanced around the room. "My maiden will be back shortly. She wanted to pray in the gardens."

"Of course, Princess. Ivonne and the council are assembling. You're welcome to wait here—"

"Won't be necessary. I know my way, Helena."

Astra flashed her a saccharine smile and hustled down the hallway into the council chambers.

The room's energy was very similar to the Celestial Hall back home, but the similarities ended there. Where the Celestial Hall allowed for a splendid view of the Empyrean Sea, the Ellumian chambers were closed off, basking in dim torchlight along walls that boasted portraits of High Priestesses and queens from years gone.

The room dripped in crystals around a metallic dais with a stately amethyst throne, one that Ivonne enjoyed sitting upon far too much. She'd beat everyone else into the room and took the opportunity to test out the chair.

It was quite comfortable, even if she hated looking down

on the rest of the eight seats below. Councilwomen trickled in as their maidens informed them of Astra's arrival, wrapped in icy blue robes and necklaces boasting Ellume's stunning aquamarines, plucked from the cliffs below the city. She smiled as they entered, filling in their seats at the table and whispering their plans for the upcoming Full Moon.

If you can locate a ledger of the councilors' salaries, snag that, too. Astra beamed to Ameera as she listened to them discuss which of their homes they thought had the best views of the Harvest Moon.

"Princess!" A silken voice spilled into the room, snapping Astra's attention from the councilors to the doorway. Ivonne bowed, her ample curves hugged by velvet and pale lavender hair twisted into a dozen braids falling down her back. Her eyes flickered from the full chairs below the dais to Astra, who pointed toward a maiden at the door.

"You, what is your name?"

The maiden blushed, shocked that the princess was speaking to her. Her chest exploded in bright yellows and pinks. "Me? Shoshanna."

"Shoshanna, might I bother you to scrounge up a seat for the High Priestess?"

She nodded, half-bowing her way out of the room as she rushed to do as requested. Astra let the room rot in silence, Ivonne's lips twisting into a tighter knot by the second as a bitter scarlet bloomed in her ribs.

"There we are," Astra chirped as Shoshanna returned with a chair from the temple, unsure where to set it. "Right there is fine," Astra assured her, gesturing toward the end of the row of councilors before her. Shoshanna set the chair down, its thin legs wobbling against the onyx marble. A ripple of nervous laughter escaped the women, the exact energy Astra had hoped to produce.

"Right," she began, setting her shoulders back. "Now that Ivonne is settled in, we have an urgent matter to discuss."

Ivonne's hazel eyes narrowed. "So urgent your mother couldn't make it down to join us?"

Astra shrugged. "The queen is otherwise engaged. She sent me to investigate the strange rumors we've heard up north."

"Rumors?" a councilwoman asked, her chest flickering an ill shade of green.

"Well, let's not call them rumors," Astra sighed. "That would imply they might be false, and unfortunately, from what I've seen over the last twenty-four hours since my arrival, they are decidedly true."

Ivonne chewed on her lip.

"Of course, I may not have confirmed them if I'd come in through the city gates or the roosts. But as luck would have it, a curious set of arrows sent me into the Rift on my way in. Ivonne, would you like to venture a guess as to where those arrows originated?"

The High Priestess tilted her head, her heart sinking into a murky charcoal ocean. "The rebels are under control, as I've told your mother—"

Astra held up a hand. "The rebels are next on my set of grievances. The arrows were Solarian, Ivonne. Now, how in the Nether would a Solarian manage to find their way not just into my court, but *your* city?"

Ivonne glanced sideways at the councilwoman next to her, a tight string in her spine pulling her shoulders together.

"Princess," she said, orange irritation curling within her gut. "Her Royal Highness has made every indication that she trusts my leadership during this tumultuous time. Just last month at the Summer summit, she—"

"Enough," Astra said, her chin held high as the command fell from her lips. "For someone so vocally unimpressed by my mother's leadership, you sure seem to think I'll be assuaged by her clear lack of interest in what goes on behind Ellume's walls. We both know her absence has emboldened you to pillage this city. Look at what you've allowed to happen!"

"You don't know what you speak of."

"I know much more than you think—"

"That goes for both of us!" Ivonne rose from her chair. "You know, we hear rumors too, Princess. Did you hear of the Lunarian who set her own mother on fire during a petty argument?"

Ivonne spoke slowly, rhythmically as she drew near Astra's perch, lathering judgment in her ancient palms. Astra's pulse throbbed under her skin, racing as the memory fought for air in her mind.

Lunelle's horrified scream had echoed off her sternum. Oestera hadn't even flinched as her robes went up in flames. She held Astra's gaze as the heat licked at her, unaffected by the heartbreak that fueled her daughter's rage.

It was over before it even started—a maiden had been standing just a breath away, watering the plants in the dining hall.

But it hadn't mattered.

She'd still done it.

Astra shook her head. "Sounds like someone I wouldn't want to piss off."

"Hmm," Ivonne said as she crossed the room. "You see, to *me*, it sounds like yet another traitor in a long line of women who wouldn't know the first thing about protecting their court."

Astra scoffed. "You sure you want to talk about mother-daughter loyalty, Ivonne?"

Something in her eyes flashed, so slightly, so impossibly subtly that no one else in the room would know the violet fear that gripped her by the throat. She swallowed her irritation and decided it was in her best interest to move forward.

"What did you really come here for, Princess?"

I found where they're keeping Lumas, Ameera beamed. *And some information I think will be helpful.*

"I came to see for myself what's happened to a once beautiful city. Shame, I'll have to report such conditions back to my mother."

Ivonne's face reddened. "That would concern me if your mother ever deigned to leave her throne and do something about the infections spreading in her court. Alas, we both know I have no reason to worry."

"I suppose only time will tell," Astra replied, rising from her seat. The rest of the council watched her as she descended the stairs and made to pass Ivonne, who stepped into her path.

"When you tell your dear mother of what you've seen, be sure to include who helped the rebels consume the city. She knows exactly what to do with traitors."

The word tickled Astra's ears, the space she kept vacant in her heart for a certain tall blonde throbbing. She'd used the word twice now—traitor. The intentions behind each syllable were laced with venom. Astra turned her eyes to the High Priestess's frigid glare.

"Do not fret, Ivonne. I'll give her every sordid detail."

Astra pushed through the room, carrying her chin high, even as a stinging flood of uncertainty crashed through her veins.

⸙

ASTRA JOGGED THROUGH THE HALLWAY, her day dress slipping against the onyx tile behind her.

Where are you? She sent across the temple, searching for the buzzing golden energy of Ameera's mind.

Lobby, she sent back as Astra rounded the corner.

Ameera leaned over the altar table, gathering a stack of documents and books into a woven bag, the kind the priestesses carried back and forth from services.

Helena giggled as she helped her stuff one more book inside.

"I'll see you this evening?" Ameera asked as she caught Helena's warm gaze.

"Looking forward to it," Helena replied, resting the tips of her fingers against her chin.

"She's quite pretty," Astra observed as they exited the temple gardens and looked both ways down the city street. "Where are you taking her?"

"*She's* taking me to an art gallery in the Sixth District. Will you be okay on your own for the evening?"

Astra wiggled her eyebrows as she spotted the creaking sign swaying in the breeze over The Waning Wren. "I'm sure I can find something to entertain myself."

"And the commander."

"Oh, shit. Yes. Forgot about him." Astra pushed the wooden door open and let Ameera enter the dim pub. The walls were already lined with people, despite the early evening hour.

"We made out pretty good," Ameera said softly. "Ivonne has been panicked over the Rift's leaks for months now. Helena wasn't sure about the details, but she's been pulling texts on the wards and origins. She also overheard Ivonne arguing with your mother at the Spring Equinox in Lunaria. She accused your mother of covering up something for Selenia."

Astra shivered. "Selenia? Why would she be in leagues with Selenia? They barely tolerated each other before her Ascent."

The girls stepped up to the bar, the busy eyes of the

bartender landing on them momentarily before pulling another pint for the man next to them.

"Forget entertainment," Astra said. "I'll spend all night rifling through your haul. Something about Selenia has always given me pause—if she's involved in any of this, it can't be good."

The bartender stopped before the girls and Ameera glanced to each side.

"We'd like the Vega Special?"

The woman nodded her head and pointed a finger toward the corner where one of the rebels from last night's gate-crashing sat, head buried in a news leaflet.

She didn't approach Astra or Ameera as she felt the heat of their stares. Instead, she stood slowly and tilted her head toward a door at the back as she stretched her neck. The woman disappeared and Astra counted to ten in her head before following, painfully aware of the stares her presence drew as patrons tried to figure out if she was really who they suspected.

"We had a bit of an issue, Princess," the woman murmured as they broke into the alley.

"What kind of issue?"

"You'll see," she sighed, yanking on the door of the building next to the pub. It pulled them into the dark under-ground of Ellume's tunnels, the cold, damp air clinging to Astra's skin as they wandered farther and farther into the city's center.

They followed her through the labyrinth until they arrived outside of a heavily guarded set of doors. The rebel closest to them nodded as she approached, allowing them passage. As they rounded a corner, the clank of a gate startled Astra.

"Are we... in a prison?"

The woman tossed a grimace over her shoulder.

"Shit," Ameera hissed.

A merlot-stained tension rose in their lungs as they followed the woman down another hallway, this time passing several cells.

Most of them were empty, but not all. Astra's stomach churned with the despair in the room as prisoners stirred at the sound of their steps. The woman came to a stop at the end of the row, standing equidistant between the final two cells carved into the dirt walls.

Astra hung her head back. "Oh misty Mother above, what did you two *do*?"

The commander's head snapped up from his slumped position against the dusty wall, drawing a gasp from both Astra and Ameera. His amber eyes burned against bruised purples and reds that spilled from his nose over the planes of his face. His forearms were covered in shallow cuts and scratches.

"Surely a human didn't do that," Ameera whispered as he hauled himself to his feet. Astra spun, her eyes landing on Daria's sullen glare, her arms folded against herself in the cell across from Luxuros. She looked better off, but still had several short gashes in her forearms.

"We have a very strict code of conduct here," the woman explained. "No physical altercations are tolerated, not even between high-ranking rebel officers like the commander." She winced as she tossed Astra a set of keys. "We'll let it go this time since I understand you've done us a favor, but next time he'll have to pay the fine."

Astra shoved the key into the lock at the edge of the iron bars, the click echoing off the stone floor and ceiling.

"What the fuck," Astra whispered as Luxuros stepped from the cell and stood beside her. Her eyes took in every mottled marking against his flesh.

"It's his fault," Daria muttered, pushing herself up and leaning against the bars. Astra ignored her, keeping her attention on Luxuros.

"Did you..."

"Did I fight a woman? Is that your question, Princess?"

She frowned at his tone, the bitterness spreading like poison in the air.

"I certainly wouldn't blame you," Ameera said.

"Oh, please," Daria sneered. "Your idiot commander is lucky to be alive. He thought it would be a good idea to get into a scrap with the hatchlings. I warned him they weren't old enough to be touched! I was trying to save his ass from their mother and the bastard caught me in the eye with his elbow—"

"I had it under control," Luxuros growled.

"You reveled in a chance to hit me," Daria spat. "From the moment I dared to criticize your precious princess, you were *waiting* for a reason to fight."

The commander looked away, the heat of his rage rising over the iron wall within him.

"What did she say?" Astra asked. When the commander did not meet her gaze she changed tactics. "What did you say?" she asked Daria, her mind wandering in a billion directions for what she might have revealed to Luxuros. The possibilities sparked in her chest, racing to her fingertips.

"There she is," Daria laughed. "Queen Blastra. Go ahead, darling, burn me again. At least I'd be even," she muttered, pulling the sleeve of her shirt back. A river of pink scars ran over her tan skin between tattoo ink and hatchling scratches.

"Healed fine," Astra whispered, shame clutching at her throat.

"She get you yet, Commander?" Daria smirked. His eyes

closed briefly, a million unreadable thoughts pulling at the corners of his lips. "Oh gods. She did, didn't she?"

"It was self-defense," Luxuros said, shrugging.

"It always is," Daria returned, a hollowness to her tone that felt rather like a punch to Astra's gut.

"Enough," Ameera said. "We found Lumas." She pulled a ledger from her bag and tossed it onto the ground before Daria's cell. "We'll be out of your hair tomorrow."

Daria, for perhaps the first time in all their years together, had nothing more to say.

NINETEEN

Ameera drew in a sharp breath as they broke through the underground door to the surface just a block from the Crescent Manor.

"She almost made it twenty-four hours without showing her ass. I'm impressed," she said, graciously waiting until they were out of rebel earshot to start her attack.

"She's a fool, Ameera. That's never been up for debate."

"Well, we should stay out of her way. She'll be miserable to deal with." She slipped the bag off her shoulder and offered it to Astra. "Are you sure you'll be okay tonight?"

"Of course. You deserve some fun," Astra said, her eyes searching the street. "Be safe."

"I'll see you back home." Ameera skipped off toward the treeline of the city's center park, disappearing on a path toward the temple. Astra should have crossed the street and gone straight back to the manor, but she wasn't ready to bury her head in books for the rest of the night. Ellume certainly wasn't the city it once was, but it still had much more to offer than the palace.

"Tavern?" she asked as the commander's mashed eyes squinted against the lamplights. "You look like you could use a drink, Commander."

She didn't wait for him to agree, but he followed her dutifully down the street and around the corner, into a dark tavern with a moonblossom carved into the door. The woman behind the bar looked surprised to see them and Astra worried she recognized her as part of the royal family, but a glance at Luxuros solved the mystery.

He was easily a head taller than anyone else in the room, and just about every angle of his face looked as if it had been mashed against the cobblestones outside. Many, many times. Astra pushed him toward a corner booth, stepping up to the bar.

"Two moonshines and can I get water and a clean rag? Oh! And two bowls of whatever that is," she chirped, pointing toward a pot heating behind her. Whatever it was smelled plenty good enough for dinner. "Thank you."

The bartender's nerves flared in copper sparks as Astra took two steins of moonshine back to the booth, setting one in front of the commander, who looked about as ravaged as her bones felt. She returned to the bar and snagged the bowl of water and clean rag she'd asked for.

Luxuros held up a hand. "I'm fine—"

"Shh," Astra dismissed him. "This isn't out of the kindness of my heart. The bartender's ribs are going to crack from anxiety due to the bloody warrior brooding in the corner. Bad for business."

She dabbed at the split in his eyebrow, the blood making it look much worse than the shallow cut was, thankfully. She moved on to a larger gash below his cheek, and then to his lip, his jaw tensing under her grasp.

"The hatchling scratches will have to be medicated. You

don't want an infection from those little fuckers. The maidens will have something back at the manor, I'm sure."

Astra slid into the booth across from him as two bowls of stew appeared, the bartender's eyes widening at the sight of the bloodied rag on the tabletop. As she turned around, Astra let the heat in her fingers sear, sending a spark to the edge of the cloth and incinerating it as Luxuros watched.

He did not say anything as the ashes crumbled to the floor. Instead, he focused his attention on the bowl. Astra tried to do the same, but the volume rose as dozens of frayed souls poured in after a long day's work. Reds and oranges and yellows flickered as they decompressed, drowning her lungs and twisting her stomach.

"Breathe," the commander said around a bite of stew, his eyes still glued to the bowl.

"I'm trying," she insisted, swallowing against the bile rising in her throat.

"You're panicking," Luxuros said, setting his spoon against the rim of the bowl.

"I'm not panicking. I'm... sifting. Organizing." She tried to tuck all the colors in the right boxes in her mind—exhausted purples in one, irritated reds in another—but they kept slipping away from her.

"Don't waste your energy on trying to process it all, Astra. The energy shifts too frequently. You need to find *you* in the noise and hold onto it."

Astra ignored him, the seeping colors running down her back and leaving burns as she shook her leg against the booth.

"Where's your favorite place?"

"Hmm?" Astra squeezed her eyes shut, hanging her head over the table.

"As." The commander gripped her wrist, freezing her

fingers as they tapped the nervous energy into the wood. "When you lived in Celene, where did you go to relax?"

She stilled her knee. Celene's hot springs steamed to life in her mind. Crystal blue waters bubbled under stars, sliding over the rocks into endless pools below. She let the smoky steam fill her lungs and the salty brine cling to her lips. Serene emeralds and lavenders swirled around her shoulders, forcing them to relax.

The nausea subsided. She could open her eyes without feeling the need to avert her gaze from the colors hovering over the heads of the patrons. She could see them without absorbing them; acknowledge them without inhaling.

Her lungs unfurled.

"Better?" Luxuros pulled his hand away, leaving five hot fingerprints branded around her wrist. She nodded, picking up her spoon and eating a few cautious bites. She let the stew warm her, making an effort to breathe slowly through her nose with each new wave of drinkers. Halfway through her bowl, she felt brave enough to wash it down with some moonshine, numbing her chest even more.

Luxuros felt her eyes on him before he met her gaze.

"Go ahead," he muttered. "Ask me."

"What did Daria say?"

"It's not worth repeating," he sighed, his amber eyes flickering between her curious face and the moonshine remaining in his stein.

"If it was worth getting socked in the nose—"

"It was her elbow."

Astra grimaced. "Even worse. If it's worth that, it must be worth repeating."

Luxuros breathed in deeply, finishing the moonshine in his cup before he spoke, weighing his words carefully.

"Daria implied that allowing you to marry Mirquios would

be too much of a risk to the mission. She believes that in your heart you are your mother's daughter, and you'll always choose the crown. She seemed to think that your family has a history of putting the throne before even each other."

Ivonne's words from earlier struck Astra again. They twisted even deeper into her spine now.

"She told me it was my duty to the Nova Rebellion to put an end to your engagement."

Astra flinched, the pain striking her just below her ribs. "Well? You've said as much, haven't you?"

The commander frowned. "Anything I've said to you was expressly to motivate you, Astra. You're capable of stunning amounts of power, and you've been kept in the dark your entire life. It was obvious from the moment we met. I do worry about your discipline, but it's not because I think you're a hopeless danger. I think you're just a little hard work away from great potential. If I didn't believe in you, we would have picked Lunelle when your mother—when..." Luxuros scratched at the back of his neck.

"What?" Astra set her spoon down.

He shook his head, running a hand through his hair. "I didn't mean—"

"Yes. You did. When my mother *what*, Commander?"

"I misspoke. I shouldn't have said that."

"And yet you did, so please, enlighten me, Luxuros." She swallowed, her head swirling again, the careful grip she'd held through dinner vanishing.

"Oestera is not always the villain you believe her to be. I meant what I said to Daria yesterday. She knows the danger lurking in every court, gods, even her own! Mirquios can offer you the safety you need, but that wasn't the only reason we agreed to come here, okay? We need you, too. The cause needs you, Astra. When your mother invited us to come, there was zero hesitation on our part because we knew what an addition you would be to our court. We never dreamed that you'd Tether... that was... it was a happy accident, of course. And a sign we made the right choice."

Heat rose to Astra's cheeks. "So all of this, this whole time, it was just a plot with Oestera to get me on your side? Was Mars even a factor, or was that yet another manipulation?"

Luxuros held up his hands, begging for her mind to slow down. "It was all your choice, As. Oestera didn't want to force you. No one was trying to trick you, but she knew you'd resist Mirquios if you thought she had anything to do with him, so yes. Yes. She pushed you toward Mars to curb your interest, but I swear to you, if you didn't show any sign of genuine intrigue, we'd have left well enough alone."

Astra didn't believe him. "Ah, yes, of *course* you would have. The hypothetical right choice is always easy to make." She should have known her mother was working behind her back instead of coming to her directly with her plans.

She should have suspected it immediately. She'd never been able to outsmart Oestera, and this was no different.

"We should get home," she whispered. She slammed back the rest of her drink and left a few gold coins on the table. As she rounded the corner, she shook her hands, letting a few errant sparks flicker against the cobblestone street before they consumed her.

"Astra!" Luxuros called from behind her, but she did not slow her pace. His long legs would catch up with her in no time, anyway. "As."

She pulled her hood over her head, tucking her hair back into her cloak as Ellumians passed them on the street. They didn't have far to go, but her nerves tangled as more faces entered her space with the commander at her back.

He followed her in silence, even as she scaled the steps of

the Crescent Manor's porch. Before they could enter the house, Eileen was in the doorway, eyeing every movement between them.

"A note came for you, Princess." Astra's head tilted. "And flowers."

"For me?"

"From the Bloodmoon girl," Eileen sighed. She pushed the doors open and let them pass, handing a note to Astra as she stopped before an explosion of roses in the foyer. "Commander! What happened?"

"Long story," Luxuros said. "Astra—"

"The commander needs something to disinfect his arms. Hatchlings got the best of him," Astra said to Eileen as she stroked a soft petal between her thumb and finger.

"Of course. This way, Commander," Eileen cooed.

"Roses," Luxuros scoffed as Eileen led him down the hallway.

"What's wrong with roses?" Astra asked, sliding her finger through the envelope she'd been handed.

"Nothing." He shrugged. "If you liked them. Wouldn't you have preferred moonblossoms?"

Astra felt a soft blush rise to her cheeks as he disappeared down the hallway, leaving Eileen with a magenta explosion in her ribs and Astra with a spray of roses she never would have chosen for herself.

S he'd stared at the note for an entire hour and still couldn't quite bring herself to descend the stairs and join Luxuros for dinner.

The letters blended into two long black lines, slipping off the page and melting onto the desk beneath her lantern's heat as she hid in her bedroom.

The card burned under her fingertips. It was a curt note. A warning, really. Three maidens had already knocked on her door to inform her dinner was waiting and when the fourth knocked, she lost her hold on herself.

She rose from the desk and yanked the brass handle inward. "I said I'd be down in a minute," she sighed into a leather-bound chest much taller than she expected.

Luxuros, in all his bruises and bloodstains, stared down at her. "There's something you need to look at," he grumbled, turning quickly and taking the stairs two at a time. She followed him into the study off the second landing, the floor littered with books and documents they'd taken from the temple.

He pointed to the leather tome in the center of the desk, a linen bandage wrapped neatly around each forearm. Elegant script ran across the pages, the midnight-black ink bleeding out in a few spots.

"Shadow Bargaining," she read aloud. Luxuros wound his finger in the air to keep reading. As she read, he set a cup of black coffee beside her. "The dark art of bargaining one's Shadow should only be attempted in dire circumstances. The Court Below does not dabble in casual whims or indulge changed minds. To trade one's Shadow is to make an eternal commitment—what is this?"

"Skip to the next page," the commander said over the rim of his own cup.

"Once the trade is complete, the Shadow remains in the possession of the Nether Queen, granting the bargainer access to her dark magic in direct proportion to the weight of the Shadow offered. Though difficult to trace, the bargainer should be aware of certain after-effects that, to a trained eye, may reveal their trade. An aversion to light, for example, or even to the more sensitive of the realms, an unnaturally cold signature or dark aura may be detectable."

Luxuros leaned against the table, sipping his coffee. "A few weeks ago we heard Selenia was spotted in the Mercurian Bazaar. It's not uncommon for Ascended gods and goddesses to appear in the Living Courts—we assumed it was meant to be a blessing after the engagement. The two women she spoke to at a stall both mentioned that Lunarians were much more frigid than they expected, based on the rumors. You *are* noticeably colder than Ameera or other courtiers, but I wouldn't describe you as frigid."

"Imagine how much easier your life would be," Astra said, flashing whispers of fire from her fingertips before reaching for her coffee.

He chuckled, pointing to another stack of papers. "Ivonne was studying this. She has pages of notes—I haven't gotten through even half of what Ameera took, but she seems certain your grandmother bargained her Shadow."

"To give up your Shadow..." Astra inhaled, shoving down the unease in her bones. It was a dark trade, indeed. "She'd never be able to reconcile her Soul and Shadow in the Court Below. She'd be doomed to spend eternity there instead of Ascending again. What could possibly be worth something like that to the Lunar Goddess?"

The Ascension journey took the bravest of Souls decades on their first go-around—a century or two. Some never even attempted. Astra shivered. To damn oneself to the Court Below for eternity was not a lighthearted decision.

Luxuros considered this. "But if she stayed in the Court Above for the rest of her existence... the risk that someone could kill her as an Ascended goddess is quite low. Maybe she figured it wouldn't be an issue."

Astra arched her ruby brow. "To kill a goddess, especially in the Court Above, is difficult, but not impossible. It's not as if the rivalry between courts ends at the Eternal Gate. Maybe the power she exchanged it for would help her avoid the consequences?"

"You can only outrun your choices for so long," the commander said, leafing through Ivonne's notes.

"I've noticed her aura before," Astra said, thinking back to the last time she was in the same room as Selenia—it was a rare occurrence but she attended some of the more significant events. "I just assumed it was part of her emotional disposition. But it was there."

Luxuros tilted his head. "Do you typically see auras?"

"No, not necessarily. I see colors I've learned to correlate with emotions. The Solstice. I knew you were behind the hedges because of the shitstorm happening in your heart. Whatever you did to tuck it all away was impressive, but I still caught it. All that midnight-black torment... it was a lot to carry, Commander."

Luxuros stared at her for a moment, fighting a war within himself that manifested in something halfway to a frown. He chose to avoid himself as a conversation topic.

"How likely do you think it is that Selenia traded her Shadow?"

"I can't say for certain. I did not know her well, but that leaves everything on the table at this point. Ivonne said something about me being just another in a long line of traitors. Daria implied the same. Whatever Selenia did, whatever my mother knows—it can't be good."

"Anything that requires more power than an Ascended goddess already concerns me. You should finish that." Luxuros said, gesturing to her coffee. "I think we're in for a long night."

Astra rolled her eyes. "Yes, Commander." She sat back into a squeaky ancient chair, sipping the coffee as she pondered what her grandmother might have been capable of, all too aware of Luxuros's stare resting on her.

"So you *are* capable of taking orders," he mused.

"When they bring me pleasure, sure." She enjoyed the sizzling heat that rose to his cheeks as she winked.

He cleared his throat, pointing back at the open book as his fingers pushed at the muscles in his chest.

"We need to figure out the common thread between all of this—the Rift, the Shadow, the novel Ehlaria gave you. It all has to connect somewhere."

Astra agreed. "We should visit Ehlaria when we're back."

"Do you think she'll share more?"

"Ehlaria always knows more than she lets on. I need to read that book first."

"Fair enough. I owe her a visit, anyway."

Astra crossed one leg over the other, pursing her lips.

"Intriguing, Commander."

"Just checking in on some old friends," he said. He studied the pages of the book for a long moment before asking the question she'd felt perched on his lips all evening. "Did she at least write a good apology?"

"Who?"

"Daria," he murmured, his eyes never leaving the book's pale pages.

"And why would you care?" Astra rose from her chair, leaning against the table beside him.

The commander shrugged. "You're to be my queen. It's pertinent that I know who your enemies are." He turned the page, his calculated casualness flickering under the weight of her stare.

"There was no apology at all, actually."

"Bold choice," he scoffed.

"She was warning me," Astra said, leaning closer toward him, the heat from his skin buzzing in the space between their hands. "About you."

His shoulders tensed, something flashing across his eyes— maybe anger, maybe fear, it was always impossible to tell with him.

"What about me?"

"She suspects you to be a spy," Astra said, choosing her words carefully.

His lips twitched and he turned toward her, holding the embers in her eyes. "A spy?"

"For the Solar Court."

Luxuros did not flinch like she thought he might. Instead, he blinked slowly. The corner of his mouth slipped upward into an amused grin.

"What's funny?" Astra asked, sinking back into herself.

He broke into a deep laugh, the sound bouncing off her shoulders as he closed his eyes. "She remarked how warm I was after all that hatchling nonsense. If she'd ever met a full-blooded Solarian she'd know just how wrong she is." He shook his head, seeing the concern in Astra's eyes. "We've gone over this, As. I'm not lying to you. I may have Solarian blood but I've no Solarian loyalty. I've never met a Solar courtier, certainly not the king."

"That you know of," Astra corrected him. "What if you *were* a Solarian spy and have no memory of it? You go on and on about my lack of discipline, but what about your fear of who you might be, Commander? You're so afraid to touch any of it, you don't know where your loyalties may truly lie."

He moved closer, an anger she seldom saw rising in him as he prepared to argue with her, but the damned truth of it all was that she was right.

Devastatingly so.

"You really remember nothing?"

Luxuros tried to turn his attention back to the book, but she was so close he could smell the moonblossom petal scent of her perfume. Something about it disarmed his ironclad will as he chewed on the inside of his cheek.

"I'm overstepping. I apologize."

"No," he said. "It's okay. You have every right to be concerned. I realize we're asking a lot of you to just take me at my word. I am sincere when I say I have nearly no memories, Astra. Sometimes I dream of a library in Solaris, I think. Everything is so warm and brightly lit it couldn't be anywhere else. I'm usually playing a marble game of sorts, with these little glass orbs that clink together when they cross paths. That's one of the good memories." Luxuros paused, closing his amber eyes to try and recall things he'd worked hard to erase.

"I have nightmares of The Flare frequently," he continued. "It's nothing concrete, just an intense fear as I float. I was only a child when it happened, As. We don't think I'd started my primary schooling yet. When I showed up at the Mercurian Gate, I only remembered my name and enough languages to piece together that I was at least partially Solarian. I spoke the common tongue, but Mirquios's father had a palace tutor run me through every dialect they knew of and identified that I was fluent in Solar Elvish and several regional Jovian dialects. We think perhaps one of my parents was a Jovian ambassador. But that's as far as we ever got. I doubt I was a spy, given how young I was, but I've often worried who my parents are. Were," he added.

Astra reached forward and rested her hand above the bandages on his forearm.

"I'm so sorry, Luxuros. That must be incredibly difficult to not know about your family."

"When I was younger, sure. But I've lived a lot of life since then. I know who I am, even if I'll never know who I was. There's freedom in that."

"I could help you," Astra offered. "I have more tricks up my sleeve than just fire and fury."

"Is that so?" He laughed, leaning into her touch before remembering himself and moving back.

She wiggled her fingers between them. "I haven't practiced appropriately, but Lunarian women used to access all sorts of strange planes. It's how I found you in the woods. Perhaps we could help you remember."

"No need to waste your energy on me," Luxuros said. "We have bigger things to worry about."

Astra giggled. "The mighty commander fears nothing but himself."

"Not nothing," he sighed, his eyes falling over her. "You scare me."

"Good." She grinned. "I have one more question for you. Did you... did you train him on me?"

"Who?"

"Mirquios," Astra said, her voice dropping to conceal the emotion building behind her words. "Everything was just so easy. Too easy. Did you craft it all to win me over?"

"No," Luxuros assured her. "Of course not. We came with intentions to court you, but I swear to you, it was all him. Your mother may have passed along a few notes—"

"Favorite flowers, for example?" she snapped.

The commander rolled his eyes. "No, Astra. Believe it or not, I'm very observant. It's the job. You drink your coffee black unless you're hungover. Then, you take it with a little sugar and follow it immediately with a cup of tea. You prefer to wear your hair down, but always pin it up if your mother or sister are around. I have my theories about why, but won't bore you with them. You're a big fan of Capella's poetry. You've blown through at least three of her anthologies just since I've been in the court and you leave notes in the margins for someone. I thought Ameera, but she doesn't seem to be as much of a fan. She tends to reach for history books."

"I leave them for Lunelle," she murmured.

Lux continued, "And you always take the moonblossom centerpieces back to your room after dinner. If there are roses or violets, you leave them."

Astra leaned away from him, the air too thick around her throat.

"And besides all that, it doesn't *really* matter if I wrote him a damned encyclopedia on you if you Tethered, does it? The gods themselves ordained it. Who cares how well-studied he was or wasn't?"

216

"Right," she said, unable to look at him.

"Unless..."

"Unless what?" she repeated, her fingers tightening against her palms.

"Nothing," he said quietly. Her lungs flared with violet wisps she resented immediately as she felt the urge to push him, to dig out the truth.

"As?" Ameera's voice broke the scarlet web forming in her chest, her footsteps echoing off the stairs below. Astra moved away from the commander, grateful for the breath she forced down.

"As!"

"In here!" She called, Luxuros's eyes glued back on the book.

Ameera sighed as she entered the study. "I think we should leave for home first thing in the morning."

"Oh?" Astra asked. Luxuros closed the book, his ears perked by the alarm in her tone.

"Helena told me that the wards have been down for months, at least. Ivonne has been hiding it from your mother, insisting on handling it on her own. She thinks the priestess is letting them in intentionally, hoping they'll find their way to Lunaria and—well—do exactly what you think they'll do. Technically, if the Aurellis line ends, the Bloodmoons are the next to the throne."

"Gods above," Astra gasped. "All that talk of traitors and she's giving the enemy free reign of the Rift!"

"Do you think she's safe one more night, or should we leave now?" Luxuros asked, stacking the books and documents together and shoving them back into the bag.

"I think leaving when most of the city is sleeping is better," Ameera said. "We could wait until moonrise, but we shouldn't linger."

"We'd have to take horses," Astra muttered. "And stop to get Riv in Celene."

Ameera sighed, a spark of something pink twirling in a wine-red river settling in her stomach. The commander slung the bag over his shoulder and looked to Astra to make the final call.

"I'll speak with Eileen. We should leave within the hour."

"Cam won't want him here," Ameera said as Astra slid off her horse, leading her through the crumbling gates of Celene's facade.

No one shuffled within the small village at the late hour, but Astra and Ameera knew a spotter was probably on her way to the city below to alert the council of their presence.

"I can handle myself," the commander said. "I'll camp."

Astra twisted toward him, struck by a need to show him the city they'd built, a craving to see Celene through his disapproving glare.

"You can't camp out here. I've been shot at in these woods more times than I can count. I need you to understand that the women in this city are my *family*, they are my top priority, and if ears outside of the rebellion were to hear about them—"

She cut herself off, unwilling to imagine the things that could happen. "You will not speak to anyone unless spoken to. You will not make eye contact. You will not tell a soul what, or who, you've seen, okay?"

"I understand, As," Luxuros said, a softness in his tone she hadn't heard before.

"I still don't think Cam will appreciate the surprise," Ameera said, looking out over the cliffs for signs of life.

She was right. Cameren would be worried on behalf of the women she'd sworn to protect. It would take more than just his word to make them feel safe.

"A blood oath," Astra barked, her eyes falling to his hands. She reached for the sharp pin in her hair, releasing the knot at her neck into a waterfall of curls. She held her hand in front of his face, pressing the blade into her palm. The same blade that had been in his neck not so long ago.

It was reckless—would he even care if she tied her life to his honor? But it was the insurance she needed. Celene needed.

Ameera balked as Luxuros stared at her, taken aback by her swift movement. He folded his arms as he eyed her.

"That seems a tad dramatic, Astra, even for you."

"These women deserve to feel safe, Commander. They need to be certain." She held his gaze, drawn into the intensity behind his eyes as she stepped closer, toe to toe with his worn leather boots. "If you're squeamish—"

A dark laugh rippled through him as he glared at her and shoved his sleeve up his arm, the pink hatchling scars already sealing themselves over.

"Please, Princess. I've bled for you before, I've no problem doing it again."

She didn't notice his right hand wrap around the handle of the dagger he kept on his hip, slicing the flesh of his palm open in a rapid movement that startled her. His jaw hardly twitched as he shoved his bleeding palm forward and flipped the dagger in his other hand, sheathing it before Astra could let out the breath she held.

Astra carved a shallow line into her flesh, extending her

hand to meet his. "You will never speak of Celene or anything you see within her walls. You will protect them like your own, as long as we both breathe."

The commander nodded, wrapping his large hand over hers as a searing pain gripped their nerves. As they touched, a sizzle and pop made them both jump, as if a bolt of lightning struck between the wounds. Just as quickly, a soft warmth spread over her hand, easing the sharp pull of the raw wound as she pulled away. Astra's brows furrowed, her mouth falling open to ask a dozen questions, but she paused when she saw the same confusion settle over his jaw.

"Well, then," Ameera huffed, rolling her eyes. "If that doesn't do it, I don't know what will."

Astra rubbed at her palm, marveling at the way the skin fused back together as Ameera charged ahead through the silent village. They wove beyond the dilapidated homes, no fires warming them, and traced a path Astra knew well even in the dark.

Her boots gripped the cliff's loose gravel as she stared out over the Somnia slipping away into the sea.

"Where is everyone?" Luxuros asked, his eyes narrowing in the night.

Astra smirked. He was looking the wrong way, exactly as they hoped. The river's sweeping beauty made for a sparkling distraction, leaving the city built into the cliffs below to slumber peacefully unnoticed. Astra pointed to a small wooden cart tucked into the edge of the cliff, just a short hop from the ledge. She dropped onto the platform, followed by Ameera, but the commander hesitated.

"I'm not getting on that thing."

"It's *fine*," Astra insisted. "We just had it built last Summer. It beats repelling."

He eyed her skeptically but dropped over the cliff's edge

onto the platform. Astra did not wait for him to stabilize before pulling the rope overhead and ringing the bell on the ground, laughing quietly as the cart lurched to life and the commander cursed under his breath.

The platform descended several stories, dust from the cliffs crumbling over the handrails as they sank into the canyon. Astra turned to watch the commander's face as Celene's sapphire and jade tower homes came into view, carved into the cliffside. They descended over the Somnia River and her many rivulets that wandered through the city, carved bridges dotting gardens that sang with the sweet petals of late Summer, early Autumn blooms.

"Unbelievable," he whispered.

"The Forgotten City used to be a wasteland," Ameera informed him. "But after decades of neglect, the restoration is quite something."

"You did this?" Luxuros asked, watching Astra's face as she scanned the rapidly approaching transfer station.

"I paid for it," Astra said, shrugging. "The women did the work."

"She's being modest," Sephone chimed as she stepped onto the platform and tied off the cart with a thick rope, extending her arms to wrap Astra into a warm embrace. "We had no pulley system before she got here, and the crystal bridges were her idea. Built from a tower that fell some decades ago."

"Seph," Astra mumbled into her hair.

"You brought a friend," she said tentatively.

"He's oath-bound," Astra assured her, holding her palm up, though the wound didn't appear as fresh as she'd intended. "You can trust him, but we don't want to cause any upset. Can you bring Cameren here?"

Ameera straightened her back at Cam's name. "Of course," Sephone said, breaking into a jog across the platform and disappearing into the nearest tower. She tossed one glance over her shoulder at the commander before disappearing.

Is she still mad? Ameera asked.

In a hot, want to fuck about it, kind of way, Astra thought back, enjoying the caught breath in her friend's chest.

The commander looked between them but thought better about intervening.

"The Fire Queen returns!" Cameren called as she left the tower, pulling a velvet robe tighter across her slender frame. Her long, midnight-black curls were twisted into dozens of braids, tied off with quartz beads of all sorts of pinks and blues. "And she brought a treat." Cam's eyes slipped over Ameera. "And a *man*," she said, unable to keep the word from tilting into a shocked question.

"Sorry for the late-night surprise," Astra offered.

"It's probably best this way, fewer eyes around. You should take them to your tower. There's hardly anyone there these days."

Astra nodded, though it stung to hear it. Her tower was overflowing with women when she'd left. She gestured to the sapphire spire closest to them, a steep staircase winding in a spiral leading up several stories. Salt from the breeze off the Empyrean clung to the facets carved into the walls as Astra led them to the top floor through a smooth moonstone door, much like the ones in Lunaria.

She'd opened her door to hundreds of women without hesitation at all hours of the night, but shoving the stone inward and taking in her home with the commander behind her sent a flurry of blues and purples across her chest, the vulnerability foreign.

The entry was dark, too dark, as she stumbled against an altar table she'd left covered in dried florals. She sighed and stilled her breath, letting a whisper of heat leave her fingers before touching them to the sconces in the hall, following a trail of bronze lights to her densely furnished study she'd left in quite a state. Books and letters lay scattered across her desk. A bottle of moonshine was still out on her coffee table. She lit the lanterns around the room and pulled the glass doors open to her balcony, letting the cool night air flow through the silky white curtains. The study gave way to several other rooms, usually inhabited by various women who didn't feel like walking home after a few too many drinks and listening to Cam's wild stories all night, or Sephone's long, olive fingers dancing across the harp tucked in the corner.

Gods, she thought, *I miss it here.*

"You can stay in that room," Astra gestured to a door off the study and then to the one across the hall. "That's mine."

Lux shrugged his tense shoulders, setting his eyes on the sofa in the middle of the study. "I can sleep here. Ameera can take the bedroom."

Astra mumbled as she straightened up piles of books, "I think Ameera will find other arrangements." She tilted her head toward the balcony, where Luxuros could see two silhouettes through tangled curtains move into one another.

"Oh," he said quietly. "I suppose I could have pieced that together."

Astra watched their long limbs twist around one another, a rosy glow blossoming between them and dissolving into a violet layer of yearning. She felt something rise within her as she watched, a pain scraping at the inside of her ribs.

"They're never ready for each other at the same time. It's complicated."

"It always is," Luxuros responded as he sank into the sofa.

Astra sat across from him, flipping a set of glasses over on a metallic tray and pulling the cork in the moonshine bottle out with her teeth. She poured them each a healthy glass.

"Am I allowed to ask you questions?" Luxuros leaned back, crossing one leg over his knee as he sipped the liquid fire.

"Am I allowed to ignore the ones I don't like the answers to?"

"*I* have questions first," Cam said, slinking back into the study. She sat on the arm of Astra's chair, plucking the glass from her hands and throwing the moonshine back before pouring another glass. "Namely, is this the king of yours I keep hearing so much about?"

Astra choked on a laugh, sitting straighter as she explained. "No, Cam, this is Luxuros, Commander to the king of Mercury. Luxuros, this is Cameren, one of the leaders here and, most days, one of my best friends."

Cam rolled her eyes but draped an arm around Astra's shoulders. "It's a pleasure to meet you, Luxuros. I assume those twin scars on your palms are Astra's way of ensuring I didn't have you arrested upon entry?"

Luxuros only nodded.

"Excellent."

"The commander can be trusted," Astra assured her. "He went with us to Ellume to investigate some strange happenings."

"The rebels?" Cam asked.

"I—" Astra pouted. "Am I the only person in the court who didn't know about the Novas?"

Cam shook her head. "No, of course not. But the commander's cuff," She pointed to the leather band around Luxuros's wrist, emblazoned with runes Astra never did understand. "I've seen them in documentation from the Venusian Court. Daria came and had one tattooed on her arm a few months ago. What the Nether did she do to Riverion, by the way?"

Astra sighed. She'd nearly forgotten that she'd sent Riv back to Celene with an injury. "Oh, you know me and Daria.

We love a good quarrel. The rebels are the least of our worries," Astra said, eager to move Cam off the topic. "The Rift's wards aren't working. There are Solarians all over the Midwood, and likely in Lunaria."

"Solarians!" Cam sprang to her feet at the word. There were some fears so deeply woven into the fibers between muscle and tendon that one can't help but jump at the mere mention.

"We know nothing concrete," Astra assured her. "But yes, they're in the court. There's movement in the Outer Courts, as well. We have every reason to expect war, Cam."

"Shit," she whispered. "*Shit.*"

"We can strategize in the morning, but I want Celene fully prepared for what's ahead."

Cam rested a hand on Astra's shoulder. "Of course, As. We'll assemble the council after breakfast. I'll have something sent up here," she said, glancing at Luxuros. "I assume you're aware your presence here might be unsettling for some residents?"

The commander nodded. "I'll stay out of the way."

"Until morning, then," Cam said, squeezing Astra's shoulder one last time before dropping the glass in her hand to the table and heading back to the stairwell.

She left the door open—an invitation.

"Go," Astra smiled. "Please."

Ameera darted to the door and whispered, "See you tomorrow!" and disappeared.

The commander waited in silence as Astra's face readjusted, the ambient energy in the room gone.

"How long were you here?"

She drew in a slow breath, letting the tingling feeling in her chest fade as she came back to herself for the first time in weeks. "Three years, give or take."

"How did you find it?"

"'Find' is a generous term. I, uh, was exiled here by the queen herself after an incident."

"A fiery one?" Luxuros raised an eyebrow.

She considered adopting his method of communication and merely nodding, but something about the commander's interest in her begged the truth.

"There's a village in the Midwood, not far from here. Three years ago they suffered a strange illness. The priestesses thought it might have come from another court. They were dying at record numbers and needed help, but Oestera refused to send us. She was too afraid Lunelle or I would get sick. We had a bit of a blow-up." Astra winced as she spoke, the memory sticking to her throat like tar. "I'd battled the fire before, many times throughout the years, but I'd never hurt anyone. I'd never burned so out of control. I barely caught her gown on fire, but it was enough."

Luxuros sucked in a sharp breath. "That'll do it."

"She was fine, but obviously, she couldn't let it go without punishment. Really, it was the last thing on a long list of reasons she wanted to send me away."

Luxuros pondered his next question long enough that she wondered if they were done conversing for the night. "How many Lunarian demigoddesses are gifted with fire magic, Astra?"

She held his stare. "Very, very few."

"Leona?"

She nodded. "Leona."

His face twisted with intrigue.

"I'm not particularly proud of it," she said through another sip of moonshine, the warmth spreading through her chest. She rose and made her way to the balcony, letting the cool breeze wash away the heat on her cheeks.

He leaned against the rail beside her, watching the river flow quietly below. "If anyone can understand resenting what flows through your veins, it's me."

"Yeah, well, at least yours isn't costing you much."

The commander's jaw clenched, an unrestrained slip of misery snaking through whatever failsafe he held so tightly. It was gone before she could get her mind around it.

"What's over there?" he asked, pointing across the river.

A series of pools and waterfalls bubbled softly in the night, glowing in shades of blue and lavender under the Moon.

"Hot springs," Astra mumbled, her bones aching for the soothing waters. "Actually, I could go for that right now."

"You're certain it's safe for you here?"

Astra rolled her eyes. "Yes. Well, no. I'm uncertain of anything these days, Commander."

He closed his eyes, wrestling with himself for a moment before sighing and gesturing to the door.

"I'm coming with you."

CHAPTER

TWENTY-TWO

Astra set the moonshine bottle and two cotton blankets on the edge of the smooth rocks bordering the water, warm ripples and steam pouring from stacks of pools above their heads.

She wasted no time in pulling off her dress and leaving it in a heap next to the blankets, peeling off layers of linen and a thin chemise before slipping under the warm water.

She let it wash the tension in her body away, sending her hair into a ruby halo.

When she resurfaced, Luxuros still stood on the edge, debating.

She laughed, leaning over the rock ledge and watching the surrounding water slip over the smooth surface and into the pool below.

"Surely you've encountered scarier things than a body, Commander?"

His eyes landed everywhere but on her.

"I'm sorry," he said, nervously pulling at the leather ties in his vest. "In Mercury, this would be inappropriate, to say the least."

"Lucky for you, you're not in Mercury, and we're both exhausted and sore. I won't watch."

Astra winked at him, which he did not find amusing, unsurprisingly. The whoosh of leather and linen dropping to the ground cut through the gurgling springs, followed by several falling blades—two more than she'd counted on him earlier—heavy boots, and a soft splash as his body slid into the water. The heat ticked up a few degrees in response to his skin.

She perched on a worn rock at the edge of the pool, pulling her hair over her breasts to ease his discomfort. He sat across from her, leaning against the crystalline rocks with his eyes closed. If Luxuros was anything, it was exhausted. She saw it then, the weight of his station in life.

His body was marked by tough decisions. Lost sleep left its evidence in ravines beneath his eyes.

She told herself to stop staring, but her eyes remained fixed on his broad frame. His shoulders rose above the springs, golden swirls inked along the tops of them. They ran down his back, the skin on his left shoulder still pink and marred by her reckless reaction in the Midwood.

"They're from a Jovian artist in Mercury. Most Nova Rebels have them. I thought you weren't watching," Luxuros said, his voice dropping into a soft Summer storm, the harsh edge she usually earned dissolving into the steam.

His eyes hadn't been closed, then. A faint rose washed over her face, embarrassed at how long she'd been staring.

"May I?" Luxuros asked, circling his finger in a gesture to turn around. She stood from her seat, pulling her hair to one side and revealing the ribbon of sparkling Moon phases inked along her spine. He stood, the water rippling around her hips as he moved forward. The warmth of his fingertip hovered over the curve of the first crescent Moon at the base of her neck, refusing to actually make contact. "It's beautiful work," he breathed, moving back a step.

"I had it done at a silent retreat. There's an artist here who makes ink from the Somnia and the dust from altars to the Mother. It took two full days."

The commander smirked—she felt it in the silence. "No way you stayed quiet for that long."

She rolled her eyes. "Ha, ha. Let me see yours up close." She reached out and spun him by his shoulders, his back tightening under her touch. Where she'd once seen chains in a dream sat a gilded phoenix rising out of the water and across his shoulders. Beneath the tattoos ran dark purple scars, faded with time, but there nonetheless.

The same burn scars she knew lay under her mother's gowns.

"It's not as meaningful as yours, I'm afraid. Really, I wanted something to cover the Flare scars." His shoulders shrugged away from her curious stroke, the golden ink bouncing with the movement. Flames engulfed the bottom of the bird from what she could see above the water. "Mirq and I decided for each other. He picked a phoenix for me, I picked a lion for him."

Astra ran a finger over the wing of the phoenix, glowing with an iridescent shimmer. "What's in the ink?"

"Pixie dust," he laughed, turning to face her.

"I'm serious!"

"So am I," he grinned. "Jovian specialty. Wait until you see it in the sunlight."

She shivered. "If I don't catch fire the second I wander into it."

"I believe Mirquios has already ordered his courtkeeper to add shades to the windows," he teased.

"So thoughtful." The mention of the king's name was a stark reminder that she was not just a friend enjoying a relaxing evening, but a future queen he needed to guard. She should have been more considerate about the position she put him in.

The leather cord around his neck pulled her from the thought. She'd seen it before, peeking over the top of his shirts, and once in Ellume, but she'd never gotten such a close look at the raw moonstone hanging from the leather. A delicately carved gold Sun and Moon hugged the iridescent moonstone, catching the starlight above.

He jumped back as she reached out to touch it, returning to his side of the pool.

"I'm sorry," she gasped, surprised by his sudden movement, intrigued but also kicking herself for intruding on his space. He dropped his eyes toward the sea beyond the springs, squinting in the low light.

"It's fine. It's just, no one else should touch it."

She nodded, afraid to pry further. He briefly looked back toward her, touching the amulet with a wince. "Apologies, Princess."

"Lux." She crossed the pool, moving closer but careful to give him time to react. "Must we fight about this constantly?"

He chuckled. "When you're married, you know I'll have to refer to you as 'Your Highness,' right?"

She groaned. "*Please* don't. You know I hate the honorifics. They just feel so unearned."

"Most of your court would kill for the title, but you hold it in such little regard. I would say it seems ungrateful, but that doesn't fit."

Her brows curved in curiosity. "Then what is it?"

"You feel unworthy of it."

Astra held her breath, her eyes giving away how right he was.

"You move through this world with the grace of a queen and the grit of a dragon, but the discipline of a feral animal. It's bewildering how your mind runs in all directions at once. But you don't see what an asset it would be if you mastered it. You see what a danger you are if you don't. I know I've contributed to that. Perhaps I was too quick to judge."

"A feral animal," she repeated, scrunching her nose as she laughed, ignoring the near-apology.

Lux nodded. "I've seen many atrocities in this life, Astra. One of the biggest is that you don't have the faintest idea of your potential for destruction."

She opened her mouth to protest, but he stopped her. "That wasn't an insult." His amber gaze held hers, the hard line of her brow softening. "This time," he added.

She considered this. She was used to her demeanor being boiled down to untamed impulses, but rarely did the critics of the court acknowledge what ran beneath her flesh in unseen currents. The control she'd worked at for years. So much of her strength lived between breaths in what she *didn't* show them.

She narrowed her eyes, trying to understand what he was getting at.

"The women here have done me a great honor by opening my eyes to the injustices of the system within which we operate. You'll notice not one of them calls me princess unless they are mocking me—that is where my aversion truly comes from. We're all equal here. We're working toward the same goals. Everyone agrees on the rules, and if there's any opposition, we examine the issue from all sides and hear each other out. Everyone cleans, everyone cooks, everyone rests. It's a system that works, but not if I'm a princess."

"You sound like someone I know." Lux grinned, leaning his head back again. "Mirquios dreams of a titleless world."

"So he's said. I look forward to introducing him to Cam and a few of the other leaders, and showing him how we work."

"I imagine your mother opposes the idea."

Astra snorted. "She won't even hear of it."

He lifted his head again. "Minds can change, Astra."

"Sure." She smiled weakly. "Just look at you. A month ago you thought me nothing but a spoiled princess who would destroy everything you love. "

He flashed a wicked grin. "Yes. And someday I may just change my mind."

Astra paced forward, a dark laugh from him drawing her toward the melody.

"Well, if nothing else, you've stopped sighing every time I open my mouth."

He nodded, spreading his arms back over the rocks behind him, his chest expanding as he inhaled.

"Earlier," she whispered. "What was that between our palms?"

"I'm not sure what you're talking about," he said through tight teeth, his eyes shifting away from her.

She shook her head. "I think you are."

"I truly don't know," he insisted, his eyes silently begging her to move on. "A trick I learned between battlefields and bar fights." He changed the subject. "Daria..."

She sank back against the rocks, her head swirling with memories and regrets. The steam rose around them, like the haze over cups of warm tea Daria would bring her in the pale morning moonlight. "Daria and I were..."

"Complicated?" Lux arched a brow.

"Actually, no," she sighed. "It was supremely uncomplicated at first. I had just been shipped to Celene. I happened across her path in the Midwood one day, and that was it. We were simply together. And it was nice until it wasn't." Astra swallowed. It caused her physical pain to reduce Daria to a nice time, but it was certainly easier that way.

"You loved her."

Astra fought the urge to curse at him, but he was not judging. He was genuinely curious.

"I did." She pressed her lips together into a wistful smile. "That was the problem, as it so often is. We were great together, but she wanted more than I could give. The clock was ticking until Mother needed me as a bargaining chip. She wanted to run away together, find some little city in Venus or Mars, and disappear. Which had its appeal, trust me."

"What stopped you?"

She glanced over her shoulder at the sleeping city behind her, at the thousand women traversing their subconscious desires as they rested. The low hum of their dreams wafted over, like walking to a room after someone applied a floral perfume.

"I couldn't leave. I saw the state of the city. They needed my help. She couldn't understand why I would choose strangers over her, but that wasn't it. The weight of a court... so few people understand the way a crown breaks your neck and straightens your spine." Emotion climbed her throat, digging its skeletal fingers into the soft flesh.

"You chose to be a queen."

"Queen-adjacent," she snorted. "I might never be on the Lunar Throne, but I still love the people who serve it. It was my fatal flaw with Daria. I couldn't choose heart over duty, and she resented me for it. Things ended in a plume of smoke, as you've gathered. I never meant—"

She bit back a violent wave of tears, searching for a breath.

"I never wanted to hurt her. You may think me a feral

animal now, but a few years ago... feral almost feels too generous a term."

"It must be lonely," Luxuros murmured, his throat tightening, a familiar ache in his chest. "Always feeling for everyone else, but never being allowed the same grace."

Her eyes flickered over him, the warmth in his tone unexpectedly comforting. It was so rare for someone to even consider how it wrecked her, wading through the court's internal wars day in and day out, let alone give her the space to explore it.

"I can count the number of times I've been completely alone with my thoughts on one hand. Even now, you're a brick wall, but the women beyond us... they dream in such divine palettes... it's lovely some nights, but on others, their nightmares take root in my lungs. It costs me days when I can't find the energy to block it out. It's like my mind is constantly on fire and no one ever smells the smoke until it's too late."

He stared for a beat too long, his eyes swirling like pools of molten honey. Something about him this way, in the starlight, surrounded by a warmth she understood, a warmth she expected, pulled her in. She couldn't have fought if she wanted to as she stepped forward, a strange insistence in her chest.

The crash of her knees colliding against his sent her back in shock. The heat of his skin—the one she understood so much less—flooded her senses as she lost the focus that constantly ran in the back of her mind to disarm his lineage.

"Sorry."

"It's fine," he assured her, reaching for his chest—closing himself off. "We haven't slept. We've been drinking. I'm not being a complete hardass for once." He laughed at himself as he looked beyond her, toward the glow of her windows. "Just a body, right?"

"Right," she breathed.

"We should probably get some sleep, Astra."

She agreed, knowing it wouldn't be possible with all the wild thoughts convalescing in her mind.

She didn't look to see if he turned around as she climbed out of the pool and wrapped herself in one of the cotton blankets, nor did she wait for him to get out before heading back to the bridge.

THE STEAM from the springs combined with the moonshine pulled her mind downward, into a spiraling haze. She'd have to extinguish the blazing rivers of him again in the morning when she wasn't so dizzy. Now was not the time.

She could already feel the dream coming on as she sank right back into those damned hot springs.

She should have known she'd find herself here—standing before Lux, staring him down. Her knee brushed against his again, but she did not flinch this time.

She didn't move at all as she waited, watching his body unconsciously rearrange for her, his eyes dropping from her face to the bare skin between her breasts.

They flickered back up, a blush creeping over his throat. A throat she'd once nearly slit—now she felt her fingers twitch at her side, begging to reach out and touch the taut skin across his collarbones. Yearning to twist them into the bronze hair on his chest.

"What are you, Luxuros?" she asked, eyes dropping pointedly to the twin scar on his palm.

"You don't have a monopoly on magic, Astra," Lux said, his resolve to adhere to his Mercurian propriety crumbling with every step she closed between them. Emboldened by the swirling smoke in his eyes, she did what her body begged—she slid over his lap as he froze beneath her. Her knees landed on either side of him, his breath

stalling as she took a moment to explore the feel of the commander beneath her.

"Astra, please," he begged, hands tightening around the rocks behind him, hanging on to any shred of loyalty he could bleed from the stones. The siren call of him was unstoppable—is this how human women felt about Solarians in the real world? Entranced by the heat in their veins?

She should have moved, should have gotten up, should have apologized.

She should have felt worse about the position she put him in.

In reality, she did the right thing. She ignored the knocking in her ribs and stepped back. But here, where she could lock her decisions away in the dark recess of her mind where she kept all the things she pretended didn't occur to her in the moonlight, who could blame her for sinking lower?

Shit, when did the blazing current under his skin become so tempting to her cool fingers? It was like the call to reach out and touch a singing kettle, just to ensure the boiling tea within wasn't imaginary.

His eyes slid along her bare skin, smoke and flame, drowning any logic she might have clung to in reality. Her heart pounded so loudly there was no way he couldn't hear it, but as she leaned forward, she felt his drumming wildly, too.

Maybe she imagined the pulse of scarlet in his chest.

She lifted her hand, the need to touch more of him all-consuming, but she couldn't bring herself to commit the next crime.

Lux sighed, the warm air tickling her neck. His lips brushed her bare skin so slightly that perhaps it was only a passing breeze. "You have to stop."

"Me?" she asked, daring to reach out and touch a loose curl. It taunted her, the curve of it begging to brush against her fingertip. She'd lost any ability to think about the consequences as it slipped

between her fingers and sprang back toward his face. She ran her forefinger along his jaw, forcing him to look into her eyes.

"Astra," he breathed, his hands breaking free of their perches. They wrapped around her back under the sizzling water. "What are we doing?"

She rocked her hips over his, letting his fingers brush her hair behind her shoulders, his lips finding their way to her throat.

"What we've always done," she said, a quiet gasp escaping in the space between them as she felt his desire for her between her legs. A shock of white lightning lit her spine up as she slowly rolled her muscles forward, creating a delicious friction between them. His breath hissed between his teeth. "For centuries and centuries. Sun and Moon, destroying one another."

She woke up gasping, her heart racing, her head swirling with a thousand justifications.

Not one of them quelled the midnight-black guilt consuming her soul.

TWENTY-THREE

The commander left his room first.

His heavy boots thudded against the obsidian floor, stopping briefly in the study before heading for the balcony. Astra had been awake for hours, listening. Trying to decide how to look him in the eye after her dream.

It was just a dream, she told herself. Her spine tingled as her mind wandered back to the warm water, his hands even hotter as they slipped over her skin. She shook her head, the smell of coffee percolating wafting into her room. It *was* just a dream, after all. She hadn't consciously traveled there, not like before. They'd been drinking. She was lonely. He didn't need to know, and she needed to forget it.

Astra pulled on a pale lavender dress and boots from her closet. She glanced in the mirror on her dresser to twist her hair into a half-back knot, sliding the crescent pin into the mess of curls. She smoothed the wrinkles in the linen of her dress, officially out of reasons to linger in the bedroom.

The coffee smelled so divine to her hungover senses—at least she could soothe one headache.

"Morning!" she chirped, passing by the balcony and heading straight for the pot of coffee he'd brewed on the small stove in the corner. The balcony doors opened to a fair breeze where Luxuros sat on an iron patio chair, dwarfing it as he sipped on one of the coffee cups next to him. Her eyes landed on the second cup as that tingle in her spine begged for attention again.

Enough, she hissed at herself.

She sat beside him, the heat she'd worked so hard to keep at bay stronger now. He glanced at her quickly but did not speak, which would have been expected, but this morning, his silence suffocated her. She fussed with the skirt of her dress, watching the breeze ripple across the lush grass along the Somnia's riverbed below. Women were shaking off the night and starting in on their daily chores, their eyes flickering up to the man on Astra's balcony as they passed.

Waves of moss-green curiosity and amber discomfort floated on the late Summer air, but they seemed to settle when they caught sight of her ruby curls beside him.

"I want you to train me," she blurted out. "*Train*, train me."

Luxuros nodded. "I can do that."

"It's that easy?"

"I think it's for the best. We know more about the dangers you're up against, Astra. But I'm not just going to train you on the mental game, you need to learn basic self-defense. And some diplomacy—"

She huffed. "I hardly think I need lessons in diplomacy from your pissy ass."

The commander only stared at her, waiting for the words to echo against her skull.

"Fine," she sighed, setting her coffee cup on the glass table. "I heard it. I'll learn anything you want me to."

"Very good," he mumbled, his eyes turning out toward the

sea beyond the city. "One more thing," he said, the fire behind his gaze sparking with something that made her nervous. Something that felt rather like the ghost of last night's simmering flames.

A bead of sweat rolled down the back of her neck, despite the cool morning.

"You're getting greedy, Commander," she muttered. She drained her coffee and leaned forward, spotting Cameren and Ameera leaving Cam's building and heading their way. They wound over a bridge, a basket of what Astra hoped was something Sephone baked between them.

"Lux?" she asked, his condition still hanging in the air. She turned back around and met his strange stare, a wickedness within his smile she couldn't begin to read. He took his time as he wrestled with whether he should say whatever sat on the end of his tongue, but as she heard her door scrape inward, he murmured softly for her ears only.

"You have to do something about the dreams, As."

Her chest exploded in a symphony of mortified reds and oranges as heat rushed across her limbs. "Wh-what?"

The commander's lips curled into a truly diabolical grin. "Were you unaware, Princess?"

"We brought breakfast!" Ameera cheerfully burst into Astra's living room, poking her head onto the balcony and displaying her basket proudly. Astra barely heard her over the rush of blood in her ears. "Oof, what are we fighting about now?"

"No fights here," Lux sighed, smirking still as he finished his coffee. "We were just discussing a dream Astra had last night."

A scarlet blush unfurled over her chest. She growled, "Commander!"

"Was it serious?" Ameera asked, her vivid yellow concern wrapping around Astra's heart. "A vision?"

"No," Astra bit. "A nightmare, actually."

"You should have heard her scream," Luxuros teased, resting his boots on the balcony railing as he leaned back.

"Luxuros!" Astra hissed, kicking his feet back onto the floor. "Which one of us needed lessons in diplomacy?"

Lux opened his mouth to argue with her, but Cam cut him off.

"We have a job for you, if you're willing to lend us your strength, Commander," Cam said, cutting through the tension as she tossed Astra a scone. "The younger girls managed to jam a boat under the bridge. They've been working at it all morning but have made little progress."

"I don't want to distress anyone," Luxuros said.

Just me, Astra groaned internally.

Cam waved a hand. "These women know Astra would sooner fling herself off the cliffs than endanger them. Her word is good. Though you may want to watch out for your own sake. They aren't too happy that your king is taking her away from us."

Astra sighed, a purple pang of guilt tightening around her wrists.

"I'll take you to the docks, Lux," Ameera offered. "We'll check on Riv, too. Cam says he's in rougher shape than we thought."

"We can send him home in a few days, but I wouldn't ride him for a while, As. His wing took some damage when you landed."

"Perfect," Astra whispered. Ameera and Luxuros were hardly out of the door before Cam slid closer to Astra, aware that every wall in Celene had ears.

"Ameera showed me the Shadow Bargaining manual. I pulled a few texts to send back to the palace with you. It's not an exact match, but there's a book of Saturnian mythology. Their patron goddess, Saturnia, promised the Nether Queen a black diamond ring if she granted her the ability to see auras. Saturnia went back on their deal and the Nether Queen blew her soul into a billion shards of black diamond, forming a ring around Saturn so her people would never forget her betrayal. There are a few other similar exchanges between ancient gods and the Nether Queen. They may not be speaking of Shadow Bargaining, but it's a start."

"Thank you," Astra said, a chill crossing her arms.

"I also pulled some texts on the Ascension process. If Selenia truly made her full Ascent, which she would have had to in order to take the Lunar Throne in the Court Above, she would have reunited with her Shadow and Soul in the Court Below. If she did trade her Shadow, it had to have been recently."

Astra shook her head. "I'm not sure about the timeline. We have records in the library of the palace, but I think she Ascended before I was born. I don't have many memories of her, but she was already on the Lunar Throne Above when I was old enough to form memories."

"Whenever it happened, it's not good. That kind of power has to be up to something nefarious. The Court Above is not the end-all-be-all, Astra. There are powers even the gods fear."

"So it never ends, then?" She smiled weakly. "Thank you for compiling all of that. I know there's a common thread somewhere. I just need more information. But Solan," Astra whispered his name as if the crests of the rivulets below might be spies. "He's moving, Cam. We need to be ready."

"I was born for this, Astra," Cam grinned. "As were you."

AFTER LUNCH with the Celenian council, Astra mounted her horse with a long list of needed supplies in hand.

She wasn't sure *when* war was coming, but she knew Celene would be ready. She'd managed a quick visit with Riverion before taking the pulley cart back up the cliffside and darting through the village as woman after woman stopped her to speak.

"Add some pigments for Seph to our list," Astra said to Ameera, her mind a steel trap for Astra's scattered thoughts.

"What for?" Lux asked. It was the first thing he'd said to her since breakfast.

"She's a gifted painter. Whatever happens, someone needs to document it. She reminds me of my father, quietly absorbing everything happening around her to capture it permanently."

The commander considered this as Ameera galloped ahead of them, her eyes scanning the perimeter of the forest for any strangers.

"You love them so deeply," Luxuros finally said.

She only nodded, surprised by the tears that sprang so freely to her eyes. Leaving the first time had felt like a temporary mission.

Leaving now felt like the last time before everything changed.

She did her best to swallow the feelings. She'd been vulnerable enough with him that morning, even if it was against her will. Now, she couldn't stop spiraling into memories of the dreams she'd had since he first appeared in the court. All the times her mind had painted a softer portrait of him after arguing all day. All the times his warmth had reached out to touch her.

Mother above, she was blushing again.

"Celene is the only place in the world where no one recoils

when I express a strong opinion," Astra said, desperate to cover the shaking feeling inside her. "No one rolls their eyes or sighs when I pose an idea. And better, if it's a bad one, they tell me without fear. They don't eye my fingertips because I'm not a monster to them. I'm passionate. No one manipulates or plots to shape my will. They trust me to be the leader they know I am."

Luxuros kept pace beside her, smiling as he replied. "The little girls down by the bridge this morning were using berries to stain their hair red. They called one another 'Fire Queen.'"

If she hadn't been blushing before, she certainly was now. "We need to move faster, Lux. We have to figure out what's happening before they get hurt. I can't let them down."

"You won't," he assured her.

She smiled, the ease of it sending another blaring reminder of last night's dream to the forefront of her mind.

"I'm sorry about the dreams," she said quietly, watching Ameera ahead as she spoke. "I didn't know. I thought... I thought they were just dreams. Before, when we met in the Midwood, I'd been cognizant of it. It was intentional. These were... not."

The commander's lips twitched as he reached for the cord around his neck. "It's all right. I was only teasing you this morning. You've been left alone too long, Astra." He pressed his fingers against his chest as he sauntered beside her. "The Tether must be driving you to madness."

"That's not—" Astra stopped herself. He was offering her an out. "Yes. Quite maddening."

"But I would like to set the record straight," Luxuros murmured, his voice edging into a lower register that raised the hairs on her arms. "The blood of the cruelest warriors in the universe flows through my veins. I'm the decorated commander of one of the strongest armies in all thirteen courts. I won wars in four realms before you were out of your governess's care."

He yanked on his mare's reins, circling in front of Astra and cutting into her path. She reared back, her horse huffing as she held his blazing gaze.

"I wouldn't beg."

Lux dug his heels into his mare's sides and sped away, the rhythmic thumping of her hooves perfectly paced against Astra's heart. She rolled her eyes and told herself the sudden rush of fire-orange adrenaline filling her lungs was a pathetic attempt on her body's part to regulate.

She told herself it was just a little lust.

What she hadn't noticed was the way the alarm curled around her ribs and pulled, crushing the bones together in a desperate warning. She didn't notice it rising from her right side, not hers to hold at all.

The force of something, *someone* slammed into her and sent her soaring off her horse and crashing against the muddy forest floor, an explosion of furious color and sound shoving her into the brush.

A scream ripped through her lungs as she pushed back, but her arms were pinned beneath a suffocating weight.

The last thing she heard before her assailant smashed her head against the ground was the metallic ping of a sword and the fury of a warrior unleashed.

A scarlet rage settled over her like a blanket as the world released her mind into the ether.

She came to seconds later, the base of her skull protesting at the very notion of opening her eyes as the world faded back into view.

She coughed, the Midwood's grainy dust coating her throat as her ears rang.

Shuffling feet and cracking twigs—no, was it bone?—revived her from wherever her mind slipped when she hit the ground. Everything hurt as she rolled to the side and shoved herself upright, her boots tangled in the overgrown ryegrass.

"Get down, As!" Lux roared as his arms swung over her head, Ameera's dagger clutched in one hand and his sword in the other.

Ameera! Astra glanced around frantically, searching for her.

Behind you! She panted back, a strange echo around her words. Gods, her head was a mess. Astra spun, locking onto Ameera a few dozen paces away, scrambling through the brush to gather as much as she could from Astra's pockets.

Astra twisted back at the sound of metal on leather to find

Luxuros tangled with a large wall of a man. They blurred into two bronze ghosts grappling with one another's speed. Lux kicked him square in the chest, sending him flying, a streak of crimson fury and disdain lighting up the Midwood as he landed with a thud to her right. Astra reached for her pin, but everything she'd had on her was gone.

"You hit the ground *hard*," Ameera called out, throwing her pin at her. She pointed to the grass, Astra's various belongings strewn about.

"Shit!" Lux screamed as his arm twisted behind his back. The man used his weight to spin and throw the commander to the ground. He skidded across the clearing, hardly coming to a stop before he rolled over his shoulder and popped back up, ready for another hit. There was just enough space between them to make out the man's face, grizzled in the same deep tones as Lux, a recognizable heat rolling off him in waves.

Astra glared, the fire in her blood sparking at the sound of Lux's pain. She let it boil and build in a crest she rarely permitted, ready to send it across the clearing—

You'll hit Lux! Ameera cried against her skull.

She was right. *Fuck.*

She watched as her assailant's eyes fluttered in her direction, his chest alive with a fluorescent rage—no attempt to hide his hatred for her behind a wall. But there, in the center, a small twisted knot of something else.

Fear.

Fear was the quickest route to desperation, and desperation scrambled even the most dangerous of minds. The man's eyes widened as she let sparks fly from her fingertips, wincing at the shock. He struck his sword into the commander's ankle, a blunt thud sickening Astra's stomach. Luxuros hissed in pain, reaching for the injury as Astra let another flare cut through the clearing, distracting the Solarian.

She tried to focus it, to bottle up the fire and still everything else around her. She let her mind hold the flames, concentrating them into a direct line the way Luxuros had taught her before. She let the Solarian slip into the space in her mind as well, his hatred and fear and vicious pain whirling into a funnel of reds and oranges around her unholy light. His eyes raked over her once more and she let it all break away from her control, pushing it into his chest.

He knew, she realized, from the moment he saw her glowing palms. He knew it was coming, but he also knew there was nothing he could do to stop her.

The fear combusted, sending a ripple of fire and smoke through the soft flesh of his lungs, consuming them. In her mind, he burned from the inside out, the cloud of anger in his chest churning brightly into something like ash, floating down to the forest floor.

His eyes turned on her once more, frenzied as a scream left his lips.

"As!"

Her shoulders shook under his touch, but she was trapped somewhere liminal, not quite hearing him as she watched a tendril of smoke rise from the Solarian's throat.

He collapsed to the clearing, his knees hitting the floor with a muted thud—so much quieter than she'd imagined death to be.

"Astra," Luxuros said again, his hands gripping her shoulders tightly. "Come back," he whispered.

Her eyes fluttered open to a hand clasped over Ameera's mouth as she took in what Astra had done. She risked a glance to the clearing. The lifeless body of the spy toppled over, smoke still rising and dissolving from his lips.

The horror of what she'd done tied her veins into knots as her vision blurred, searing white at the edges. Everything in her drained somewhere ethereal, somewhere she hadn't just immolated a man, pulling her energy into another dimension altogether.

"It's alright," the commander murmured against her, but she was no longer present to hear his words.

Her mind spiraled in on itself, and she was gone.

"You have to wake up," Luxuros whispered against her neck as his hands lifted her knees and shoulders. "Please, wake up." He jogged across the palace gardens, her head bouncing with each step in a way that made Ameera's stomach churn.

"I'm awake," Astra tried to say, her eyes unable to prove it. "I'm right here."

"Please," he hissed, setting Astra on her bed as the room filled with maidens. Shadows crossed over her as an herbal scent filled her lungs, the smoke sticking to the walls of her ribcage the same way it rose over the Solarian.

She felt sick again.

"As," Luxuros pleaded, but his voice was distant, slipping away as she fell deeper within herself. Heat consumed her feet and ankles as she fell into a lake of fire, the raw flames licking at her thighs and hands, scraping her flesh.

She opened her mouth to scream, but only smoke came out.

"Astra! Wake up!"

"How long has she been out?"

Nayson's voice was the first she heard as her eyes fluttered against her cheeks, the moonblossom scent of Lunaria slipping in through her nose, soothing her.

"A little over six hours," Luxuros said, his voice low, strange.

Scared, she realized.

Scared of what she was.

It came rushing back at once. The twisted expression on the Solarian's face as he crumbled to his knees, the putrid stench of singed flesh. The wisps of smoke or soul leaving his corpse, perhaps both.

Ameera hovered at her feet, the tides in her chest vacillating from violet terror to navy regret.

"Astra!" Her father's voice cut through the buzzing between her ears. She blinked as the bedroom came into focus. Several sets of eyes peered back at her as she pushed herself up, the pain in her back jarring any remaining haze from her mind. Nayson clasped her hand between his, scanning every fragment of her as she shuffled to rest against the headboard. "Darling?"

"Did I—"

"Yes," the commander cut her off, his head tilting softly at Tula, the High Priestess, resting a hand on the foot of her bed. She was already trying to spin this for Oestera's ears should the queen return soon. "You fell off your horse," Luxuros explained.

"Are you all right?" Nayson asked.

"I think so. No? My head," she groaned, reaching for her forehead and finding a silk bandage wrapped around it. A throbbing pain at the side of her skull demanded attention.

"Here," Ameera said, offering her something in a glass cup. "It will help with the pain." Astra took a long sip and regretted it immediately as the bitter tea burned a path down her throat.

Was that even a fraction of what the Solarian felt as she roasted him alive? Had she killed him? What if there were more?

As if he read her mind, Lux stepped forward. "You hit your head on a boulder, Princess. You may not remember for a few days, but you are safe now."

Safe. It felt demonstrably untrue.

"I did?" she asked, unsure if she was playing along or genuinely confused.

"There was a snake," Ameera chimed in. "Your horse got spooked. You couldn't have done anything to avoid it." She sounded much more like herself within Astra's mind now than she had in the Midwood as she beamed to her, **Get that guilty look off your face, As. You saved our asses.**

"I'm so glad you're awake, Princess," Tula breathed. "You gave us quite the scare. I'll have dinner sent up, stay in bed and rest." Tula faded quietly out of the room, but Nayson remained by her side.

She tried to piece together what she remembered, but the second her eyes closed, the pain reverberated around her head in a cursed halo and she saw two hateful eyes staring at her. Perhaps Luxuros wasn't lying about the boulder. It certainly *felt* like she'd smashed her head on something.

Nayson placed a kiss on his daughter's hand.

"I'll be back in a bit with dinner." He glanced toward Ameera and then Luxuros. "You three better get your story straight before Tula asks questions. Astra could ride Riverion blind through a storm. A snake?"

"Father," she whispered, tightening her grip on his hand.

"I'll buy whatever you sell me, my love. As long as you're okay. But your mother will want answers when this reaches her."

Astra nodded, Nayson's cerulean haze retreating into the hall.

"Don't let it consume you," Lux said quickly, her breath

coming in ragged gasps. He sank into Nayson's now empty seat. "He was going to kill you."

"He was going to kill *you*," she said, the rage that flashed within her when Lux screamed in pain still lingering in her blood. "Is your leg okay?"

Luxuros shrugged. "Don't worry about me. Though I have taken quite a bit of damage in your honor lately."

"I think we're even now," she whispered, her eyes hollow.

Lux nodded solemnly, the smile falling from his face as Ameera shuffled around the room, fussing with anything she could. "How did you do it?"

She shook her head, unsure she could relive it, or even articulate it.

"It was... impressive," Ameera said.

"Impressive!" she cried, a miserable violet bloom choking her. "It was *awful*. I killed him!"

"As," Lux said, his voice dropping into a soft, soothing tone she'd never heard before. Managing her, she realized. "The first kill never stops haunting you. I know it well. But that man was seconds away from killing me to get to you. You felt it. He was Solarian, and he was bloodthirsty. You had no choice."

"I saw it. His hatred for me."

"There are more where he came from," Lux sighed. "Ameera warned Archera. She's agreed to keep it quiet for now. But whatever you did, we need to hone that. Sharpen it."

"Not tonight," Ameera added. "You really did hit your head on a boulder. Did you... did you set him on fire with your mind?"

"I think so," she admitted.

"We've never really explored the talents you may or may not have," Ameera mused. "I wonder... you can sense emotions, but do you think you can influence them?"

"Oh gods," Luxuros chuckled. "Just what we need."

"Next time I'll let you die," she said, wincing. It was so clearly a lie, it nearly hurt to say. Something in her back ached at the mere concept. She'd burn a thousand men alive before letting them hurt Ameera or Luxuros, and they knew it now.

He rested a searing hand on her arm. "It will get better. You just have to keep reminding yourself what was at stake." His fingers tightened against her skin and she realized that there was really only one stake that had crossed her mind when she acted.

And it wasn't her own interest in survival.

He rose, stopping in the doorway. "Get some rest, Fire Queen. We've got work to do tomorrow."

"AGAIN."

Lux's excitement was nearly visible to her, a misty green flickering beyond his closed-off chest. She sighed and did as requested, holding another rose from across the garden in her mind as she imagined it going up in flames.

When she turned to look, it was falling toward the cobblestones below in a plume of smoke and ash. They'd learned through hours of trial and error that if Astra could visualize it, she could almost certainly bring it to pass in reality, though it cost her dearly. Her head was foggy, and her eyes tired as she fought a wave of nausea.

It took two full days of incinerating roses for her to stop vomiting the moment she was alone again. Each cluster of petals took on the shape of the Solarian's face.

She leaned back in the garden chair as Ameera's eyes snapped to her, still watching for any signs of discomfort. Her headache had subsided quickly, but her bones still ached.

"I did want to try something else," Luxuros said, taking a

step toward Astra. "Ameera got me thinking the other night. You can see the colors of someone's feelings in your mind… if you shift the hue, would it influence anything?"

Astra shrugged. "It's never occurred to me to try, but if you're volunteering, you'll have to let down that iron wall of yours."

He shook his head, dark curls bounding off his shoulders. "Not a godsdamned chance. Meer?"

Astra choked. "Meer? Since when are you 'Meer?'"

Ameera rolled her eyes. "Lux and I trauma-bonded," she said, shrugging. "There was a good hour where we thought you were dead. So shut up, okay?"

Astra let loose a clipped laugh, the navy concern in Ameera's chest swelling. She watched it ebb and flow around her ribs, washing them in a dark sea. She held the image in her mind, cradling it as she tried to shift the oceanic blues into something brighter, lighter. They slipped into a lively green, a gilded glimmer in the center as if a star was born in her heart.

"Mother smite me," Ameera whispered.

"Not exactly what I was going for," Astra laughed.

Lux stared at them, eyes wide. "Did it work?"

"I think so," Ameera said. "Try something more extreme."

Astra spun the glittering green into a deep violet she'd experienced many times over the years, usually as she slipped her dress over her hips and—

"Astra Leona!" Ameera burst into a fit of giggles, the violet churning into a nervous petal pink, reflected across Ameera's cheeks as the blush wrapped around her sloped neck.

"Well, that's fun," Astra mused.

"I hope you know you just created a monster. I'll spend the rest of my life wondering how I actually feel," Ameera sighed.

"I can teach you some tricks," Lux chuckled.

"Trauma-bonded or not, *Meer's* loyalties lie with me," Astra grumbled.

"Maybe. Maybe you've been forcing her to like you all this time and we've caught on to your game," Lux said.

"If I had that particular skill available to me when we met, I would have made sure you found me much more charming, Commander."

Lux's eyes glazed as he ran his fingers over his chest, his attention lost momentarily.

"Actually, I should teach you both how to shield yourselves," he finally said, his serious tone such a stark contrast to the girls' lighthearted rousing. "Especially you," he glared at Astra. "You're ripe for the taking if you run into someone else with your proclivities or worse."

"Worse?"

"I believe I told you that Lunarians did not have the sole claim to magic." Lux looked over her head, into the gardens, recalling what he had said to her in her dream when she asked about his own abilities. A rush of heat blossomed in Astra's cheeks, but she quickly imagined herself as calm and stoic as he always seemed to be, the flush retreating.

"You are a powerhouse," Lux murmured. "But you are far from the only one with considerable power in the courts. You need to protect yourself physically, mentally, and spiritually. In war, it's all on the table."

"Anything stand out?" Astra asked Ameera, her lanky body stretched out on a blanket in the gardens, stacks of books anchoring the corners in the early Autumn breeze.

"Not particularly. I'm beginning to think we're crazy."

"Me too." Astra flipped through Ehlaria's translation for the third day in a row, waiting for something new to jump out at her. She'd made it halfway through the story without anything appearing relevant to the Rift, or Selenia, or Shadows. So far, it read as a jumbled string of plots between two star-crossed lovers.

They met in a vague realm between realms—a Shadow Witch and a Light Mage. They were too afraid to touch, but couldn't stop wandering back to one other over the decades.

Perhaps it needed to be read in its original tongue to make more sense. She could convince Lux to read it, probably, not that he had much free time these days.

He'd spent the last few weeks either working on tricks with her or organizing things back home. A few days after they'd returned from Ellume, Mirquios sent along a novel's worth of notes for Lux to tend to, worried that their prolonged stay left Mercury vulnerable. They'd been engaged in intense debates and negotiations from what Lux reported and what Lunelle wrote. Her sister was overwhelmed, homesick, and unsure she belonged in Pluto, her letters riddled with the things she missed about home.

Astra still received brief notes from Mirquios with each post drop, usually something sweet and meaningless. The way two strangers would write to each other, she'd remind herself. She rolled onto her back, holding up the book to cover the nearly full Moon above, the light washing them in a cool glow.

A litany of questions she'd avoided rolled through her mind unstoppably fast.

Would she ever adjust to the golden light of the Sun? Would her heart ache forever for the cool tones of the Moon— its presence gone from half her life, just like that? Would she ever feel more than a tepid tolerance of the king's touch?

Was that something she could make do with? Before she could stop herself, she slipped back into Celene, strong hands running across her back under the springs. The heat in her spine as it arched against the commander's touch... could she really sacrifice that? Or something like it, of course.

Ameera interrupted her. "You're leaking your bummer mood all over me."

"Oh," she laughed, that had become more of an issue as she expanded her abilities. They'd been working on shields, but the concept of keeping her feelings in had always been foreign to her. She'd been an open book her entire life, to everyone's detriment, but especially to her own. "Sorry. Ameera?"

"Hmm?"

"What do you know about Tethers?"

Ameera closed her book, pushing herself up from the blanket. "Quite a bit," she said, a rush of orange skepticism between them. "They're a much larger deal in Venus than they are here."

"Of course."

Her eyes narrowed. "Ask what you *really* want to ask."

"Are they always instant?"

Ameera's lips smiled tightly, a release of something in her chest Astra could not trace. "Not always. There are plenty of cases where they take time to develop. I had a cousin who was with her husband for a decade before theirs snapped into place. It was after their first child—something changed within them both and that did it."

"Fascinating," Astra breathed. "So there can be a right person, wrong time?"

"Something like that. But my cousin still knew. Deep down. Sometimes even the gods get the timing wrong."

"But do they get the Tethers wrong?"

Ameera sat with that in tense silence for a moment.

"No. They do not. The gods stitch Tethers together the same way they weave Souls and Shadows into one. Once attached, it's irrevocable. You'll find each other in a million lifetimes if you have to."

A group of maidens crossed the garden, fiery orange blossoms, red roses, and yellow daisies falling from buckets in their hands.

"It can't already be the Equinox," Astra said.

"It is, indeed," Ameera confirmed. "Tula didn't want to burden you with planning the ball. She's still worried you got hurt on her watch."

"Good enough for me," Astra replied. "I may not even attend this year. I owe Ehlaria a visit."

"You don't think the court will notice the only Lunar Princess missing?"

Astra crumpled inward, her shoulders falling. She'd forgotten about her duties on nights like these, taking part from the sidelines most of her life. "Damn."

"Your mother picked out a stunning gown for the occasion..."

"You knew I wasn't leaving the moment I got here, didn't you?" Astra sighed, Ameera's eyebrows wiggling.

"Oestera missed you, As. I know it's hard to believe."

"So I won't."

Ameera only glared at her.

Astra laughed at the familiar expression. "You're spending too much time with the commander."

"You have got to stop leaving your right side open when you block me on the left," Lux groaned.

She heaved a sigh. They'd been at this for an hour already.

Roll, rise, block, attack. Over and over again until her head drowned in delirium.

"If someone attacks me, I'm not wasting my time with a physical altercation. I'm much more powerful in here." She tapped her forehead with one hand, flashing a flame between them with the other.

Lux shook his head. "There are a dozen situations I can think of without even trying where your magic wouldn't matter. Your hands could be bound, or someone could dampen your abilities. There are ways to ward against elemental magic. You can't always rely on that."

"Fine," she relented. "Again." Lux dove for her ankles, taking her down for the hundredth time as she rolled from his grip, kicking his bad shoulder.

"Fuck!"

"Shit," she whispered, crawling back toward him, "Are you okay? I forgot which side—" He cut her off with a push onto her back. He slid over her, knees squeezing her sides, and pinned her hands above her head, pinching her skin. The ryegrass in the same meadow they'd met tickled her wrists. Mocking her.

"Roll, rise, block, attack," he hissed against Astra's face. "If I was your enemy, would you stop to make sure I wasn't hurt?"

She grunted, attempting to pull her wrists from his grip, the weight of him making it impossible. "Let me go!"

"You have no clear firing path," he ground out, pushing her wrists into the ground harder. "What's your move?"

She scrambled, trying to think. She held him in her mind the same way she had the Solarian in the Midwood, sending a spiraling cloud of smoke into his face. He backed off, but he only lost his concentration for a second.

"If I'm trying to kill you, I've already done it. Think, As."

The weight of him over her, the leather and oak scent of him, the heat rising as she lost her grip on his bloodline—it was all-consuming. She wriggled again, hoping to get a knee free, but he was just too heavy.

"I can't think! You're drowning me!"

"Come on, Fire Queen, you're better than this," he whispered against her ear, hands tightening. A dark thought rippled through Astra's mind for a second. From here, it would take only an accidental brush of her hips, or a whisper of something utterly distracting to break him. She shook her head, clearing the fog in her mind, embarrassed she'd even let herself imagine such a thing.

He was the king's commander, not a plaything. She was to be his queen. The king's wife. She was supposed to be Tethered to the man for gods' sakes.

"And you're dead," Lux muttered, releasing his grip on her

wrists and rising off of her. Astra's head swirled, the heat rolling away like a smothered campfire. He held a hand out to help her up. She reached for it, letting just a slip of flame lick at her fingertips. Searing his palm enough to cause him to pull back, but not enough to melt flesh.

"Do better tomorrow." Lux flexed his hand, refusing to give her the satisfaction she sought as he left her on the ground. She would happily let him sit in his disappointment. The alternative was to drown in this dizzying haze as sparks of white-hot guilt for feeling anything come alive under his touch blazed against her.

He was right before, on the way out of Celene.

She'd been left alone too long.

ASTRA WAS three-quarters of the way through the novel Ehlaria gave her.

She had notes sprawled across her desk and several empty coffee cups forming a ring around her. She hadn't left her study all day.

The plot had finally gotten interesting.

The Shadow Witch could summon the Shadows around her and use them to cast spells. The man, a Light Mage, was born to keep the Shadow Witches in check.

She thought they were on the precipice of confessing their love to one another when she heard three quick knocks on the study door. No thoughts behind it, no emotions to scan.

"Luxuros," she said, setting the book down as he pushed the door open.

"You're up late," he murmured, closing the door behind him. He sat on the sofa from which he'd spent most of his

Summer lecturing her, his eyes unfocused in a way she hadn't seen often.

"Sleep has eluded me lately," Astra confessed, organizing her notes so she didn't lose her place.

Lux nodded toward the book and the translation, sitting next to each other. "Anything interesting?"

"It's a captivating story, but I'm not sure any of it is relevant," she sighed, frustrated. "It's a romance story between forbidden lovers." Lux didn't respond. She continued, "I was just about to get to a good part when you interrupted."

He smirked. "A good part, huh?"

"You're foul," she laughed. "Not that kind of good part. A love confession."

"Ah." He leaned back, crossing one leg over the other. "So it's only a matter of time, then."

Astra snorted. "I'd certainly take the payoff at this point. Though they're forbidden from touching, so I'm not sure it would be all that gratifying. She's afraid to eclipse him, he's afraid he'll expose her. It's all very tragic."

"Sounds familiar." He leaned forward, his eyes hardening as his thoughts solidified. "Leona and Solan... what do *you* know about what happened in The Flare?"

Astra shook her head as she leaned back from the desk, readjusting her simple dress. "Only what the history books report, which isn't much. Just another enemy bloodbath on a long list of Solar Kings and Lunar Queens who couldn't tolerate the other."

Lux dropped his eyes to hers. "What if they were not enemies?"

"What do you mean?"

"I've been thinking a lot about it. There's only one thing that I know of that might drive two smart, confident leaders to such madness. And I don't think it's hatred."

Her cheeks flushed. "Are you suggesting—"

"Leona was your mother's sister. Your mother is a sane woman by all accounts. Could she really have just lost her mind one day and sacrificed herself on the Solar Throne?"

Astra's brows furrowed, a rush of orange fury like the sunset canyon above his head flowing into her veins. "Sacrificed herself? That's not what happened."

"Oh?"

"Solan killed her, stabbed her in the heart."

His expression mirrored hers. "Is that how you learn it here?"

"Is that *not* how you learn it in Mercury?"

"No." He stood, pacing in short lines in front of her desk. "We were told that the Lunar Queen went mad, begging Solan for a truce, for partnership. And when he said no, she slit her own throat on the throne in a final act of madness in an attempt to start a war between the Inner and Outer Courts."

Rage flashed across her bones. "No. That's not... no! Leona *did* go to Solan, but it was because he asked for a meeting to discuss a ceasefire. To open up the trade routes in the Courts Between. Leona thought it was a trap, but Selenia thought it was a genuine offer. No other Solar King had ever offered it. They thought perhaps it was time for the fighting to end. And then he had her bow before him as a sign of her commitment to the truce, and stabbed her in the heart as her eyes dropped to the floor. She didn't even see it coming."

Lux stared at her as she spoke, running through everything he thought he knew. "What if we're both wrong? The truth is always the third version of the story, right?"

"It's possible," she sighed, her eyes heavy at the late hour. "We really need to speak with Ehlaria. She's survived hundreds of these wars, she would know." The clock on the wall chirped a delicate melody, drawing her attention. "I should get to bed. Big day tomorrow."

"I'll walk you back," Lux said, his face shadowed by something like concern.

"Back... two doors down?"

She laughed, but saw the fear settle in his eyes. "Archera would never let anyone get into the palace, Lux."

He shrugged. "I'm here, aren't I? You're the only one who batted an eye."

The thought ran her blood cold. Shards of ice prickled through her veins as his implication settled across her chest. "Point taken," she whispered, letting him stroll beside her.

"Mirquios would have my head if he came back and I'd let some asshole in the forest take you down."

"Lucky for you, *I* was there to save us all." Astra let the sarcasm coat the regret in her voice, still struggling to accept the life she'd ended, no matter the stakes. She leaned against her door as he frowned.

"I was moments away from getting the upper hand," Lux insisted, his amber eyes flaring with irritation.

"Sure, sure, Commander. We're all very frightened of you." Her teasing only fueled the fire in his eyes, a twisted rage darkening them.

"*Never* forget," he murmured as he leaned close to her, holding her captive against the bedroom door. "As long as my heart beats Solarian blood, I am only ever one moral crisis away from destroying you."

Her breath caught between them, the smoke of him enveloping her. "Lux—"

His mouth turned up in a crooked smile, a thunderous laugh washing over him. He was so close to her, she could hear the breath drawing into his lungs as he pushed away from the wall.

"Goodnight, As."

"You're better than this, Fire Queen," he whispered, his voice catching as her eyes fluttered open, fixed on his lips. Astra pushed back against him, surprised to find herself in the meadow, under his weight once more.

"You shouldn't be here," she hissed.

"No," Lux agreed, lips hovering over her jaw. "I shouldn't." The burn of his mouth on her skin was as tempting as it was terrifying. Scarlet lust ran up her spine, setting fire to the space between her arched back and the meadow.

If he was here, if he wasn't leaving...

She let her fingers crawl over his back, dark linen scratching against her skin.

He sighed, and the worst part of her hoped it was an invitation, not a warning.

His hips pressed into hers, a quiet sigh slipping from her lips before she could get control of herself, but he was only pushing himself away from her, rising quickly to his feet. He offered his hand again, and this time, she took it. A crackling heat sang between their fingers.

"What am I doing here, As?"

She blushed, alight with an acute misery in her chest, the adrenaline demanding she move.

Closer. Away. It didn't matter as long as she did something with the sparking fire in her muscles.

"I don't know." She fixed her eyes on the wavering walls of the garden, moonblossoms unfolding in the early Autumn air, floating to the grass below.

Lux nodded, his lips pursed.

"Get some sleep. Without me."

TWENTY-SIX

L ux did not show up to the gardens after breakfast.

They'd made it a habit to meet there after they ate, spending a few hours on whatever trick he wanted to hone next. They'd break for lunch and then fill the afternoon with self-defense lessons.

But this morning, Astra was alone, left to her own devices, still wrestling with a lingering ember in her chest and guilt picking her apart. It was unconscious, pulling him into her dreams like that, but didn't that mean something alarming about the wants hidden in her heart?

She needed fresh air and a break from his relentless sear. Perhaps he needed a break, too.

She took her book to finish in the quiet of the rustling moonblossoms, tendrils of green rapidly fading to brilliant oranges as Autumn tightened her grip. She slipped into a chair, unfolding the stack of parchment, and flipped back to the spot she'd left off last night.

Aurelle reached for Gladrious's face, her hands cupping the sharp jawline, worried his light would scorch her as she pressed their skin together. She marveled at the faint glow that seeped from his jaw to her palm.

"What if I destroy you?" Her heart was at risk of bursting.

"Then I'd find you in the next life." Gladrious shrugged. She knew it was true.

She pressed her lips to his, a spark pushing her back for just a moment before he stepped forward, sweeping her up into his arms. The world around them fell away, the space between swirling as the light within him ignited her Soul and her Shadows drowned him.

They dissolved into color and dust and deep darkness and brilliant white, twisting together until they were no more than a whisper of who they used to be. They stretched across the sky in dazzling colors, a river of what could have been, now bursting with the potential for something new.

"Wait," she whispered, flipping the next page. "Are they... did they become the Rift?" Her heart thumped against her ribs.

"Who?" Nayson slipped into the seat across from her, already dressed in his golden Autumnal hues for the holiday.

"It will only bore you," she laughed, folding the pages back into their paper wrapping. "How are you holding up? Big night without Mother."

A sharp pain ran through her father's chest, concentrated in the center, a purple and black bruise.

"I miss her terribly," he said, his tone something between sorrow and reverence. "She thinks they'll be home soon." He said it for his own benefit more than Astra's.

"Good," she breathed.

Nayon's eyes narrowed, studying his daughter's face. "Not

exactly the excitement I'd expect from a young bride waiting for her betrothed to return."

She winced. "No. It wasn't, was it?"

"You know you don't have to marry him, right? A Tether is a Tether, but you're still Astra. You have a say."

She glanced around the garden, all too aware that this was a dangerous topic.

"Do I?" she scoffed.

"Of course! Your mother would certainly be the first to understand."

"Mother would never understand a damn thing about me," she snapped, his eyes softening.

"Your mother understands you much better than you'll ever know, Astra."

She shrugged. "You're quite biased, Father."

"And you only know Oestera Aurellis as your mother. You never knew her as the Rebel Queen." He smiled just at the thought of her old nickname.

"By *her* design," she sighed. "Can I ask you something I've always wondered?"

"Of course."

"Does she keep me at a distance because I'm too much like Leona? Does it just hurt too much to look at me?"

Nayson held her gaze for a long moment, a whisper of a smile pulling at the corner of his lips.

"You do not remind your mother too much of Leona," he said, rising and waving to a courtier across the garden, arriving for the festivities. "You remind your mother too much of herself."

He left Astra to ponder that shocking observation, the fire in her veins stirring at the comparison.

THE CELESTIAL HALL glittered in oranges and crimson. Gold cords tied off curtains at the archways over the sea, letting the crisp Autumn air circulate over the heads of the Lunar and Mercurian courtiers.

The room lacked a certain tension that lingered when Oestera's eyes scanned the crowd, but it also lacked her gravitas. Her flare.

Astra touched the delicate fabric of the wide ballgown Ameera had kept tucked away, designed for a much more significant event by her mother.

A wedding, surely.

Gilded twigs constructed the bodice, woven over and under to create a shimmering lattice from shoulder to hip, flaring out slightly as the golden twigs faded into gossamer wisps.

The bodice gave way to a thousand layers of fine-spun silk, a pale golden hue just kissing the layers, the subtle warmth to the fabric highlighting her fiery tones. The same silk, hardly visible in a single layer, spilled over the shoulders, creating a sloping cape that caught the moonlight perfectly.

Crystal flutes of moonshine flitted around the room as the quartet staged at the center played on, their hands painted with golden flames as they pulled their bows across their instruments.

"You'll have to open the dancing," Nayson said from beside her, his brows lifted.

"Only if you'll join me." She smiled, holding out her hand. His dark eyes lit up with the chance to spin about the room with her, like they had when she was a girl. Astra pulled him out onto the floor, her dress swishing against the polished onyx tile as they turned.

"That's quite the gown," Nayson thought aloud.

"Your wife picked it."

"Seems she knows her daughter somewhat, then," he said.

She'd hurt him by coming after her mother earlier.

"I know I could try harder with her," she said, the hem of her skirt brushing against the stage and the feet of the courtiers waiting along the edge of the floor. As they glided, the onlookers' assessments rose in plumes of red and blue, setting her nerves on edge.

"I will implore her to do the same," he smirked, twirling Astra out and under his arm, bringing her back in and touching her shoulder. The short song ended with a sweet whine of the violin. As she bowed to him, she glimpsed a tall, dark, and grumpy commander circling the edge of the room, eyes trained on every entry point as he scanned over the heads of spectators.

She'd worried about seeing him most of the day, embarrassed after pulling him into another dream, but she hadn't done it on purpose.

She just needed to break the tension.

Astra plucked two glasses of moonshine off a maiden's tray and slipped into the crowd, weaving between courtiers until she came to one of the dozen arches lining the walls of the hall. She dipped into the evening through the arches, the slight chill forcing her forward until she saw him again.

She counted the archways between them, trying to stay silent as she tracked toward his broad shoulders, his deep crimson tunic glowing against the pale moonstone pillar he leaned on.

Setting her back against the opposite side of the pillar, she held her breath as she prepared to strike. Astra stretched her back around the pillar, hoping to catch him off guard, but he was gone. Her shoulders fell in disappointment as she scanned the ballroom.

She closed her eyes, the hum of the room hitting a pitch she couldn't hold off. It snapped at her skin, biting her heels and running talons over her shoulders.

"Looking for someone?"

"Shit!" She jumped, spilling liquid from both flutes over the rims and splashing on her dress.

"Oh no," Lux chuckled. "I'm so sorry."

"It's my own damn fault," she huffed as he took the half-full glasses from her dripping hands. She ran her fingers over her dress, flicking the moonshine away from the dozens of metallic twigs.

He watched her for a second too long, shaking his head as he spoke. "Bet if you were careful enough, you could use a little bit of heat to dry that up."

Astra shook her head. "I don't trust myself in a room so packed, the heightened anxiety is already making me crazy. I can hardly breathe, let alone control myself." She leaned against the archway, stilling a breath that threatened to choke her as she lifted her hand, showing the commander her jittering fingers. "Everyone is on edge without my mother here."

His eyes dropped to her other hand, clenched in the ruffles of her skirt, trying desperately to relax in the crowded space.

Lux leaned close, lowering his voice so only she could hear. "I've heard the Lunar elves throw a damned good Equinox party."

She glanced up, half-expecting him to be joking, but the smile across his lips was genuine, a rare beam of light from the stoic soldier. She should have known he'd meant it. He was probably just as miserable as she was in a room full of courtiers who could be anyone, with any intention. At least in Ehlaria's realm, they knew they'd be safe. She would never let anyone through the barrier that didn't belong.

If anyone asks, I was feeling ill and went up to bed, Astra beamed to Ameera.

Where are you actually going?

She grinned to herself, *Don't worry about it.*

I'm very worried about it, she huffed.

Lux owes Ehlaria a visit.

Ah, she sighed. *Just don't do anything stupid, okay?*

Now, you know I can't promise that.

"Nothing for the commander's passage?"

Loleena Nightlark, Ehlaria's most trusted advisor, materialized against a tree a few paces from them, her stunning features bearing gold paint across her face, a blush pink gown dripping off her lavender skin.

Astra sighed, plucked the second golden comb from her hair, and laid it down with its twin she'd offered just moments before.

"Well, come on then, you interrupted the party." Loleena grinned, her pearlescent teeth gleaming under the moonlight.

Four other elves slipped between the trees as they walked, flanking them as Lux's head stayed on a constant swivel in the forest.

"Fascinating. You make the commander nervous," Loleena whispered.

"We had a run-in."

"I heard," she mused. "I also heard the bastard burned alive for it."

Astra flinched. "Something like that."

Loleena's eyes fixed on her as they climbed over a fallen log.

"If you hadn't done it, the commander would have ripped him limb from limb. You did the right thing. Besides, it was time he got a break." Loleena glanced over her shoulder, her starry eyes flashing to Lux. "You must be tired of managing the Solarians in the Midwood single-handedly, hmm?"

Astra stopped. The buzz beside her indicated they'd reached the invisible wall between the Lunar Court and Ehlaria's hidden city, though the charged energy wasn't what gave her pause.

Lux grimaced, rubbing the Mercurian emblem across his chest. He could have run, that might have been preferable to the fury he watched bubble across Astra's eyes.

"How many?" she demanded.

Loleena's chest tightened into a scarlet spiral. "I'm sorry, I assumed she knew. It's hard to keep things from the Fire Queen." Lux did not break Astra's stare or respond to Loleena as her veins sang with a miserable heat.

"How *many*?"

"Some." He glanced at Loleena who could not fight the wavering within her lungs. He corrected himself. "No more than a dozen."

"A *dozen!*"

Lux reached around his neck, pulling on the cord of the amulet beneath his tunic. "Mirquios brought me here to protect you, and I've done my job. They've all been one-off assassins, trying to be heroes, we think."

"There's that *we* again—"

"*We* as in myself, Loleena, Archera, and Daria. We've been working together over the last few weeks to ensure the Midwood and Ellume are thoroughly swept for Solarian activity. There's been a decrease in spottings since your... encounter. We believe the nature of his death may have sent a message."

Astra shook her head, baffled at his report. "I'm so tired of being the last to know things, Commander—"

"Astra," Loleena interrupted. "This man has intercepted—what number did you say?"

Lux flinched. "A dozen... ish."

Loleena rolled her eyes. "A dozenish assassination attempts on your life and we only kept it from you so you could focus on figuring out what's going on with Selenia and the Rift. We *all* made the decision. He actually wanted to tell you after last week's incident, but with how hard you were taking the kill, he didn't think you needed the blood of dozens of other spies on your hands."

Astra turned to Lux. "Dozens? Plural? How many, really?"

He sighed, his eyes squeezing shut. His hand wandered into his pocket, pulling out a long string of gilded beads. He tossed them at her feet.

"That many." She scooped the chain from the twisted grass and swallowed. Each bead was carved with runes like the ones she'd seen on the Solarian cuffs in the crystal ball. She wondered briefly which bead belonged to the Solarian that used it to locate her in Celene.

There were at least thirty of them. "What are these?"

"Solarian soldiers wear a signet bead braided into their hair to identify their specialties and rank. The one on the end technically belongs to you." Astra ran her thumb over the most recent bead, the metal absorbing the heat from her hands. "He was higher ranking than the others we've seen. They've been escalating over the last few weeks."

"Don't let it ruin your night," Loleena cooed. "The Midwood is flooded with sentries from all over the court to protect you and your family, Astra. Not that you seem to need it, these days."

She sighed, her shoulders much heavier suddenly. She handed the beads back to the commander, a swirl of emotions coalescing into something resolute in her heart.

"I want a full briefing with all of you the second the Equinox is over."

"Even Daria?" he asked, a slight smile returning to his lips.

She snorted. "Okay, most of you."

"Done," he said, stuffing the strand of beads back into his pocket.

"Well, my buzz is sufficiently dwindled. Might we get back to the celebration?" Loleena did not wait for them to reply before disappearing into the realm between. Lux did not share Astra's same hesitation at the shimmering barrier between here and there, fading into the mirage before she could muster up the courage. She'd always struggled with that first step.

Between what she'd just learned and the gnawing feeling in her gut anytime she passed into the barrier, she needed a moment to breathe.

His hand reached back through the shimmering wall, bronze fingers suspended in the forest air. Astra held her breath, forcing her mind to still for a moment before she reached for them. Lux tugged her through the strange mirage and into the glowing trees of the vibrant Elven village. Every tree was wrapped in golden ribbons and freckled with amber lights. The branches teemed with elves in their very best.

It was a breathtaking distraction. Loleena cocked her head toward a set of oak stairs lined with gilded moonblossoms. Everything was coated in a fine sparkling dust and music came from all directions in the village, each little pocket filled with its own flavor of jovial sounds—dancers, drinkers, and gamblers. Children lit paper lanterns and released them from the tops of the trees, letting them fly off into the night, drifting on their giggles.

Astra had never been there during a holiday, and she regretted every single one of them she'd missed.

"Ehlaria thought you might be our guests this evening," Loleena said, leading them through a swinging moss-covered bridge across the village. Dancers spun in circles below them on a large central deck. Astra was too busy watching them to look up at the mighty oak as they drew near, only snapping her attention as she felt the sweet lavender calm of Ehlaria. The Elven queen lounged on a wooden throne, a series of golden swirls painted across her thighs and arms, painted constellations speckled her face.

A face that smiled softly at the sight of Astra—of both of them, she realized.

"Our honored guests!" She rose from her throne, elves flowing quietly around her, ready for anything she might need. She reached her long arms out to them, grabbing each of their hands and dragging them into the fray, a jingling percussion pulsing against Astra's heartbeat. Behind her, an Elven male ran a worn bow over his fiddle, a female sang a high soprano note to match.

"You need drinks," Ehlaria purred, two goblets popping out of thin air as she handed them over. "Cheers, my loves, I'm so glad you finally made it," she sang, clinking their hands together as she fell back onto her throne. "Please! Make yourselves at home. Dance!"

Astra sipped her wine, turning to the dancers in the middle, their feet moving quickly as they spun each other around, so unstructured and free. Her heart was still gripped with anger—what else was whispered about in clandestine meetings on her behalf?

Luxuros drained his goblet and set it on the ground. He

extended his hand to her, but she wasn't sure what to make of the gesture.

She held his gaze as she tossed back another gulp of wine, setting her cup beside his.

"Don't you hate dancing?"

"I do," he said, glancing at the crowd as it turned about itself. "But you don't."

Astra imitated his best scowl. "Doing something I like will not make me forget you're plotting behind my back."

Luxuros sighed, his outstretched hand folding away from her. "Are you going to dance with me, or do I need to find another partner?"

A deep crimson thrill raced through several of the female elves standing within earshot of them.

The right motivation, as always.

He whisked Astra away the moment her hand fell into his. They floated on the breeze alongside the whisper of a chill— Summer was well and truly gone. Lux spun her, gliding them around the bonfire, the flames throwing their warm reflections on her dress.

"Where were you this morning?" she called out over the sound of the fiddle and feet pounding on the wooden deck.

"I wasn't in the Midwood, if that's what you're asking. I was called back to Mercury," he replied, twisting her the other direction, his fingertips caught on the golden twigs as she twirled.

"Is everything well?"

Lux shook his head. "It was nothing overly interesting," he insisted. "Mirquios wanted me to check in on a village not far from the city. Nova connections live there. He hadn't heard from them in a few weeks and got nervous."

She arched her eyebrows as he passed her under his arm,

twisting their hands so they tangled around each other in an elegant knot. "And?"

"All was fine. The Rift's communication paths may be compromised, however, so we'll need to figure out a new system."

She nodded as if she had any idea what they were facing. She supposed she would soon. Lux spun her again, untangling them and pushing Astra away from him, a buzzing tension stretching between their hands. He pulled her back sharply, chests colliding as he wrapped an arm around her waist and held her other hand away from them.

For a moment, she lost her grip on the heat of him, her lungs catching fire as she stared into his eyes. The smoke and steam and flame overtook her thoughts as she tried to cling to refreshing images. Waterfalls, the first frost of Winter, a plunge into the Empyrean Sea. Unfortunately, that thought only led her right back to the springs in Celene, the steam rising from the pool around Lux's bare shoulders.

Something knocked against her ribs, that same force from the springs, begging her to move even closer. She inhaled, shaking off the haze. She swallowed. Hard.

"Did Mirquios mention coming home?"

Lux winced. "I believe they will soon. They've reached an agreement with the Plutonian Prince, Arcas, but he seemed concerned with some terms still. He's only writing half of what he means these days, I'm sure you've noticed."

And she was sure that Lux had noticed that they had written little to each other at all after the first few weeks. The thought gnawed at her as they spun, a knot forming in her gut. "Luxuros—"

"Princess!" A horde of giggling girls rushed them, their little pointed ears pierced with sparkling hoops that bounced up and down as they all spoke at once.

"One at a time," she called over them as Lux backed toward Ehlaria, reclaiming their space near her throne.

One girl stepped forward, the ringleader of their glittering circus.

"We want to paint you!" She looked at their hands, chubby purple fingers gripped around long wooden brushes. Several jars of golden paint threatened to escape from two overly excited little ones. She stooped to her knees, letting them have at her arms, the wildfire in her mind burning out.

The brushes tickled against her shoulders and hands, glimmering swirls inking across her skin.

"Okay! Okay," she laughed, pushing a hand away before it threatened to coat half her face. "I think I am sufficiently gilded!"

The girls admired their work before moving on to claim their next victim, disappearing in a whoosh of giggles and bare feet against oak. She reached for her goblet from Lux, who watched in amusement as she wiped paint away from her ear.

"How do I look?" she joked, swigging whatever remained of her wine.

Lux cleared his throat, his eyes drifting over the tangle of branches around her ribs. "Exactly as a Fire Queen should."

"Why do they call you that?" Ehlaria chirped from behind them, leaning over her throne. The lilt from her throat suggested she was speaking more freely than she otherwise might have. "Don't they know it's not fire?"

"What?" She twisted around, Lux mirroring her confusion.

"Well." She pursed her lavender lips. "I suppose it is fire in the end," she corrected herself. "But you must know, you must realize, dear girl, that it's not merely fire." Ehlaria rose, stepping toward them, bangles ringing against each other.

"Then what is it?" Astra asked.

Ehlaria only looked to Lux, who choked on a breath. "You

cannot mean it's sunlight," he croaked. Ehlaria watched them both, a soft smile slipping over her delicate features. Lux argued, "That's not—"

Ehlaria held up her ancient hand. "It's very possible."

Astra gasped, her head swirling. "How could that even be?"

"Young Luxuros here was not the only one in The Flare, Astra. You may have been safely tucked away in your mother's womb, but you were every bit as present for Leona's death as he was."

"You were there?" She turned to Lux. Her heart might have actually stopped beating.

"I... I'm not sure." He shook his head, his own confusion so palpable she had no choice but to believe him. So rarely did he lose his grip on his guard.

"I assumed you'd have sorted that out weeks ago," Ehlaria stared between them. "You've never been one for patience."

"Me? What can I do?"

Ehlaria rolled her eyes. "You mean to tell me you finally figured out how to go within and you wasted all your energy on me?"

"I didn't mean to do it!" Astra cried, a rush of adrenaline sending her heart back to a brutal pace.

She smirked. "There are no accidents, darling."

"What is she talking about?" Lux finally formed a full question.

Ehlaria gestured between them. "You can help him remember, Astra." She glared at the commander. "*You* just have to let her in. She would be a powerful tool for you, Luxuros." Something passed between them Astra couldn't grasp hold of. "Don't get hung up on it now, Astra. Tonight is a celebration. Enjoy it. Both of you."

She twisted away, finding her footing under the sweet melodies of the fiddle behind them as she danced away.

Lux rested a hand on the back of his neck, unsure what to make of this new information.

"It makes sense," she said. "The Flare and all."

"Of course." He nodded.

"You look out of place, now," she said to Lux, pointing to the abandoned jars of paint. She snatched a brush and held it up, waiting for him to protest.

But he didn't.

They were both desperate for a distraction. Lux rolled the sleeves of his tunic up and held his arms out for her.

"No obscenities or appendages," he said, arching a brow.

She cackled a rather unbecoming sound as she dunked the brush into the glittering paint. Astra dragged the brush's thin side over his forearms, swirling along in slithering rivers and matched the strokes on his other arm. The gold pigment flooded the valleys between scars, covering the evidence of his spat with Daria and the hatchlings in Ellume.

"That's what it feels like," she said as she set the brush down. "In my veins, when the sunlight rushes through." He rotated both arms, flexing his hands as the lines shimmered under the torches.

"It's also how it feels," he returned, leaning closer to her. "When I'm sucked out of my dreams and thrown into hot springs and gardens."

Astra's mouth dried out, the nausea rising from her stomach and fluttering into her lungs. Her inner and outer worlds competed for who could flush a deeper shade of pink.

"You two coming?" Loleena pranced by, several elves falling into a line up the oak stairs, goblets of wine in their spindly lavender fingers.

Astra was happy to follow her, grateful for anything else to focus on.

They climbed through rustling leaves and glowing orbs of

light until they reached a break in the treetops. A series of round decks spanned the village, each connected with foot-bridges that flowed under amber lights. Hundreds of elves made their way to the treetops, rustling paper lanterns in their hands.

"Grab one!" Loleena pointed to baskets overflowing with lifeless lanterns, painted with curved shapes and flowers that made Astra's heart twist and yearn for something she didn't quite understand.

Lux plucked two from a basket and pushed them toward the edge of the deck, leaning over the rail to look below as more elves journeyed up the steps.

Loleena explained, "You make a wish as you light them and let them free. The winds will carry them to your ancestors in the Court Above."

Lanterns floated up into the night sky around them, splat-tering the black velvet with glowing spots, dancing gently on the breeze. Music started again, this time slower, pensive, a soft rise and fall of notes that gripped Astra's heart.

"Can I get a light?" Lux's eyes dropped to her fingers.

"Only if you tell me what you're wishing for," she laughed, a considerable effort given how tight her throat was as it filled with questions she dared not ask herself.

Loleena's head whipped around, preoccupied with her own lantern but always listening. "Don't tell her! The wish should be a sacred secret between your soul and the ones that came before you."

"Well damn," Lux chuckled. "I would have told you, but it's against the rules." She swatted at his arm, sending a tiny stream of fire, or rather sunlight, to her fingertip. She touched the candle inside softly and it sparked to life, washing Lux in a soft glow.

He held up her lantern as she lit the candle, passing it back as they turned to look over the trees, hundreds of lanterns taking off from the whispering branches.

Lux sent his skyward and her mind turned toward the last wish she requested from the gods, standing ankle-deep in the sea with Mirquios. She thought she'd wanted him—needed him—to accomplish what she dreamed of.

But the gods did not agree. This time, as she pushed the lantern into the plume of lights, she did not make a wish.

She asked a question.

What do you want from me?

"A million wishes," Lux said beside her, resting his arms against the banister as sparkling lights arose around them. "What do you think your chances are?"

"Slim," she laughed. "But not none."

Lux's eyes settled on her face as she watched another wave of lanterns bubble up over their heads.

"That sounds about right," he agreed.

TWENTY-EIGHT

" I believe I have something of yours, Commander."

Ehlaria motioned for them to follow her, weaving through the crowd of wobbling dancers and into her mighty oak home. Astra's feet hurt from hours of dancing and drinking. Her head swam in a hazy mist of Elven wine.

She'd never made it this high into Ehlaria's retreat before, the opulent home carved into the center of an impossibly large tree. The hollowed home buzzed with elves, who were drinking, eating, and tangling themselves up with one another.

Astra did her best not to absorb the rising clouds of petal-pink lust and desire. She had enough nerves of her own to contend with. Ehlaria pointed to a deep blue velvet cloth hanging over a round object on a console table.

Astra knew what it was immediately.

"You were the Solarian spying on me?" She turned, the fire in her—no, the sunlight—bubbled to her fingertips.

Lux held up his hands. "I used the looking glass to locate you, that's true, but—"

287

Ehlaria clucked her tongue. "Not here, you two." She glanced around at the dozens of eyes trying not to stare.

They followed her up the spiral stairs and passed two more floors before she veered off the landing and into a hallway, pushing a tall door inward.

"You can stay here tonight. Discuss whatever you need to, but please, no blood on the rugs."

"We can't share—" Astra protested, but Ehlaria cut her off.

"You two have wasted enough time. All of our time," she sighed. "Figure it out. And Commander," she said, the tone cutting. "Thank you for letting me borrow your toy. We're paid up."

She shut the door behind her, shaking her head the whole way out.

Astra surveyed the room—small, but cozy, exactly what she pictured a guest room in the Queen of the Lunar Elves' home to look like. Curved shelves lined the walls, boasting books and crystals and potions of gods only knew what.

Layers of soft rugs flopped over the floors, glittering silver threads woven through them. In the center of the room, a large, lavish bed begged her to collapse into its luxurious bedding. A sheer black silk fell over it, creating an inky canopy with stars embroidered in constellations across the sky.

She tried to still her heart as she crossed the room, pulling off her slippers and flopping against the black velvet bedding, smelling of lavender and smoke and spices. Lux did not speak, folding himself into an armchair in the corner, leaning his elbows on his knees, his eyes brimming with misery.

"Get on with it then," she sighed.

"We wanted to make sure you weren't involved in anything nefarious, that was all."

"How long did you watch me?"

"Not long! Just a few weeks, and only a few times. I promise you." Lux ran his hands over his face.

"Why does she have it?"

"She borrowed it," he shrugged.

She shook her head. "Try again. Ehlaria borrows nothing. You made a trade."

"I did." He did not offer more.

"Luxuros," she growled, a furious plume of red smoke rising. "What did you do?"

"I traded her for this," he said, snatching the leather cord around his neck and pulling the moonstone pendant out from under his shirt. "Okay?"

"And what does it do?" she asked through clenched teeth.

"What it needs to."

The crimson fury in her lungs threatened to spill out as she glared.

He threw his hands up, sliding it back under his shirt. His eyes narrowed. "It dampens my emotions. It protects me from your prying eyes, okay? It blocks you."

"How?"

He rolled his eyes, annoyed at the vulnerability she was requiring of him. "I'm not an elf! I do not know how their magic works."

She glared. "You have that much to hide from me then? That you'd trade something so useful for a way to dampen it?"

"Astra," he whispered, his head hanging. "It's not that I have so much to hide. It's that I don't know what I need to hide. When we watched you, we realized you were much more powerful than your mother let on. I was afraid you'd be able to sense things about me I myself don't even know. Whoever I was before, whoever The Flare erased, I have no affiliation to. I am a Mercurian. I did not want there to be any questions about that when you met Mirquios. I did it to protect him."

"You did it to protect you!"

His eyes flickered to hers for a second. "I did it to protect *you*. Above all."

"Me?"

He nodded. "I could have been anyone to Solan. I was a boy when it happened, but I was still raised in Solaris. You saw the fire within the Solarian in the Midwood. What kind of cruelty is carved into my bones? At what point do generations of hatred erupt? It's all I think about. When I left Mirquios here on your birthday, I half-hoped you'd put him out on his ass just to ensure I never brought any harm your way. But then you two... you two did whatever it is you did and I had to have a fallback plan."

"Whatever it is we did," she scoffed. "You really have so little respect for the Tether, then?"

Lux leaned forward, a curl at the corners of his lips alarming her. "I respect Tethers. When they're real."

Her eyes narrowed as blood rushed to her ears. "What did he tell you?"

"He didn't have to," he snarled. "If you two had actually formed that bond, you'd have lost your damn mind weeks ago. When was the last time you even wrote to him?"

"I've been distracted by a million other things!"

His eyes flared as they locked on her, refusing to release her from their heated stare. "You've been distracted by your king's commander. None of those dreams would have happened if you were truly Tethered to Mirquios nor would I have allowed them to continue. I love my brother. I wouldn't betray him, and I don't believe you're the kind of woman to trifle with his heart."

Astra swallowed the shame rising in her throat. "So you've known this whole time?"

He nodded. "I suspected."

She folded her arms, anger and regret swirling into a gray mass in her chest. "Why didn't you say anything?"

"Who am I to interfere in what's best for the courts? We need you. And you need us. Who cares how messy the truth is if it means we're that much closer to our goals?"

She stared at him for a long minute, trying to understand the desperation in his voice. The fear of who he might have been. The respect for his king. The protective instinct over her. It was all genuine—she could feel the regret in his chest even over the shield, the fear that at any moment he might slip and she'd learn something neither of them could unlearn. Even if he didn't let her see it, anyone could feel it.

She could understand that, couldn't she?

"Fine then," she relented.

"That's it?"

She dropped her head back, an irate laugh escaping her throat. The war commander, muscles always wound tight, prepared for a battle.

"If anyone can understand fearing who you might be, and forsaking it all for the benefit of your people, it's me." Her eyes dropped to her fingertips, buzzing with sunlight after years of flickering in flames.

"I didn't know about the sunlight," he murmured.

She shrugged. "Many, many surprises this evening."

"I am sorry. For what it's worth."

Her lips twisted into a half smile. "It's not worth much, Commander."

"You should sleep."

She furrowed her brows, the irritation still twisting in her gut. "You're going to stay up all night staring at that door, aren't you?"

He didn't respond. He simply scooted the chair so that it faced the door straight on.

Astra rose and reached behind herself to loosen the ribbons holding her dress together. There was no way she could sleep in the stiff bodice.

"Shit," she whispered, her fingers just missing the top loop.

Lux tensed behind her, his eyes still fixed on the door. She struggled for another moment before she heard heavy boots brush against the rugs. Searing fingers pulled gently at the laces, first unraveling the tight bow Ameera had carefully constructed, and then loosening them loop by loop.

"Thank you," she whispered.

She felt another tug, and the bodice sighed in relief as she held the front of her mother's masterpiece against her chest. She expected a rush of cold when he inevitably darted back to his perch, but he stayed.

He lingered.

A rough fingertip traced the petals of the moonblossoms jutting out from the full Moon at the center of her spine.

She held her breath, afraid if the ink so much as twitched, he'd disappear. Lux exhaled, the warmth tickling her neck.

"Goodnight," he mumbled as he circled the Moon one last time, leaning beside her to extinguish the sconce on the wall, plunging them into darkness. She let the breath go, dropping the gown to Ehlaria's floor and sliding under the velvet quilt. She watched the constellations woven into the canopy glint in the faint glow from the window, revelry still floating on the late-night air.

She understood why he lied, logically. She even understood why he left so many unspoken threads floating in the air between them—why he could only bring himself to trace lines and never cross them.

She nearly preferred it that way.

But in her gut, under all the rationalizing, there was still a bright white heat that burned against bone and vein. How many times now had she caught him in a lie designed specifically to control her actions? To curb her decisions?

It was hard to be angry with someone who believed they were protecting her, even if it was from herself.

As she drifted to sleep, a nagging thought percolated at the base of her skull. If she could be so forgiving of his well-intended meddling, didn't she owe her mother a similar grace?

Another question nagged at her—one she feared the answer to even more as his words echoed in her chest.

You've been distracted by the king's commander.

"Lux?" she whispered.

She felt him shift in the chair, tensing against the back.

She took a slow breath—he counted the seconds between the end of her exhale and the sound of her lips parting in the dark.

One.

Two.

Three.

Fo—

"I'm not the only one distracted... am I?"

Lux stayed silent for a long, brutal moment, at war with the *right* way to answer. She could feel it, pull together in a tightness between them—she damn near thought she could hear the thoughts spilling over his iron wall.

"As..." he said, unable to string together any of the dozens of words wandering from his mind.

Deep in the space between her beating heart and bleeding soul, she understood.

SHE WASN'T ASLEEP LONG *before she slipped further into herself, falling, falling, falling into nothing, just color and light blinding her.*

"Go, go," a woman's voice screamed from above, her anguish a stab in the chest. The pain was unbearable. She couldn't right herself, couldn't see anything. It was like drowning without water, her lungs collapsed all the same.

Above her, everything exploded into a furious bright white. An unholy pain ripped through the air. She couldn't tell if it was hers or someone else's. Everything faded as her heavy eyes closed. The last thing she saw was a spray of ruby flames.

And then there was nothing.

She fought for breath, the pressure in her chest too much to take, her eyes starting to swell.

"As," someone called from far away, their voice barely a whisper.

"Astra!" they yelled again, more firmly. Her lungs were on fire, begging for air.

A cold gasp tore her from the dream. Her eyes fluttered open, Lux hovered over her in Ehlaria's guest room.

"Are you hurt? As, talk to me," Lux pleaded, his knees on either side of her hips, eyes wide with the same fear she'd seen in the Midwood.

"I'm okay," she breathed, her lungs finally filling again. "I'm okay."

"You were dreaming about The Flare," he said. "You were dreaming a memory. My memory."

"Who called to you?" she asked, the woman's terror still so fresh in her mind.

"I don't know."

It was the pain in his whisper that did it, she told herself, that broke her into a thousand pieces. The pain drew her in as she reached her hands to his face, drawing three curved lines along his cheek and his neck, where his hand caught her fingers.

"Go back to sleep," he said, but he made no move away from her. His fingers wove between hers, pushing them against his chest.

"Will you ever let me in?" She held his gaze, hardly visible at the midnight hour.

He shook his head, swallowing as he rolled off her, hands still tangled. His eyes dropped to their fingers, resting against his chest before he released her hand, moving for his station on the chair.

A silent shock of betrayal crept up her back—a gnawing knowledge that his place was there, beside her.

"Just stay," she whispered, everything within her begging to close the distance, no matter how traitorous it might be. "Stay with me."

Luxuros put as much distance between them as he could without falling out of the cursed bed, his chest tightening with each of her movements.

The *right* thing to do seemed less and less viable by the moment.

TWENTY-NINE

*S*he was significantly warmer than she'd expected, cocooned against some sort of mystic light, cradled in its soft embrace in her half-awake state. She sighed, her eyes still heavy, caught halfway between reality and a dream.

Astra floated in the Rift again. This time, she slowly bobbed by a gilded gate, the light pouring from it hard to stand. It was so bright.

But she had to touch it.

The light reached back, touching its fingertip to hers, exploding into brilliant stars the moment they met. She pushed herself even further into it, letting the warmth slip over her. It embraced her in a gentle song that pulled on something within her, dragging her very soul to the surface of her skin.

She spiraled into the song, desperate for it to touch more of her, the warmth so intoxicating she thought perhaps she'd died last night. Perhaps she'd skipped the Descent altogether and risen straight to the Court Above, embraced by Mother Glory herself.

Her skin came alive, simmering under the heat, craving more as she fell into a sweltering rhythm. She moved like a leaf on the Autumn breeze, swept into a freefall she never wanted to end. She *needed more of it. She wanted to drink it, to stand in it as it rained down on her in a quiet Spring shower, to let it cleanse her in holy fire.*

As, it whispered, *caressing her shoulder, blazing against her skin.*

Don't, she begged, *don't go.*

Astra, it whispered again, *fading quickly from her, the devastation more than she could bear.*

Please, she whimpered, *I need more.*

She chased it, rolling through the mist of the Rift and clutching to the rapidly fading beams. Her fingers grasped madly for a holding point. Gods, all she wanted was to drown in it for one more moment. She wrestled against it, wrapping her legs tightly around whatever she could find, the shock in her spine at the electric current lighting up her blood enough to end her.

She'd never felt a rush like this, burning in a pillar of fire from head to toe—

"Oh, gods," she heard her voice whine, her muscles aching in a way she hadn't felt in ages.

A wave of oak and leather pulled her out of the haze with a sharp start, her arms wrapped around a very warm, very asleep commander. His hands tangled against her hips, his dark curls splayed across her pillow.

She leaned into him, desperate to find the light in his chest.

"Shit!" she hissed, flying out of the bed, unable to breathe in the heat of his blood. Lux's eyes shot open, startled.

"*Shit*," he breathed, his head snapping in the other direction as they both realized she wasn't wearing anything.

She snatched last night's dress from the floor, holding it around her chest as she shot to the wardrobe in the corner, her heart audibly slamming against her ribs.

"Apologies, Princess."

"Apologies!" She threw her hands up, pacing as she tried to

get her head back down to this plane. Her body cried out for him, despite the litany of reasons it was completely unacceptable. She groaned, "Now we're back to 'Princess?'"

"Can you let me wake up before berating me?"

She rifled through the wardrobe's contents, delighted to find a light silk shift that would at least get her home.

"We should get back," she said. She couldn't bring herself to glance in his direction as she dressed. Had he been there with her again? Sharing in the dream? Had he been the dream? Had he heard the way she begged—oh misty Mother smite her.

"Right," Lux agreed, tugging his boots on. She held her shoes in her hands, darting out from the room and into the hallway, hoping that Ehlaria wouldn't be—

"Good morrow, Princess." She leaned against the doorframe across the landing. "Luxuros." He gave a half-hearted wave. "A bright morning, is it not?" She rolled her eyes, fading back into her room.

A blush threatened to suffocate Astra.

Lux didn't wait for her to recover, taking the dozens of stairs to the bottom of the tree two at a time, desperate for the fresh air as the Moon rose outside. She followed him in silence to the edge of the village. Several elves were still scattered across benches and rugs, not quite making it back into their homes.

They didn't speak through Ehlaria's mirage. They didn't speak as they wound through snapped twigs and gnarled trees. They didn't speak as they came upon the clearing she'd made home so many times.

She couldn't take the awkward silence any longer. Her mouth barely opened before Lux called out, "Quick!"

He dipped low, tackling her legs out from under her. Her body twisted over his back, his arms clenched tightly around her legs. The world rolled in a blurred circle. She hung upside down behind him, her head slamming against his back.

"The Nether are you doing?" she yelled, her lungs struggling to inflate properly at the angle.

"What are *you* doing?" he shot back, breaking into a run. "How are you going to get out of it?"

A fucking drill. After everything last night and this morning. Anything to avoid talking about his godsdamned feelings.

She shook her wild curls, trying to force the image upside right in her mind so she could determine her best chance, but the throbbing headache from the elf-wine hangover was almost as loud as Lux's playful mocking.

"Congrats, you just got kidnapped by a Solarian," Lux chuckled, rounding a fallen log and bounding into the meadow. Her squirming had absolutely zero effect on the mighty oak of the commander.

His ribbing was the exact trigger she needed to clear her head. She let her light flow freely, throwing her hand out above them. A twisted branch severed with a thunderous crack from the birch above, stopping Lux in his tracks.

"Shit!" He fell back, stumbling, giving her time to calculate her next move. Her hand was still blazing hot when she brought it down to touch the back of his leg, causing him to shout and loosen his grip. She yanked one leg free and used the momentum as it swung down over his shoulder to capture his arm between her thighs and bring him to the ground.

His heavy body fell to the side of her with a thud so loud she'd surely knocked the wind out of him.

She scrambled out from under his weight and hopped to her feet. Just as she was about to shove her boot in his neck, he grabbed her foot with both hands and pushed back, sending her flying onto her ass.

"Fuck you," she groaned. "I was going to win that one!"

Lux pushed himself up across from her, reaching out his hand to pull her up from the forest floor, both their chests heaving. "You were doing okay," he said, gesturing to the broken branch. "That was quick thinking, but it was sloppy. Could have just as easily landed on us and knocked your ass unconscious, or worse."

"But it didn't," she argued.

"This time," he pushed.

"Would it kill you to just let me have one win?"

His face flushed red. "It wouldn't kill *me*, it would kill *you*! You need to be a thousand times more focused than that if you're going to keep yourself safe."

"I can focus," she insisted. "I've been working at this for months now. The goal was to get out of my assailant's grasp, and I did that!"

"That's not the point." He shook his head, clutching his chest. "Blindly throwing fire or sunlight or whatever the fuck will not get you far in hand-to-hand combat. It'll probably just cause you more pain than your attacker."

Fire rose in her chest, the anger hot on her tongue. The last twelve hours roiled inside her and there was no amount of meditative thinking that would stop the floodgates from opening.

"You're such a fucking bastard," she said through clenched teeth. "You know I can hit any mark you give me at this point. Why are you being so impossible about this?"

He didn't respond, which only fueled her rage. Fine, he wanted to be a prick about it? She could show him just how focused she could be.

She narrowed the flame behind her index finger, envisioning it the size of a sewing needle. She fired the tiniest spark across the space between them, landing right on her target.

The leather cord around his neck broke in two and slipped beneath the collar of his shirt, disappearing.

He wanted to be stubborn about it? Fine. She'd force him to show her the feelings driving his mystifying commitment to belittling her.

She smirked, victorious as he reached for the cord. "How's that for—"

Whatever she might have said, whatever she wanted to say, was silenced instantly by the look of pure horror on Lux's face, falling into absolute dread as everything in the meadow stilled.

More shocking than the expression on his pained face was the way she saw the dread, black as night, tightening within him, spiraling into a glittering cloud.

His eyes widened, and she felt that tug in her chest again. The one that had gotten her into nothing but trouble lately, starting deep in her lungs, but it didn't crash against her ribs and stop like it had when they were training. Like it had last night.

It did not stop at the contracting muscles around her bones.

It did not stop at her skin, flushed with sweat and dirt and goose flesh.

It did not stop until it collided in the space between them, wrapping itself around its invisible twin, tangling into a sacred knot.

"As," Lux gasped, his hand flew forward to reach for her, but he thought better of it.

It wouldn't have mattered if he had grabbed her and thrown her into the meadow, claiming her as his own right then and there. She wouldn't have felt it. She was no longer in her body. She was floating somewhere above, watching the consequences of what she'd done unfold in a fever dream.

She was dust on the wind as the early Autumn breeze swept through the meadow, the only sound she processed as the tension between them stretched and pulled against her heaving chest.

The Tether strained, collapsing her entire world into a single gilded thread, the end and beginning of everything she was now woven deep within the commander's very soul.

I t was silent in the Midwood, save for the ragged breaths settling between them, neither of the two sure what came next.

"Astra," Lux said again, "Look at me."

She stammered, "Wh... what just happened?"

He only stared at her, wordlessly. His eyes brimmed with so many layers of feelings she had to parse through them one by one, untangling the muddy quarrel in his chest.

She saw every last one of them.

Every midnight pang of guilt, every violet flare of angst, scarlet terror, peony pink desire... the palest drop of blue hope, like the Somnia under a full Moon.

Every imaginable emotion, laid bare in a palette of rich colors she never knew existed.

She moved first, leaning back onto her heels, pushing up to stand before him. The turmoil within him wasn't all she could feel now. Between them, a tightrope of stardust and sunlight and shadow stretched. She felt the gentle shift of his soul as Lux's body leaned forward in response.

Lux whispered, "Please, say something."

The heat in her veins was gone, extinguished by the icy chill of his betrayal.

"You knew," she cried. "This whole time? Last night—*you lied*!"

"I will explain, I promise, but please, just tell me what you're feeling first. I can't, I don't, I never—" He fell into a silence, tripping over his words.

His demand astounded her. "You want to know what I'm feeling?"

Lux rose, stepping closer, which only pushed her back. "Of course," he said, his eyes pleading with her for a mercy she had no access to.

"After months of hiding this from me, of hiding every feeling you've ever had, you want me to bare my soul to you? Can't you see how unfair that is?"

"Astra," he begged, his voice so unlike that of the man she thought she trusted. "I know. I know. But this was never supposed to happen. It was never going to happen. Fuck! I should have moved faster, I shouldn't have pushed you—"

"Luxuros."

One word, but it held so much.

A command. A prayer. A dismissal.

A plea for him to come closer. A fear that he might.

"I'm so sorry," he whispered, his voice breaking at the top, so faint she almost didn't register it.

She could do nothing but stare at him, pain from depths she might never understand washing over his sharp features. Regrets and secret wishes spiraled within him, fighting to be seen.

He'd asked how she felt, and she had no answer.

She'd spent her entire life desperate to be seen—starved for someone to wonder about her beyond her talents.

She let her eyes fall over him again—his skin so scarred from years of fighting for someone else. Everyone else. She took one step forward, the tension on the Tether loosening, sighing. She reached for it, her fingers finding nothing but buzzing energy between them, invisible but undeniable.

Humans and gods alike faced death before they faced denying this little slip of space.

They traded their prized possessions to prevent them from destroying their plans.

They started wars in the hope they could sever them.

She drew in a shaky breath, unsure if she would use it to kiss or kill him.

Every longing stare she thought she imagined, every hostile argument about her safety, every brush of his hand... dozens of moments from the last three months crashed down on her at once, the weight of it unbearable.

Every dream she'd shoved down, every burn, every call to lean forward and touch she'd denied.

The man I'd met on my birthday.

My destiny.

"Astra," Lux said once more, his hands thrown up in surrender, a white flag waving within his ribcage. She stepped forward, chest to chest with him, so overtaken she wasn't sure she was breathing. "Please, you must know..."

She wanted no apologies or explanations. They would have to come later.

For one moment, she only wanted to let the forbidden static of the Tether brush against her skin. She only wanted to give in to it. It would all be gone soon, but here in the meadow, she could indulge in it.

She wondered as they stared at each other if he could feel the way her entire being centered around him the moment she stopped fighting and just let the Tether bloom. Her muscles shook with a desperate need to reach out, to surrender.

There was no fear within her, no hesitation, but she felt it all in him.

A war raged within his chest, a thousand shades of gray spinning and whirling in on themselves. It overwhelmed the brilliant bouquet of pastels and deep maroons and ocean blues that fought for the light.

The guilt.

The pain.

The doubt.

Those dark masks pulled at the light, tainting them and embedding them deep in his chest.

The yearning. The desperation. The overwhelming need to protect her.

The same colors she'd been painting against her ribs for weeks without even realizing it. She only ever felt the guilt, missing the hope entirely.

She'd missed the challenge of him, lost in the taunting. She'd missed the respect that blossomed despite the rocky soil.

She fought for air as the feelings rolled over her, the warmth of him evaporating against her skin. His eyes met hers and she saw it so clearly.

She would not be winning the war within his heart.

She ignored the doubt she found there and went on the offensive instead, bringing her hand up to the golden planes of his face. Lux leaned his forehead against hers, but his soul was already retreating.

"I'm so sorry," he whispered, pulling back from her.

"Please," she begged. "For a moment, forget about every-thing else. Just one minute. I know it can't last, but please." She wanted to reach within him and pull the shame and anger and guilt from his muscles. She wanted to pluck them out one by one like needle-tipped feathers and use them to ink a sacred prayer into her hands.

"Don't do it," he whispered, his eyes closed against her skin.

"Why?"

"Because the dreams are hard enough to let go of. If you kiss me here, in the real world, where I can taste you, I'll never recover."

Even before Lux left her hands she felt everything within him vanish, sucked back into the vortex of his mind, shoved into drawers and baskets.

"What if you don't need to recover?" she asked, her empty arms falling to her sides.

"I can't," he groaned, his face flushed in the moonlight.

"You can't or you won't?" She reached for him, but he stepped back, hands digging into the leather across his legs. Ryegrass crept over his ankles, holding him in surrender.

"I won't," he sighed, the weight of it settling between them.

"Oh." She tried to catch her breath, but it caught her first, the air ripping through her lungs like a knife to the heart. She backed off, trying to get out from under the haze of him, the Tether stretching and groaning as she ventured farther.

"We can't," he said again, his shoulders falling as he finished fastening the cord around his neck. Everything between them dulled slightly, but not enough to survive. "You know the stories. Even if you weren't a princess and I wasn't his commander, his *best friend*," he swallowed. A fresh wave of pain rolled over his shoulders. "We were born to hunt one another. I was honest last night when I told you I was terrified of what might happen... of destroying you."

As she watched him steep in his own self-loathing, she

couldn't help but think it would be a godsdamned privilege to be destroyed by him.

"Why? Why would you torture yourself like this—*me* like this? You've said yourself a million times you have no loyalty toward Solaris, you've never hurt me and you've had every opportunity! When I had your life in my hands, before I even knew who you were, my bones knew I had to spare you. It was never even a question!"

His eyes remained focused on the ground, a warrior defeated. They closed gently against his bronze cheeks, his lashes wet with all the emotion he'd been burying for weeks. She moved toward him, unable to fight the Tether's insistence, even muted by the amulet. Her fingertips were cold against his chin as she turned his face toward her.

"You have a king," he whispered. "You don't want some warrior with nothing to offer you. Ask your mother how much it cost her."

Everything in her twisted into a furious supernova, ready to burst and birth an alternative universe where kings and queens didn't exist.

"I don't need a king." She gripped his chin, holding onto him, forcing him to stay in the tension with her. "I don't want a king! Surely, he would understand. It's not as if we had anything deeper than a mutually beneficial arrangement. It's not like this—not like—"

"There are ways to sever a Tether," he said, his voice distant, poisoned with something so bitter. He pulled his chin from her grasp. "It would be painful, but not impossible."

She scoffed, "So that's it, then? You've just decided for both of us? I suppose I shouldn't be surprised. You've been making decisions for me all along," she said, the Tether between them threatening to snap as he got farther away.

"This isn't about what we want. This is about entire courts

and what they need right now. You have faced this decision before, and you know the pain it's causing me, but it's the right thing to do." Lux turned, glancing up to the top of the ashen treeline.

"You're a coward."

"And you're reckless!" Lux raised his voice, his temper flaring to protect himself from the other feelings dancing below his skin. "For millennia, our ancestors have stumbled over one another and left nothing but devastation in their wake. I come from a long line of men bred to hate you, to hunt you. It may lie dormant now, but I cannot spend the rest of my life wondering when the final thread will snap. When my cursed bloodline will drag you into some horrible danger I can't protect you from. This godsforsaken bond might make you believe we're special, but we're not. No one is above the gods' sick twists of Fate."

"What if—"

"No. No what-ifs! No maybes. We're not playing some lighthearted game here. The gamble is that we either will or won't cost one another our lives. That's why I did what I did to stop it. It's why I'll find another way to stop it." Lux stomped through the meadow, set on a path back to the palace.

"I might be reckless, but at least I'm honest about how I feel," she spat. "I didn't need a Tether to force me, either, Lux. It would have happened anyway, and we both know it."

He spun and she crashed into him, the contact a delicious relief in her chest. He grabbed her by the shoulders, dipping his face so that he was staring directly into her eyes as he ground out the next few words, battling his emotions into submission.

"You will marry him. You *must* marry him. You two will do good for the courts, please," he said, his voice shaking with a twist of rage and fear.

"And what of you?"

His eyes softened, the anger fading into something even more horrible. Acceptance.

"I will stay until I can't take it anymore. I'll find another way to dampen it. I'll make another trade with the elves. I will do whatever it takes to keep you safe until the only threat that remains in your world is me. And then I will go. I'll find another court to continue the fight in, but I will not be the reason all the work we've done fails."

His words hit like bricks.

They could give in and become yet another duet of star-crossed enemies in centuries of failed attempts—fodder for tragic poetry and paintings—or they could suffer apart and have an actual shot at change for their people.

It didn't matter which option she'd choose. Lux had decided, and there was nothing she could do to convince him otherwise.

And as much as she wanted to deny it, he'd made the right one.

THIRTY-ONE

L ux was at least gracious enough to stay quiet on the walk back.

He left Astra in the safety of the palace gardens, one last devastating look before disappearing into the halls.

Except he *didn't* disappear.

She felt every one of his movements from the warm waters of her bathtub. Every line he paced back and forth, every circle he wore into the floor of the Andromeda wing, the cord in her chest pulling and releasing.

The amulet might have dulled the physical sensation, but her heart knew all the same. It was agony.

She leaned her head against the curved edge of the pool, the water now uncomfortably cold. She'd been hiding in here too long. She knew it, but she could hardly get her head around what happened, let alone what to do about it.

Not that there was anything *to* do about it.

He'd made himself clear.

And he was right. Centuries of bloodshed couldn't be

311

wrong. She attempted a deep breath, but the Tether tightened and suffocated her.

"As?" Ameera was in her bedroom, looking for her. If she sank under the water now, she'd hear the bubbles, surely. "They're back from Pluto!"

As if this day couldn't get any worse.

"I'm in here!"

"Your mother and the king are in the Celestial Hall."

She nodded, making no movement.

"You're being requested," she said hesitantly, appearing at the edge of the pool. "For obvious reasons."

"Thank you," she whispered.

"Whoa," she breathed, her eyes landing on Astra's fallen face. A river of orange alarm slithered up her arms. She eyed her, clearly distressed by what she saw. "What happened?"

"Elf wine."

She faded into the dressing room across the way, a faint blossom of anxious orange crawling her shoulders.

"Shake it off, Fire Queen. It's showtime."

It took a good ten minutes to find the strength to leave her dressing room, shoulders rolled back as if her entire world hadn't just changed. As if she couldn't feel the very center of that world walking quickly along the Andromeda halls, probably beside Mirquios.

Naturally, her mother was irritated with her the moment she entered the Celestial Hall.

A distraction she welcomed, frankly. "Good of you to welcome us home with such enthusiasm," Oestera huffed between instructions to her maidens.

"I was in the middle of something." Astra shrugged, her heart simply not up for another battle today. "My apologies. How were your travels?"

Oestera ignored her question, bustling past her as the room

filled in. The palace was a flurry of activity in the wake of their return. Tula spoke quietly with Archera as councilwomen took their seats.

"Where is Lunelle?" Astra asked Archera first. Her eyes widened, but she shrugged. She felt the wave of nerves in the room as dozens of eyes set upon her. "Is she harmed?" She tried to search for her sister within the walls of the palace, coming up empty. "Did she not return?"

No one answered.

She stomped her foot. "Mother, *where* is Lunelle?" Oestera's head whipped toward Astra, disrupting her conversation with another councilwoman.

"She's tired from the journey. Don't be hysterical." She turned back to her conversation, but Astra didn't feel any better.

"Astra," a low, velvet tone rang out against the hall. Mirquios crossed the onyx floor, his hands extended to greet her.

"You're home!" She forced a smile, but her heart felt like a stone tossed into a lake. How was she supposed to even look at him after what happened?

"Are you well?"

"Of course," he said, placing a quick kiss on her cheek, but as he pulled away, she couldn't feel a thing from him. He read the confusion on her face immediately. "It's been a long, hard trip. I didn't want to burden you all at once."

"Of course."

"I need to debrief with my advisors. Can we catch up this evening?"

"I'll see you then."

He squeezed her hand and marched away, taking his stone wall with him. She waited for a spark, a longing to follow him, anything. But it did not come.

"Ladies," Oestera announced, every head in the room turning toward her. Astra found her seat, wondering where her father was as the queen addressed them. "As you all know, Pluto has declared their intentions to join the Lunar Court and Inner Courts as tensions build with Solaris. Solan's armies are gathering in the rings of Saturn and Neptune's seas. We cannot hesitate to send a message of unity."

As Oestera spoke, a body settled into the seat next to Astra, Lunelle's silvery hair pulled into a gentle braid, her eyes tired from the long journey.

There you are!

She didn't so much as glance at her sister. *Sorry. I needed to freshen up.*

Are you okay? I couldn't even sense you.

"In an effort to show our firm support for Pluto's wise decision to join in our fight against the oppression and tyranny of Solaris..."

She shrugged. *I'm fine. Just tired. It's a long trip.*

Everyone is being weird. What are you hiding?

"It is my honor to announce to you that Arcas, the Prince of Pluto, has joined us along with his court for Lunelle's trial. He'll be the sole Lunar champion, signifying—"

"What?" Astra barked, unable to stop herself.

"What part aren't you clear on, Astra?" Oestera sighed, her eyes blazing.

Astra shrieked, "The part where you—the Queen of 'tradition matters, Astra'—are shucking centuries of ritual by only nominating one champion? The part where you've invited a court full of people who were our sworn enemies until a month ago, and then promised your successor to them? Have you lost your mind?"

"Astra," Lunelle warned, but she couldn't stop.

314

"Why even put her through a trial if you're going to dictate the outcome? Just plan a wedding instead!"

"Astra Leona, that is enough!" Oestera's words cut through Astra's hysteria, the silence in the hall deafening.

"This is insanity," she cried, Lunelle's bright eyes pleading with her to sit back down. "How could you do this to her?"

Oestera heaved a massive sigh. "Your sister is not a child, Astra. She understands the role she plays. This is not the time to be soft. If you were more willing to do what was necessary for your court—"

She threw her hands up, exasperated, flashing the ring on her hand at her. "I'm more than willing to do what needs to be done to further the well-being of my court, something I would argue you have never done!"

She didn't need a divine intuition to feel the rage boil in her mother's heart. Oestera spoke carefully but seethed beneath every syllable.

"Perhaps you should be down the hall with your intended's court since your allegiance is clearly not to your queen."

She held her icy stare, unwilling to break as Astra landed a blow she knew she couldn't take back. "My allegiance is to the people upon whose backs you'll fight this war. My allegiance is to my sister and the court she'll have to piece back together after the mess you're making of it."

Oestera's eyes broke from Astra's, dropping to the floor for the briefest of moments. Decades of conditioning kicked in before her eyes hit the punishing glare of the polished stone beneath her shoes.

"You're right," Oestera growled. "What would I know about piecing together a broken court?"

Astra opened her mouth to respond, but Oestera cut her off. "You are dismissed."

Astra hid in her study for the rest of the evening, flipping through Ivonne's notes once again. If Oestera was willing to throw Lunelle into the hands of strangers who had, for centuries, sided with their mortal enemies, what else was she willing to do?

What else was she willing to hide?

SHE'D FELT the soft shift within her ribs several minutes before the commander finally worked up the nerve to knock on her study door.

"Princess?" His voice broke her from a blurry stare at the Shadow Bargaining manual.

"Come in," she mumbled, unsure she could take seeing him again as her stomach churned. Her heart only beat faster when the door widened and Mirquios joined him, neither of them readable to her.

"Mirquios!" She pasted on a smile, aware it didn't do enough as he looked over her with a quiet concern. "I'm sorry I missed dinner," she offered, closing the space between them and blocking his view of her desk. "I started a project this morning without realizing everyone was returning."

"We didn't give much of a warning," he excused her.

Everything inside her screamed, desperate to touch the wrong man. She tamped down the lava flowing beneath her skin. "I suppose we have a bit of catching up to do."

"That's why we're here." The king smiled softly, a kindness she didn't deserve. "I was hoping you'd join us on a special mission this evening."

Astra watched Lux's lips seal into a tight line. "Mission?"

"The commander has informed me of what happened while I was gone."

As if her body could burn any hotter, a flare in her chest sent a crimson hue to her face. "He what—"

The slightest head shake from Luxuros shut her up.

Mirquios continued, "You met the Nova Rebels in Ellume?"

"Oh!" She sighed, hoping for a wave of relief, but it did not come. "Yes. Daria Bloodmoon is an old friend of mine."

"My time in Pluto allowed me to meet with the captain of their Nova chapter. I learned some key information that I need to get into the hands of Mercury's captain, but it's far too dangerous to send written communications through the Rift, as you know. So... how would you like to see Mercury?"

Her lips fell open, shocked at the request. "Mother would never—"

Mirquios stepped closer. "I imagine your mother and father will be quite distracted this evening, will they not?"

Astra swallowed. "You mean to sneak me out of the Lunar Court?"

"Three hours. Four, tops." He smirked, a mischief playing in his bright eyes.

"The Rift. It's incredibly dangerous, now more than ever."

The king waved a hand. "From what the commander tells me, we have no need to worry about your ability to defend yourself. We're moving the rest of the Mercurian courtiers back home to avoid clashing with the Plutonians. Luxuros will escort you and I'll meet you there."

"Oh, no, that's okay," she protested. "I'm sure I can figure it out—"

"You've never taken the Rift out of your own court," the commander cut her off. "Don't be ridiculous."

"Fine," she huffed. "Let's go."

THIRTY-TWO

"Y ou just have to do it," Luxuros growled, his patience wearing thin as they teetered on the edge of the Lunar Gate, the Rift's mystic waves rippling beneath them. He'd hit his limit three "just jumps" ago.

"It's easy for you. You practically lived in it," she said.

He was not amused. "Astra, it's not as complicated as you think. You did it before with Riverion!"

"*You* did it before with Riverion. I was just along for the ride." She rolled onto the balls of her feet, trying to summon the courage to tip forward. The maidens guarding the gate wondered if the gold coins Astra slipped into their palms were really worth their silence.

"Okay," Luxuros breathed. "We're already late. I'm going to count to three."

Astra frowned. "It's not going to work."

"One."

"I will not jump into an unknown void just because you're a big boy who knows his numbers!"

Lux scoffed, the slightest hint of amusement at his lips. "Two."

"You can count to one hundred, Commander. It does not matter!"

"Three."

"And I'm *still* not ready—"

She didn't get to finish the rest of her argument as Lux hauled himself in her direction and wrapped his arms around her shoulders, throwing them both into the Rift.

The freefall only lasted for a split second, but it took her breath away all the same as her body landed amongst streaks of brilliant pinks, yellows, reds, and blues, each buzzing with its own specific frequency. The vibrations gently cradled them as they slipped along the blurred river.

White lights sparkled around them, blinding her. "Are those stars?"

Lux didn't answer. He was too busy searching through the haze of color and light, his eyes fixed on a pale green thread, glowing like the stone on her hand. He released the arm around her back and looped his fingers around the thread, their speed accelerating as she buried herself closer into him.

"Why is it so fast?"

"Stop asking questions and look around," the commander laughed. "You're missing it."

She absorbed as much as she could, but everything whizzed by at such a fast clip she could hardly keep her wits about her. They passed a portal of gleaming blues and purples swirling into space, veering off from the rest of the colors.

"That goes to the Outer Courts," Lux explained.

Another lightning-white streak flashed by them, the heat of it warming her face. "Where does the white go?"

Lux glanced down at her. "Solaris." He looked over his

shoulder. "Brace yourself, we're coming up on the Mercurian Gate."

"Brace myself?"

The thread pulled them into the carved pale green stone gate, brilliant facets reflecting off each other. It spat them out onto a sandy platform, a crash landing Astra hadn't, in fact, braced for.

Luxuros landed and rebalanced himself, but Astra pulled him sideways as her boots slipped out from under her. Her knees buckled under the sudden force.

"Steady," Lux huffed, tightening his grip on her shoulders to stabilize her. Though it was more of a ghost with his amulet on, the Tether still bounced between them, their eyes both dropping to it at the same time.

"You can let go of me," Astra sighed.

Luxuros released his hold but kept her hand in his, yanking her from the platform and into the beige halls of the Mercurian palace. He moved quickly, dipping into the servants' passage.

"It's early morning here, not many will be awake, but it's easier if we aren't stopped at every turn to introduce you. The Mercurians are excited to have a queen," he sighed at the last few words, dropping her hand as he led them down the narrow corridor.

She followed close behind, her chest tightening as he rounded a corner ahead of her. He stopped without warning and she collided with his back. She pushed away from him and folded her arms over her chest.

"I asked Mirquios to station me somewhere else," Luxuros said, still facing away from her, eyeing a fork in the halls. "He denied my request."

Astra sighed. "And that should concern me because..."

"I just—I didn't want you to think I was trying to make this harder for you."

That riled Astra.

She couldn't help the rage that seeped from her lips. "Oh! So *now* you want to be proactive about your communication. You know, if you had just told me from the very beginning what happened, we could have worked something out. I never would have cut that amulet if I knew what you were trying to prevent. If I had known, I could have spared us!"

Lux's breath caught, his voice low and strained as he twisted to face her. "Would you have?"

She could have said yes, but it would have been a lie—and it was too late. He already saw it all over her face.

Instead, she glanced at the sparkling alabaster tile they stood over, their boots just a breath apart. Her hand reached for his chest, resting over the spot she'd watched his fingers push into for months, soothing an ache she was only just starting to understand.

"As," he whispered, a golden heat simmering under her fingertips. His eyes closed for a moment, covering her hand with his. A deep crimson smoke billowed between them, drowning Astra's senses. He leaned forward slightly before backing off, restraining himself.

His palm weighed against hers in the silence, a memory slipping over her into her mind.

Not her memory, she realized.

His.

The rich scent of the soil in the palace gardens filled her lungs as he stood on the other side of the hedges under the Summer Solstice Moon.

"Hello?"

She heard her hesitant voice call out, his feet poised to run, the tension in his muscles begging him to get as far away from her as possible.

Lux's chest exploded as she ventured toward the hedge and he scrambled to shield her from what was now clearly a Tether taking shape, a nightmare in his heart.

She called again, "Is someone there?"

Her skirt dragged against the cobblestones. He'd already committed the way it moved to memory. As she'd swirled in a circle with his king, his best friend, he'd felt himself caving inward and panicked.

"I can feel you," she whispered. He needed to run. He needed to breathe. He needed to find the Lunar elf queen and beg for her help.

But she was so close.

Just one last look wouldn't kill him. Probably. He stepped toward the hedge, peering at her through a hole in the foliage. Her ruby curls tumbled over her back, licking at the pale green gown he'd already started resenting.

To see her at all was a certain kind of punishment, but in his own home court's colors? Devastating.

"Fine," she relented. "Stay hidden, but it's my obligation to warn you that the Midwood will not take kindly to intruders. It wouldn't be surprising if the Lunar elves decided they could use a meal. Especially one so warm," she said, and he watched her sink into her hips.

It happened before he could stop himself, the craven desire for her to hear his voice.

"Oh, please," he rumbled back. The leaves rustled as he got too close, sending him backward. "Everyone knows the price of a Lunar elf is but a handful of gold coins."

He could practically hear her eyes roll. Her confidence was misplaced but alluring all the same. "For the average citizen, perhaps. But you..."

Gods, she was as stubborn as she was gorgeous. "What of me, Princess?"

She hesitated for a moment, a pause he wished to reside in forever. "Take your chances then. Between the elves and my army, *you'll find yourself in quite a predicament. Or, you could surrender yourself now. I'd be happy to deliver you into the queen's hands myself."*

"As much fun as that sounds, I have somewhere to be."

"Who are you?" she demanded.

"No one you need to worry about," he lied. He was exactly the thing she should be worried about—terrified of.

"Surely, that's not true. Who are you here with?"

He laughed darkly, amused at her insistence. "I have somewhere I have to be." His eyes caught the edge of the row of bushes. If she got too bold, too curious, she'd only need to poke her head through.

He'd already taken enough from her.

Lux darted away, the hedge rustling behind him as she hollered after him, "Suit yourself!"

"How did you do it?" She asked, daring to look him in the eyes. "How did you tolerate it?"

Luxuros shrugged, the movement pulling her hand up with his shoulders. "I do not fully know."

He dropped his hand from hers and ran it over his face, wiping away the shame he felt prickling at his skin.

"I've run into magic similar to yours before. I know how to protect myself, but it took everything in me to keep the Tether at bay. I slept for two days at Ehlaria's after I begged her to help me, to give me anything to stop this from ruining both of our lives. She enchanted the moonstone in exchange for the looking glass, but even her magic wasn't strong enough to stop the pain. Every moment in your presence has been an unbearable struggle, Astra. I have not drawn a full breath once since meeting you for fear that I might fuck this up."

She stared at her hand against his chest, his heart beating beneath her touch.

"Oh," was all she said. She had held him in such a firm

category for so long, it was difficult to imagine him any other way.

But then again, it wasn't.

"I'm a very pleasant person, actually," Luxuros added, chuckling against her palm. "But between the physical strain and the emotional pain of being near you and your stubborn attitude, I can admit I haven't been my easygoing self."

"I did think it strange how much my father liked you," Astra wondered aloud. It pained her, the realization that there was an entire other version of the commander she might never meet. "And then I tortured you in your sleep," she groaned, pulling her hand away, a rush of misery washing over her.

"Yes," he said, a slight smirk pulling at his lips. "I could have stopped you earlier."

"You *should* have!"

"I am *trying* to do the right thing. But I am only a man at the end of the day."

"A man who is so certain that this would never work?" She gestured between them, her nerves tangled in knots.

"If Solan found out, what do you think he would do? Or, shit, the Court Above. They have laws against this very thing. You know that, don't you?"

She did know. She'd memorized them as a child. At seven and eight, the thought of a union with the enemy was repulsive. It never occurred to her to question the laws against Solar and Lunar courtiers marrying.

"It will settle. The discomfort. It gets easier, though I can't lie to you. It never goes away."

"Fantastic," she huffed. "I can't kindle a damn spark with the king, but his commander sets my entire soul on fire and wants nothing to do with me."

Lux swallowed.

"You know that's not true," he said softly. "Maybe Ehlaria could help, she helped once."

Astra's ears perked at the mention of Ehlaria's name.

"I'm not certain this isn't exactly what she wanted to happen. The book she gave me—I told you it's about two star-crossed lovers. A Light Mage and a Shadow Witch, when they finally..." Astra cleared her throat, aware of how close he was. "When they finally connect, they dissolve into a spectrum of color and light. They become the Rift."

Luxuros considered this for a moment, turning it over in his head. "So what, you think if we... *connect*, we save the world?"

Astra balked, a scarlet blush running from her cheeks to her chest.

"Is this you being pleasant and easygoing, then?" She moved to pass him, but he caught her arm.

"I am sorry, Astra. Truly."

"I wish you weren't," she mumbled.

He held her gaze for a moment longer before blinking away whatever thought crossed his unreadable mind.

"We need to move quickly if we're going to see it," the commander said, dropping her arm.

"See what?"

Lux didn't answer her question. Instead, he bolted down the hall, his long legs taking the distance quickly as she trailed behind, slipping through hallways and tumbling into the palace's main hall. It glowed in ambers and pastels. Pale aventurine tiles accented the floors as his boots skidded to a stop outside of an ornate crystal door.

Two guards watched them, curious but trusting of their commander. As she stepped closer, she felt a strange warmth from the other side of the door.

"Are you ready, Fire Queen?" he asked, his voice tight.

"Ready for what, exactly?"

Lux's mouth tilted in a quiet smile. "For your first sunrise."

He pulled the handle of the door inward, washing the hall in a golden bath of light. Her eyes squinted against the glare, struggling to adjust to the boldness of the early morning rays. He stepped into the shimmering beams, his dark skin lighting up in a dazzling display of golds and bronzes.

Astra's heart squeezed. The commander was handsome in the dim silver glow of Lunaria. She would never deny him the compliment, but here, in the gilded tendrils of sunlight...

Luxuros was a god, and she was struggling against a call within her very soul to worship him.

"You coming?"

She stepped out tentatively. The heat was not all that unlike touching Lux, but stronger as it danced across her skin. The world outside faded into view. Brilliant oranges, reds, and pinks painted the sky in glorious auroras, all radiating from a central ball of fire just beyond the city gates.

The Sun perched on the horizon over a valley of orange dunes speckled with pockets of flora in all sorts of interesting shapes and shades of green.

"Mother above," she whispered. Her stomach twisted in a nervous knot, the warmth tickling the tip of her nose as she watched the Sun slip higher into the sky. Tears welled in the corners of her eyes, threatening to betray her.

"As," the commander breathed. "Your face!"

"Shut up," she said, flicking the tears away. "This is a big deal for me."

"Not that," he laughed, brushing his thumb across her cheek, a tear sliding between their skin. "You're covered in golden freckles. You don't see them in the Lunar Court."

She reached to her face as if she could see them, running her fingertips along a sunkissed path over her nose and cheeks. She fought the dangerous desire to lean into his touch.

"Does it live up to your expectations?"

"Beyond," she whispered.

His finger slid down her cheek, trailing the freckles as he held her eyes.

"Whoever you are, whatever you are, Astra Leona, the gods did not craft you to hide in the shadow of night."

And yet you deny me your own sunlight, she thought. Instead of confessing the feeling aloud, she sighed, his finger pausing at her chin as if to catch the whisper of her discontent.

"Astra!" Mirquios boomed across the street, his voice bouncing against the beige walls of his palace. She hadn't even looked around. She was so entranced by the golden light of the Sun. They were perched atop a paved street on a hill, looking down at the rest of the city. Everything glowed in shades of sand and red clay.

Luxuros pushed her chin toward his king as if it was perfectly within the scope of his job to touch her like this.

The king stopped just short of them. "Whoa."

Lux dropped his finger, the print embedded in her skin in a sizzling scar no one would ever see. "That's intriguing," he whispered. "Who would have thought a Lunar princess would be even more beautiful in the Sun?"

"Perhaps I belong here, after all," she suggested. She half-meant it.

Mirquios only smiled and gestured toward the street, unfurling before them. "Shall we?"

"Where are we heading?" Astra asked.

Lux flashed a devilish smile at his long-time companion, who mirrored his expression. She saw it then, the bond between them, a seal that blood couldn't touch.

"No place fit for a princess," the king said.

Astra followed him through a series of alleyways, Luxuros stalking behind them to keep an eye on the empty streets. The homes in Mercury were vertically oriented, much like the homes in Celene, but on a grander scale. Tall towers rose one after the other, with pastel green and blue domes crowning their roofs. Balconies boasting plants and hanging laundry loomed over the city sidewalks, teeming with evidence that a few hours from now, the streets would bustle with life.

Everything the Sun touched sparkled.

Mirquios banked left at the end of an alley, throwing his hand backward to grasp for Astra's. He yanked her into a narrow opening between towers, bathed in cool shadows. He stepped lightly as he guided her to a back door, cracked open with a metal crate.

"Welcome, Princess," Mirquios said, sweeping his arm toward the door. "To The Dune, home to the Mercurian Rebels." He pulled the door open and entered first, scanning the room before waving her forward, the commander close behind her.

It was dim inside. Her eyes struggled to adjust after taking in so much light, but the bar slowly came into focus. It was empty save for someone stocking curved glass bottles behind a slab of aventurine stretched across the room. It glimmered under beams of morning light sneaking in through the open door. Velvet-lined booths hovered around metallic tables across the majority of the floor. A stage littered with instruments took up the far edge of the room.

"She's downstairs," the barkeep called out without looking up. Mirquios and Luxuros exchanged a glance before the king plunged down a narrow staircase beside the door, his tall frame swallowed by the darkness immediately.

Astra craned her neck to peer into the darkness, but a gentle push from Luxuros at her back prodded her forward. She descended into the inky black, her eyes relaxing as they found their comfort in the haze.

Her feet hit cold cement at the bottom of the stairs as Mirquios disappeared behind a door that had seen better days.

Perhaps better centuries.

"Maeve?" he called.

Luxuros pushed Astra aside, poking his head through the door and holding her back as they spoke with someone in hushed tones. When a velvety feminine tone replied, his fingers curled around her wrist as he pulled her into the basement.

Before her eyes could even take anyone in, a gasp followed by amused giggles prickled at her skin.

They'd entered a workshop of sorts. Shelves held tools and trinkets spread out and numbered, neatly organized into rows of similarly shaped objects. In the corner was a sitting area comprised of worn-out, mismatched chairs, their fabrics faded by time.

Rising from one of them was a woman who stood eye to eye with the commander, her tall frame weathered by fine lines at the corners of her amber eyes. Her deep skin was marred on one side of her neck with a shallow series of scars, healed over gods knew how long ago. As Astra's eyes settled on them, she pulled her onyx braids forward, letting them spill over her neck in a waterfall of beads that bounced off her leather vest.

"Astra, this is Maeve Maelstrom, the Captain of the Mercurian Nova Rebels." Astra extended her hand, but Maeve's wide-eyed stare gave her pause.

"You're her spitting fucking image," Maeve said quietly, scanning every freckle on Astra's face. No colors flowed from her chest—she must have been trained by the commander.

"Oh," Astra said, shrugging. "Yes, I look a great deal like my aunt." A rivulet of crimson pulled at her nerves.

"Not Leona," Maeve snorted. "Oestera."

"My mother?" Astra tried to cover the shock.

"She doesn't mean your face," Luxuros said.

Mirquios flashed a grin. "Maeve has tricks, much like you. She sees auras that tell her about a person's past, present, and future."

"And you," Maeve said, her bold red lips parting in a wicked smile. "Are a dead fucking ringer for Her Majesty the Queen."

"You know my mother?" Astra asked.

Maeve snorted again, setting something on the shelf closest to them. "She knows nothing," she said to Mirquios. She turned her gaze on Astra. "You know nothing."

"Apparently."

"You aren't here for me to regale you with tales of our glory days," Maeve said, pointing to Mirquios. "What have you got?"

"Lumas has been located," Mirquios started.

Gods above, Ellume felt like a decade ago, Astra thought.

Maeve laughed, "Who broke Ivonne? Surely Daria didn't suddenly grow a spine and stand up to Mommy." Lux cleared his throat, eyes sliding over to Astra. "You, Princess?"

Astra frowned. "I might not know much, but I'm not completely useless."

"And does your mother know the apple didn't fall far from the Rebel Queen's tree?"

Astra shook her head. "If she knew I was here right now, she'd have my head."

Maeve flinched, her eyes widening, but she talked herself out of what she wanted to say. "Where is Lumas?"

"We've already dispatched a team to extract him. He was being held in a Lunar prison. As of this morning, he's been relocated to an outpost in Venus."

"Excellent. And Kwan?"

Mirquios shrugged. "Kwan's numbers are outpacing the Lunarians, though he's made little progress with the prince.

The Plutonian Court will join us in Lunaria for the Winter. Arcas is to be the sole champion, though we're doing everything we can to prevent the union." Mirquios cleared his throat, something tightening in his chest as he stood taller and smoothed his shirt.

Maeve turned her eyes to Astra again.

"Speaking of unions," Maeve said. "What are we doing about this little mess?" She gestured between Astra and the commander, their eyes both flashing in panic. Whatever Maeve saw between them, whatever sparked as she stared, she understood in a heartbeat. She pushed her hand back toward the king.

"I thought we were to have an Autumn wedding, but we've clearly missed that mark."

Mirquios nodded, his eyes avoiding Astra's. "The timing was off. Now that we've returned, I'm sure we can remedy it soon." He swallowed, a shiver settling in the spaces between Astra's spine.

"Good." Maeve's eyebrows tucked together, unsure where to look.

"I've compiled an extensive report on my time with Pluto. Is Gnor here? I'd like to give them a full rundown."

"They're paying our friends in Mars a visit," Maeve said, leaning over another table to search for something. "Seems they're still struggling to get their communication networks built. That prince of theirs is green, but he's trying his best."

"Omnir?" Astra asked. "Is he a Rebel?"

Mirquios nodded. "He joined us last year. His father would crucify him, but he's brave for a child."

"You knew even during the Solstice?" Astra's eyebrow raised, her arms folding over her chest.

The king's lips twisted into an apologetic grin. "I had to

knock him out of the running for your hand. He's too inexperienced to let you rise to your fullest potential."

"Well, how lucky I am to have such an *experienced* man paving the way for me."

Luxuros choked on a laugh, leaning against the wall as he watched Astra's cheeks flush. Mirquios sighed. "That's not—"

"No!" she barked. "I am thrilled to have all of you plotting on my behalf. Between you, my mother, and the commander, I merely have to decide which pretty dress I'll wear each morning. Imagine the godsdamned mess I'd be in if someone actually presented me with information and let me make my own decision. The havoc I'd wreak!"

"Princess," Mirquios protested.

Astra held up her hand, letting a spark flicker to life on the end of her fingers, controlling the burn into a perfectly curled flame.

"Go on." Astra's lip curled in a sneer. "Or do I need your permission to speak, my king?"

"Spitting fucking image," Maeve chuckled to herself.

Astra blew out the flame, a wisp of smoke rippling between them.

"Allain is in her office," Maeve said to Mirquios. "Why don't you and the commander—"

A clambering in the stairwell broke her concentration, feet slamming against the landing and ripping the door open. The barkeep from upstairs huffed and clutched his chest as he stormed into the room.

"What in all two thousand and forty-eight gods is a Lunarian Queen doing in my bar?" He glared at Astra, her mind hazed by his question.

"I'm no que—"

"Not you. Her." He pointed upstairs and a dozen eyes followed his finger to the ceiling.

She closed her eyes, honing in on the energy above. An icy cloud of rose petals and silver stars waited, tapping her foot.

"Oh, shit," Astra whispered.

Lux watched her face.

"Send her down," the king said to the bewildered barkeep. "She knows why we're here."

As she stepped into the basement, Astra realized she'd never seen Lunelle in pants.

Gone was the demure princess who nodded and smiled at all the right moments. Before them was a warrior queen, seconds away from destroying each of them.

Lunelle was wrapped in black leather, her hair braided into a tight crown at the top of her head, glowing softly as she pulled back her hood. Her eyes glowed with a rage that felt an awful lot like Oestera's.

Maeve's eyes danced at the sight of her, darting quickly between the four of them. "Well, now. What a strange turn of events."

"We had a deal," Lunelle said softly, but sternly, to Mirquios.

The king gestured toward Astra. "I'm not breaking any of our rules." His tone struck a familiar cord in Astra's ears.

"Did she walk here?" Lunelle asked, pointing to her sister. It was perhaps the angriest Astra had ever seen her. "I was clear about taking her into the Rift, Mirq."

The edge in Lunelle's tone took Astra by such surprise, she physically stumbled. Lux's hand reflexively reached for her shoulder to steady her.

"Lu," Mirquios started, holding his hands out to calm her. Her silver eyes flashed with another lightning bolt of rage.

"Good gods, Mirquios, now you've pissed them both off." Maeve clicked her tongue and chuckled as she crossed the room. "Who do you put your money on for the final blow, Commander? Fire or Ice?"

"Fire." His gaze settled on Astra's bewildered expression. "Always Fire."

"I need everyone in this room to start talking, now," Astra hissed, her blood boiling in her ears. The tension in each of their carefully guarded hearts hit a point that even the strongest of their shields couldn't contain, drowning her in purples and reds.

"As," Lunelle said, her voice falling into a softer note. "You need to get back home. It's not safe for you here."

"Mother above, not you, too. I'm so sick of everyone telling me what I need to do with zero explanation!"

"The basement is yours," Maeve said to Astra, moving for the stairs. "I just got things cleaned up down here, Fire Queen. I don't want to return to a disaster." Maeve climbed the steps behind the barkeep.

Mirquios gravitated toward one of the worn armchairs, settling in as Lux strode to the end of the basement, distancing himself. The Tether whispered a complaint in Astra's ribs and she watched as his hand drifted over his chest. Lunelle sank into the seat to Astra's right, her heart as heavy as ever.

Astra looked at each of them. "If someone doesn't start speaking, I'll volunteer you."

They exchanged glances, but no one spoke.

"Very well." Astra turned to her sister. "Ladies first."

336

Before we speak, Lunelle's soprano voice rang in her ears. *I need your promise that Mother never finds out about anything you hear.*

Not telling Mother things is one of my favorite hobbies, Lunelle. Go.

Lunelle reached for her sister's hand, locking their fingers together like they did as little girls. "May the Mother bless us," she said.

"Within and Without Oestera's knowledge." Astra smiled, the catchphrase of their youth springing back to the forefront of her mind easily.

Lunelle's eyes narrowed. "Fine," she inhaled. "I don't know where to start!" She let the breath back out, releasing months of tension. "There is no easy way to say what I want to, and I had planned on having a few more answers before we did this —" she tossed a glare at Mirquios, who blushed a deep shade of crimson, "—but frankly, we're running out of options and time."

She hesitated, her eyes squeezing against tears as a navy well opened within her chest.

"Just tell her," Lux cut in. "She can handle it."

Lunelle moved forward, her eyes lowered as she spoke. "I don't think Selenia is who we think she is."

"Princess—" Luxuros groaned, but Lunelle shook her head.

She continued. "I spent a lot of time with... people who think differently in Pluto. They heard rumors when Leona died that Selenia sold her out to the Solar God in the Court Above. He didn't know what she got out of it on her end, but the Outer Courts all hold it as common knowledge that Selenia betrayed Leona and Solan, leading to her death."

Astra paced as Lunelle spoke, the buzzing in her bones a confirmation that Lunelle was right. She turned to Lux. "Does she know about the Shadow Bargaining?"

Lux shook his head. "I figured you'd want to brief them."

"Shadow Bargaining?" Lunelle rose from her chair.

"Ivonne Bloodmoon was researching Selenia. She thinks Mother is covering up the fact that Selenia traded her Shadow to the Nether Queen for some of her power."

"What would she need more power for? She's already an Ascended Lunar Goddess!"

Astra sighed. "That's where we got stuck, too. Lux and I brought a dozen texts back with us from Ellume but we can't think of a motive. The Outer Courts believe it had something to do with Leona?"

"Will you show me in the morning? I tried to prod Mother on Selenia a few times, but she always clammed up."

"Of course."

A silence fell between them, their hearts clouding over with the possibilities.

Lux cleared his throat from the corner of the basement. "There's something else."

"Luxuros," Mirquios warned.

"What is it?" Astra asked.

Lunelle's eyes cast to the floor as she searched for a crack to melt and disappear into.

"Lunelle," Astra whispered. "You can tell me anything. I'm your sister."

Lux rubbed his chest, stepping closer to them. "She deserves to know."

A deeply troubled crimson embraced Lunelle's throat as she swallowed.

"While we were away, I Tethered."

Astra gasped. "Oh gods, not the Plutonian!" She rubbed her temples, pushing down the bile in her throat. There was something off about Arcas, something she couldn't understand, something—

"Not Arcas," Mirquios said, his eyes closing as he let out a slow breath.

Astra stared at the space between them, their bodies leaning toward each other unconsciously.

Orbiting one another.

"As," Lunelle whispered, her chest swelling with all of the suppressed colors she'd been holding back from her sister. The only set of eyes Astra cared to look for flickered over her, his burning amber irises assuring her he hadn't told their secret.

That she shouldn't tell it now.

Lunelle bit her bottom lip, unable to look away from her sister as she absorbed the information. Mirquios left his perch from the wall and set a hand on her shoulder.

With all the gentleness of a king attempting to prevent war, he explained, "I never would have agreed to our deal and put you in such a precarious position if I so much as suspected. I'd crossed paths with your sister a dozen times before we left. I never dreamed..."

He glanced down at her, a slip of rose smoke rising to his lips as he smiled.

"We were trying to find a solution," Lunelle whispered. "A way to sever it. We weren't going to tell you until we had a plan." Another glare left Lunelle's face, but her hand rose to rest on Mirquios's, and at once Astra saw it.

The portrait of a king and queen perfectly suited for each other. Their mild temperaments and soft pastel hearts swirled into a jade breeze.

"Oh." She let the vision wash over her.

Lunelle's eyes welled with tears, but before they could spill over Astra felt a snap inside her lungs, and a whoosh of relief flooded into her bloodstream, springing forth from her chest in the form of hysterical laughter.

"Oh my gods," she cried, falling into a chair and covering

her mouth. "Oh," she laughed again, her face twisted in horror. "No wonder you've been so strange!"

Lunelle let a short chuckle escape. "The day you told me you Tethered to Mirquios I felt a piece of me die. I thought it was because I was losing you... but I think I was losing both of you and didn't even realize it. We've had every historian we know between the two of us hunting for a way to sever the Tether."

"No!" She stood, pushing the chair back behind her. "You shouldn't! You can't!"

Lunelle shook her head. "Well, we certainly cannot—"

"Yes, you can! It makes perfect sense, Lu. You're both so similar, so calm. Like tranquil seas."

"Boring," Mirquios snorted. "You mean?"

"No," she laughed. "The world needs more of you two and less of my uncontrolled burn, I assure you. And besides, it's not like we had chemistry on our side. I'd begun to wonder if I could go the rest of my life without—" Astra cut herself off, blushing. Mirquios frowned, but it was the strain in Lux's forearms as he gripped the back of a chair that caught her eye. "Sorry."

Mirquios sighed. "I'd be lying if I said it hadn't been a concern for me, too. Forever is a long time."

Astra nodded. "Indeed."

"So you're not angry? Or hurt?" Lunelle watched her face closely.

Astra shook her head. "Who am I to fight Fate?" Her eyes darted toward the commander in time to see his lips twitch in a pained smile. "We signed no contracts, there are no hard feelings on my end. I assume Mirquios told you the truth of our deal? And it's not the first broken engagement Mother has navigated." The thoughts rushed out. "This is a good thing, sister."

Lunelle sighed. "It's a tad more complex."

"Arcas," Mirquios muttered. *Ah, the Plutonian Prince.* "Your mother is determined to marry Lunelle off to him. She does not know anything transpired between us. I didn't want to erode her trust in you. When the Tether happened, it caught us both off guard. We were so in shock we didn't speak for three days."

His mouth tilted into that smooth smile, the one that until five minutes ago promised her a kind, if not unremarkable, future.

"Wait," she turned to him. "You said she knows why we're here." Astra turned back to Lunelle. "How!" It wasn't a question so much as a shocked exclamation.

Lunelle grinned. "I know you think me soft and perfectly groomed by Mother, but I have my secrets. The Plutonian Rebels contacted me for a meeting when we arrived. I'd heard rumors of their rise in council sessions. I followed Mirquios to their base."

Mirquios added, "She forced me to bind her into the rebellion. When our palms touched..."

He couldn't fight the grin that spread over his lips. An emerald thread of jealousy tugged at Astra's lungs, and for once, she was grateful to have such an isolating ability.

"Between running into one other at The Underground and the Tether, we were both overwhelmed. We decided to deal with it when we returned, but then we were there for so long. We became good friends. But nothing more for your sake."

Lunelle and Mirquios exchanged a heated glance, unable to stop the maroon shades within their chests.

"No need for details," Astra insisted, shoving down the dreams that sent a rush of blood to her cheeks.

"Lu made me swear I'd tell you before getting you involved in any Rebel activity, but when Lux informed me of your run-in with the Lunarian Novas, I may have skirted that rule."

"I also made him promise not to let you into the Rift." Lunelle rolled her eyes.

"That wasn't my doing," Mirquios chuckled. "The commander insisted."

She turned to Lux. "You?"

He did not respond.

Mirquios glanced between them. Astra wondered what he thought he knew—what Lux had told him. "He wanted you to see the Sun, in case you didn't get the chance depending on what happens next."

Astra fought tears that burned at the back of her throat and the urge to throw herself across the low table between them and embrace him. Instead, she drew in a shaky breath and forced out the question, "What *does* happen next?"

"I'm not sure," Lunelle sighed. "I was hoping we could figure it out together."

"I have another question," she said, drawing both Lunelle and Mirquios's attention. "When did my prim and proper older sister get so interesting?"

Lunelle threw her head back in laughter. "I've always admired your spirit and ideas, sister," she insisted. "I'm just more willing to play the part than you ever were. I knew someday I'd sit on the throne and be able to enact the changes we hoped for, but patience has never been a virtue of the Fire Queen."

Astra considered this. Lunelle was never *not* on her side, that was true. She just had so little freedom compared to Astra, and she was on a short leash as it was.

"I think I need a second to get my head around all of this," she admitted.

"I'd actually like a word with the king here, anyway," Lunelle said. "I met with Mother again last night before bed. We need to talk about my trial."

Her eyes softened as Mirquios pressed his lips into a tight line, the pain there evident to anyone, not just Astra. As she brushed past them, Mirquios caught her arm.

"If you'd like to see the palace, Luxuros can give you a tour. We'll meet you at the gate in an hour."

"Of course." She tried to hide the disappointment on her face, all too aware that Lux wouldn't make the trip back with them.

"My heart broke." He lowered his head, hanging before her. "I was ready to conquer the world with you. Never doubt that."

Astra patted his shoulder. "Do not mourn for me. It seems we'll be conquering the world alongside each other, anyway. I'll make sure of it." She squeezed Lunelle's hand, putting on her bravest face as she strode beyond the table and through the door, taking the stairs two at a time, focused only on getting back to the Sun.

She needed to feel that warmth on her skin again, one more time, for fear that it might be her last chance.

"You haven't said a word in thirty minutes."

Lux stood against the sandy wall of the Mercurian palace behind her. He'd brought Astra to a tower that overlooked the city so she could marvel at the early morning light until they had to go.

She stood against the balcony rail, the city shaking to life below, dozens of people strolling along the golden streets in a soothing array of pastels.

"I never thought I'd say this, but your silence is insufferable."

She spoke without turning, afraid to peel her eyes from the

life below, like it might be a mirage that disappeared if she looked away.

"Have you changed your mind about anything? Now that you aren't betraying your king?"

He swallowed. "I have not."

"Then what is there to say, Commander?"

He stepped forward and then thought better of it. The Tether in her chest spun with the back and forth. Another breath and he fell forward again, hovering behind her as she leaned over the railing. She followed a little girl skipping along the street, a gauzy pink scarf wrapped around her hair floating in the gentle breeze.

"I'll be fine," she sighed as pity filled his eyes. "I'll forge ahead with my plans, either in Celene or Lunaria. Perhaps the Martian Prince has an opening."

Lux scoffed. "Governess seems like a step back, no?"

Astra glared. "I'd rather that than be stuck watching the rebellion from afar."

"With Lunelle in place on the throne, I imagine the Lunar Court will have a much different role now. They'll need you."

Two thrones flashed in her mind, sending a chill down her spine. She glanced at him, the fear she'd ignored for weeks now returning to her chest.

"If she makes it."

"What do you mean?"

She turned to him, leaning her back over the balcony rail, the metal pushing against her spine a sharp distraction from the pain in her chest. His eyes searched hers.

"I had a vision," she whispered. "I was in a throne room, wearing her coronation gown... it felt ominous. Like a prophecy."

"Show me."

Her nose scrunched. "What?"

"Earlier, when we... when we were touching, you were able to see my memory, yes?"

She nodded.

"Try it the other way."

She rolled her eyes. "You'll have to open up those iron gates," she sighed.

"Don't pry," Lux smirked, moving closer. The flood of feelings was as overwhelming as it was that morning.

"Fuck," she gasped at the weight of it all.

"Sorry." He rearranged boxes on shelves, making just enough room for her. Astra closed her eyes, conjuring up the vision as she'd seen it all those weeks ago, trying to place it in his mind.

"Do you see it?"

"No." He squinted as if his eyesight prohibited him from seeing into her mind. His hand reached for hers, resting it on his face. Her fingers scraped along the harsh line of his jaw and his muscles flexed beneath her touch.

"There," he said.

Astra stepped forward in the room, the glow of the Sun and Moon washing her in golden waves and silver swirls as she approached the throne on the right. She let him feel the call of it, the siren song that pulled her in and made her want to fall further into herself.

The strange twin to the Lunar Throne beside it was now clearly a Solar Throne—the same runes from his cuffs were emblazoned on the back of the gilded crystal arch. She dropped her gaze, showing him the Lunarian coronation robes around her feet, moons embroidered along the hem. When she glanced back up, running her fingers along the arm of the Lunar Throne, he pulled away from her.

Lux shook his head. "Was that the Court Above?"

"I don't know," she said, confused. "It might not even be a real place, it could be symbolic for all I know."

"The music you heard, the call to the throne, it was Solarian."

"What music?"

"You *didn't* hear it?"

"I felt something *like* music, but not clearly."

Lux cupped her chin in his hands, enveloping her easily in his grip.

"Who are you, Astra Aurellis?"

"Who are *you* is the better question, isn't it? What secrets are hiding within you?"

They stared at each other, frozen in the golden glow of the morning light, unable to detach, unable to move forward.

"The looking glass. Does it sing, as well?"

"Yes," he whispered. "You heard it?"

"Barely. Just a distant buzzing, but it's like I *knew* it was singing."

"Fascinating." His fingers lingered against her skin, burning his fingerprints into her face, marking Astra as his whether he meant to or not.

Where are you? We should get back, Lunelle's crisp voice bounced in the halls of her mind, making her jump back from his touch.

"They're waiting for us," she said. "For me," she corrected.

Lux cleared his throat.

"I'll escort you back. Wouldn't want you grabbing the wrong thread and throwing your ass into enemy territory," he explained.

"It's no longer your job to worry about my ass, Commander."

L unelle and Mirquios waited at the edge of the Mercurian Gate, now filled with courtiers and their daily travel plans.

Most of them politely pretended not to know who they were, but a few stopped and stared, leafy green curiosity ruffling their chests. It had been thirty years since a Lunarian Princess was spotted outside of the Lunar Court, and now here they both were.

Fire and Ice.

"You're confident Mother doesn't suspect your affiliation?"

Lunelle nodded. "Yes. And I intend to keep it that way. It will make things easier when I take the throne." Astra hesitated to say what she wanted, causing her eyebrow to arch.

"What is it?"

"What if Mother *is* part of whatever Selenia did? What if she helped her set Leona up?"

Lunelle turned this over in her mind. "I don't know. I can't imagine them in leagues with one another. When you were first born, Selenia and Mother frequently fought about you. I was little and didn't understand most of what was going on, but it always felt tense. She doesn't seem to have much affection for her mother. "

Astra wasn't sure exactly what to make of that information. "She doesn't seem to have much affection for anyone."

She winced. "You're not wrong. What exactly did Ivonne say?"

"She didn't, we stole some documents and notes from her office. I'll take you through them tomorrow. Maybe Ameera and I missed something."

"What does the commander think?"

"He's suspicious as well but seems to be on Oestera's side more than not. I think he knows more than he lets on about her and Leona. We've compared notes on The Flare, and I have to say, I don't think we know even the beginnings of the truth."

She glanced across the courtyard where Lux and Mirquios spoke in low tones.

"Mirquios and I have had similar conversations. I know you and Mother have a very different relationship than we do, but I don't think she's the enemy. Selenia, however... something was always off there, don't you think? The rebels have eyewitness accounts that she was present in Solaris before The Flare."

She nodded. A group of courtiers edged closer to them as they waited to jump.

You and Luxuros, Lunelle mused in her mind. *You two seem to have gotten past your differences.*

He's a stubborn bastard, but I suppose we have. Astra tried not to scream internally for fear Lunelle would hear it. The differences that had developed in her absence were insurmountable.

Lunelle's eyes fixed on the men. They laughed about something at the edge of the gate with several guards—two brothers reunited. *What's up with how hot he is?*

"I wouldn't say hot," Astra sputtered aloud. "I'm sure some women would find him to be quite handsome, but with his attitude—"

Lunelle cut her off with a giggle. "I meant his temperature. It's insufferable."

Her heart raced, was Lunelle more sensitive than she'd thought?

"You feel that?"

Her nose scrunched. "Do you not?"

"Remind me to teach you a trick to stop it when we get home."

"Are you ladies ready?" Mirquios asked, crossing the platform as he offered his hand to Lunelle, who only winked as she let him pull her into the Rift. No hesitation. No fear as she took to his side.

Lux watched them disappear into the mist, his eyes far away. "One last dance, *Sol'ah*?"

She crossed her arms, ignoring his outstretched hand. "Is that Mercurian for 'pain in the ass?'"

"Solar Elvish." He leaned forward, brushing a finger across the bridge of Astra's nose. "Something like stardust. It's what they call freckles."

"You do not fight fair," she groaned. She didn't have time to stew, he wrapped one arm around her waist as he pushed them off the platform and into the swirling river.

They tumbled for a second, Lux working to steady them as colored threads tickled her face.

"Find the Lunar thread," he rumbled against the top of her head. She watched for a silver strand, glinting above her head, and reached for it. Her fingers clasped around the tendril, colder than she'd anticipated, and away they went.

349

Lux leaned his head down to her—getting closer to her ear, she realized—as other bodies flew by them.

"When you get to the gate, imagine yourself landing upright in your mind like you do when you're igniting things. It'll help you stick the landing."

"Got it," she said, watching as other gates raced by, gleaming moonstone coming into view ahead. As they came up to the gate, the silver thread faded out of the mist. She did exactly as he said. Her feet collided with moonstone pavers in the palace garden, only faltering for a heartbeat before she steadied them.

She hit her hands against his chest. "See? That would have been a useful instruction the first time. Imagine what I can accomplish with the right information."

Lux pointed at her feet, his face twisted in irritation. "Where's the fighting stance I taught you? You're too loose on your feet. You land like this and anyone waiting at the gate will have you on your ass before you can see straight!"

"Must you always do that?" she growled, pushing away from him with more force than needed.

"Hey," he hissed, grabbing her arm and pulling her back to him. "I'm not going to apologize for ensuring you're safe. Especially if I'm not going to be around to protect you."

She rolled her eyes, yanking away from his grasp, fire sparking in her veins.

"I protected myself for thirty years without your help. I hardly need a bodyguard. You've seen what I'm capable of firsthand!"

Lux scoffed, "And how much progress have you made with me? You're a completely different woman than the one I met in these very gardens. That's because I pushed you! And don't you dare act like you hated every second of it—you get off on proving me wrong at every turn, Princess."

She stomped forward, seething. "Mother above, if you spent half as much energy on getting to know yourself as well as you think you know me, we wouldn't be in such a fucked up—"

A throat clearing stopped Astra mid-sentence.

They turned toward Mirquios and Lunelle at the same time, both of their faces perplexed. Lunelle spoke first, already settled back into her perfect princess mask.

"Do you two need a moment?"

"No," Astra swallowed, stepping away. "The commander was just leaving."

"Are you not staying, brother?" Mirquios asked, clearly unaware of his commander's plans.

Luxuros did not so much as glance at his king before turning back toward the Rift. "Send word if you need me."

Astra did not wait for either of them before stomping off to her bedroom, desperate for sleep, the Tether mocking her with each step.

"Hello?"

Astra wiggled bare feet against the soft dirt and pavers of the palace gardens, all the right elements but in all the wrong order. The moonstone pavers formed criss-crossed lines across the courtyard instead of a central square around the fountain. The hedgerows swayed gently in strange ripples.

Astra glanced at her hands, a golden glow contrasted under the moonlight.

"I know you're there," she called out to the ether, a dark chuckle echoing off the fountain in response. Heavy boots knocked against the pavers as Lux rounded the hedges. He stopped fifteen paces away from her, a satisfied smirk painted across his lips.

"Did you bring me here to apologize?"

Her eyes narrowed. "Even in my dreams, you're a nightmare."

"Is that how you really feel, Fire Queen?"

"I don't think you want to hear how I really feel."

"That's probably true," he whispered, a wave of purple guilt rising over his shoulders. He had no need to block Astra in this version of reality, she already knew too much.

"The night we met," she started, taking a few steps forward, gesturing to the hedges. "Why engage me at all? You could have kept running."

His jaw tightened, falling in line beside her as they strolled across the garden. "You ask as if you wouldn't have run after me."

"You didn't know how stubborn I was yet," she laughed.

"Oh, yes I did," he countered, tucking his arms behind his back as they reached an arch in the hedges, now on opposite sides of the carved opening as they were all those months ago. "We'd heard a great deal about the mighty Fire Queen at that point, and every report was a harrowing tale of the fierce leader who couldn't be stopped."

She shook her head. "You're avoiding my question."

"I tried to run," he answered, his eyes holding onto hers. "Knew I should have. I begged at least a dozen goddesses for the strength to do it, but you were right there. I knew I was leaving that evening and I didn't plan on returning until I'd severed the Tether or sorted it out somehow. I just wanted one moment with you."

"And you used it to tease me?"

"I used it to scare you," he whispered, his words harsh. "I used it to make you hypervigilant of your enemy. If I was going to leave you, I'd at least ensure you had your wits about you. You saw how many Solarians I caught in the Midwood. I needed you to feel fear for once in your stubborn life."

"How did you walk away?" She caught his hand, leaning into

his palm. *"I keep telling myself that if you could do it, so can I, but here I am."* She drew a shaky breath.

Lux snorted. *"Is this what walking away looks like? I made it a few days at most. I came back over and over again to check on you. You almost caught me a few times."*

She pressed her lips together. *"Everything aside—our blood-lines, your beliefs about them at least, the war... if I was just me, and you were just you, and we ran into each other somewhere..."* She smiled, despite the pain in her chest. *"If our hands both reached for the same cup of coffee in a village market and the Tether connected us before you could stop it..."*

He frowned. *"If everything about our circumstances were completely different, what would I have done? Is that what you're asking?"*

She nodded. His fingers twitched, hard lines carving into the edges of his mouth.

"If absolutely everything were different," he sighed, a hand skimming her jaw as he held her cheek. *"I'd have introduced myself, first of all."*

"Good start," she breathed, lost in the scent of the leather cuff on his wrist.

"And then I would have done one of these." He pointed to his chest and then hers, eyebrows arched, a wry smile on his lips before silently mouthing, 'Did you feel that?'

Astra laughed, so unused to this lighter version of Lux, his head finally over the water her presence drowned him under on this astral plane.

"And then, you would have wounded me with a biting remark that secretly only made me want to impress you all the more." He grinned, the magic of it shoving her off a cliff she'd never recover from. *"I'd play it off like I wasn't affected by your cutting words, but*

really, I'd think about them that night, in my bed, about the delicious way your lips curl around insults... well. A man can't help but think about the way they'd curl around other things."

He backed her into the trellis, the length of his body fitting against hers like two broken shards of the same crystal. She watched his eyes drink her in, taking his time.

Even here, in a plane that numbed the heat between them, she suffocated in his shadow. Her fingers traced lines in his chest, slipping under the band around his waist. Scarlet lust filled her lungs, begging to spill over.

He shook his head, pushing her hands away. "It'll only make this more difficult."

"I'm not afraid of difficult," she insisted. "I can handle difficult. What I can't handle is never knowing."

"You're not missing much. I'm nothing special." Lux laughed, sliding his hand from her face to her shoulder, his fingertips fussing with the ruffled neckline of the white nightgown she'd pulled on before falling to sleep.

"Surely you don't believe that," she whispered.

"I used to, before you started looking at me like that." He dropped his hand to her hip, settling into the curve. "You have to stop looking at me like that."

"Would you prefer a withering glare?"

"No. That'll only make me want you more." He stepped back, a rush of cool air filling the void. Lux took her hand and strolled with her once again. "I'll never forgive myself for what I've done to you."

"Me either," she chuckled. "I'll stop torturing you for tonight, then. We haven't really talked about Oestera yet."

"I was wondering if you'd spoken with your sister about her thoughts."

"Lunelle doesn't think she's involved with Selenia, or at least doesn't believe she'd do anything to defend her. They've always had a strained relationship."

"I think you should talk to her," he said, stopping as they met the gnarled trees of the Midwood, sparkling in silver moondust on this plane.

"And ask what? 'By the by, is your mother actually evil? And are you covering it up?' Didn't seem to go well for Ivonne."

Lux snorted. "I trust you can be more tactful than Ivonne."

"Ah yes, that's what they call me. The Tact Queen."

This earned her a laugh from his chest, a sound she'd give anything to be the reason for again and again and again.

He leaned his forehead against hers, the red haze within him fading into a gentle rose pink—a feeling she was hesitant to name. He pushed a soft kiss against her temple, catching his breath. "Maeve knows someone in Venus who can sever a Tether safely. We're visiting tomorrow to see what all it entails."

Her heart stopped for a moment, the hollow space in her chest where she should have felt a tugging empty.

"And there's no convincing you to find a market coffee stall somewhere?"

He frowned. "Run away together?" His eyes held a million futures, none of them theirs. She made a mental note to find Daria when this was all over and flog herself at her feet.

"Just for tonight, I want to hold you like I wish I had on the Equinox. Before."

"Before?"

He nodded, pulling her backward, the garden around them swirling into a blur of greens and purples. They fell onto a soft bed, a lush black silk canopy falling over them, stars vibrating with a soft glow.

"Before," he said again, beside her now, draping his arm over her hips as she curled into him. She laid a hand on his face, his eyes closed against the pressure, afraid to see where his vulnerability landed him.

Before Fate struck, damning her into an irrevocable attachment *without a choice, he meant. When Astra was just her, asking just him to stay in the dark of night, no cosmic obligation.*

Tomorrow, he would end it all, just as confident that he was right as she was sure he was wrong.

They lay under the canopy, neither of them speaking.

Sun and Moon, bound by Fate, broken by blood.

The ache of waking without him tugged at her muscles, every space between bone and cartilage yearning to stretch, but there was nowhere to spread out.

Astra hadn't heard a word said at breakfast until her mother dropped her fork and turned her eyes on Astra from across the table.

"You're uncharacteristically quiet, Astra." She looked around the table. Father, Lunelle, Mirquios, and Tula watched.

"I did not sleep well." Reaching for her coffee cup, Astra sipped and prayed to whatever god had not yet abandoned her that it would be enough to move on.

"Something on your mind?" Nayson asked.

"Never." She grinned, but she knew her eyes did not reflect the curve of her lips.

"I'm sure you'll perk up in time for your wedding gown fitting this afternoon," Oestera sighed. Astra felt the lurch within both Mirquios and Lunelle's chests.

"Some coffee and a little fresh air, I'll be the portrait of a glowing bride," she insisted, squeezing Mirquios's hand over the table, the movement purely for show.

Easy now, Princess, she shot at Lunelle as her cheeks reddened.

You have no idea how difficult it is, Astra.

Astra set her eyes on Lunelle as she pulled her hand away, *I'm sorry, Lu, but until we have a better plan...*

She sighed, leaning her chin in her hand. Oestera huffed, "Oh, not you, too."

"Sorry," Lunelle said, straightening her back and moving her silver hair from one shoulder to the other, deflecting from the blush creeping over her neck.

Breakfast passed slowly, agonizingly so, but as the table cleared and everyone went on their merry way, Astra lingered behind. It occurred to her sometime between staring at the ceiling and staring at the wall that Lux was right about talking to her mother. She had never outright asked Oestera what happened during The Flare. She'd thought about it all morning —if she implied Selenia was involved, perhaps she'd jump to her defense. Slip somehow.

It was mostly out of politeness that Astra never asked her or anyone else who was alive for it. Lunelle was only a small child when it happened and even her mouth ran dry when the topic came up.

"May I speak with you, Mother?"

"Of course," she agreed, setting down her tea. She nodded to her maidens, permitting them to take their leave. Nayson eyed his daughter carefully as she tilted her head toward the door. He was happy to exit the conversation.

"What is it?" She looked so tired of Astra already.

"I had a dream last night. It was unsettling, and I would keep it to myself, but I fear it might mean something. I was hoping you could help me separate fact from fiction."

Oestera's grip on her emotions slipped for just a moment, a bright orange flame of fear shooting from her navel to her throat, but before it could force anything from her lips, it smoldered.

Astra took her silence as permission to keep going.

"I dreamed I was in Solaris, during The Flare," she lied. "And Leona was there, as well as the king. And you, of course."

"Oh?" she asked, her face somehow even more pale than usual.

"But there was someone else there that I found peculiar. Selenia."

Oestera's eyes narrowed, her curiosity outweighing her reservations. "I see. And what was her role?"

"I'm not sure. She wasn't really there, of course?"

She did not answer right away. "Not that I know of."

"An odd dream then. I know so little of your mother."

Her mother sighed. "I do not wish to speculate on something so painful."

She nodded, "Understood, but—"

"Please," Oestera said, her eyes finding Astra's in a rare moment of sincerity. "Whatever you think you know, leave me out of it. You must," she said, the words landing like harsh winds against her skin. Her face took on a shade of pink that Astra recognized many times over. "I cannot give you more."

She stood, brushing her dress back with a violent whip, her chest caving in as she turned to leave.

"You're afraid." Astra narrowed her eyes, the orange ripple rising off her shoulders. *What a strange reaction.* "What does she have on you?"

Oestera closed her eyes and gripped the bridge of her nose. She glanced at Astra one more time and something within her turned over. Her eyes widened and refocused.

"Where did you find that dress?"

"What?" She looked down, a gentle green silk draped over her frame. "Ameera left it out for me."

"Of course," she said, sweeping from the table and disappearing into the palace, leaving Astra with more questions than answers.

SHE TRIED to shake off her mother's strange reaction all day, but even after the wedding dress fitting and dinner, Oestera's frozen glare was still fresh in her mind as she finished a few letters to Celene in her study.

If Oestera didn't want to tell her the truth, she was going to have to figure it out herself.

She'd waited until it was late enough in the night that no one would catch her and sat on the study floor, trying to let the entire cursed day melt away. Her mind stilled and she let it slip, following it down the trail as she fell inside herself. The feeling was less alarming now. She knew what to expect, concentrating on finding her mother in the moments before The Flare.

Astra's feet hit the ground, but instead of the obsidian tiles of the Lunar Palace, she found herself smack in the middle of a sunstone courtyard, everything bright and airy, the smooth walls rippled with reds and oranges.

But it was the scent that drowned her—sweet orange blossom and warm, toasted honey floated over the afternoon breeze. Everyone around her wafted across hallways in breezy linen and cotton robes, their skin the same deep bronze as Lux's.

She moved quickly, unsure how much time she would have or if others could see her the way Ehlaria or the commander had. She'd surely stick out with her pale face and velvet Winter dress.

She waited for her mother's signature chill to call to her,

Oestera's energy frenetic as it moved through a room nearby. Astra shuffled quickly along the hallways. The walls dripped with gilded artwork and sparkling tapestries. Slipping by sentries and servants, she stopped only when she felt Oestera through a wall.

Astra did not give herself time to second guess before simply passing through the wall, finding herself in a cozy study, a glass pane in the ceiling spilling golden light into the room.

"It cannot be done," said a baritone voice, fraught with regret and fear.

The Solar King Solan rose from his desk, his face set in a familiar reluctant expression. A suffered blend of challenge and sorrow. Solan stepped forward, the light above illuminating his deep-set amber eyes as they fell to a face she knew so intimately. A face that could be hers in just a few years.

Leona kneeled on the floor, her crimson curls spilling over her shoulders as she tucked her chin to her chest.

Not a posture Astra would have expected to find a Lunar Queen in.

"Then do not attempt it," another voice said from the corner. One that echoed off the canyons of her mind frequently—criticizing, cutting. Oestera sprang forward, her face not yet touched by the burdens of raising her children, her belly swollen beneath her ornate gown.

Leona warned, "I did not bring you here to stop me. I brought you here to witness."

"You're both fools," Oestera hissed, shaking her head.

Solan nodded, the grim lines in his forehead worn and tired. "Unfortunately, I've always been a fool when it comes to your sister."

"Her mind is made up," Oestera cried. "You have to stop her!"

Solan stared at Oestera, their eyes speaking in a language that couldn't be translated.

"I'll do it myself," Leona ground out, a crimson fire lighting

inside her chest. "It's the only way we break this curse, Solan. If we don't, the gods will maintain their grip on our courts for yet another generation. For a thousand years, they've pitted us against one another and bound us to make it impossible to rise against them... if we don't do it, who will? Your heir? His? How many more centuries will we tolerate their cruelty?"

"Leona," Solan breathed, his heart sinking into his chest, drowning in blood-red anxiety. He kneeled before her, and that's when Astra saw it.

The knife in her hand.

"It is impossible to sever a Tether. If it weren't, one of our predecessors surely would have done it by now."

Leona set her face, drawing in a deep breath and resting her hand on his chest. "Selenia said it could be done."

"Is that true?" Solan looked to Oestera, who looked rather like she was about to vomit.

"She assured us it was."

"But you don't believe her," he said, his eyes searching both sisters' expressions.

Oestera shrugged. "If it were possible, why would we still be here, millennia later?"

"Because no one has ever been brave enough to do it," Leona muttered. "They'd rather destroy each other's courts or murder each other to avoid fulfilling some prophecy we both know isn't true."

Leona leaned forward, brushing her hand against Solan's cheek, opal and bronze fusing together in a shimmering heat. "They've told us for centuries one touch was instant death, and you know it's not true. We're proof it isn't true!"

"Leona—"

"I know you are not like us. You do not rely on intuition and gut feelings the way we do, but ask yourself, really search yourself—what's the truth, Solan? It lives within you just as surely as it lives within me. Selenia is sure that we can sever the Tether and break the bond because we've been the only two strong enough to accept it."

Solan leaned into Leona's palm, the swirling in his chest shifting from anxiety to devastation.

"What if I'm not strong enough to let it go?"

"We have to," she whispered. "I will come back to you, Tether or no. If we sever it, we're free from the gods' interference. If they can't control us, they can't stop us from rebelling. We could end this for everyone," she pleaded.

"I can't live with myself if something happens, Leona, I can't—"

Leona cut him off with a desperate kiss, her hands clutched around the blade between them. When she pulled away, everything had changed within both of them.

The choice to do what is right, not what is easy, rolled through them like a Summer storm.

"You have to do it," she rasped. "Selenia said the Solar heir had to choose heart over head."

Solan glanced at Oestera. She nervously twisted her fingers together over her womb, deep purple dread climbing up over her spine.

"It's what she said," she confirmed.

Solan turned back to Leona, his eyes welling with stinging tears, lips trembling as he spoke. "Tether or no, I will choose you in every lifetime, Leona."

She smiled reassuringly. "This is neither first nor last for us, my love."

The Solar King held her gaze as he wrapped his hands over hers, curling around the handle of the blade. For a moment, neither moved. Time ceased. He held his breath as they communicated a lifetime's worth of words in a single glance, the blade shining in the sunlight as Solan rotated it.

He carved gently through the invisible tie, both of their breaths catching as he worked.

When it sprang free from the tension, Leona's eyes widened as a clipped scream escaped her throat. Solan's hand clutched at his chest, her breath cutting short as her body collapsed into a heap on the floor. No sooner did she hit the floor did Oestera's scream follow, a guttural wail that sent shivers through Astra's chest as Leona lay lifeless.

"N-no," Solan stuttered, his eyes wild and searching Oestera's for an explanation. "What-why?"

"Solan—" she started, but a seismic shift shattered the room, a loud thunder brewing as Solan's hand covered his mouth to suppress the horrified shock that echoed in his chest.

"No!" he shouted again through clenched teeth, throwing himself over Leona's body. The rage inside of him broke every rib, every tangled vein, every muscle. It burst from his chest, a light so hot even Astra felt it from decades away.

"You took her from me," he roared.

"Run!" Astra shouted at her mother, Oestera's face frozen in horror. "Run!"

She could have sworn Oestera's eyes flashed to her. Oestera came back to herself, Solan's devastation pouring out of him in a hurricane of strained screaming and dangerous light. She twisted toward the door, moving as quickly as possible as others in the hall began running, all in the same direction.

The Rift.

Astra could see it overhead, shimmering in the midday glow. Dozens of Solar courtiers ran from the fearsome rumbling in the palace's heart. A shoulder checked her as she watched the Rift reflect the Sun.

Astra's head jerked back, shocked to feel someone in this state. Her eyes locked on the silver stare of Selenia for a mere moment, weaving her way through the crowd. For just a heartbeat, they looked at one another before she disappeared into the whirring mist.

"Oestera!" a voice cried over the crowd. Her mother's head

whipped around to find a raven-haired woman's wide-eyed stare burning into her.

"Oestera!" she cried again, reaching for her from across the courtiers as they rounded a corner and landed on a sunstone platform. The panicked faces of dozens of linen-wrapped bodies fell away into the Rift.

Oestera gasped. "I'm so sorry, we didn't know," she said with no explanation, an understanding passing between them.

She yelled over the courtiers again, "He won't go without the girls!"

Oestera shook her head, standing on the edge of the platform, courtiers pouring between them.

"I'll take him!" she yelled over the roar of screams as a bright white light moved over the horizon of the palace, making it hard to watch them. Astra tried to search through the crowd to understand who they meant, but had to narrow her eyes as the light barreled toward them.

She could hardly see her mother's face as she screamed over the bronze heads of the Solarians.

"Give him to me!" A small voice screamed the names of the three princesses Astra recognized from history texts. The Solarian princesses who would never make it into the Rift. Oestera shoved past Astra, leaping into the colored mist as the light overtook them completely. Astra tumbled with her, the lamenting of the woman on the platform echoing off her chest.

Astra watched in horror as her mother's body flung against the edge of the mist, her hands desperately grappling for a thread. Her fingers wrapped around a ruddy brown line to the Earthen Court.

Home, where she'd been hiding from the fallout of eloping for five years. To her father. To Lunelle. To the modest manor Selenia would pluck her from in just a few days to take over the throne.

The Flare had consumed many in the Rift. Astra needed to move. To grab a hold of something. If Selenia had seen her, could the *light destroy her all the same? She pushed herself over the flailing bodies of courtiers who reached for a thread, any thread.*

Below her, the young boy's body floated, his eyes closed. He needed to move. She needed to move. She could feel heat prickle against her arms.

The boy was still breathing, but barely. Gripping his hand, Astra shoved his fingers around the first thread she could find, sending him flying across the Rift. Her hand ached with the heat, an electric sting brewing beneath her skin.

She blinked hard, willing herself back to the surface of the present, pushing herself up, but she couldn't move.

The light was too bright, too hot. She couldn't breathe.

Astra was stuck, the heat of The Flare evaporating the breath from her lungs, her consciousness slipping away.

Leona and Solan were not warring enemies. They were Tethered.

"Astra!"

Selenia told them they could sever it and break the curse.

"Where did you go?"

Solan hadn't murdered Leona in cold blood—he'd been trying to save them.

"Oh gods."

Everything they knew was a lie. They were rebelling, too.

"No, no, no, no, no."

Oestera was there. She knew.

"Wake up!"

The Flare was Solan's grief, not an attack on the courts.

"Come back to me!"

They were Tethered.

"As!"

THIRTY-SEVEN

Astra's eyes shot open, no longer floating in the Rift, but back in her study, on the floor, wrapped in warm arms that smelled like oak and leather.

She gasped for a breath, her head swirling from the lack of air. Two brown eyes came into focus, hovering before hers.

"Oh, thank the gods," Lux breathed, sitting back on his heels, untangling his arms from her body against every instinct within him.

"What are you doing here?" She pushed herself to her feet, rising over him, a wild expression set in his jaw.

"The Tether disappeared," Lux gasped, clutching at his chest, "I thought—I thought you were gone," he rasped, his chest heaving. "I thought you were dead!"

The anger within her melted away at the panic gripping him, so unchained it flowed over whatever walls he maintained with such a rigid grasp, spilling onto the floor in flaming currents. She kneeled before him, gripping his shoulders and forcing him to look her in the eye. "I'm unharmed! I'm here."

"You were gone," he said again.

"I was stuck," she nodded, rubbing small circles on the hard muscle of his shoulders with her thumbs. "You pulled me back," she insisted, moving her hands from his shoulders to his chest, his heart hammering against her fingertips.

Astra pictured a calm breeze wafting through a red canyon during the brilliant colors of the sunrise, just as her father had painted them, and pushed it against the wall within him. She met nothing but resistance.

"Let me in." Astra pushed the image again, searching for a crack in the wall. She slithered her way into his head, his heart slowing as she set him on the edge of the canyon with a gentle breeze, a bird singing. His breath relaxed and settled into a steadier rhythm. Astra watched his face smooth over, the terror easing from the lines in his forehead.

She tried to wriggle from his grip, but his arms did not loosen their stronghold. Something about the desperation in his hold coaxed more out of her than she'd planned to tell.

"I went to The Flare," she whispered.

Whatever calm she'd achieved disappeared into a crimson mist. "You did fucking *what*—"

"I know! I know. It was dangerous."

Lux dropped his hold on her, grasping her face in his hands. "Dangerous! It was—it was beyond danger! You're trying to kill me, I swear to the gods."

She pushed through the flailing tendrils of anxiety from his chest as he worked to tuck them away again.

"Leona and Solan were Tethered. You were right. It wasn't an attack. Selenia told them they could sever the Tether to stop the gods' interference. They were trying to rebel, but it didn't work. It killed Leona. The Flare was a reaction to Solan's grief—"

Lux shook his head, a thick fog gnawing at his senses. "Wait, wait, wait, go back."

"It's easier to show you." She cradled his face in her hands, reliving Leona's last moments for him. His heart stuttered and jumped as The Flare's unholy light began consuming the realms. It had taken Solaris first, and then claimed the Inner Courts before dissipating in the rings of Saturn, only just brushing Pluto with its lethal kiss. His arms tightened around Astra's waist as Selenia's chilling glare caught hers. When she dove into the Rift, she dropped her hold on his stubbled jaw.

"Gods," Lux sighed, smoothing a curl behind her ear. "This changes everything."

Astra nodded, holding his gaze, daring to prod at his statement. "Everything?"

He squeezed his eyes shut. He knew exactly what she meant. She leaned forward, pushing into him the way she'd stopped herself from doing so many times. Her hands crawled his chest and explored those golden dunes of his face. She nipped the edge of his jaw, reveling in the salt of his skin like she had in their dream.

Lux's fingers wrapped into her curls, a reflex as she moved against him.

Emboldened by the way his body unfolded against hers, like two stars thrown into the same orbit, she snagged his earlobe between her teeth and whispered, "How did you get here so quickly, Commander?"

Lux hung his head back, a blush creeping over his neck she wanted—*needed* to chase. She laughed against his searing skin as she read the vulnerability in his posture.

"You were already here."

One side of his mouth curved upward as he looked toward the study door.

"I went to Venus today. I came to talk to you." Her heart

sank. The Tether desperately tried to lasso around it and hold it in her chest where it belonged, but she was plummeting toward the Court Below at a rapid pace. Astra leaned back on her heels, putting space between them.

"Don't look at me like that. History may not have happened exactly how we thought, but war is still racing toward our courts. We are still each other's biggest threats—"

"No." She said it simply and felt no need to elaborate.

"What?"

"No," she repeated herself, shaking her head. Everything in her body pulled taut as she spoke with the conviction that, in this moment, she was exactly where she should be.

"You're wrong, Luxuros. I know it in my bones. We were born for one another." She touched one hand to his chest and pressed the other to hers. "I was forged with sunlight in my veins, just like you. The same black shadows wrap both our hearts. You cannot escape the shades of me any more than I can exhale the smoke of you, and I will not pretend I want to. I belong to whoever you are, whoever you were, and whoever you will be—you only have to summon a shred of bravery to claim what's yours."

The commander's gaze fell to her fingertips, pulling at his chest as if to wrap her palm around his very heart and squeeze his thrumming pulse back into a regular rhythm.

"I don't want to keep extinguishing this for the sake of your nerves. You saw them—you saw Leona and Solan. They let their fear destroy one another. They thought they had to fight it to win, and they lost everything. We aren't bound to that same Fate!"

"Astra."

A single word. Not a question.

A boundary.

She released her hold on him and rose to her feet. She

couldn't look at him. Everything within her rolled into a black ball, tightening with each breath she took to cool the flames rushing to her fingers. She sat in the chair behind her desk and pulled a stack of parchment to the center, unable to see Cam's elegant script through the tears that boiled against her amber irises.

The commander's shadow moved over the letter, hovering across the desk.

"Just go," she choked out. "I've laid myself bare at your boots enough times. I've left nothing tucked away in my soul and it's *still* not enough. I cannot show you any more proof, and I am far beyond the years of thinking I can wait out a made-up mind. Go and leave me to gather whatever shreds of dignity I still have."

"*Please.*" He reached for her chin, but she pulled away, leaving his hand hollow in the space between them. Gripping the edge of the desk, she tapped her foot against the rug beneath her, ready to burst. She lifted her eyes, willing the tears to stay behind the rims of her lashes. He begged again, hopeless in his resolution.

"Please."

Astra snorted, chewing on her tongue but unable to bite back the words. "I believe you said you don't beg."

She'd seen Luxuros angry plenty of times. She'd seen him frustrated, irritated, annoyed. She'd seen him perplexed by his irrational affinity for her, plagued by his denial. She'd even seen him outright pissed.

But she'd never seen him seethe.

She'd never seen him *burn* the way she burned.

His eyes flickered with a single flame as he leaned over the desk, hands planted on either side of her. He dropped that terrible wall within him, releasing the flood of blacks and maroons and blues and golds he'd kept at bay for months.

Lux spilled out the anger, the guilt, the loathing all over the desk, racing toward her fingertips.

He poured so much of it out before her, she finally saw what lived beneath it, cowering in the corner of his soul.

The ache for her. For *them.*

She drew in a stilted breath, unable to get enough air between them.

His voice was chillingly strained against the current of emotions. "Is this what you want? To drown in all my misery?"

She shook her head in disbelief, rounding the edge of the desk to stand before him. Her eyes drank him in, every frown line carved into his face, every twitch of his jaw as she let him rot in his confession.

"Is misery what you think I feel?"

He whispered, "Isn't it?"

Astra reached for him but stopped herself, still unsure where his iron will and scarlet desire intersected.

"All that hurt within you, it's there. Of course, it's *there*, I won't deny it. But it only lasts for a moment. Do you not recognize what's living just under that black blanket you cling to?"

A well of confusion opened up in the center of his chest, pinks and reds and oranges swirling beneath the stormy sea he couldn't see beyond. She lifted a finger, running it over his heart to his stomach. "Here."

His chest expanded with a breath he'd been holding for thirty years, covering her hand and resting it against the edge of his lungs. Lux's eyes closed as he dropped within himself, further than he'd ever ventured. His eyes flashed open, fixing on her.

"None of this was supposed to happen."

"Do you think you're the first man in all the courts, *shit,*" Astra laughed. "The first man in these very palace walls *this week,* to say that?"

He laughed, but it didn't touch his eyes. "What makes you think we'll be any different from Solan and Leona?"

The image of them kneeling across from one another flashed in her mind, sending a shiver down her spine. Yes, they'd destroyed each other. But Selenia had made sure of that and her mother allowed it. Her muscles pushed her into his arms. Nothing inside of her fought anything about him.

Her trust in her intuition may have been foreign to him, but it was all she needed. "I'm not afraid of you. I'd take you out before you could kill me, anyway. I'm much more powerful," she chuckled.

"Fuck you, Fire Queen." But he gifted her a real laugh this time, creating just enough space within his chest for something else.

"You know, some men woo ladies with poetry." She slipped her hand against his chest as it filled with another low rumble of laughter in response. She was hooked, desperate to replicate the sound as often as possible, to let it cleanse the sorrow that clung to his bones.

Lux pursed his lips. "I've read the poetry you like. I'm afraid I'll disappoint you terribly."

"You've never worried about disappointing me before." Astra glanced up at him, his face stoic as always, but he'd left the wall in his chest open. A flurry of colors raced over his lungs, a thousand shades at once.

He caught her chin in the rough grip of his thumb and forefinger.

"I've only ever worried about disappointing you. Every single time I hurt your feelings, or distanced myself, or lied to you, it was not without great personal cost. I felt it in my soul, a thousand weeping wounds, I swear it. I'd rather never take another full breath again than hurt you any more than I already have."

"But you're no poet," she whispered, her heart pounding.

He tilted forward, and it was over.

Kissing Lux was like touching a star. Whispers of molten light slipped under her fingertips as his arms contracted around her waist, pressing her into him where she belonged. She let her hands drift, slipping under his linen shirt, the skin beneath toasted and rippled with soft hair. She had to focus acutely to prevent a flicker of light from breaking through her hands. Everything in her was on fire in a new, thrilling way, equally uncontrollable. Lux broke from their kiss, hissing in pleasure as her fingers crawled further over his hips.

"Astra," he groaned. She wasn't sure if it was a plea to stop or a desperate cry for more.

"Don't stop me," she begged, dragging her fingers down again and hooking them along the top of his pants, the leather smoldering to the touch. She moved her lips to his neck, his arms squeezing tighter around her as she tasted every available expanse of him.

"I've never once been successful at stopping you, *Sol'ah*. Why start now?" He pulled at her skirts, his fingers clawing at the soft fabric as he backed her onto the desk. He settled between her legs, her soft skin bare as he shoved her skirts toward her waist, and she felt just how much he *wouldn't* stop her straining against his pants, the rush of riling the commander beyond anything she'd ever experienced.

She tore at his shirt, letting it float to the floor as threads slipped from her dress. She tried not to choke on smoke and flame as his lips moved over her neck and chest, any semblance of control over his bloodline vanishing into the ether. Her fingers grazed the scarred flesh on his shoulder, the skin remarkably healed but still tight where she'd hit him. Before she could catch sight of it, her head fell back as fingers traced the curves of her sides. Stars fell from his lips as he trailed from her neck to her shoulder, stepping back to dispose of his pants.

Only wisps of lace underthings remained against her skin, a sight that darkened his eyes as they committed every gentle slope to memory. His chest lifted and fell, a hesitation settling within him.

"You've seen me less clothed than this." Astra's mind slipped back under the steamy waters of the hot springs in Celene.

His lips twitched into a simmering smirk.

"I didn't get to appreciate it then."

"I wouldn't have minded."

His hazy gaze narrowed. "Yes, I know. You felt it then, didn't you? The Tether? I was so afraid it was happening, but you stopped..."

She slipped a finger beneath the lace strap over her shoulder, pushing it down over her arm and letting the fabric fall away, baring her breasts as he spoke. His sentence trailed off as his eyes glazed over.

"I didn't know that's what it was, but yes. I felt it knocking against my ribs. It was all-consuming."

"I remember." Lux flashed a devilish grin that undid any lingering doubts she *should* have been considering. The risk was never being with the commander—it was being without him. Whether he saw it or not, she felt it in the way her blood called out for his, singing through rippled time just like his looking glass or the thrones.

Searching for him.

He moved closer, finally satisfied with his staring, trailing a fingertip from her collarbone to her navel. His voice was dangerously low.

"I've thought about that dream every night since we left Celene."

"Oh?" she managed, thoroughly hypnotized by the proximity of his mouth.

He dipped his head, placing a long, smoldering kiss on her lips, holding nothing back from her now. If he was going to cross this line, he might as well cross all of them and enjoy his Descent into the Nether below.

When he reluctantly broke their contact, desperate for a breath as she ravaged at any remaining sanity clinging to his mind, she whimpered, her breath catching.

"You have no idea," he hummed into her ear, fingers closing around her neck, wrecked by the rhythm of her pulse in his hands. He'd worried so many times it would awaken something dark within him—but what stirred in his chest was a bloodlust of another nature entirely.

"No idea how badly I wanted to cross the hallway and tear off that moonstone—tell you everything."

He kissed her cheek with a reverent brush. His eyes sparkled with memories of lying across the hall, counting her breaths, not even allowing himself the relief of imagining what it might be like to hold her—steeping in the fear it would create an unstoppable beast no moonstone or man could fend off.

"Gods, I wanted to bury myself inside of you. To hear my name on your tongue. To be claimed by your fire for good."

She snagged his lips in a blazing kiss, slipping her tongue over his softly as his hands found their way over her breasts, worshipping at a crested altar. The room went up in smoke and ash, flames bursting between them as the rest of their clothes vanished—she wasn't sure if only she saw the embers or if they'd burn the whole damned palace down, nor did she care.

He pulled Astra by the hand to the chair he'd spent hours sitting in, watching her read or write, lecturing her, teasing her.

Wondering what it would be like to be the man who put that blasted ring on her finger.

"Don't go wherever you just went," she breathed, climbing over him and resting a palm on his chest. "Stay right here, stay with me."

Her knees dug into the soft velvet on either side of his thighs, hesitating as she waited for him to close the gap between them. Lux's hand carved a burning trail through the tattoos on her spine, lingering at her hips. She closed her eyes against the soft pressure between her thighs, holding her breath as he gently guided her over him, a thrill rising from her belly to her chest as they fit together.

"Gods be damned," Lux sighed, inhaling sharply as she wrapped one arm behind his neck and let the other rest on his chest, gently weaving her fingers into the dark hair that guided her down to where they met. "Dreams don't do the truth of you justice."

She rolled her hips forward, enjoying the slow, sweet sting of him inside her. The motion drew low sighs from both their throats, the sound of his hushed need spurring her into a steady rhythm.

His chest bloomed in shades of deep violet and peony pink, scarlet waves, and glittering gold. The Tether between them shimmered awake as they moved together, though still choked by that damned cord around his neck. His hands and lips were everywhere, setting little fires all along her freckled skin, connecting the gilded dots as he went.

"Just like that," he groaned as she sank deeper and twisted her fingers into his curls. "Gods, you're fucking perfect."

"Finally," she laughed, gasping for breath. "The commander has no complaints."

His eyes closed, and his hold on her hips tightened. Baritone notes poured from his chest and shattered her ability to focus on anything other than doing whatever it took to keep him singing.

He snapped his head forward when she pressed her fingers lightly around his throat, letting the leather of his amulet slide between them.

"Leave it," he said, his breath hot on her neck. She twisted to catch his heavy gaze, the question on her lips. She tightened her grip on his shoulder, nearly abandoning asking it in favor of the tension building in her stomach, but her eyes gave her away.

"I want you to *want* me, not *need* me because of some god of Fate's meddling."

Astra savored the heat in his stare before kissing him again, dragging her nails along his chest and sighing his name. He reached for her face, the edges of his vision blurring.

Lux squeezed her hips. His voice strained as he whispered something in another language against her neck. He buried his face in her curls.

"You first," he whispered, holding her closer to him.

And away Astra went.

Golds and stars and pinks and flames consumed her, consumed both of them. She drowned in the color exploding within his ribcage, blinding her as she gripped onto the new skin she'd burned across his shoulder. She cried out, forgetting they weren't alone in the sea or on a mountaintop somewhere. His bronze hand reached for her mouth, covering her lips as he followed her over the edge.

She clung to him, afraid that if she let go, the walls might ripple and the seams of time would fall apart in yet another dream. But when she finally worked up the courage to look at him through the sweat and heavy breathing, she knew.

He'd never leave her side again.

Not for Above or Below, Sun or Moon.

She brushed a curl from his forehead, running her finger down the knotted bridge of his nose, marveling at all the hills and valleys of him she'd never allowed herself to notice.

He unleashed the wicked smile she'd grown to quite like. She considered saying as much, but she'd been vulnerable enough with him. She drew the line at stroking his ego. He cocked his head to the side as if he read the string of thoughts in her mind.

"What?" she asked.

"Nothing," he laughed, running his hand through her hair, tickling the bare skin of her back. "Just wondering what comes next."

"Hour by hour, Commander. Hour by hour."

Her knees ached as they slammed against white marble.

Her neck hung forward, the weight of her dazed head straining the muscle.

She squeezed her eyes, something in her chest screaming, as if a pillar of fire was spiraling from her heart. A metallic blade hit the floor, pinging against the cool marble as sparkling gold liquid pooled around her knees.

"Good man," a deep voice said behind her. "Now finish it."

Astra woke as another fire burst within her spine, screaming.

"As?"

She'd forgotten he was next to her. She was so used to waking up from her strange dreams alone, forced to slow her breathing and will the images away in silence. Lux's arms encircled her and pulled her close, her ragged breathing settling as she grounded herself to this plane of existence.

"Who was that?" he whispered in the dark, gently stroking

her bare skin as she pushed her hand against her drumming chest, the dull pain still lingering.

"You heard him?"

He hesitated. "I saw him."

"It was just a nightmare," Astra assured both of them. "Not everything has to mean something."

He pressed a kiss into her forehead, not buying the line. She could feel it in the tension burrowing into his shoulders.

"We need to be careful with who we trust. Careful about who knows we're..." Luxuros trailed off, realizing that there was no word for what they were to one another.

"Whatever we are," she breathed.

"Whatever we are," he agreed, his tone dropping into the problem-solving commander he only shook with her. "There's a reason Selenia wanted Solan and Leona dead. It's only a matter of time before someone sets their sights on us."

"Of course," she whispered, curling her leg over his hips and pressing her lips against his neck until a low rumble answered.

He sighed into her curls.

She cut whatever argument he was about to make with a kiss before saying, "If I have to go back to playing the doting fiancée of your king tomorrow, I'm going to enjoy every second of you I can tonight."

Luxuros hardly let her get the last word out before he covered her mouth with his, dancing in the shadows of her before the Moon rose, and they faced whatever came next.

THIRTY-EIGHT

"Didn't take you as the type to sneak out the morning after," Astra said from the warmth of her bed, tangled in the soft silk of her sheets.

The tattoos along his back stretched as he pulled his shirt over his head, glinting in the dim beams of moonlight cutting through the window behind him. A slow smile unfurled over his lips as he pulled his boots on.

"You looked so peaceful. I didn't want to disturb you."

"I've heard that before," she chuckled, her sheets slipping over her skin as she sat up and searched for her clothes. "Shit, I've *said* that before."

He tugged on his bootlaces and jolted forward, snagging the silk robe he'd peeled off her last night before she could grab it.

Luxuros held it between them, a lavender flag suspended in the air, his smile darkening with something wicked. Astra lunged as he pulled it away, the movement of her body as she sliced through the speckled light stirring a deep maroon storm within his chest.

"Fine," she said, shrugging and pulling her hair into a loose knot at the nape of her neck, all too aware as her arms raised behind her head she offered him a view he couldn't pry his eyes away from if he wanted to.

He certainly did not want to.

But he needed to, she realized, the ticking of the clock on her nightstand drawing her attention to the hour. Soon, maidens would shake off the night and begin their daily chores. Ameera would be close behind them with a tray of coffee and breakfast.

She closed the distance between them, his arms reflexively reaching behind her to drape the robe over her bare shoulders.

"I wasn't sneaking out," he insisted, tracing lines down her arms.

"Sure, Commander," she whispered, pushing up on her toes to catch the edge of his jaw in her lips. His chest eased at her touch, a feeling he feared would make it impossible to think clearly for the rest of his existence. His hands moved on their own accord, pulling her into him by her hips.

"Does it even matter what I say? You can see the truth, anyway, can't you? I couldn't keep it from you a moment longer." He brushed his fingers against her hair, shivering as her hands found their way beneath the hem of his shirt.

She nodded, shades of rosy pinks and scarlets swirling between them. She could see it, amulet or not, and while much of him remained a mystery, there were two things she was certain of:

1. The gods were even more cruel than she'd believed prior to watching the stars within him contract and implode beneath her

and

2. They were *so very fucked.*

He didn't need her intuition to come to the same conclusion.

"I should get back before Ameera comes to wake the mighty Fire Queen." Luxuros placed a soft kiss on her forehead, the warmth branding her.

"Are you staying in the Lunar Court, then?"

He glanced at the door, an amused frustration rumbling against his throat. He rubbed the outside of her crossed arms, the heat of his fingers once so alarming now a source of comfort.

"If I were a smart man, I'd be on the other side of the universe by now, trying to forget the way you taste. But as you've pointed out many, *many* times, I am not a smart man."

Her eyes fell to his lips, satisfied that she'd broken his resolve, no matter the mess poised to crash over them. Astra followed him to the door, leaning against the cool stone, a chill forming at her back.

He loomed over her. Heat whispered between them, no longer emanating solely from him, but from the space between their chests, the Tether a lightning rod stitching them together. Lux's eyes searched hers, finding a thousand answers to questions he'd never asked.

"You're thinking too loudly," he laughed, a soft curve to her lips holding back a comment. "Ameera will hear you."

Her nose scrunched. She beheld his face—and it *was* something to behold, merely looking would never be enough. The worry lines she'd carved beneath his eyes had been replaced by fresh, new fears.

"I'm still unsure what to make of you."

"Make whatever you desire of me." He touched the freckles across the bridge of her nose. "Make me your sunlight, make me your darkest secret," he murmured, leaning into her, letting himself pour over her one more time before that door opened and he'd have to do the impossible and return to his king's side. "Make an irreparable mess of me."

She tucked into the space below his throat, craving the sound of his heart beating against hers.

"We'll find a way to fix this—all of this."

He said nothing for a moment, the fear that fled in wisps of smoke last night now rekindling.

"We need to be scared. Much more scared than you are right now. What happened with Solan and Leona..." He would not dare speak the dark thought to life.

She heard it, nonetheless, rushing in reds and violets beneath his shirt.

"Once you leave this room, I promise I'll behave."

"We both know that's not true," he chuckled. His fingers brushed her shoulder as he lifted her chin toward him. "We *cannot* be reckless."

"Of course," Astra said, pushing her bedroom door open, the moonstone edge scraping gently across obsidian tile.

The door stopped as it came into contact with something.

Someone.

"Oh!" Nayson yelped as he caught the knuckles of his right hand on the handle, sending a coffee kettle flying across the hallway.

"Father!" Astra gasped. She pulled the trim of her robe tighter around her neck, scarlet smoke choking her lungs.

"I was—*oh, gods*—I was just leaving some coffee, and your lights were on. I know you've been having a hard time with your mother back. I thought you could use some comfort..."

Her father stood and turned away, the commander's heart slamming hard enough against his sternum the Tether between them pulsed.

"Nayson," Luxuros said, but the king held up a hand, waving in surrender.

"I didn't see anything," Nayson mumbled. "I—well—I should let someone know to clean this up." He darted down the hallway, not risking a glance over his shoulder.

Astra bit her bottom lip, her fingers twisting into the silk of her robe. She looked to the commander, a similar wince taking hold over his countenance.

She rubbed her forehead. "You were saying?"

"I'll see you at breakfast."

He squeezed her hand in a farewell gesture, stepping over the puddle of steaming coffee pooling in the middle of the hall.

Do you think Mother and Father are fighting?

Lunelle caught her sister's eyes halfway through a miserable breakfast across from the Plutonian prince as a leather boot tapped Astra's foot under the table.

She shot the commander a warning look, still in a daze from this morning's run-in with Nayson, and though she tried to rise above it, she was all but drowning in the heat of the commander in new, wholly consuming ways.

What makes you ask that? Astra replied, her eyes searching the end of the table where her mother sat stiffly in her carved chair, her lips pursed in a fashion not unfamiliar to Astra.

A general disappointment, not directed solely at her for once, but there all the same.

She saw Nayson as Lunelle did—somewhat disheveled, strangely fixated on his plate, and ignoring Tula beside him as she asked after his latest painting.

They just seem at odds, Lunelle sent back. She smiled numbly at something Arcas said, the Plutonian prince's grim demeanor absorbing any light from the full Moon above. Astra studied him. She'd ignored him before, so certain he would hardly be a memory in her life, but as the days wore on she realized it would behoove her to understand the stranger.

His face was long, drawn constantly into a sharp, arrogant point at his chin. His skin was a pale cerulean, the same shade Astra imagined the Earthen sky stretched over a fair Spring day might be. He was young, starved for power, and dangerous after the ego check of the Outer Courts ousting him.

"Princess?" Astra and Lunelle's heads both snapped toward the end of the table, where Mirquios stared at them expectantly.

Lunelle forced her gaze away from him. He'd meant Astra.

"Sorry," Astra winced, the chill of her mother's stare settling into her bones.

"I was telling Arcas here what a talented rider you are. He has an affinity for dragons."

"Oh," she sighed. "Do you ride?"

Arcas shook his head, hardly letting his eyes leave his teacup. "I don't. But I find them fascinating. We don't have them in the Outer Courts."

"Perhaps you could introduce him to Riverion," Luxuros said, lifting his head from his plate for the first time since breakfast was served.

"Do not take the prince near that beast!" Oestera declared, the sturdiness of her tone drawing the eyes of the entire table. "You'll forgive me, Arcas, but Riverion has a history of unpredictable behavior around men," she followed up, smoothing her skirt as she spoke. Her eyes blazed against the morning moonlight, two silver flames burning through Astra.

"Odd," Mirquios observed. "Luxuros seemed to find him quite amiable. I've yet to brave the introduction." The commander set his fork down, glaring at Mirquios.

Lunelle's voice shrieked in Astra's mind. *Astra Leona, you let the commander meet Riverion!*

No! No. Astra set her lips. *Lux snuck up on me in the roost. He threw himself in Riv's claws before I could get the warning out!*

Lunelle eyed her sister carefully, an amused smirk crossing her fair lips.

"I'm sure Riverion would be nothing but kind to you, Your Highness," Nayson declared, louder than necessary as he gestured toward Mirquios. "He respects the worthy. Right?"

Astra looked from her father's bewildered expression to Mirquios's deeply entertained grin.

"What do you say, Fire Queen? Would I stack up to the commander in your beast's eyes?"

Luxuros hung his head forward, reaching for another cup of coffee.

"Only one way to know for certain, my king," Astra said, her breath strained as a rush of giddy pink ran through Mirq's chest.

"The commander can have Riverion's affections," Mirquios said, sipping his tea as Lunelle watched him. "I will not fight that battle."

Nayson arched his eyebrows and drew in a long, unsteady breath as Tula attempted again to engage him.

Astra had little else to contribute for the rest of the meal.

"You TOLD HIM!"

Astra shoved Luxuros against the damp cellar wall of the distillery. She'd hauled him down the stairs after breakfast, her nerves wound tightly in her back, sweating.

"I had to," Lux hissed, hands dropping around her waist as she batted at his chest. "*I had to*," he repeated, holding her blazing glare. "When I returned to our rooms this morning, he was... also... on his way back and we ran into one another! We've been friends for thirty years, he knows me *too* well. He saw it all over my face."

"On his way back from—oh. *Oh*," she breathed, tapping her fingers against the commander's leather vest. "I see." She bit back the blush warming her cheeks, glad for her sister but distressed that their secret had already gotten away from them twice in one morning. "This is impossible," she sighed. "Maybe we need to keep our distance, at least until we figure out the Mirquios and Lunelle of it all."

His hand splayed against the small of her back, the cool air beneath the palace driving her closer to him.

"Perhaps you're right. I could go back to Mercury for a few days. Let things cool off."

"Right," she said, muffled by his stubble as she climbed his throat with her lips. "You could do that."

"I *should* do that," he whispered, his fingers tightening their grip on her hips as her lips brushed against his earlobe. "As," he warned.

"You know," she said between nips of his skin, even warmer than usual as blood rushed to the surface at her touch. "I could still be your queen yet."

He did not speak, but a quick release of his breath encouraged her.

"Perhaps I should remind you of your duty?" She tangled her hand into his thick curls, pulling to the right and exposing more of his neck to her. His eyes closed against the pressure, hands clenching into fists against the soft fabric of her dress.

A smile tugged at his lips. "And how might I prove my loyalty to my queen?"

A scarlet ripple curled around his heart, beckoning her to

press her fingers tighter around his throat as she ran her teeth along his jaw.

"On your knees, Commander."

Luxuros did not hesitate to hit the floor, the cobblestones of the cellar cracking against his knees as he crawled his hands over her thighs, prepared to worship her in any way she saw fit.

We're in the library. Ameera's voice interrupted the tightening spiral in her belly as she threaded her fingers through his curls.

"Godsdammit," Astra huffed.

Luxuros gazed up at her, full lips parted, a purple disappointment rippling through his chest.

"Go," he sighed, rising to his feet. He brushed his thumb over her bottom lip, caressing the pout that formed as he glanced at the stairs.

"I'll return in a few days. I can properly worship you then, my queen."

ASTRA TAPPED her finger against the soft velvet of Ehlaria's novel, watching her sister as she scanned the Shadow Bargaining manual in the back corner of Lunaria's library.

Maidens hovered, but most knew they were out of luck when it came to intriguing gossip between Ameera, Astra, and Lunelle. Anything even remotely sensitive would travel between them in silence.

The halls of the library rose over them, glass ceilings bare to the Moon and her cohorts. Astra counted the stars she could name as she tried to take her mind off what she was missing in the distillery.

You know, I always thought Selenia had a strange coldness to her, Lunelle sent across the table.

Astra nodded. *I said the same thing. I don't want to give too much credit to Ivonne, but she may have been onto something.*

"I found a few more notes in this journal," Ameera said quietly, flipping open a navy-bound volume overflowing with elegant script. Prayers, incantations, and diary entries fell off the pages. "This one in particular was interesting."

Astra stood over Lunelle's shoulder to read.

Cycle Day 28
Wolf Moon 2,486

The queen has finally enacted her revenge for Spring's argument. This month's funding was three-quarters of the typical allotment. She cited the need for more military protection along the Rift as the cause, but I'm certain it's a reprimand for daring to question her mother's motives.

Ellume will pay the price for Selenia's bloodlust.

"I saw her at The Flare," Astra whispered. "Selenia."

Ameera turned to her, a twisted violet flooding the walls of her lungs. "You didn't—"

Leona and Solan were Tethered, she sent to Ameera, and then to Lunelle, both responding with the same sharp gasp.

Lunelle's lips tightened into a line as Ameera asked, "How did you—"

"I went within," Astra whispered. "You can spare me the lecture. The commander already gave me an earful."

"You told Luxuros?" Lunelle sat back in her chair, crossing her arms.

"I had no choice," Astra admitted. "I was trapped in the Rift within. I'm lucky he found me when he did. He pulled me back."

"Astra!" Ameera groaned.

She held her hands up in surrender. "Again, I've had the lecture. Selenia told Solan and Leona they could sever the Tether, but it ended up killing Leona. Solan wasn't trying to hurt her, *he was devastated*. The Flare was a response to his grief —not an attack. I know it was a dangerous endeavor, but this information changes everything, does it not?"

"It certainly does," Lunelle breathed. "These Tethers are troublesome." She half-laughed, unsure how else to process this revelation.

"We need to understand *why* she did it. Whatever she was after, she had to trade her Shadow for the power to do it."

"Was it purely political?" Ameera asked, sinking into the seat beside Lunelle. "The Solar and Lunar Courts have been enemies for millennia, but if Leona and Solan were Tethered... the gods wanted something from them. But what?"

Astra nodded. "That's what we need to find out. And soon."

LUX WATCHED *Astra pinch the stems of a handful of wildflowers from the edge of the meadow.*

"Where are we, anyway?" she asked, soaking in the fragrant floral. Though dulled on the astral plane, the perfume was still sweet enough to catch.

"Not far from your father's home village, actually," the commander said, propping himself up on his elbow as he let the Earthen Sun warm his face. "The Mercurian outpost is just a few

minutes that way." *He pointed into the forest, dense with lush greens and peeling browns.* "I used to come here for some peace."

"It's lovely," *Astra said, returning to the picnic blanket he'd summoned her to moments after her head hit her pillow.* "I can see why my father misses it so terribly."

"I spoke to him this afternoon," *Luxuros said, picking at a blade of grass.* "On my way back to Mercury I caught him in the gardens. He said he can only keep our secret for so long, that the truth always has a way of revealing itself."

"He is, unfortunately, always right." *Astra let her head fall back, enjoying the sensation of the Sun her mind conjured from the memory of the Mercurian streets. He reached for her bouquet, wrapping a long blade of ryegrass around it and tying it off.* "We'll sort us out after we sort out Lunelle and Mirquios and, well, the war, and, I suppose Selenia."

Luxuros frowned. "Quite the to-do list."

Astra's lips parted with a snarky comment, but something at the edge of the meadow caught her eye—a glimmer along the rippling seams of the dream.

"Did you see that?" *she asked. Lux followed her line of sight but the shimmer vanished.*

"What?"

"There was something strange." *She pushed herself up from the blanket and edged toward the ripple, waiting for it again.*

Come on, Fire Queen, we've got somewhere to be, *a voice whispered quietly. Her eyes snapped to the commander, who didn't seem to hear the voice. He was still watching the spot in the woods, now on his feet behind her.*

Astra hesitated—a push in her spine begged her to move forward.

If you won't come to me, I'll have to come to you, *the voice said again.*

"Who are you?" she asked aloud, drawing a confused stare from Luxuros.

If you don't come play, you'll never find out. *She stepped forward and then rocked back on her heels, arguing with the strange impulse in her bones to keep moving.*

She turned to the commander. "I have to go."

Luxuros darted forward and reached for her hand, but she was already disappearing into the thicket, compelled by a force she did not understand.

An olive hand reached for hers through the trees, glinting against the Sun, wrapped in a pristine black cuff. She shuddered against the warmth of his touch, so different from the commander's.

His fingers closed around her wrist and the training she'd spent months on with Lux kicked in. She dropped back on her hip as she felt the commander's arms wrap around her waist, pulling her from the stranger's touch.

"Ah, ah, ah, Fire Queen," the voice said. "We'll have none of that now."

He reached out and touched Astra's forehead, and she was gone.

CHAPTER

THIRTY-NINE

"Don't panic, Princess."

His voice rang like a gong as Astra's eyes cracked open, a thick fog descending over her mind.

A glittering white hall materialized before her, decked in silver and gold, the floor polished to a pristine finish.

She only knew because she kneeled over it, wrists bound behind her, head hung forward. She'd been changed into a silk dress, the fabric hardly concealing anything as it hugged every curve, falling into a pool of moonlight on the floor. Her hair was swept away from her face and secured with a silver crown of stars. The points dug into her scalp as she blinked, trying to shake off the strange clouds around her mind.

The bags under her eyes suggested she'd been out for a while.

"Astra," an alluring voice hummed. Her head snapped up, three figures before her. One was the man in black, his fingers resting against his chin as he studied her, his face round and tan, two dark eyes staring down his knotted nose. The second

394

appeared to be a woman of Elven descent, though Astra couldn't place her. Dripping in rosy shades of blush and pink, her skin glowed in a subtle shade of lavender, set off by iridescent pearls falling from the pointed tips of her ears. Perhaps one of Ehlaria's ancestors.

She looked at Astra as if she was trash left in her path. In the middle stood a proud queen, even more frigid than Oestera. Her sharp glare sent a shiver down Astra's spine.

Selenia.

"Grandmother!" She dipped her head, unsure how to address her in this setting.

"No Lunar princess should ever kneel. Get up."

She shook her head, desperately trying to disperse the fog. Selenia sighed. "Alastair."

A single command.

The man in black stepped behind her, wrapping his hands sharply around her wrists as he yanked her to her feet in one swift movement and tugged at the binds, freeing her. He returned beside Selenia, looking bored with the entire affair.

"You'll pardon his attitude," she said with little effect. "He detests when I send him down to the Courts Between."

Alastair glared. "Worse than that, I found this one in the Astral. She didn't put up a fight, at least."

"I didn't have the chance!"

"Now, now," Selenia silenced her. "I did not bring you here to argue. I want you to join me as my honored guest this evening. We're celebrating the Ascent of Neptune's late queen. You'll stay, of course."

"Do I have a choice?"

"There's always a choice, darling." The way her eyes washed over Astra with a searing disdain told her she did, indeed, have two choices—stay or suffer Selenia's wrath.

"Why me?"

Selenia chuckled, "I think we *both* know why I'd want to see you again."

"Again?"

She glanced at the woman beside her as they shared a sly smile. "Have you forgotten our run-in the other night?"

"Oh," Astra breathed. Unforgiving eyes flashed to her mind in the crowd at The Flare.

She stepped closer, the icy chill of her screaming at Astra to back away. All three held thick walls around their inner worlds, locked down from every angle. Astra should have expected as much.

"Stay for a few drinks. Alastair is a fine dancer. And after you've enjoyed yourself, we'll have a little talk. Sound fair?"

"I assume I'm dressed appropriately?"

"For a half-human," Alastair mocked.

"We're late." Selenia swept out of the room as the woman trailed behind her.

Alastair clicked his tongue and tilted his head toward the door, offering his arm.

Another "choice."

She rested her hand on the crook of his elbow. He pulled her in tight, straightening her back as they slipped through the doors and into a brilliant courtyard. Glowing white lights hung from metallic trees. Gilded roses blossomed under the moonlight. The courtyard buzzed with gods, humans, and the in-between, all draped in various metallics and pastels.

Surrounding the courtyard were twelve thrones, carved with the names of each of the ancient gods the Living Courts prayed to. Only Neptune sat on his throne, his hair falling in watery waves as he picked something off a plate held by a young woman with pointed ears. The rest of the thrones were empty, their gods mingling amongst the crowd.

"You seem confused," Alastair said as Selenia disappeared into the crowd with the Elven woman hot on her heels.

"It's not how I pictured it." Astra took in the rest of the courtyard. "They seem so... similar to us."

"Gods are only what we make them," Alastair said quietly. "You'd do well to remember that."

Her eyes scanned the thrones one more time, catching on a thirteenth behind the Solar and Lunar thrones.

"Is that for the Nether Queen?"

"You ask all the wrong questions. Stay on my arm, do not talk to *anyone* if you can help it, and I'll get you back to your little boyfriend in no time," Alastair muttered, low enough for only her ears. Her eyes widened, his wicked sneer gone. His eyes softened, and his smile was genuine.

"What—"

"Your life depends on your acting skills here. You might be a fearsome creature in the Lunar Court, but the Court Above will eat you alive if you give them any shred of anxiety to feed on," he said from the side of his mouth as he pulled her through the crowd and toward a marble bar laden with foods and wines. He plucked two goblets from the spread and placed one in Astra's hand, whispering into her ear, "I apologize in advance for the next hour. I'm afraid I'm going to be a bit of a bastard."

She sipped the wine, the bitter liquid slipping over her lips easily as he rounded the center of the courtyard where a mass huddled. A trio of strings and a mesmerizing harpist played through an enchanting melody. They listened as she followed his lead and drained the wine, letting it bolster the fog around her head into a warm wave, rolling over her bare shoulders.

Selenia stood across from them as they took in the sweet notes, her eyes trained on Alastair, a slight nod communicating something Astra couldn't understand.

But, as he plucked the goblet from her hand and dropped it onto a garden table, she knew what came next. The strings sang a new melody, and her hand floated upward as Alastair pulled her to the center of the floor, dozens of eyes sizing her up. Several other couples joined as he spun her around, the silk skirt sliding against the dance floor.

"Smile, Astra," he whispered. "You're a spectacle to the gods. Their humanity died centuries ago, they'll lap up fresh blood eagerly." Then he did something unexpected—he lowered his guard. A careful concoction of confidence and charm slithered off of him, warming her as they turned again. He leaned in close. "Better?"

She nodded.

He turned her in a half-circle, pushing her back against his chest, perfectly aligning his lips to her ear. "She's going to make you a deal. Take it."

Astra faced the crowd. Like living marble statues, the Ascended gods and goddesses of all the courts assembled to watch—to judge. Most of them had made their triumphant Ascent to the Court Above centuries ago. They'd long forgotten what the rush of red blood beneath flesh even felt like. Liquid gold slipped through their veins now.

They watched like they knew who she was, knew *what* she was.

She turned her face toward him so they couldn't read her lips, though she wondered if that mattered here.

"Why should I trust you, Alastair?"

He lifted his arm, twirling her in a full circle, facing her once again.

"Have you forgotten who you are, Fire Queen? What does your intuition tell you?"

He was right. Just like Lux had been when they met all those months ago. Nothing screamed to run from his arms.

Nothing within his spirit felt like a threat. Something about the way he moved, the way he felt, was so familiar. As if they were crafted from the same dust.

"Who *are* you?"

"You've never heard of me?" He chuckled, bowing to her as their dance concluded. He moved back, looping her arm through his again, pulling her back into the crowd and weaving between prying eyes. "Alastair Obyss. Right Hand to the Lunar Goddess, Weaver of Dreams."

"Sorry." Astra watched two goddesses whisper as she passed. "I'm unfamiliar."

He sighed. "That's disappointing. You Lunarians have been robbed of all your fun."

"That we can agree on. How did you get me here from a dream? Aren't the gates only open on Equinoxes and Solstices?"

Alastair dropped his eyes to hers, his lips tilted into a crooked smile.

"Gods aren't bound to such silly laws like time. I'm surprised you've never tried the Divine Gate yourself. Most don't, but every so often one of you slips through—it makes for an amusing anecdote at dinner parties. The Nether Queen, on the other hand, keeps a very tight lock on her gate between holidays—she's not one for surprises."

He stiffened as Selenia approached, her eerie chill rolling ahead of her like a morning fog.

"I see your mother, at the very least, kept up with your dance instruction," she tossed.

"Of course." Astra forced a smile.

"I want you to meet some friends," Selenia mused, gesturing for them to follow her.

Astra spent the next half hour listening to the Goddess of Mercury preen on and on about how excited they were to have a Lunar Princess inherit the court. She tried her best not to frown every time she mentioned Mirquios. As the goddess started on her third round of stories about her time on the throne centuries ago, someone in an all-white tunic approached and whispered in Alastair's ear. His lips fell into a tight line.

"Pardon me," he said, handing Astra to Selenia. "I'll just be a moment."

Selenia wrapped her arm around her granddaughter's and nodded along to the goddess's tales, stifling a yawn.

Alastair did not return before Selenia grew bored with the party, introducing Astra to several other ancient gods, always beaming as she revealed she was her granddaughter in a way that tugged at Astra's heart.

In a way her mother never had.

Selenia pulled Astra from the courtyard back to the white room, giving her more time to absorb the fine details she'd missed earlier. On one end was a set of sofas, accented with velvet pillows stitched with the lunar cycle in iridescent thread. Metal frames filled with ethereal portraits hung on the walls, the white tile on the floor reflecting them as they strode across the room. She plopped onto one sofa and gestured to the other, the woman in shades of pink hovering in a corner.

Astra felt a breeze as the doors opened again, Alastair returning with a smug twist of his full lips.

"I did not just bring you here to show you off," Selenia confessed. "I believe you and I have a shared goal."

"And what is that?"

"You weren't revisiting The Flare for fun, Astra. What *were* you trying to glean?"

"Nothing." She tucked her lip between her teeth, realizing as her eyes narrowed that was the wrong answer. "I was only trying to understand what happened with Leona. As you know,

I am engaged to the Mercurian king. His version of events was quite different from mine. I was hoping to learn the truth."

"And what truth did you learn?" Her eyes sliced and examined Astra, sinking back into the sofa, her hair blending into the crushed velvet.

Alastair's lips twitched as his shoulders tensed. It was a trap she'd need to navigate with great caution.

"That it wasn't the brutal attack I thought. It was mutual destruction. Both of their faults."

Her pale pink lips dropped into a frown. "Tragic, wasn't it? A shame your mother couldn't talk them out of it. Perhaps, if she had tried a little harder in the end."

Astra flinched. "Perhaps."

"Then you'd understand," she said, sitting up straighter. "Why I might have an interest in speaking with Leona again. To clear the air. I thought I could trust the person who gave me the advice about their situation."

Astra fought the urge to push, to ask her exactly who advised her.

"How would I facilitate something like that? Is she not... here?"

The woman in pink sneered, a wicked grin chasing it.

"Leona has not made her Ascent. I'm afraid my daughter suffers greatly from the guilt of what she caused with her reckless behavior. She's never been able to look her Shadow in the eye. Which is why I need help."

Selenia leaned toward her, a dark, cold shift pushing a wave of nausea through Astra's stomach.

"Your sister's trial is coming up, yes? The Court Below is open to the Courts Between and the Living Courts on the Solstices..."

"Why can't you go?"

Selenia and the woman behind her exchanged a fraught

glance. "I am not exactly welcome in Luciela's domain. The Nether Queen and I have our differences, darling. Long story."

"So you want me to go to The Court Below... and get Leona?" The fog she'd been battling all evening cleared instantly as adrenaline rushed into her spine.

"The Nether Queen will be distracted by Lunelle and the champions. It would be the perfect time to visit the River of Souls. Take something of hers, use it to call her."

Selenia reached into the pocket of her robes, producing a locket, engraved with the Aurellis crest. "Contain her in this and bring her to me so we can handle our unfinished business and I'll grant you a favor. You've already seen what I can offer you here."

Ah, so this evening was not about showing her off to the gods, but the gods off to her.

"Nominate Mirquios as a champion," Astra spat out before she could stop herself. The woman in pink and Alastair both leaned forward, caught off guard.

"Fascinating," Selenia said, her eyes lighting up. "Why would I do that?"

"Mother has only identified one champion in the Prince of Pluto. He is not *worthy* of Lunelle. Or the title. He has nothing to offer. But Mirquios... he is a king. A true leader."

Selenia's lips pursed. "What about the Tether?"

Astra drew in a breath, letting the truth—as much of it as she dared—guide her response. "The Tether was a politically motivated farce. We made a deal. Nothing more. But it's why I need a goddess to intervene and change Fate, if you will."

"My blood *does* run through you," she scoffed. "Of everything I could offer you, that is what you want?"

"It is what I want."

"Your mother will not appreciate my interference."

"What *does* my mother appreciate?"

Selenia laughed, a sound Astra couldn't help but return.

"It is done. Next week, at Lunelle's Trial Ball, I will declare my nomination. Do we have a deal?" She reached a hand across the space between sofas, glimmering chains around her wrists clacking together.

She glanced once at Alastair, who nodded so softly anyone could have missed it.

"We have a deal."

"Excellent. Alastair!" Selenia turned to her right hand, satisfied with how the evening turned out. "Do make sure our princess gets home safely."

He rolled his eyes, extending his hand to Astra, exhausted by having to make two trips to the Courts Between in one day.

"Let's go, Fire Queen."

She took his hand, wrapping her arm around his as he guided her out a back door, onto a terrace that backed into the Rift, the colors much more brilliant from the Court Above.

"I believe I have something of yours," Alastair sighed. He pointed toward the treeline, a soft golden glow illuminating two ancient oaks. Lux's eyes widened as he saw her, his legs springing into action.

"Don't," Alastair called. "I sensed you from a mile away, Luxuros. The rest of the gods surely will, too. You have enemies here you cannot even fathom."

Lux's shoulders stiffened as Alastair walked her toward the forest, the Rift tangled between the trees. Astra was about to ask how he found her when she saw his fingers working to refasten the moonstone amulet around his neck. He'd followed the Tether.

Alastair halted just as she could feel his warmth, releasing her arm.

"You did well tonight, Astra," he said quietly, scarlet panic climbing Lux's spine as he strained to get his hands on her.

"But Selenia is dangerous, so much more than you know. And she answers to even more frightening figures. Do what she asked, but don't entangle yourself further."

"Who does she—"

Alastair cut her off with a finger to his lips. "Another time. If anyone asks, I escorted you back to the palace personally." He leaned in, brushing his lips against her cheek, and whispered, "I won't tell Selenia who whisked you away, but do be careful, Princess. The gods who do not get a say in Fate's tapestries will do just about anything to unravel the threads."

Astra leaned away, Lux's face stoic as heat rolled off him. "Goodbye, Alastair."

"Good luck, Fire Queen." He tossed one last glare toward Lux, who reached his hand out for her, not wasting a second more as he crashed them through the trees and into the Rift, clutching his hand around an aventurine thread as Astra held her breath.

CHAPTER

FORTY

"You found her!"

Lunelle's voice echoed off the halls of the Mercurian palace as they landed at the gate and ducked inside. Lux dropped Astra's hand as they rounded the corner and Lunelle's arms collided around her sister's shoulders.

"Are you hurt? Who took you? How did you find her?" She directed her last question to Lux, who hadn't spoken since leaving the Court Above.

"I'm fine," Astra insisted as she struggled against Lunelle's grasp.

She dragged Astra down the hall and into a lush library. Red tapestries and carpet glowed under the sunlight trickling in through the windows—the scent of something herbal rose to Astra's senses. Ameera perched beside a table overflowing with pastries and fruit, nervously picking at grapes the same color as her concern.

"I'm *fine*," Astra said again, easing everyone's tension. She felt a sharp tug at her chest as the commander crossed the room, the unexpected pull stealing her breath. Her eyes flew toward him,

405

but the pain was gone almost as quickly. She watched his fingers fasten the leather cord around his neck. Beams of Sun brightened his dark countenance, but not enough to comfort her.

"I cannot believe I let this happen." Lunelle's chest was a pit of black loathing. "Anyone could have grabbed you. I told you she shouldn't be in the Rift!"

"You sound like Mother."

Lunelle stopped pacing, a flare of bright red resentment blaring within her chest.

"Sorry," Astra apologized. "But I wasn't in the Rift. I was dreaming, Lunelle. It could have happened anywhere."

"You were gone for hours! The Lunar Court will awaken any moment and we're lucky we aren't bringing back a corpse!"

Astra flopped onto a chaise lounge. She'd forgotten how little she was wearing until the embroidered cushions touched her exposed back.

"I attended a ball with a bunch of deities and drank some wine. That's a Tuesday in the Lunar Court."

Mirquios snorted in the corner. A quick dart of Lunelle's eyes wiped the smirk from his lips.

"What did Selenia want?" Ameera asked. It was the first question she wanted to answer since Lux had dragged her back into the Rift.

"To make a deal."

Lunelle kneeled in front of her, searching her sister's gaze. "What did you do?"

"She wants me to go to the Court Below with you and Arcas to retrieve something for her," she said as if describing the weather in the Court Above. "And Mirq."

Lunelle gasped, resting her hands on her silver silk-coated knees.

"Mirquios?"

"In exchange for my help, Selenia will nominate Mirquios as a champion."

"What—no. No!" Lunelle argued. Lux's body stiffened in the window, his fingers clasped around the trim.

"Lu, it's the solution we've been looking for. If Selenia nominates Mirquios, no one can argue. Not Mother. Not Arcas. It will be seen as a formal decision of the gods."

"It's too dangerous!"

"You'll both be there with me," she shrugged. "When I'm not knocked unconscious by an Ascended god, I actually handle myself quite well."

Lunelle leaped forward from the ground, throwing her arms around Astra's shoulders, a sob ripping from her chest.

"I do not deserve a sister like you," she whispered against Astra's neck. Over her shoulder, Mirquios nodded from the corner, a faint smile bubbling up over his lips, but his eyes flashed to Lux and Lux alone.

"What does she want you to retrieve?"

Astra pressed her lips together. "Leona."

Lunelle's brows folded inward. "As—"

"I know it sounds crazy! But she wants to make amends. Leona has never Ascended. Selenia believes that there's been a misunderstanding." She felt the heat of Lux's eyes land on her shoulders.

"She can do it," Mirquios said mostly for his brother's benefit. "If anyone can do it, it's Astra."

Lux did not respond.

"And there's no catch? You bring her Leona's Soul and she'll leave it at that?" Ameera asked. Lunelle leaned back on her heels, tears still spilling over from her eyes.

"There's always a catch," Astra sighed. "I just haven't

figured it out yet. But until then, I have her word. She's going to crash your Trial Ball and announce it."

"Oh, Mother is going to hate that." Lunelle stifled a nervous giggle.

Astra grinned. "A big part of the appeal for me, if I'm being honest. Now, if you all don't mind, this crown is becoming a permanent part of my skull and I am drunk on the wine of the gods. I desperately need to get home."

"Of course. We can talk more tomorrow," Lunelle said as she crossed the room and placed a hand on Mirquios's shoulder, their eyes holding the gaze of infinite possibility once again.

"I'll have breakfast sent up to your room," Ameera said softly. Her eyes slid from Astra to Lux, sending a flush to her cheeks.

One tray or two?

Astra fought the urge to shrug. *Your guess is as good as mine*, she sent back.

Ameera patted Astra's shoulder. Before leaving the library, she hugged her sister once more, the joy radiating from Lunelle's chest worth anything that might happen in the Court Below.

"Thank you," Mirquios said as Astra left, his eyes still fixed on Lux. "Will you make sure Astra makes it back to her chambers safely, Commander? I'd rather she not enter the Rift alone, after tonight." Lux's head snapped toward his king, his answer in the form of a shallow nod.

Luxuros followed her in silence, his hand lightly skimming the back of her dress, a twisted knot of fury working itself out into a straight line in his gut.

It wasn't until they made it back to her dressing room that he spoke. She reached for the crown of stars when his hands stopped hers.

"Let me," he whispered.

She dropped her head as she leaned against the vanity. He took his time untangling the delicate metal and mess of curls with the utmost care. A satisfying burn sizzled against her scalp when he finally freed it.

Lux set the crown on the crystal countertop, stars reflecting in the white quartz as his fingers moved to the braids in her hair. He loosened each of them, letting his hands rake through her ruby curls as they sprang free, brushing against her shoulders. Before he moved from behind her, he reached for a crescent pin on her vanity and twisted her hair off her neck, the way he'd seen her do a million times in the gardens as they'd worked in the late Summer heat.

With her hair neatly tucked away, he slipped the silk straps over her shoulders and let the dress fall to the floor. Astra was relieved to find she still had underpinnings on, she'd never learned who dressed her in the Court Above.

"Get in," Lux said as he dragged the ivory lace off her body, tilting his head toward the simmering pool beyond the arch in the wall. She was about to ask if he'd join when his fingers went to work on the buttons and laces of his leathers, his boots falling next to the pile of silk her dress became.

She slipped into the pool and leaned her head back against the tile floor. The water was perfectly warm, exactly what she needed. Her eyes drifted closed as Lux joined, the water heating as he crossed the pool and sat beside her.

The fog Alastair had placed around her mind still lingered, turning her to clay in Lux's rigid hands as he pushed his fingers into the muscles beneath her neck. He placed a quick kiss at the top of her spine before moving lower, digging into the sore tissue between her shoulders.

She leaned back into him, letting her head fall against his shoulder, his lips resting gently against her neck.

"You're so quiet," she said.

"There was a time when you would have preferred I keep my opinions to myself," he murmured into her skin, working his fingers into her lower back.

"Not when I can feel how distressed you are," she returned.

"I'm working through it."

She smiled. "I feel that, too. But you don't have to do it alone."

"You're busy saving everyone else. You don't need to listen to me whine."

"This only works if you talk to me, Luxuros."

"Luxuros," he mimicked. "Full-naming me."

"And you say *I'm* stubborn."

"I'm not avoiding it. I know that you would tell me if anyone... tried anything."

"You mean Alastair?" She turned around, folding her legs under her so she could watch his face as he spoke.

"Is that his name?"

"Yes." She reached for his hand under the warm water, twisting her fingers into his. "And you're correct. I would tell you. He's Selenia's right hand, Weaver of Dreams? Or something to that effect. He seemed to understand our plight. Like he knows what we're up to. He kept me safe."

"He was less kind to me." Lux's brows furrowed. "Though I couldn't fault him for wanting you to himself."

"Nothing like that," she assured him.

"Thank you." Lux reached forward and tucked a loose curl behind her ear, the warm water on his hands dripping over her neck.

"Better already," she said, gesturing to his chest as the red knot settled and unwound into something more manageable, though fiery anger still lingered at the edge. "But you're still pissed."

"I'm angry at myself, not you. I didn't even consider the possibility that might happen. This is now the second time you've gotten hurt because I was distracting you. I should have sensed someone there. I should have protected you."

"Easy, Commander. I *also* got distracted and failed to protect myself. I'm not a child."

He nodded. "I'll work through it. I promise I'm not usually a possessive asshole but there's something about him. I don't know. I don't trust it." He leaned forward, cupping her face. "The thought of something happening to you makes me physically ill. It's overwhelming."

"You're talking to the woman who burned someone alive for a little tap on your ankle." She pulled him closer, enjoying the warmth settled over her—she no longer drowned in him, she reveled. "*Some* of your stress could be rooted in those identity issues we like to pretend aren't a problem, no?"

She poked him in the shoulder, his eyes rolling.

"I promise we'll work through those, too. When I'm ready."

"When you're ready," she agreed.

He closed the narrow gap between them and placed a soft kiss on her lips. "I *will* be ready someday."

"Mmhmm," she hummed, pulling his lips back into hers. A pale pink wisp of smoke rose in his chest, tickling her fingertips as she dragged them through his dark hair. Something glittered in the swirls, clinging to the moonlight pouring in through the port in her ceiling. "That's a new one," she whispered, glancing at her hands.

"What?" he asked as he broke from her mouth to her neck. She grabbed his face, forcing him to look at her. The smoke intensified as his eyes flared, sparkling as fingers found her hips. She let it fill her lungs, soothing an ache within her.

His hand slipped further, dancing against the inside of her thigh.

A question.

She pushed into his touch, a soft note of delight passing over her lips and encouraging him. As he stroked her skin, the smoke rose, filling every cavern within her heavy heart. Claiming spaces within her she'd never given up before.

She leaned back, allowing him more access to every piece of her, the Tether between them singing in anticipation, even if quieted by the amulet resting beneath the water.

His tongue found hers, burning up every thought she'd had rolling around in her head, crumbling them to ashes. The flames whipped around her heart, flaring into a deep magenta at the ends, expanding from her belly to her lungs and her throat as he moved faster, as he gave her more.

She rested her head against the tile, lost in the wildfire as he moved over her like a shadow. Lux brought his other hand to her cheek, stroking the path of freckles he admired so much. She laughed, her voice pitching up as he leaned forward and she felt how much he enjoyed pleasuring her against her thigh. She closed her eyes again and pulled his forehead against hers, letting the flickering pinks and reds and silvers slip from her mind to his.

Gods above. Low tones bounded off the base of her skull, shocking her. The flames within her chest curled in on themselves and retreated at the surprise intrusion.

"Ah, shit," Lux groaned, feeling the release she was so close to vanishing.

"It's okay—"

He grabbed her face, his expression serious. "It's not okay. I didn't—I didn't mean to. I've been playing with the motion, trying to figure it out. But it's never worked before."

She perked up under him, water splashing over the edge of the pool as she caught her breath. "Have you just been screaming at me in your head for weeks?"

His lips tilted upward. "Well, I've been screaming at you in my head for months, but that was usually unrelated." He leaned forward again, brushing a thumb across her lips. "I see it now, the path into your mind. It's only fair, considering you've lived within mine all along," he breathed against her ear. The vibration was enough to spark the fire in her belly back to life.

Do it again, she beamed, holding his gaze.

Which part? His dark laugh rumbled through her, her back arching into his waiting hands. She pushed him away, climbing out of the pool as he protested.

Where are you going?

Swiping the water from her legs with a towel, she shot back, *To my bed. I believe you said you'd worship me.*

She heard a splash and footsteps behind her.

Lux caught up to her and spun her around, pulling the pin from her hair as he tangled his fingers in her waterfall of curls. He pushed her back onto the bed, disappearing from view as he fell to his knees. The magenta flames leaped to life again as his fingers pushed her thighs apart and made way for his lips.

Shit. She wasn't sure if she meant to beam it or hiss it into the ether as he crawled one hand over her body, digging into the curves of her soft belly.

You taste exactly as I dreamed you would, Fire Queen.

No invite to those dreams? She giggled. His eyes snapped to hers, lit with the same fire that threatened to choke her out.

I'll figure that trick out next. His hand kneaded her breasts, desperate to hold on to her as the base of that fire burned out, exploding into a fine mist as she bucked against him. She gasped as the embers collided with each other, resettling against her spine as she came back into herself.

He rose from the floor, climbed over her, and replaced his tongue with his hand, giving her no time to recover.

"What does it look like?" He nipped at her jaw, moving against her in a slow spell, conjuring a brilliant flame of yellow pleasure in her spine.

"What—" She could not focus enough to finish her question. She cried out again, his fingers on their way to coaxing another release from her. Yellow sunlight lit her vision, blinding her as he caught her lips in his.

Lux leaned back, a scarlet need for more building in his hips. His eyes scraped her body, drinking her in before he pulled one leg over the other. She rolled, his breath hitching in approval at the sight of her back.

"Does it change?" he asked again. "Or does every release look the same?"

Ah, he meant what she saw within herself. She thought for a moment as his fingers crawled her back, tracing the lines of ink.

"It's different from person to person." She gasped as he nudged her knees apart, hovering against her. "I've seen oceans, stars, flowers."

"And me? What do I look like when I sing the praises of the Lunar Goddess?" A strained moan rolled off her tongue as he entered her, an appreciative gasp radiating from his chest in return. He ran his hands under her hips, pulling her back into him. The friction kindled another fire, though there was so little oxygen left in her lungs to stoke it.

"Flames," she rasped, a black fire roaring between them, white-hot on the edges.

"Show me," Lux groaned. "I want to see."

She reached back, her palm gripping the muscle of his thigh as he moved within her. The onyx flames rose to her throat, unfurling in a desperate cry against the soft velvet bed linens. She pushed the image into him as she held on for dear life, losing her senses completely. His arms hooked around her waist as he pulled her back to lean against his chest.

"One more for the Fire Queen's most devoted disciple," he rumbled. His hand snaked over her hip and between her legs. His breath was hot on her neck as the fire between them flashed, no longer fathomless black but pure gold.

"I cannot," she forced out, looping her arm around his neck, anchoring herself to this world in any way possible. She clutched at his leather cord, twisting it between her fingers.

He tangled a hand over hers, wrapping them around the moonstone pendant. "I know you, you're far too stubborn to quit." He held her to him the way he'd ached to a million times, willing to offer her anything she needed—anything she wanted—if she'd only bless him with one more release.

"Lux," she whined, drowning in the golden smoke, the edges of her vision blurring.

One more, Sol'ah. Just for me.

After all the arguing she'd done, all the denying of his wishes, the pushing against his better judgments... she could happily give in to his command.

The flames roared, bursting into smoke and shadow and stars as they spiraled together. The Tether hummed between them as if pulling all the heat from the embers between their bodies and storing it away for a cold moment.

"Good fucking gods." He pulled her hair off her shoulders, running his lips over her sweat-speckled skin.

She fought for breath, nothing left within her but a pleasant warmth. "If that's how I'm rewarded every time I'm kidnapped..."

Lux laughed, falling back onto the bed. He reached for her hand and pulled her into him.

"Don't tempt me. I'll throw your ass back into the Rift right now."

She ran her fingers over his chest, an emerald flare of jealousy so slight she might have missed it, but she felt it—the simmer of it needling at him as the ecstasy of being inside her dwindled.

She twisted in his arms, tangling their legs together as he reached for her quilt.

"Green looks better on me, Commander."

FORTY-ONE

Astra teetered on her heels outside of the Celestial Hall, the room beyond the doors already bubbling with a myriad of colors and speculation. A trial was always a spectacle, beginning with her sister's trial ball, an occasion her mother had spared not a single extravagance for.

She'd watched the maidens spend weeks on the delicate starry decor, watched her mother pass over a dozen floral arrangements that were not big enough, strong enough, enough, enough, *enough.*

Though she was drowning in a spectrum of worries, no one was as conflicted as the king on her arm, his lips twisted against the anxious purples rolling over his shoulders.

"Are you ready for this to be over?" she asked.

"I'm ready for *all* of it to be over." Mirq smiled weakly, the hurricane of nerves tinged with golden sparkling hope dancing in his chest.

"Here's to your last night pretending to be in love with me." She extended her hand to wrap around his arm as he rolled his eyes.

"It's not all pretend. You're family, whether you like it or not. Lunelle aside, I've known Luxuros for thirty years. He is my brother in every way that matters. Whomever he chooses to shine his light on will always have a place in my court."

She blushed at his sentiment, unprepared for his outright embracing of their tangled relationships.

"You know," she mused as they watched the hall fill with courtiers. People filtered in from all corners of the universe, their glittering gowns throwing multicolor rainbows across the floors. "You may just be the only man good enough for my sister."

Mirquios's eyes held hers, a sorrow pooling behind them. "Let us hope that's still true tomorrow."

The benefit of being the second-born heir and settled on the arm of a king was that Astra was no longer the object of the court's curiosity. She could watch and observe—follow stolen glances and intrigued stares, listen to trite gossip between maidens as they circulated the room, and no one watched her with their judging eyes.

By the time the evening ended, that would no longer be true, but for the moment, she could rest in a low tide.

It helped that no matter where she roamed, no matter what circle she inserted herself into, she felt that eternal thread pull and release as Lux trailed. He kept his back to the walls of the ballroom, his eyes on everyone and everything as she and Mirquios played the doting couple.

Lux let his thoughts slide over the Tether. Teasing chuckles as he watched her fuss with her champagne glass or force a laugh at a councilwoman's flat joke. She'd never craved the kind of security he offered before, but now, it was unfathomable that she ever walked this realm without him to anchor her soul.

He felt the emotion pour from her. She was sure of it. His

eyes slid over hairpieces and tiaras to find hers, his lip twitching in a sacred smile only for Astra's eyes.

Selenia had to show up. This had to work. She would fling herself off the cliffs of Celene before she condemned her sister to live a lifetime without the same heart-stopping attachment.

"Princess Lunelle Silverswan Aurellis, the future Queen of the Lunar Court. May the Mother bless her Within and Without."

Three hundred pairs of eyes turned at once to the top of the grand staircase in the center of the room. Lunelle's sparkling cosmic gown painted her an angel as she descended into the crowd. Her heart soared as she caught Mirquios beaming, and then plunged to the depths of the sea when Arcas stood at the base of the steps, his cerulean arm offered to her.

"Steady," Astra whispered as Mirquios's body lit in enraged flames. "You can do anything for one dance."

He didn't respond, but his grip on her hand loosened slightly. Lunelle and Arcas swept across the dance floor, sparkling stars floating off her gown and slipping through the air in a meteor shower.

As they turned about the room, the strings of the orchestra swelled with the same heightened anxiety Astra felt in her heart.

When exactly is Selenia supposed to join us? Lunelle beamed, her voice fraught with the tension running through her spine as she carried herself and Arcas across the floor.

We didn't set an exact time. You can do this.

We may not even have to rely on her. I think Mirq's glare might vaporize Arcas and solve the problem for us.

Astra smirked. *And that's with my attempts to calm him.*

I only hope you find a love like this one day, Astra.

One day.

She could tell her. Lunelle had trusted her with her deepest secret. But something stopped Astra, a gut feeling she couldn't quite place. It wasn't the same with them. Lunelle and Mirquios certainly had bad luck, but they weren't forbidden in the all-powerful-gods-will-kill-them-for-touching sense.

"You two should join them." Oestera appeared behind Mirquios, shooing the pair toward the dance floor.

Mirquios held her hand high as he bowed his head and searched for the rhythm to step in time with the orchestra. His hand rested on the small of her back as he spun her in a delicate arc.

Tell the king to watch that hand. Lux's voice rumbled through her mind like a late Summer rain. She searched for him as they rocked back and forth, Mirq spinning her out and back in.

She caught Lux just behind the crowd, watching them closely. He smiled from his station against one of the pillars coated in moonblossoms, arms folded across his chest as other couples flooded the floor.

She caught his eyes. *You could cut in. It wouldn't be so odd, would it? You're a leader of my soon-to-be court.*

Lux scoffed, she couldn't hear him across the ballroom but she could see his eyes crinkle. *That blush of yours would give us away in an instant. And even if you could control yourself around me, I'm not sure I could do the same.*

"I'd love if you two could at least keep your drooling behind closed doors," Mirquios muttered.

She threw her head back and laughed. "I'm *so* sorry!"

"Mmhmm," he grumbled, dipping Astra low. As her head fell back, she saw a whip of white gauze parting the sea of courtiers. A rush of whispers around the room followed the shift of energy at the edge of the crowd—brilliant swaths of red and blue swirled through their chests.

"Shit," Mirq hissed, pulling her back up as Selenia stood at the edge of the dance floor, her hands on her hips. "Showtime."

Oestera cut across the ballroom as dancers froze, their eyes trained on the ethereal goddess soaking up every drop of light in the room.

"Lunelle," Selenia cooed, her voice dripping with honey and venom. Her hands outstretched to cup Lunelle's chin, placing a soft kiss on each cheek.

"Grandmother." Lunelle bowed, her tiara glinting in the moonlight above.

"What an exciting celebration!" Selenia announced, her voice taking over the orchestra as the strings cut to an abrupt stop.

She cast a stare at Oestera, ice in her eyes. "No need to stop on my account! I'm merely here to deliver a message on behalf of the Court Above." Oestera stopped dead in her tracks and Arcas searched for her, his eyes narrowing as Selenia began speaking again.

"We've been waiting with bated breath to see who our champions will be, but it seems my daughter has failed to provide much competition for your hand, my dear girl." Selenia held Lunelle's silver-gloved hand, squeezing it to make a point.

Whatever color might exist within her mother's heart drained.

Selenia continued, "We try not to involve ourselves unless absolutely necessary, of course, but that time has come."

Oestera maintained a perfect mask of composure as her heart raged.

"You there, Mercurian child, look how you've grown under the harsh Sun. Your great-grandmother was just bragging to us at a party about how excited they are for a Lunar Queen."

Selenia held her hand out for Mirquios, who did not have to act terrified. It came quite naturally.

Astra relinquished her hold on him. He tentatively stepped toward her, joining the Lunar Goddess in the middle of the floor.

"I understand there's an arrangement made here already, but Astra, my dear girl, surely you understand that bigger games are at play?"

Astra nodded slowly, unsure of how she should be reacting. The confusion aided in the illusion as Oestera's eyes flickered between them, horror rolling off her. Nayson was ready to burst.

"Mercury has proven themselves worthy of a Lunarian woman already, but perhaps the Lunar Court needs young Mirquios's eyes more than Pluto's... modest offering."

Arcas's temper flared, his lips tightening, but he was raised in the same calculated void they all were—his muscle memory snapped his rage into submission.

Selenia sneered at him. "I suppose only the trial will tell."

"Mother—"

Selenia held her hand up to Oestera's face, silencing her in a way Astra had never seen done. "It is decided, Oestera. What happens tomorrow is up to Fate."

"But Astra... the Tether—"

Selenia's eyes trained on Astra, a blaze of holy fire within them.

"Sometimes we get things wrong, Oestera. Surely you can understand that. Astra is a strong girl. She'll do whatever it takes to secure her court, will she not?"

Astra nodded, swallowing, reminding herself that this should be devastating. She let a single tear fall, wiping it gently with her gloved hand.

"There we have it. Mirquios is to compete in the trial

against Arcas, and we'll have a real show to watch in the Court Above. Although..." Every eye in the room slid from Selenia's face to Astra's, then to Lunelle's in synchronized disbelief.

The sharp edge in her tone dragged over Astra's skin like a blade.

"One champion is so *very* dull. Two is interesting..." Selenia stepped in a circle, soaking up every ounce of apprehension in the room. "Three," she laughed. Her cold eyes fell on Astra. "Three's enticing. You're in quite the predicament, Oestera," the goddess continued, pacing along the edge of the crowd. "The Solar king is mounting an attack, he's already invaded Saturn and Jupiter. Is Pluto *really* the best Outer Heir you can do?"

Arcas opened his mouth but shut it just as quickly as she pivoted on her heel.

"Did you even attempt to find a stronger alliance?"

Oestera's jaw tightened. "I—"

Selenia huffed, "Spare me, Oestera. Luckily, as always, I've done the work for you. My right hand discovered something *quite* fascinating when your second-born came to visit me."

Astra's mother's eyes widened, any evidence of her calm mask now disintegrated. Astra watched the floor, ashamed at the pain in her expression.

Selenia continued with little regard for her daughter's emotions. "It's always the secondborn that breaks your heart, wouldn't you agree, Oestera? Now, you younger lot may not know this—it's not well documented in the Living Courts— but there's only one way to get through the Court Above's gates outside of a Solstice or Equinox. No mere mortal can pass."

Astra felt it before she said it, in her bones, bouncing between vein and vessel.

"Now, a demigod has certain privileges. So color me

intrigued when a certain commander came to collect my granddaughter."

Astra searched for Lux, the panic crawling through her chest in muddy rivers of colors too complex to name. *Lux*, she sent, but nothing connected. His mind was too fogged over.

"And now that I see you, Commander, the resemblance is *truly* uncanny. Wouldn't you say, Oestera?"

Oestera twisted, finding Luxuros in the crowd. He stepped forward, his chest a hurricane of alarming sunset oranges. Astra flinched. Her feet strained to cross the ballroom and get between them, but Mirq's hand caught her arm.

Selenia frowned. "Well?"

Oestera did not speak, but Astra saw it in her eyes, the spark of recognition. The details she'd missed when she revisited The Flare. The slope of his bronze nose, the amber eyes, the proud shoulders bred to carry courts, scarred by Solan's pain.

"Luxuros Soleras," Selenia gave a sick grin—a wolf spotting a wounded rabbit. "The heir to the Solar Throne. Two thousand years of trials and we've never had a champion of your lineage for obvious reasons... but it does make one wonder."

Astra, Lunelle's voice rang like a bell. Ameera shifted at the edge of the door, she felt her amber glow flare into a fully stoked fire as she paced. Lux did not move, frozen to his place, a thousand thoughts racing over his skin, drowning him.

"You seem confused," Selenia cooed, stepping closer to Luxuros as Astra pulled her hand from Mirquios's grip.

Lux did not reply.

"No matter," she sighed. "It's settled. You will join your king and the Plutonian prince to compete for Lunelle's hand. Good luck, Commander." Selenia gave the onlooking courtiers a sinister smile. "Now, we were celebrating, were we not?"

She clapped her hands twice, and that's all it took.

The music flooded over the tension in the room, covering the soft gasp Astra finally managed to force out. Selenia disappeared into a glittering mist, a chill rippling over the room.

The Solar Heir.

Here in her court—in her own hands, and she'd never even considered it.

Astra's head swirled, a dozen different outcomes flashing before her, each more disastrous than the next. Lux moved for her, the shock on his face too painful to be manufactured, mirroring her own. A dozen threads snapped at once, Lunelle and Nayson both weaving through uneasy courtiers to get to Astra.

The careful grip Astra had learned to hold around her heart shattered, all of the confusion and angst in the room crashing over her in a vicious myriad of colors.

It sucked the air from her lungs.

"Not here, *Sol'ah.*" Lux gripped her arm tightly as he hauled her into the crisp night air, the Winter wind a fraction of the relief she needed. She gasped for more of it, trying to push out every ounce of crushing surf with icy air, the sting of it giving her something else to concentrate on.

She felt Ameera, Lunelle, Mirquois—each of them trailing behind the commander, but something stopped them from approaching.

She looked at Lux, his chest filled with just as much misery as hers.

"I didn't know," he insisted, his hands wrapping around her, clutching to her shoulders. She wasn't sure which of them was holding the other up. "I never dreamed—"

"I know," she breathed. "I believe you." She reached for his jaw but stopped herself, cognizant that everyone was watching.

"Nayson," Lux called out as he released his grip on Astra, fading back into the hedgerow. Her father's boots stomped against the cobblestones as he rushed to them.

He grabbed his daughter, wrapping her in the kind of embrace a child received when they fell and scraped a knee. When she didn't respond, Nayson looked to Lux.

"Luxuros? Are you well?"

"I–I don't know," Lux murmured, stepping closer to Astra, the release on the Tether one less pull on her grated nerves.

"Astra Leona!" Oestera's voice was tight as she rushed into the gardens. Astra's head snapped toward her, a scarlet flare of anger in her chest settling between them. Their eyes met, her cold irises searching her daughter's flickering gaze.

"We didn't know—"

Oestera stepped forward, tilting her head to the side.

"What have you done?" she asked.

Astra pushed away from her father's grasp, her heart lurching forward.

"What?"

Oestera was frenzied as she spat her questions. "Why did you go to her? What did you offer her?"

"I didn't—"

"Do not lie to me!" Oestera shook as she yelled, her nostrils flaring. "I can feel it! *What did you do?*"

Astra slammed her foot against the pavers between them, all but baring her teeth as she snarled. "I did what you wouldn't!" Her lips curled as hot tears fought to escape. "I protected my sister!"

"You have no idea the kind of evil you just put yourself in leagues with." Oestera rubbed her forehead, a red flush washing over her, no attempts at hiding it. "You just couldn't be patient with me! You couldn't *trust me!* And *you.*" She cast her blazing eyes toward Luxuros. "Was this your plan all along? Infiltrate my court and destroy it from the inside out?"

Astra's eyes locked onto her mother's, a merciless cloud of burgundy rage spiraling against her ribs. Oestera squinted from Lux to Astra, the anger shifting to something much less manageable.

Fear.

Astra winced. "Why would I trust you? On what merit, Mother? You've never once trusted me! Did you think I would just blindly hope that you'll *do something* when you've sat here and let the court rot for decades?" She was yelling, she knew she was out of line, but she couldn't bring her voice back down where it belonged. Her eyes flared, a dangerous warning behind them.

"You've just wrecked a plan thirty years in the making," Oestera all but whispered, tucking any trace of passion safely inside of her.

"What?" Astra looked to her father, who sighed as he hung his head. She asked him, "What does she mean?" He only glanced between the women.

"It doesn't matter," Oestera snapped. "None of it matters now. Whatever you did, it's too late. You made your decision and now we will all burn for it!"

She swept out of the gardens, leaving behind a shocking silence as Nayson followed her.

Astra couldn't breathe, glaring red filling her lungs like blood. She wanted to run, but her feet remained rooted to the moonstone pavers.

"As," Lux rumbled, pulling at her elbow. Smoke built within her, her mind on fire with the possibilities of what Oestera meant.

"Brother," Mirquios said, stepping into the courtyard from the edge of the hall. He placed a hand on Lux's shoulder, exchanging a glance that asked a million questions. Lunelle slipped from the shadows and looped her fingers through her sister's. They stared at each other in silence for a moment.

"Well," Lunelle said, clearing her throat. "This is certainly more complicated." Her eyes fell on Lux's hand wrapped around Astra's arm. "*Much* more complicated."

"We need a new plan," Astra said, her skin flushed pink as she swallowed the bile rising in her throat. "A good one."

"I'll get coffee," Ameera whispered from behind them, darting into the halls.

"The Solar Heir," Lunelle whispered to herself, watching Lux's face carefully. "I suppose you've always had a flair for the dramatic, sister."

Astra managed a shallow snort, her pulse still racing through her body, but that was nothing compared to the torrent within Lux's chest.

"We'll meet you in the Andromeda wing in a moment," Astra said to Lunelle. She listened to their footsteps fade as she tried to sort through the tangled emotions within them and the real, logical sentiments that drove them.

"I told you I would destroy you," Lux whispered, afraid to look her in the eye.

"And I told you," she reached for him, letting her palms rest against both sides of his face. "That I don't care whose blood runs through your veins. I care what runs through your heart. And whatever happens, whatever Selenia or any god throws at us, I am yours Luxuros Soleras." She leaned forward, pressing her lips to his briefly, all too aware that anyone could be watching.

"Now let's go figure out how to keep you from having to marry my sister."

SHE HADN'T BEEN ASLEEP LONG *when she sank into herself, falling fast through a disorienting ribbon of shapes and colors, her feet landing with a thud against the forest floor.*

"Don't panic," a voice said smoothly. Astra's eyes adjusted, taking in the ground covered in silver and gold leaves.

"Alastair?"

His hand reached out and lifted her chin, Alastair's dark eyes finding hers. He pulled Astra to her feet. Black trees groaned and creaked in the Winter air.

"I'm sorry to call on you at such a late hour. But it's important."

"Where are we?"

"You're dreaming," he laughed, waving his fingers beside his face. "Weaver of Dreams, remember?"

"Ah," she breathed as if that explained everything. The night came screaming back to her as she found her footing. "Why are you here? Why am I here? What did you tell Selenia?"

He held up his hands. "Relax! This wasn't my doing. I told you that I could sense you both, Selenia picked up on Luxuros and tortured it out of me." He swept his midnight-black curls away from his neck, a fresh wound climbing the column of his skin below the faded pink scar. "You're in deep shit, but I'm here to help."

She shook her head. "I don't trust you."

"Yes, you do," he smiled, pointing at her chest. "He doesn't." Alastair was right, upsettingly so. "I brought you something, consider it a gesture of goodwill." Alastair reached into his black jacket pocket, producing a thin chain, moonstones tangled in delicate gold threads. "This was Leona's. Selenia kept it. You can use it to summon her from the River of Souls."

"I was going to use the locket—"

He shook his head. "The locket wasn't hers. It will hold her, but it won't bring her to you. She was wearing this when she... appealed to Solan. Selenia kept it as a trophy. It will invoke a more visceral memory in Leona's soul. Thirty years is a long time to forget who you are, Astra."

She reached for it, but he shook his head, stepping behind her. He laid the necklace across her collarbones, fastening it at the back of her neck. "You're not good enough at this to get it back safely," he chuckled.

"A trophy? So she did do it on purpose?"

Alastair sighed, a pained look on his face. "She did. You already saw Leona and Solan's connection, it was powerful—too powerful. That kind of knowledge is threatening to those on divine thrones, Astra. It's why she nominated Luxuros. She can't prove you're Tethered, of course, but she suspects it. The Threader won't tell her—"

"The what?"

Alastair frowned. "Another story for another time. There are rebels in the Court Above, too."

"Why would gods rebel against themselves?"

"Are you not doing the very same?" Alastair chuckled darkly. "I told you, there are powers beyond Selenia—even the gods have gods. And they're fucking awful."

"But why help me now?"

"You're asking all the wrong questions." He frowned, rubbing his wrist. "Wake up, Princess. Your little boyfriend wants to talk."

Alastair reached forward, touching his fingertips to her forehead, and she jerked back through the same swirl of sound and color before her eyes fluttered open.

"I'm easily twice his size," Lux grumbled beside her, his arm draped over her stomach. She laughed, reaching for her neck, the weight of a golden chain pressing into her flesh.

"You're also much more handsome than he is," she assured him. "And a prince, technically. So you have a lot going for you."

Lux winced. They hadn't had much time to talk about where he'd landed with the revelation of his heritage. He reached up and ran his fingers over the moonstones twisted in the necklace.

"Whatever game he's playing, I don't like it."

"I know," she admitted. "My gut says he's on our side."

"Then I suppose it's a good thing I trust you more than I trust him."

She rolled to her side, backing herself against his long frame and moving his arm so that he wrapped around her, enveloping her in his warmth. He ran his fingers along her stomach, enjoying the soft ripples of her skin in the quiet of the night.

"Are you scared?"

"No," Astra lied.

"Wanna try again?"

"Of course I'm scared!"

Lux sighed. "Whatever happens to me tomorrow—"

"I don't want to talk about it right now," she cut him off. "There is nothing to do but endure, Luxuros."

"Understood. But there is something I still want to do." He lingered on the last syllable, fingertips moving from her stomach to her thigh, drawing circles in the bare skin beneath the hem of her nightgown. She wiggled her hips against him, kindling the flame that sizzled between them, but he only laughed in the dark.

"Not that, well, *always* that, but something more important, Astra."

Luxuros sat up and leaned away from her, rifling through his clothes. He returned with a silver blade, the small one he'd used against his own palm outside of Celene.

"What are you—"

Lux's gaze flashed to hers, pulling her to her knees across from him.

431

"You cannot be a Nova unless you're bound to one by blood," he said quietly. "If something goes wrong tomorrow..."

Lux squeezed her hand as her chest ruffled with a fierce rejection of the very idea they wouldn't both return from the Court Below.

He said softly, reverently, "I want to have been the one who bound the mighty Fire Queen."

Astra's eyes found his, a warmth washing over her in pale pinks she wished to stay beneath forever. He leaned forward, holding her palm as he delicately carved a shallow circle beneath her thumb.

"Is that a full Moon?"

Luxuros smirked, drawing a half-Moon shape into his palm. "It's the Sun. I did not think you'd appreciate slicing a dozen rays into your skin."

He held his hand up, a crescent-shaped scar smeared with crimson teardrops. She pressed her palm into his, that same strange alchemy between them grabbing hold and sizzling as they bled into one another.

"Astra Leona Aurellis, Princess of Lunaria, you will fight for the people who serve the courts alongside them, never over them. You will protect peace and reject oppression. You will never reveal your association or another Nova's, as long as we both breathe."

Astra exhaled, squeezing her hand against his. "I will."

Luxuros hauled her into a dizzying kiss that stole her breath and nearly made her forget the reason for the insistence in his touch. His arms wrapped around her back, pressing them into a fiery pillar of smoke and ash.

She whined against his lips, the sound unraveling any threads of logic he'd strung together that evening.

"As," he warned, pulling away from her for a moment before she consumed him again. "Astra," he breathed, laughing into the space between them. He gripped her face between his palms, the Moon-shaped cut already closing over.

"We should *sleep*."

"I'm fine!" she protested.

"We're descending into the Court Below and facing the Goddess of Death in a few hours," he whispered. "We are *not* fine."

Astra returned the laugh, but the sound was hollow, like listening to herself through the wall.

Tomorrow, she'd have to hold up her end of a bargain she believed in her soul to be true, but as she lay in the dark, she wondered just how many more catches the gods had planned.

CHAPTER

FORTY-TWO

"Did you get some sleep last night, darling?"

Astra glanced at her father from their dutiful perches beside Oestera on her throne in the gardens, the Winter winds kicking up as courtiers lined the Lunar Gate. They mingled and sipped on moonshine, dressed in their best, ready to celebrate the triumph of Lunelle and her champion.

Whichever one of them made it back first.

Oestera hadn't looked at Astra once since she arrived. She quite preferred it that way.

Lunelle stood beside her sister, wrapped in silver and black leather, less a queen and more a warrior. The Lunelle she'd seen in Mercury. Astra tried not to shift too much—she had similar vestments beneath her golden gown, but no one needed to know that.

"I slept enough," Astra replied, the lie leaving her lips with ease. She watched as Lux stood against the misty waves of the Rift, his long hair pulled back into a knot at the top of his head, stoic as ever. His eyes scanned the courtiers, landing on her long enough to send a soft shimmer over the Tether.

It took everything in her not to give in to the nerves ravaging her bones, begging her to run—to yank him from the platform and disappear on Riverion's back.

But they had a plan.

It would work.

It had to.

"Welcome everyone!" Oestera rose, stepping forward as heads whipped in her direction. "Thank you so much for joining us on this most sacred night, celebrating centuries of tradition. For our visiting friends, a Lunar heir's trial is not just a feat of strength or endurance, but a symbolic gesture between her and her future partner, demonstrating they are equally matched and equally capable when faced with adversity.

"This morning, in the temple, our champions were separated from their Shadows, the piece of them that holds their darkest qualities, the hardest parts of themselves to look at. The most powerful parts of themselves. They offered their Shadows to the Nether Queen herself in a ceremony few ever undertake—she has them in safekeeping. To complete this rite, they'll have to descend into the Court Below and reunite with their Shadows, through whatever means necessary. They'll rely on their Intuition, their empathy, and their magic to complete their task. The first heir and champion to return will be crowned Queen and King of the Lunar Court."

Oestera looked to her left where Lunelle stared stone-faced, her heart racing. Blood-red fear pounded against her chest, but her face displayed none of it. She'd trained for this day for years.

Mirquios and Arcas flanked Lux on the platform near the Rift, tension rolling off them.

"Whenever you're ready, dear."

Lunelle drew in a deep breath and Astra knew this was her only chance. Everyone would be distracted as they watched Lunelle cross the garden.

She sent her sister a quick message. *See ya in there, Ice Queen.*

Lunelle's smile curved slightly as she took her first step across the crowded garden.

Don't forget to stick your landing, Fire Queen.

Astra slipped away, only Nayson's quick glance clocking her as she darted behind the hedgerow, skirting the withering moonblossoms as she pumped her legs. As she ran, the tension on the Tether pulled with every thump of her feet against the forest floor.

She did not give herself the chance to break or hesitate at the rippling edge as she leaped through the Rift's smokey barrier.

She landed in the cosmic river with a soft twist, her eyes searching for the obsidian thread that would pull her down to the Court Below. She caught sight of it between brilliant blues and violets, wrapping her fingers over the shadowy cord as the rest of the courts whirled by.

By dawn, the thread would be gone again until Spring.

She sailed past the Outer Courts Gate and watched as the Rift darkened into a deep, purple haze consuming the edges. A hundred paces ahead, a black stone gate loomed, absorbing any remaining light from threads that seemed to originate from the gate's gaping mouth.

Or perhaps it was where they ended.

Her feet twitched as she braced herself, a decision she regretted as soon as she hit the slippery sand. She'd expected something more solid. A pair of steady hands reached for her shoulders, righting her as she oriented herself in the murky haze of the Court Below.

Lux hovered behind her, his chest locked down, a reminder that they had no idea what they might encounter here.

She worked to build the same iron wall around her own chest.

"I thought I told you to stick your landing," Lunelle said, glancing around at the desolate stretch of muted gray dunes.

"She never roots into her knees—"

Astra's glare silenced the commander. "Lunelle said it!"

She brushed him off. "Where's the prince?"

"Which one?" Mirquios snorted, eyeing his best friend.

"That one," Lunelle pointed to a blue streak blazing a path into the dune below. "He took off as soon as he landed. Before we go..." She reached for Astra's forearm, pulling her close and searching her eyes. "Just in case..."

"Do not 'just in case' me!" She pulled her arm away from Lunelle, frowning. "I need you on your queen shit, Lu, not your just-in-case shit."

"Astra," she said sternly, her jaw set as the sands beneath them whipped around their calves. "If anything happens to me, keep going. I mean it, don't come back for me."

"Lunelle!" she groaned.

"Promise me," she said, the desperation in her chest so intense she could hardly breathe.

"No!" A vision of Lunelle's coronation robes resting on Astra's shoulders lit up her mind, sending a wave of agony over her muscles.

"Promise," she insisted, her eyes locked on Astra's. "The rebellion will keep spinning without me, but without you..."

At once, Astra understood. She *was* being a queen.

Astra nodded, the fear in her sister's voice enough to stop

her arguing. She shoved the flash of the coronation robes to the back of her mind.

"I promise."

Lunelle slipped back into Mirquios's waiting arms, one last embrace before they plunged into whatever faced them at the foot of the dunes.

"I'll see you on the other side," he said to Luxuros, clapping him on the shoulder. Mirq gave Astra one more look, one last moment of silence before they turned and stared down the steep slope of the gray dune before them, stretching into oblivion.

He laughed, "You ready to burn it down, Fire Queen?"

Astra lifted an eyebrow and smirked.

"How long have you been waiting to say that?"

The king shook his head and in two long strides, he was over the edge of the dune, his powerful legs carrying him down into the mire. A blur of leather and might, Lunelle's silver hair was a streak of starlight behind him.

"Well, shit, I guess we're off then," Astra muttered to Lux.

"You have the locket?" he asked.

She touched her neck, chains intertwining together. "Yep."

"Blade?"

"Three," she smirked. She pointed to the tight spiral of curls at the nape of her neck, held with a golden crescent Moon.

Lux's eyes swelled with an odd mix of fear and pride as he watched her adjust the pin.

"Just say it, Commander."

"Say what?"

"That under all that fear and loathing, there's a small part of you that actually believes we can do this." A slow grin cracked across his worried face, that silver-speckled rosy hue spreading through his veins.

He held up his fingers, a minuscule slip of space between them.

"A very small part of me."

"I'll take it." She crashed into him, stealing one final kiss before they went their separate ways. "Go get that Shadow, Commander. You're not as handsome without it."

"Don't fuck it up, Fire Queen," he whispered, his lips twisting into a smile against her. If she stayed a moment longer, she'd never find the courage to leave him.

She pushed her legs forward, stumbling over the crest of the dune and urging her ankles to steady as she skidded down the soft silt to the bottom. She refused to look back over her shoulder, trusting the tension in her gut to be enough of an assurance that he was still safe.

As her feet hit the desolate plane at the base of the dune, she spun to get her bearings. If the map Ameera sketched last night was accurate, the River of Souls was directly to the West of the tangled forest they'd need to pull their Shadows from. She jogged across the cracked ground, her lungs filling with plumes of dust.

Pace herself. That's what Lux had drilled into her head all night. If she exhausted herself just getting to Leona, she'd never make it out of any altercation that may pop up.

She carved a path through a colorless valley, gray stone rising over her head in two fearful towers, blocking what little light broke through the clouded sky. Everything was silent save for a whistling breeze cutting through the canyon walls, bouncing from side to side, and peeling the strands of hair escaping from her bun off her neck.

It took her an eternity to break through the canyon. The cracks of the dirt ground gave way to a pebble beach, each charcoal shard crunching beneath her leather boots as she skirted behind a line of bleached flora along the shore.

The whisper of hushed waters slipping along the bank tickled her ears long before it came into view. Under the rushing of the water ran a low hum, like walking into a ballroom before the music started, the gossip rising above the heads of the guests.

Voices, she realized.

Souls.

She climbed the last hill of pebbles and sand and dropped over the top, carefully tiptoeing her way to the riverbank. The water swirled, black as ink, as it rushed through the Court Below. It was wider than she could see across, rippling and winding through the lifeless hills like a serpent.

The moment her feet hit the shore, she felt them.

All of them.

Thousands. Millions, more likely, slipping by every second on an endless journey out to some sea somewhere, folded between foamy rivulets. Some heavy, some angry, some bitter.

Some all three.

Others were excited about the possibilities of wherever they were going. Her eyes stung with the welling of emotions. She closed them, trying to focus.

She found the space inside of her, that peaceful hot spring brimming with color and life ready to pour into. She channeled the water, letting it flow through her fingertips and pushing the misery and fear and awe into it, giving a void to fill.

She could breathe.

She could concentrate.

She moved forward, edging closer and closer to the muddy waterline, the leather of her boots sliding along the pebbles as they dissolved into sand.

How exactly did one pluck an individual soul from a river of millions?

She reached out her hand, fingers trembling as her skin

broke the water's surface. Much colder than she was ready for, it sent a shock through her arm and down her spine. The souls slipped around her skin, sparkling against her, gripping her hand, begging her to pull them out. They clamored like fish to a lure, shimmery shadows hoping to hitch a ride back to the Living Courts.

She drew her hand back as if she'd been bitten.

The necklace. She shook her head, clearing it of the quiet hissing pleas running under the current.

Save me, pick me, release me.

She reached around her neck and searched for the cold chain, pulling it from the depths of her vest. Even the glint of the moonstones were dull in the Court Below as if no light reflected in their facets at all. For the first time, she felt a true chill of fear run down her arms, the danger of what she was trying to accomplish unsettling her stomach.

"Leona Aurellis," she called out, holding the necklace above the waters. "Come claim what was taken from you!"

She didn't know what she expected to happen, but the silence that followed wasn't it.

"Please?" she asked, feeling as stupid as she sounded.

But then, midway across the babbling waters, she saw it. She saw her.

Rising from the depths, her wild hair fell into shadowy ribbons as she materialized on the beach. Leona's faded face stared through Astra as she glided along the shoreline.

"Who calls me?"

The voice was not alone. It echoed against all the other tenors beneath her, stringing them into one dissonant chord.

"You don't recognize your own namesake?"

Something about Leona's barely-there countenance sank, twisted in on itself.

"Astra," she murmured, her voice softer, calmer.

"Sorry to bother you," she managed, dangling the necklace in front of her. Her fingertips wrapped weakly around the gold, trembling.

The shadow slinked closer to Astra, her feet never leaving the surface of the water. "I see you've been conspiring with my mother."

"Would you like it back?"

"No," she said, bowing her head. "Keep it. Whatever she traded you for must be worth the trip here."

"I don't want it."

"You will, darling. Oestera... is she..." She let the question linger, her voice so similar to her mother's, but curved where Oestera's angled.

"She doesn't know I've come."

"Of course, she doesn't. She'd kill you first just for thinking of putting yourself in such danger."

"Might have been a more efficient way to speak with you." She stretched her legs, aching from slipping against the crumbling dunes.

"You're so much like her," Leona hummed, the admiration rolling off her form.

"That's what I keep hearing," she chuckled.

"You may have inherited my name and fiery mane, but the way your eyes take me in, the way your lips fall into a tight line, it's like I'm looking at her again." Something in Leona's velvety chorus of voices caught, and she stopped.

It all rushed out, everything that lingered within her spirit. She may not have blood and muscle and bone to store it, but the pain was still there. Perhaps it never dies, then—the love we carry when we're living. How unfathomably horrifying, to be haunted by life even when you're haunting in death.

"It's not so bad," Leona mused.

"You can—"

"You, yes." Her shadowy head nodded. "Not everyone. You wear it all right there on your precious face, don't you?"

"It's frequently cited as an issue of mine, yes."

"It's a reminder of the love I had for her," she continued, ignoring Astra's self-deprecation. "That before I was here, bound to an eternity of slipping away, I was her sister. Her soulmate. The pain, it's only a whisper now."

Astra swallowed, Lunelle's silver eyes searing in her mind. "I see."

"Why are you here, Astra?"

She shook off the dread pooling in her fingertips and drew in a short breath, the truth leaping into her throat that she'd been trying to talk herself out of since it occurred to her last night.

"I'm here to capture Selenia's Shadow."

FORTY-THREE

I f a soul could balk, Leona's did.

"What?"

"She traded it to the Nether Queen, in exchange for something. We don't know what, but we believe Selenia intentionally led you all astray about the results of severing a tie," Astra explained.

Leona wilted before her. "I don't understand. Solan attacked the court, he—"

"The reaction after the release wasn't planned, Leona. It wasn't an attack. It was pain. The Flare was Solan's grief over what he cost you."

Leona's shadow turned away, caving in on itself.

"He's never recovered, Leona. They call him the Mad King. He's been alone all these years, festering in Solaris."

"How do you know this?"

"I went within, I went back to The Flare. Selenia saw me and she brought me to the Court Above to make a deal. She sent me down here to bring your soul back to her, she said she wanted to clear the air between you so you could Ascend, but I think she has an ulterior motive."

"She doesn't want you to have access to me," Leona whispered. "If she knows you can go within, she knows that you can find me, or any other Shadow Goddess. She'll take my soul and she'll destroy it, Astra. She doesn't want me to be able to train you."

Astra's heart drummed against her ribs, the words falling off her so casually. "A what? What do you mean 'train' me?"

"In some ways I already have. Every time you read someone's emotions or illuminate something... every time you move shadows or cast a spell, that knowledge flows in your blood—"

"Hold on," she gasped. "Move shadows? Cast a spell?"

Leona frowned. "Are you not casting?"

"No! What did you say about the shadows?"

Leona suppressed a sigh. "Your mother really stuck to the bans then?"

"Everything. We aren't allowed to practice any of it. I just thought I was extremely intuitive. We chalked the sunlight up to The Flare."

Leona drew closer. "You are a Shadow Goddess, Astra. One in a line of hundreds of generations of women who have carried on the tradition. You were blessed and cursed by the same ancient magic that sent me here."

"I am an intuit—"

"That's not a thing," Leona snorted. "But it *is* a convenient explanation for what you must be able to do without even trying. They fear you. They've always feared us. You were chosen by the Mother. Did you say sunlight?"

"Yes, we thought it was fire, but Ehlaria said it was sunlight!"

"Ah," Leona whispered, chewing on her bottom lip. "So you Tethered to a Solarian, then?"

"How did you—"

"How do you think I got into this mess, dear girl? When I Tethered to Solan and inherited his light, the clock started ticking with the Court Above."

Astra touched her forehead, a bead of sweat rolling down her skin as she tried to take this in.

"My gods," she sighed. "But I've always had the sunlight, I didn't Tether to Luxuros until—"

"Luxuros Soleras?" Her wispy fingers tightened into fists.

Astra winced. "We didn't know who he was. He was thrown into the Rift during The Flare... where Mother and I both touched him," she said, realizing now that they'd always been Tethered in some way, then. "He's been training me, but we didn't know anything about Shadows or casting."

She shook her head. "He wouldn't. Even an experienced Light God only has so much to teach you."

"A Light—"

"The Solar and Lunar Courts are not what they seem, Astra. You need to speak with your mother. She knows all of this!"

Astra clenched her jaw. "She never speaks of any of it, Leona. It's too painful for her. I think she blames herself for not stopping you."

Leona's shoulders sank. "It was all my fault, not Oestera's. But of course, she blames herself. She always kept me on a pedestal."

"You didn't cause it, Leona, we're sure of it. I saw it with my own eyes, Selenia lied to all of you!"

"Perhaps I could still make my Ascent then." Her eyes lit with the notion. "I don't understand why she would do this to me?"

"We aren't sure, either. We've only been able to piece together a small part of the story. But she did indeed bargain her own shadow with the Nether Queen in exchange for something, and we think my mother knows."

"Oestera would never betray me," Leona snapped.

"She certainly is covering *something* up."

She shook her formless head. "The only secrets Oestera would keep are to ensure your safety, Astra. Oestera's loyalty is the only thing I've ever been certain of."

Astra's chest tightened, immediately rejecting the notion her mother did anything out of protection. "I didn't come here to fight with you, Leona. I need to know what Selenia got in exchange from the Nether Queen, and the only way to do that is to get her shadow."

"You could always ask the Nether Queen yourself," Leona said. "She won't be too fond of you barging in here with demands, but sometimes Luciela surprises us."

Astra ignored her suggestion, wholly uninterested in tangling herself up in any other ancient being's strike list.

"If I captured Selenia's shadow instead... if I used the locket to hold it hostage and destroy it... what would happen?"

If Leona could have frowned, she would have. "I don't know what kind of deal she made with Luciela, but she definitely wouldn't be able to Ascend again."

Astra flashed her a smile, feeling in her soul that she was making the right choice as the plan came together in her mind.

"I have to go. This has been incredibly helpful—is it possible to come back to visit you?"

"Not here," Leona sighed. "Too many eyes. But we can make arrangements."

"I would very much like that, Leona."

"Astra? When you figure out why she did it... how she could do it... find me and tell me."

She felt the pain again, unbearable to hold.

"I will," she promised.

SHE BEGAN the journey back through the canyons, her legs aching from balancing in the gray silt as it shifted under her boots. When she stumbled back onto the set of their diverging footprints, she followed four strands of boots back over a dune and to the edge of the Shadowlands.

Gnarled trees wept over each other, tangling their branches into harrowing tunnels and murky pits. The air was so still within the black leaves she could hear her heartbeat as she stepped over fallen logs. Lux was close. She could feel the pull in her chest loosen as she made her way toward the forest's center.

A high-pitched cry yanked her attention from Lux.

Lunelle?

Over here!

She followed the trail of her sister's wild emotions, Mirquios's own signature blend of cerulean calm fading into angst and stress as she got farther into the twisted woods.

"On your left!" he called out, Lunelle grunting as something came into contact with someone.

"They don't need your help," a slithering voice hissed in her ear. "At least not yet."

Astra spun, face to face with a black serpent, onyx scales towering over her head as she wound around the hollowed-out log of a fallen tree.

"You don't like this form, then," she said. "So be it." A fog of deep black shadow twirled around her and in the serpent's place stood who could only be the Nether Queen.

Her cold eyes fell over Astra, black as night set in sickly gray skin, deep charcoal waves of hair slipping over her back. She was clothed in shadows, an ink-black dress rippling into waves of night sky at the hem. Her skeletal hands bore black diamond rings on all but her thumbs.

"Astra Leona," she said, stepping closer and washing her in an insufferable cold. "What in the Nether are you doing here?"

She could lie, but something told her the Nether Queen was not one for asking questions she didn't already know the answers to. "Selenia sent me to retrieve Leona's soul."

Luciela's lips curled, amused at her explanation. "Oh, is that all?"

"It's why I'm here." *Still not a lie.*

"Hmm." She paced back and forth, her skirts whispering awful secrets against the dusty forest floor. "Take what you came here for, and nothing else." She shrugged. "I'm curious to see what you do with it."

"That's it?"

"What, you want the Goddess of Death to pay more attention to you? It's the Solstice, I have celebrations to attend."

"Oh," Astra sighed, relieved.

"Besides, who am I to get in the way of the age-old Lunar Queen, Solar King Tether cycle? It's always an interesting cleanup for us down here. Gives us something to talk about."

"I hate to disappoint you," Astra grumbled. "But neither Lux nor I sit on thrones. We'll only bore you."

She twisted back, her skirt swirling in an unholy wave of grief and sorrow. "I suppose we'll see. I do have one question for you." She slinked closer, running a frail finger across Astra's face and tilting her chin toward the muted light filtering through the trees.

"Why risk it at all? You know the stories. You've seen where your dearly Descended aunt ended up, you've seen what the Tether did to your rotten grandmother—"

"Selenia?"

Her brow sloped, forming an amused arch. "She doesn't know," she said to the Shadows that clung to her. "I *love* that I get to tell you this." Luciela tapped Astra's forehead with a shriveled finger, sending her falling backward through a sulfuric mist.

"You're a fool," Luciela mocked, resting against a throne built from the spines of who knows how many creatures.

Astra stood at the edge of a dull palace, the walls carved from onyx stone. In the middle of the room, just a breath away from Luciela, stood Selenia. No dark ring around her, no chill, but the silver glimmer of a newly Ascended goddess.

"I did not ask for your opinion. I asked if it could be done."

"Anything can be done for a price, Selenia."

Her face contorted, lips pursing as she weighed what she was willing to give up. Something inside her broke, a violet pooling in her chest drowning her. "Name it."

Luciela swallowed, her appetite for tragedy piqued. "Your Shadow."

"And you can promise it will work?"

"Hmm." She glanced from the window to her right, eyes falling on glass etchings in runes Astra didn't recognize. "I guess you'll just have to trust me."

"Fine." Selenia did not hesitate. Whatever she asked for, she needed desperately. Luciela lifted a hand, rotating her palm toward the ornate carvings in the ceiling. By the time she stopped moving, a silver dagger rested against her decaying skin.

"It's a shadow blade. Only one in the realms. I need it back when you're done," she said flatly, as if she wasn't handing over a one-of-a-kind treasure. "He has to do it, though. The Solar God must choose heart over head for once."

Luciela's eyes flashed toward a massive sphere floating above an arched column at the back of the room. It seemed to buzz with a steady rhythm.

"You best be on your way, Selenia. The gates will close soon, and without your Shadow, you'll no longer be welcome in the Court Below. I'll take the shadow blade back in the Spring if we have a deal?"

Selenia nodded, opening her mouth to reply but a scream bounced off the hall as she crumbled to her knees. Black raced from her veins toward Luciela's outstretched hand.

"Sorry, I should have warned you. Hurts like a bitch." Luciela drew the last dregs of the Shadow from her, Selenia's chest heaving. "Off you go!"

Selenia rose, her face gaunt, a dark ring gleaming in the low light around her. The icy chill she'd come to associate with her rippled through Astra as she left the room.

Astra blinked, returning to the Court Below.

"Why did she do it? Why tear Leona and Solan apart?" Astra asked, stepping back into the Court Below's forest.

"Oh," Luciela winced. "I suppose I dropped you too far into the conversation. I've had a few cocktails. You understand. *That* trade was not to sever the Tether from your aunt's soul, but Selenia's."

"Selenia!"

"It's a tragic story. It always is," Luciela chuckled, delight floating on the dark notes. "Your grandmother was *not* the first-born heir to the throne, a burden I know you're intimately familiar with. She had a sister, Athene. They were close as girls, but Selenia was a bit of a rebel at heart. Runs in the family, I suppose. She knew her Shadow Goddess abilities were off-limits, but curiosity is a damned good high, Astra. Selenia was working with the shadows along the edge of the Empyrean. She didn't know Athene was in the water. She was just fifteen when she drowned, and Selenia never recovered from the guilt.

"Athene was a bit of a bore. She was hardly here before she Ascended, didn't come to a single one of my dinner parties. I suppose the one benefit to dying young is it's much easier to confront your moral failings when you don't live very long." Luciela twisted as she spoke, pacing before Astra. "Athene took her place in the Court Above, sitting beside the Solar God, Lucian, on the Lunar Throne above. Well, you can imagine, two powerful, attractive ethereal beings don't spend that much time ruining everyone's lives together and avoid falling in love.

"But it wasn't Fated. No Tether blossomed, though Athene waited decades with a pathetic hope in her heart. And then your dear grandmother made her Descent. Now Selenia *loves* a good party. It took her ages to embrace her Shadow and I was almost sad to see her go. But don't tell her that.

"She strode through those gilded gates Above and embraced her long-lost sister. Their reunion was the stuff of poetry, truly. Until Selenia met Lucian, and their chests caved in and souls brushed one another, blah, blah, blah. You did it, you know what it's all about. Selenia couldn't take the guilt. She'd drowned her sister in one life and was well on her way to doing it in the next. So she came to me and she made a deal, one that I'm sure she regrets to this day."

Luciela leaned back, folding her arms and touching her hand to her chin.

"You look like you need a second. Please don't vomit in the woods, it attracts the *worst* sorts of creatures."

Astra *was* considering vomiting as a way to process all of this. She took a sharp breath, trying to shift the colors within her chest from an overwhelmed bouquet of dying roses to something more neutral, but it was pointless.

"We haven't even gotten to the most interesting part. There are powers that even the Court Above answers to, Astra. There is a throne that sits vacant and has for millennia because every Ascended Lunar and Solar god and goddess is the same in the end—*selfish*.

"The Divine Throne can only be claimed by one being who holds both Light and Shadow, Lunar and Solar. You can't hold both unless you find your missing half and Tether, which plenty of you lovelorn idiots have as of late, but I can assure you that is a new development. You lot *love* to murder each other before you can even let the Tether form. But not *one* of you has ever been able to give up power in the end for the other.

"The throne would hold power over every court—including the gods and goddesses—but because every single one of you morons thinks you're better suited for it than your godsdamned soulmate, you fuck it up. Generation after generation. It's exhausting.

"Leona and Solan were the closest anyone ever came, and Lucian saw that his son was weak. He knew he'd give everything up for Leona. So he took the only action he could—prevent them from ever uniting again. He convinced Selenia to trick them, and without her Shadow she didn't have much of a choice. All he had to do was smite her and she'd be stuck with me for eternity. She kept my shadow blade, an artifact I'm still missing, by the way, and they made Leona think it was her fault. That her selfishness cost thousands of lives. They knew she'd never face it."

Astra's stomach whirled. "Why are you telling me all of this?"

"Because you should know that you have a choice. You already saw it, didn't you? Both thrones, calling your name."

She shook her head, desperate not to let the contents of her stomach escape. "I don't want it."

"Please," the Nether Queen continued. "You can lie to yourself all you want, but not to me. I know you feckless half-humans. Your selfish hearts always win out in the end."

Astra shook her head again. "No."

"I could give it to you right now if you wanted. It wouldn't take much for me to keep him here, trapped in the Court Below. All you'd have to do is waltz right into that throne room whenever you shed that mortal coil of yours... you'd rule it all, Astra. You could finally create the exact kind of world you've been working toward, with the snap of a finger."

Astra held her frigid stare as Luciela spoke, her bones rattling within her, though she hoped Luciela didn't see it.

"Say the word, Fire Queen, and I'll throw him into the River of Souls right now. Fuck, from what I've heard, he'd throw himself into it willingly. He'd want you to take it."

Astra glared. "No, Luciela."

Luciela gagged. "You hate to see a powerful woman give it all up for a man," she said, holding up her hand. "But I will warn you, Astra, what is for you will always find you, in this life or another."

"Astra!" Lunelle's scream ripped her away from Luciela's torturous game, her stilled heart bursting to life with fear as her head snapped in their direction.

"I'll see you again, Fire Queen. When you change your mind, you know where to find me."

Astra barely heard her, adrenaline surging at the thought that Lunelle might be hurt. Another sweep of shadows through the trees wrapped around the Nether Queen, transforming her this time into a slinking black cat, long and lean.

Lunelle screamed again and when Astra turned back around, the Nether Queen was gone.

FORTY-FOUR

Astra leaped over the decaying logs between them, following the muffled sounds of screams and Mirquios in pain.

When she burst through the trees into the clearing, Lunelle and Mirquios were back to back, two shadows dancing amongst them, blurs of smoke and fury.

"He's hurt," Lunelle screeched at her sister. Astra scanned over Mirquios, looking for the source of his injury as he dodged his shadow again.

She yelled to Lunelle, cornered by a transparent version of herself. "Did they tell you how to get them back?"

Where are you, Lux beamed, his voice heavy, tired.

In the forest, Mirquios is hurt. They're battling their shadows, where are you?

Coming.

"Tula said something about listening to them, I don't know!" Mirquios yelled as he dodged another swing.

"You have to embrace them!" Lux called out from the treeline. He held a squirming blue prince over his shoulder. "You have to embrace them!"

"The more you fight, the harder it is!" Arcas screeched from over Lux's shoulder.

There, Astra saw it as Mirquios made another swift spin around his shadow. A gash in his leg, from knee to hip, bright red blood spilling from his wound. Lunelle was the first to stop dodging and slicing at her shadow, staring at it in the gnarled forest, the silence deafening save for Arcas's lithe body landing with a thud on the forest floor as Lux tossed him off his back.

Lunelle reached forward, wrapping her hands around the silky black figure, the commotion ending immediately. She turned, lifting her hands, the arms of the shadow following her exactly as they should. Mirquios mimicked her movements, screaming in the process.

Lunelle gripped his shoulder in concern. "Your leg?"

"No! You could have warned me they'd say such horrifying shit," he grunted, heaving.

"Mine wasn't *that* bad," Lunelle shrugged. "But noted for you." She patted him on the back as he stretched, shivering at whatever his Shadow whispered as they reunited.

"What happened to your leg?" Astra pointed at the injury. "What happened to Pluto?"

"Shadow," Mirquios sighed, sitting on the ground and examining the wound.

"Bastard attacked me," Lux said.

Astra turned to Arcas. "You know you don't have to be the *only* champion back, just the first, right? We aren't barbarians."

Arcas pushed himself from the ground, his deep eyes flashing wildly between each of them. "I don't know! I don't know what's going on. I didn't even *want* to be here, okay? The queen said that if I came back to the Lunar Court, and pretended to court the princess, she'd pay off Pluto's debts and help us manage our rebellion! I wasn't even supposed to make it to the trial! She was supposed to announce at the ball that Lunelle is capable of ruling the court without a man and pass the crown to her unwed but then that goddess changed all the rules and the commander somehow got roped into this and I wasn't trying to attack you!"

He drew in a heaving breath as he turned to Lux.

"I wasn't expecting to run into you on the other side of the woods, I can't track you in here, the Tethers are *really* hard to see in such a dull environment."

"What did you just say?" Lunelle huffed as she marched toward Arcas, her chest barely touching his as he backed away.

Arcas frowned and closed his eyes. "Which part, Princess?"

Astra groaned, rubbing the bridge of her nose, sure that her head was about to cave in from all the new information she'd learned in the last fifteen minutes.

"Oh, I don't know, Arcas, maybe the part where you can *see* Tethers? Have you known about the king and I this entire time?"

Arcas dropped his eyes to the forest floor. "Yes. I'm sorry. My mother was Venusian, they can see Tethers."

Astra's cheeks caught fire. "All... Venusians? And all... Tethers?"

His navy eyes briefly flitted from the flora below to hers before finding anywhere else to look.

"Yes."

"Oh my gods," she gasped, Lux's hand reflexively reaching for her hip. How long had Ameera been sitting on her secret?

Lunelle twisted in her boots, her lips parted in pure rage. "Are you—Astra? Are you two... *Tethered?*"

Astra sighed. "I think there is much more pressing information that Arcas just dropped on us—"

"Please!" Mirquios cried from the ground. "Please, just tell her so I can have some *peace!*"

"You knew?" Lunelle dropped to the ground, kneeling across from him.

"I suspected," he muttered, pulling at the sliced fabric of his pants. "They weren't subtle."

"Well, we *knew* they were sleeping together, but you never once thought to tell me you thought they were Tethered?"

Mirquios winced. "We've had a lot on our plate, dear. I assumed Astra would tell you!"

They both turned to Astra, her face as red as her hair, surely. "Again, bigger things to talk about right now—"

Lunelle forged ahead. "All that stress, all that heartache, all the worry that my little sister must sacrifice her happiness for me was for *nothing?*" She turned to Arcas, focusing her anger on him.

Arcas pointed to himself. "Oh, we're mad at me again?"

"I think we're just confused." Astra tried to smooth things over. "It's been a hard few months and we don't exactly know who to trust right now."

Lunelle frowned, her shoulders dropping. "It really has. Gods, Astra. I wish you had told me how dire this was for you, too. I put too much pressure on you!"

"No, no, Lu. You've taken the brunt of the responsibility your whole life. I was happy to do this for you! I swear it—"

"As?" Lux stepped into the space between them.

Astra clicked her tongue, still not done making her point. "Yes, Luxuros, what is it?"

"We've got about half an hour before the gate closes. Do you think you and your sister can hash this out when we're not at risk of getting sealed into the Court Below for three months?"

Lunelle sprang into action. "Mirquios is hurt. We need to get him back, but there's no way he should walk on that leg."

"I can help," Arcas said. "Least I can do, I suppose."

Astra's brows furrowed as she watched Arcas's thin limbs reach for Mirquios. She turned to Lux.

"I got him," he said, pushing past the Plutonian prince. "You good to get what you came for?"

Astra nodded. "Just get him back safely."

"Wait for us at the gate," Lunelle said.

"Lunelle, no. Go with Mirq," she sighed. "I can do this!"

Lunelle placed a quick kiss on the king's cheek.

"Not a chance, As. We're doing this together."

I'll see you on the other side, Sol'ah, Lux beamed as he dragged Mirquios away, Arcas doing his best to help.

Astra turned to her sister, her eyes sparkling even in the blunted light of the Court Below.

"Let's do this."

Astra fished the locket out of her vest, the chain cool against her hand as they stood in a clearing a few hundred paces away.

It felt like the right place to be, and summoning a Shadow couldn't be all that different from summoning a Soul, could it?

"Selenia Aurellis," Astra said, her voice shaking. She held the locket in one hand and Lunelle's in the other. "We've come to return you to your rightful place."

She closed her eyes, listening for anything in the dead silence. A black flash whipped through sticks and trees, racing across the clearing, sending her a step back as she recoiled.

Lunelle watched it race by, circling the meadow. "Steady, As. Selenia," Lunelle announced, directing her energy at the shadow that edged back into the forest. "We've come to claim you!"

Astra held out the locket again, bracing herself for impact when she ran through again. She felt her Shadow before she saw it this time, the temperature dropping ahead of her arrival, blasting through the treeline. She held the locket high, drawing her in, picturing the Shadow slipping into the silver locket in her mind before she charged again.

Lunelle closed her eyes, too, afraid to watch as Selenia darted toward them. The Shadow hit Astra's hand full force. Her arm screamed at the pain, but when she opened her eyes, the locket swung mid-air, closed shut, freezing over in icy condensation.

"Did... did we do it?" Lunelle's jaw clenched in the silence of the forest.

"I think so?" Astra fastened the locket around her neck, the metal like a block of ice against her skin.

"That seemed too easy," Lunelle mused.

Astra laughed. "I'll take easy on this end. It's what comes next that's going to be impossible."

Lunelle sighed as she turned to walk, watching the trees ahead as she led them through the gnarled branches. "What do you think Arcas was talking about?"

"I'm not sure, Lu, but the Nether Queen... she told me that Selenia was Tethered to the Solar God, Lucian. And that she severed it after trading her shadow to Luciela for a shadow diamond dagger—the same one I saw Solan use with Leona."

Lunelle jumped over a larger log, the bark peeling into crumbling layers that snapped as she passed and turned to dust in the air. "Mother asked me to wait at the Lunar Gate before I came through. She said she'd signal me."

A chill ran over Astra's spine. "Did you tell her what we planned?"

"No," she shook her head. "This was before. In Pluto. She said that she would be waiting beside the gate and that no matter what, I wasn't to come through until she reached for me. At the time, I thought maybe it was a ritual thing, a symbolic gesture. But now I don't know what to believe."

The edge of the forest came into view, more sand and dust and flat light stretched beyond the trees. Something snapped behind them.

"What was that?" Astra asked, twisting to watch for it. A spark flickered in her fingertips, ready to strike.

Lunelle walked faster, pulling her along, moving from her hand to her wrist when she felt the heat. Astra jogged to keep up with her, another snap of a tree limb driving them forward.

"We're almost out, As. Just keep going!" Lunelle increased her speed again as they heard more crackling footsteps moving quickly. As they broke through the trees, Astra turned, spotting a massive black cat slinking in figure eights between the tangled trunks.

She swore it smiled.

"Let's hustle, Fire and Ice!" Lux cupped his hands around his mouth from the top of the dune, the onyx gate rising behind him.

"For the record, I really like the version of you the commander brings out. Mortal enemy thing aside. What are you planning on doing about that?" Lunelle said between ragged breaths as they pumped their legs over the sliding sand.

"Small detail," Astra laughed, her lungs burning.

They rounded the top of the dune, stopping for a moment to catch their breath as Lux tied a torn shred of his sleeve around Mirq's thigh.

"Well," Mirquios said as he hobbled against Lux. "Are we ready to take down a Lunar Goddess?"

Lunelle slipped his arm around Astra's shoulders.

"*We* are. *You* are going straight to the infirmary."

Lux held out a hand, dragging Astra into the Rift, the chill on her neck somehow even colder as they passed through the Lunar Gate.

Astra's knees absorbed the impact, stinging as she brushed herself off, confused at the strange mix of silence and nerves that greeted them. Someone pulled Lux's arms away from her, a dark sleeve weaving around her elbow.

"Evening." Alastair ducked his head in a stilted greeting. Astra's eyes searched the garden, hundreds of faces watching her every step.

"The Lunar Goddess would like a word."

FORTY-FIVE

"Alastair," Astra gasped.

"It's fine," he assured her, pulling her forward through the frozen crowd. Their faces fell into various shades of confusion and stress. Scarlet tensions fluttered off their heartbeats, collectively throwing her into a spiral.

Are you okay? Ameera beamed, she stood against the hedges, an ashen weight on her chest.

Confused, but okay. Why is Alastair here? What happened?

Ameera tilted her head toward the center of the gardens where Oestera's throne was now occupied by Selenia. Her mother stood dutifully beside the Ascended goddess, shoulders back.

Selenia showed up shortly after you left.

Where are Lunelle and Mirquios?

They haven't made it back yet, Ameera said, confusion settling over her face.

They left when I did. That's not possible!

Lunelle's words echoed in Astra's mind—Oestera had told her to wait.

Her fear was showing. She knew it. She pictured herself sitting on the edge of the canyon in her father's painting, her feet dangling over the edge, a bronze hand on her knee. The court's inner voices slowed, the emotions running low enough for her to adjust, for her anxiety to level out.

"My darling Astra," Selenia sang from her perch. "How was your Descent?"

Oestera and Nayson both watched their daughter, analyzing every line in her face. Every twitch of her lips.

She set her jaw, searching for a word to encapsulate what she hoped would be the wildest evening of her life. "Informative."

Alastair left her before Selenia, fading into the crowd toward Lux if the pull on the Tether was a tell as he moved away. Behind her, three thuds and a soft gasp from the crowd announced the arrival of Lunelle, Mirquios, and Arcas.

"Oh, that *is* interesting," Selenia grinned.

"Get him help," Astra cried, gesturing to Mirquios, who collapsed as Lunelle lost her grip on him. Ameera darted from the crowd, several maidens trailing her with various bags and herbs. Lunelle kneeled beside him. Arcas hovered behind her, looking nearly ready to pass out himself.

"What happened?" Oestera asked, but Selenia held her hand up in what seemed to be a favorite maneuver of hers.

"I believe you have something of mine," she said, her eyes fixed on her granddaughter. Astra nodded, reaching around her neck and freeing the clasp on the locket, letting it dangle between them. Selenia pursed her lips.

"I'll admit, I'm impressed, Astra. I thought you'd end up in the Court Below permanently."

"Take it," she spat, tossing the locket onto the stone pavers between them. She stepped back, desperate to get to Lunelle, to make sure they were okay.

"Don't scurry off now," Selenia cackled. "You'll miss all the fun."

"I'm maxed out on fun for the day," Astra argued.

Oestera's eyebrow twitched.

"I hope you can find some capacity, my darling girl. It would be a shame for the Lunar Queen to miss her own coronation."

A ring of whispers encircled Astra, eyes widening as the breath left her lungs.

"Wh—"

"You *were* the first Lunar Heir to return from the Court Below, no?"

Astra shook her head, no words forming on her lips. Her stomach dropped, and she thought for the second time that night she would vomit in front of everyone as she felt the Tether in her chest loosen, Lux moving closer through the crowd.

"And yes! There's our first champion. Luxuros!"

"I did not—" She gasped for a breath. "I did not participate in the Shadow Ceremony!"

"You didn't?" Selenia stood from the throne, her deep violet gown falling into a pool of night sky at her feet. "Because I *distinctly* recall dear Alastair informing me you'd confronted the very worst of yourself in a dream. The call to power you can't give up. You touched the Lunar Throne, and yet you did not stay. And this evening, surely you encountered the Nether Queen in your travels, yes?"

Astra stared at her, a crimson flare pushing a breath into her lungs.

"If I know Luciela," she said as she clicked her tongue. "She would have made you an offer you considered taking, hmm?"

Astra's vision blurred.

"If you were a smarter woman, you would have taken it."

Astra backed away from her, the blood in her ears soaring to new heights, the buzz from the panic swallowing her from the inside out. Not only her panic. Lunelle's. Nayson's. Lux's. Every courtier who watched, slack-jawed.

It was too much.

"It's all you've ever wanted, hmm? Power. Even in small doses. A curse of the spare, I'm afraid. But you resisted, both times, didn't you? You *know* your Shadow, Astra Leona, and you wear her *very* well."

Her eyes slid to Lux, his gaze frantic, unsure if they were running or staying.

"Lest I forget! Our Lunar King!" Selenia gestured for Lux to approach her as she reached for Astra's hands, pulling them together. "What a pair you two make, don't you think, Oestera?"

"It's quite something," Oestera relented, reaching for Nayson's hand.

"I can't *wait* to see you two at your coronation tomorrow evening. You know, it's a real shame your father isn't here to see this, Luxuros. I don't suppose he'd handle the news well." Selenia leaned back against the throne, her sinister glare falling over them. "What do you think, Nayson? You're always so quiet."

"Do not drag him into this," Oestera forced through clenched teeth.

Selenia rolled her eyes. "So much energy wasted on a mere man, Oestera."

"I did as you asked, what more do you want?" Astra interjected, desperate to get away from Selenia.

"Ah, yes, my little Leona," Selenia sighed, reaching for the locket. She dangled it before her face, faking a frown. "Shame she'll never make it to the Court Above, Oestera. I know how much you miss your sister."

Oestera's blood boiled beneath her pale skin.

Selenia wrapped the locket around her neck.

"Be a dear and fasten that for me, Oestera."

Mother took a singular breath and reached for Selenia's neck, fastening the locket as her lips pressed into a tight line. Astra reached for her own mouth, finding the same expression.

"Now, Astra, you're in quite the predicament here, hmm? We can go about this a few ways. You already used your favor for returning Leona to me, but I realize that such a big ask is worth a bit more."

Selenia stood, her robes dragging behind her as she stepped toward them. She reached into her pocket and pulled out a dagger.

One Astra knew all too well.

"I'll make you a deal," she whispered, the courtiers leaning in. "Luxuros here severs that godsdamned Tether between you, and I won't tell Solan that the Lunar Court has been hiding his precious heir right under his nose, or the Court Above that another Lunar and Solar heir have Tethered. Keep it, and I tell them both."

"You cannot do this," Oestera started, but Selenia paid her no mind. She pushed the blade into Lux's hands, who never took his eyes off Astra.

"Sever it, and no one has to know. Astra is a big girl, she's strong enough to take it, aren't you, darling? It'll only hurt for a second."

Astra glanced at her mother, her face frozen behind Selenia as Nayson pressed his palms into his thighs, his stomach twisting into knots.

"You're lying," Astra said, voice wavering. "She's lying, Lux. It will kill one of us or both."

I'm not touching that Tether, Astra.

Astra's eyes searched his. *There are ways around this. Your father doesn't know the truth, he doesn't know that Leona was innocent. We can still reach him.*

"Ugh," Selenia scoffed. "The silent pleading. I had so much hope in you, Astra, but here you are. Yet another pathetic Lunar woman on her knees for the enemy." She drew in an irritated breath, turning to look Oestera dead in the eye. "I'll have to do it myself, then."

Selenia twisted and lunged forward, driving the dagger into the space between Astra and Lux. A shocking pain ripped through Astra's chest as Lux gasped against the pressure. He reached for her as his knees hit the ground. Astra's fingers sparked to life, flames licking at the tips through the pain, sending licks of light flying toward Selenia who jumped back in shock.

"I always thought Fire Queen was just an annoying nick-name," she sighed. She moved forward again, but Lux reached for her ankles, yanking back on them and dragging her across the space between them and the throne.

"The dagger!" Nayson called out, lunging from his place beside Oestera. He ducked as Selenia rolled to right herself, kicking at her hand as metal clamored against the pavement. Astra's ears throbbed, the pain in her chest still sending shock-waves through her body. Selenia pushed herself back to a standing position as Lux crawled away, one hand pressed to his chest and the other reaching for the dagger as it skidded across the garden. He shoved it into Nayson's hands. Her father sprinted through the crowd, shoving courtiers away as he leaped onto the platform and into the Rift.

"That Earthen bastard!" Selenia ground out, spinning to

face them again. "You know, Astra, I'm the least of your worries. They will never stop coming after you two if you don't sever that tie. Your court has enough on their plate with Solan's war. Do you really want to declare war on the gods Above?"

Selenia stepped forward as Astra paced back.

"I'm not afraid of the Court Above," Astra said.

We need to get that necklace back, she beamed to Lux. *We need to destroy it. If she has no Shadow, she has no hope of ever Ascending again.*

Lux rose slowly behind Selenia as she tracked toward Astra.

"You're a child, Astra. You don't know what to be afraid of."

Astra let another spark fly, hitting Selenia's skirt this time, singing it. As she looked down, Lux reached for her neck, snagging the chain and yanking it free. He tossed it back toward Astra as she swung around and searched for anything to dig her hands into. Lux dodged Selenia as she called out for Alastair.

I'm so sorry for this, Alastair beamed to Astra.

His pale face appeared from the crowd, tapping Lux on the back as he had when he took Astra to the Court Above. Lux fell to his knees, collapsing over himself. Alastair turned and looked at Astra, his eyes wide, as Selenia advanced again.

He's only asleep, Alastair's deep voice assured her, but the panic did not subside.

They had no more time to waste. Astra dropped the locket onto the ground and fired at it, busting it open and focusing all her energy on the wisps of black smoke that rose from the trinket.

"What—what did you do?" Selenia's eyes tracked the wisps, her hand clutching her chest as she watched them fade into the ether. Her rage shook her very bones, a bruised anger flowed from every pore. She scooped the locket from the ground, looking around frantically. Selenia lifted her pale hand as she heaved a breath, her glowing skin fading to a sickly gray as she struggled, grasping for any sense to make of what was happening.

"You've just begun a war you cannot win, Astra Leona," she groaned against the weight of her lungs caving in on themselves. "The gods will not forgive you," she gasped. "Lucian will never let you two get away with it. He will come after you, you fools!"

Astra shook her hands, letting the remaining sparks flicker into the space around her, her heart pounding as she stood before her, rooted to her spot. The final hazy threads of Selenia's Shadow fled from the still-open locket, twirling into a sphere that hovered over Astra's palm. She felt the weight of it, the dense anger that ran through its black currents.

The power.

"I will not seek the gods' forgiveness, Selenia," Astra pushed through a tight jaw, the onyx sphere melting into her palm, fusing into her veins. "But they will have to beg for mine."

Astra watched as the reality of Selenia's situation set in. She was at anyone's mercy now, not just Astra's. She'd given up her power again and again, and now there was nothing left. If Astra killed her now, she'd be confined to Luciela's realm for eternity, no way back. She waited for a pulse in her bones, something within to tell her what to do.

Instead, she caught a flash of movement from behind Selenia.

Oestera, her proud mask faltering, gave a soft nod so slight that Astra questioned if she really saw it—if she should trust it.

She closed her eyes, begging her body to do *something*, lean one way or the other. But it was the soft echo of Leona's voice in her ears that finally pushed her.

Oestera's loyalty is the only thing I've ever been certain of.

Astra held Selenia in her mind, the same way she'd done with dozens of roses, with the Solarian in the woods, and she pushed the flame into her lungs, filling them with black smoke so thick it may as well have been the Shadow she lost.

It did not take as much effort as Astra thought, but then again, Selenia hardly had anything left to begin with. The goddess collapsed, a wave of golden blood spilling from her lips over the pavement that churned Astra's insides.

In the silence, the courtiers' colors rushed in.

Every shade imaginable, shocked and unsure what to do about the murder they just bore witness to at Astra's hands.

Oestera stepped forward, pulling uncomfortably at her sleeve, a tick Astra had seen before.

Oestera's lips parted, a heavy breath pushing down the wave of nausea in her gut. She spoke loudly and with the same authority Astra had always wished she carried.

"Aren't we so fortunate that the Lunar Queen Astra Leona's first act upon the throne was to defend her court from a premeditated attack by the Solar God Lucian? Hardly a minute into her reign, and she's already proven herself to be a wise and decisive leader." Oestera stood beside her daughter, Astra's hands shaking, and looped an arm through her daughter's.

Courtiers exchanged glances, the tide of shocked reds melting into greens and blues of admiration as Oestera spoke. She turned to Astra, her face alive with a light Astra had never seen before.

"Now, I know this was a lot of excitement for one day, so please, retire to your rooms. The maidens have prepared an evening tea service to help everyone get some rest before tomorrow's coronation!"

"Astra," Oestera whispered, something like tears forming at the ridges of her eyes. "Hold it together. I'm afraid we're in for a long night."

Lunelle's sweet spirit moved over Astra, her slender frame rushing toward them as courtiers dispersed.

"Mother?"

Councilwomen closed in around them. Both Archera and Tula whispered to maidens, sending them in every direction.

"Archera, send for Ehlaria. Someone from Mercury, get Maeve here! Tell them to check their wrists. Commander—" Oestera glanced around the panicked garden, catching Astra's eyes as she tried to comprehend what the *fuck* was going on. They both landed on Lux's motionless frame strewn across the pavement. "Oh dear, Alastair! Wake the poor boy, please!"

Alastair appeared from the rustling crowd, tapping Lux on the back again.

"Hey, big guy."

Lux's brows furrowed, one boot in this realm and one in another, but he had the wherewithal to glare at Alastair.

The god grinned. "So sorry about that. If your queen here hadn't finished Selenia off today, I couldn't blow my cover."

Lux shook his head as Oestera stooped to meet his eyes.

"Commander, could I send you to Earth to fetch my husband? You know the court better than any of the maidens."

Lux blinked slowly and looked for Astra.

"I don't know what's going on, either," she said, shrugging.

"All will be revealed, Astra, I promise," Oestera said, turning toward another maiden who asked her a muffled question. "Yes, tell him to check his wrist. Girls! Girls," she said, resting a hand on each of her daughter's shoulders. "Go change into something comfortable and meet me in my chambers. We have a lot to discuss."

Astra glanced at Lunelle, who shared the same apprehension, twisting around their ribs in flickering yellows and oranges.

"Let's go, ladies!" Oestera chirped, disappearing into the palace, a bounce in her step that put Astra on edge.

"Was she... smiling?" Astra asked.

"I believe so," Lunelle said, astonished.

"Your Highness?" someone asked from behind them.

"You just missed her," Astra mumbled, pointing toward the palace.

"Actually, I meant you," the maiden said.

The last thing Astra heard before everything whirred into a black void was Lunelle's muffled laughter.

FORTY-SIX

Ameera's voice floated in a gentle wave through a sea of fuzzy half-thoughts. Astra's eyes fluttered open, her mouth dry and stuck together. "As?"

"Here, drink this," a familiar voice murmured as someone pushed a cup of tea between her lips.

"Ehlaria?"

"Your Highness," she chuckled.

Astra's head swirled again, the edge of her vision dissolving as she fought to hold on to consciousness. "I need everyone to stop doing that. Now."

"Is that your first official order?" Ameera smirked as Astra's vision clarified.

Ameera sat perched at the edge of the bed as Astra pushed herself up on her elbows.

"I mean it, Ameera. I've had a really crazy day, okay?"

A dark laugh bounced off the walls.

Not a laugh Astra recognized.

Her head swiveled as she looked for the source. Everything

in her lit up with greens and pinks when she realized who it was.

"Mother?"

"I'm afraid we've overwhelmed you," she said quietly. "It's only been about five minutes. Don't worry. Nothing like last time."

Astra felt a flush creep over her neck. "Tula?"

Oestera smiled softly. "Your father. We don't keep secrets."

Astra glanced around the room. Lunelle sat on the couch, looking as dazed as she felt.

"Where's Lux?"

"I sent him to get your father. He went back to the manor to hide the shadow dagger. We have a safe room there. They should be back any minute."

Oestera crossed the room and sat beside Ameera, resting a hand on Astra's knee.

"I know you have a million questions, Astra, and we're going to answer them all. But first, we need to get you out of these clothes."

Astra looked down, her lips crinkling into a frown. Selenia's golden blood splattered across her chest and hands.

"I'll help you clean up," Ameera said.

"I can help her," Oestera replied. "Why don't the rest of you go get everyone settled and have some snacks? Nayson hasn't run that fast in thirty years. He's going to be starving."

Ameera stared wide-eyed at the queen, who, until today, had never cracked a joke in her presence.

"Can Lunelle stay?" Astra asked.

Oestera nodded. "Of course."

The room emptied and Astra stood carefully as Oestera and Lunelle followed her into her bathing chambers. Sand poured from the soiled garments as she peeled them off, but the discomfort she felt being alone with just her mother and Lunelle was far more demanding.

"Grab her something soft, Lu. We're going to be working all night."

Lunelle disappeared into Astra's dressing room, leaving just the buzz from Oestera's chest, a soft pink glow rolling over itself.

Wait.

"Mother above," Astra breathed. "Is that... am I reading you?"

"I suppose you are," Oestera whispered, untangling Astra's hair from the knotted bun it sat in. She ran her fingers through Astra's curls slowly, reverently.

"I don't know how to process this," Astra admitted as Lunelle returned. She unfurled a soft knit set in a pale cream yarn, catching Astra's eye. "I don't want to be queen, Lunelle. *You* should be queen."

Lunelle snorted. "Astra, thanks to you I *will* be a queen. Just not here."

Astra's face flushed again. "But is that what you want? I never asked for this. I don't want it!"

"As," she said, placing a hand on her bare shoulder. "This is exactly what I want, I promise. And more importantly, Mother and I agree, it's what people need."

She whipped her head around. Oestera leaned against the vanity, watching her daughters in the mirror.

"She's right."

"Me? The Fire Queen? The selfish monster who will never do what's right for the crown?" Reliving the words stung.

"I don't want you to do what's right for the crown, Astra. I want you to do what's right for the court."

Astra swallowed, acid coating her throat. "I feel like I'm hallucinating."

"I know." Oestera sighed, shockingly small in this setting. "And by the end of the night, you'll probably feel like your entire world has been turned upside down. But as we untangle everything with you, I need you to remember that while you *are* demigoddess Astra Leona Aurellis, Queen of the Lunar Court, you are also human. And it's okay for you to be hurt and confused. We're all here to support you."

She turned to Lunelle. "What was in the tea Ehlaria made?"

Lunelle snorted. "I don't know, but I think I'd like some."

Half an hour later, Astra sat across from her father at the very same table she announced her engagement to the Mercurian king.

This time, they'd be telling some actual truths, it seemed.

Oestera paced nervously across the back of the room as she waited for her final guest. Around the table sat Ehlaria, Maeve Maelstrom, Lunelle, Mirquios, Luxuros, and Ameera, half of them completely lost and the other half waiting patiently for Oestera to speak.

Astra's head swirled with information already, still reeling from what Luciela told her in the Court Below.

"We can start without him," Oestera finally said, sitting between Nayson and Ehlaria. She drew her shoulders back and began her long-awaited explanation, her voice no longer the frigid trill Astra was so accustomed to, but a warmer honey.

"I know you have a very specific notion of who you think I am, and I know that what I'm about to tell you is going to be quite difficult to reconcile with that narrative, so I understand if it takes us a while to get things sorted. I don't expect you to suddenly shift your entire worldview in one conversation, but you and your friends are not the first generation of Nova Rebels."

Astra and Lunelle exchanged a panicked glance.

Oestera continued, "You are the carefully curated second generation, trained from the moment of your birth to pick up where we left off."

Astra glanced around the table, confusion rolling off Lux and Ameera's chests, but a steadfast confidence from her mother and Ehlaria gave her something to hold on to as she tried to focus on breathing.

They'd been waiting for the chance to tell this story for a very long time.

"Oestera." Ehlaria leaned toward her. "It might be easier to *show* her and not just tell her. She needs to see it."

Oestera's eyes flickered over her daughter, a breath leaving her lungs as she considered this. She unfurled her hands, resting them across the table. Astra hesitated. They did not touch often—she was rarely within arm's length of her mother her entire life.

She glanced at the commander, who picked up her other hand and squeezed.

Astra reached for Oestera's hand, warmer than expected.

"I'm a little rusty, but I can take you within. I don't want you to rely on my memory. I want you to see it exactly as it happened. Stay in the shadows, and don't talk to anyone. You never know who might be sensitive to you."

"A lesson I learned the hard way," Astra said.

"When I was even younger than you are now, my dear sister fell in love with a Solarian King. So far in love, in fact, that she Tethered to him, something that we didn't even know was possible. And when they Tethered, they each took on qualities within one another that made them both incredibly powerful—a result that made us question what we'd been told our entire lives."

Oestera's fingers squeezed against Astra's, pulling her into the strange funnel within them, passing through the haze of time.

"This is madness, Leona!" Oestera shouted, her face round with the youth Fate would soon steal from her. She couldn't have been more than twenty, twenty-two. Her silver hair was braided down her back, and a simple Summer linen frock in a pale lavender danced around her ankles as she chased Leona around her bedroom.

"It's all madness," Leona hissed, shoving another piece of clothing into a bag. "It doesn't matter what you say, Oestera. If you felt like this, if you only knew—"

"You cannot touch him!" Oestera reached for her sister's arm, clutching at her wrist.

Leona's lips twitched, a dusting of peony pink and silver Astra now recognized in her blossoming in her lungs—the kind of colors you cannot will away or deny.

"Says who, Os?"

"Everyone! Mother. The priestesses. Father said touching a Solarian is like touching fire and expecting it not to burn."

Leona twisted and jerked her wrist from her sister's hands, a lightness to her smile that confused Oestera.

"You know, you could use a little heat, Oestera." She jostled the bag to make more room. She must have been planning on leaving for a while. "Gaze upon me, sister, and tell me—am I scarred? Is my flesh melted? Because Solan had me pinned up against a wall six hours ago and I can tell you, the burn, indeed, lingers, but it does not kill."

Oestera's jaw dropped as Leona swept from the room, her slippers tapping down the hallway. Oestera sank into her bed, squeezing her eyes shut—her mind could not wrap around the possibilities.

The lies.

"Once we knew they could touch with no consequence... well, not *no* consequences, of course, but not instant death, we had to learn more." Oestera's tone shifted as her eyes fell on the Elvish queen beside her. "That's how Ehlaria and I became friends. I offered her one of the golden trinkets Solan sent Leona and forced her to tell me everything she knew."

She squeezed Astra's hands again, transporting them just across the Midwood to Ehlaria's drawing room forty years prior.

"You do realize that if your mother catches you with these texts, she'll have both of our heads, yes?"

An eternally ageless Ehlaria plopped onto a sofa across from Oestera's tired eyes, half-moons worn into her skin, despite her youth.

"Add it to the list of things my mother wants my head for," Oestera mumbled as she flipped through another worn book. *"Is this accurate? The Solar and Lunar Courts were not originally part of the system?"*

Ehlaria reached for the book, checking the title inscribed along the spine.

"It's true. They did not exist until I was well into my five or six-hundredth cycle. It's hard to remember." She raised a teacup to her lips, lost in the memories of a lifetime of lore.

"The gods did not interact with the Living Courts for millennia. They pulled their strings like puppeteers, but they were never to take advantage. It was an unspoken rule. But Silas, the first Solar God, fell in love with one of his devotees. She was a Solar Witch, a worshipper of his who used the power of light to practice magic, and their love child inherited both his capabilities and her magic. He could wield both.

"Silas was consumed with the idea of creating an army of these halflings and spent centuries procreating with as many of his Solar

Witches as he could. As they started their own families, the powers carried through their bloodlines without his interference."

Ehlaria rose, searching for another volume in the oak shelves along her drawing room wall. She pulled a black velvet book, one Astra's hands knew the weight of well.

"Rowena, the first Lunar Goddess, caught on to what he was doing eventually." Ehlaria set the book on Mother's stack. "She was jealous, naturally, but did not have the same ability to spread her bloodline, of course. So she made a deal with the Nether Queen."

"Luciela?" Oestera's bright eyes scanned through her texts. She held up a thin manual. "The Gods' Guide to Shadow Bargaining?"

Ehlaria nodded. "She told Luciela that if she gave her the Shadows of Descended Solar demigods, she would raise up an army of Shadow Goddesses to defeat Silas and take both thrones in the Court Above. Once she wielded both powers as the Divine Queen, she'd free Luciela from her bonds to the Nether and elevate her to the Court Above."

"Why would Luciela give up power over all the Nether?"

"Luciela never wanted to be the Court Below's mistress. She was sent there for rejecting a Tether with Silas. It's a long story—one for another time. What matters is that Rowena made a deal with Luciela. But there was a problem. The Shadows of the Solar Gods were given to Rowena's worshippers hoping they'd inherit the powers left behind.

"And they did. Sort of. The Shadow Goddesses were immensely powerful, but they were only half of a whole. The Shadows cried out for their Souls, searching for them, yearning to be reunited. They'd find each other, form Tethers, and then become twice as powerful as they were intended to be. Rowena was never able to overtake Silas's armies because they kept falling in love."

Oestera scoffed. "Sounds tedious."

Ehlaria eyed her, a smirk forming on her lips. "Your time will come too, Rebel Queen, and it will knock you so far back onto your ass you'll regret every snide comment you made to your sister."

Her cheeks reddened. It was then Astra noticed the ring on her finger, a ruby. "The Martian Prince does not seem like the Tethering type," Oestera said.

"No," Ehlaria laughed. "He doesn't, does he?"

"I can't focus on that today, Ehlaria."

"The Light and Shadow gods became an issue. They realized they were powerful—and numerous—enough to confront the Court Above and overthrow them. They were sick of their Fates being up to passive leaders who only cared to involve themselves when their power was at stake. Fearing them, the Court Above came up with a plan.

"To make them believe they were getting their fair share, they offered them their own courts. They divided them into the Lunar and Solar Courts Between—not quite Ascended, not quite human. They gave the Solar Court stewardship over all things logic and math, science, and agriculture, as well as time. They gave the Lunar Court the mystique—intuition, emotion, magic, and spirituality. They crowned a Solar King and Lunar Queen and then they got to work.

"The gods sowed hatred and bias between the royal families, ensuring that no new children would Tether to their better halves, hamstringing their powers. For good measure, they cut the courts off from one another, too.

"It took generations, but the Lunar and Solar Courts developed their own traditions, cultures, and belief systems. Monarchies became established, the Ascent system fully took root, feeding a constant line of Ascended Lunar and Solar rulers, and no one was ever able to claim that Divine Throne, keeping the Court Above as the final layer of power. All the things you know today are because the gods wanted you kept in the dark."

Oestera's eyes were wide, her pink cheeks sucked inward as she chewed on this information.

"I have to get to Leona. She needs to know."

"Leona knows in many ways, Oestera. Ways unspoken. The Tether reveals things in unseen, unheard riddles. Take that black novel on the top with you. Read it. If you want to do something with the knowledge you've gained, you need to understand the full story. Start with the Rift—the only reason it exists is because a Shadow Goddess and Light God fell in love."

Astra released Oestera's hands, the echo of Ehlaria's words sending a shiver through her. "How did Leona and Solan even come across one another?"

Oestera's eyes darted to Ehlaria.

The ancient queen's lips twisted into something like a smile. "Fate is a strange beast."

"And sometimes Fate comes in the form of a Lunar Elf Queen who just *forgot* she invited both the Lunar and Solar heirs to an Equinox party."

Astra turned toward the culprit in question.

"How many times have you done this, Ehlaria?"

"A few dozen," she admitted. "But we're getting close this time, I can feel it."

Astra glanced at Lux who looked like he might vomit.

"Leona and Solan tried to ignore it," Oestera said. "They did their best for years after they met. Solan married, had children, he did everything he could to be a dutiful king... but Leona called to him. Over and over. When she lost her grip on her sanity, we knew we had to stop the gods' cursed rules that made it impossible for them to be together. You two probably don't even realize the danger you're in, do you?"

Astra's eyes widened as Lux's grip tightened on her knee.

"I think we both have a decent idea of what a cruel twist of Fate the Tether can be."

Oestera nodded, her smile falling. "For centuries, the Solar and Lunar heirs that Tethered tried to ignore it. They let their hate for the other side overrule their hearts. They went mad, they killed themselves or each other to put an end to the torture. And if they didn't, the Court Above intervened. Leona and Solan were as careful as they could have been."

They twisted away again, landing in the gardens just outside.

"Hurry, Os!" Leona's voice hissed as Oestera skipped across the garden pavers. It was late at night. The palace was quiet as they both flung themselves into the Rift. Leona reached back for Oestera's hand, weaving their fingers together as she reached for a thread.

A pale green cord.

They landed at the Mercurian Gate, greeted by the kind gaze of a familiar face. "King Antares," Oestera bowed and he returned the gesture.

"Through that hall," he pointed to a door Astra had passed under before. "Solan arrived half an hour ago."

Leona nodded, pulling her sister into the servant's hall. Antares followed behind them.

They wove through alleys behind two Solarian soldiers, disappearing into the passage behind The Dune.

"Here!" Maeve Maelstrom waited for them, her bright red lips and aventurine beads illuminated by the Sun rising beyond the alleyway. She pushed open the back door, beckoning them in. Leona and Oestera bounded down the stairs into a basement's cozy sitting area, chairs Astra recognized.

Solan occupied one, his High Lady Estelle in another. Leona greeted them both warmly, placing a kiss on Estelle's cheek.

"How is he?"

Estelle beamed, "Oh, he's a dream, Leona. I hope you'll meet him one day."

A ripple of emerald pain ran through Leona's chest, but she smiled despite it.

"Enough pleasantries," Maeve snapped, standing in the middle of the group. "We've got business to discuss."

"Neptune and Uranus are in," Solan reported. "I met with both of their leadership this week. They'll back us."

"Pluto, Jupiter, and Saturn are still out. But I have hope they'll come around soon," Oestera chimed. "Mars is on board."

Astra searched for her finger, still wrapped in a red ruby.

"We're headed to Venus tomorrow," Antares added.

Leona stepped forward. "Earth is arriving any moment to the Lunar Palace. We'll wine and dine them this week and feel them out. My sources believe Mother Nature will be thrilled with a chance to stick it to the gods."

"The numbers are on our side," Solan said, his eyes holding Leona's.

"I had a full map of the courts drawn up to track our progress," Maeve said, handing each leader a thick scroll. "I didn't want to send them through the Rift, just in case. Take them with you, and Oestera," she leaned closer. "What's going on with the..." she gestured to her chest.

"The what?"

"Something in there is weird. Different."

Oestera shrugged, unsure what she could mean. She climbed the steps after her sister as they left with their charts in hand, a tearful goodbye between Solan and Leona too hard for her to watch. As they sailed back through the Rift, she pressed a hand to her chest, unsure of the strange feeling knocking against her ribs.

"I'll see you at breakfast," Leona sighed, exhausted. She left Oestera in the gardens, the Moon just peeking over the hedges. Oestera perched herself on the fountain, but no sooner did her shoulders relax than she was back up, the sound of boots hitting the pavers surprising her.

Several dozen Earthen soldiers faded out of the Rift. Mother Nature in all her gilded glory parted them like an ocean. Maidens rushed around, grabbing trunks and bags, ushering them into the palace.

Oestera waited a moment. She didn't want to get swept up in their current.

"Princess?" a warm voice called out to her, like something she'd never heard before. The notes were akin to the smooth Earthen clay coffee mug Leona had brought her back once from a visit.

Oestera spun, and she never stopped. Her entire world fell apart as an Earthen soldier, late to arrive, reached for his chest.

They stared in a stunned, reverent silence as the Tether took hold. And she knew in that moment exactly why her sister risked entire courts just for a glimpse of Solan.

Why she was about to do the same.

She twisted the ruby ring around her finger, the air leaving her lungs.

"Mother—" Astra's chest ached alongside hers. She looked to her father as he leaned in closer to his queen, placing a soft kiss on her shoulder.

Oestera sighed.

"I need you to know that I understand why you kept it from me. Why Lunelle kept it from me. The Tether is often a double-edged sword. The profound love cuts like a blade when you're obligated to something—someone else. It's hard enough when you're just two people trying to navigate the world, but layer in the political implications, it's messy at best."

"Your Majesty," Lux cut in, leaning around Astra.

She flinched. "Oestera, please. I *hate* being called Your Majesty."

Lux glanced between the mother and daughter, a smile tugging at his lips. "Oestera, then. If you started the rebellion... why stop it? What happened?"

Oestera reached for their hands again, pulling them back into another memory.

"Oestera!"

Selenia's voice tore through the bright Spring air, Oestera's bare feet dug into the grass as she watched a silver-haired Lunelle pick wildflowers behind a stone manor. She rested a hand on her belly, and Astra recognized her dress immediately. She'd seen it in Solan's study.

The Sun kissed her cheeks as they flushed. It had been years since her mother's voice chilled her to the bone.

"How did she find us?" Nayson reached for Lunelle, holding her close against his chest.

"I don't—"

"Oestera!"

She moved quickly, the panic in Selenia's voice frightening her. She was at the front of the house, her icy glare wild, frantic.

"You have to come home, you have to change her mind!"

Oestera shook her head. "What? Mother, what are you talking about?"

"Your sister!" she cried. "Her little rebellion has found its way to the ears of the gods. The Court Above will destroy her, Oestera. How could you let her be so reckless?"

"How did they—"

"Does it matter?' Selenia roared, a genuine fear in her. "She has to stop this."

Nayson tucked Lunelle's face against his chest, her eyes wide with terror.

"Go," he said. "You should go."

She kissed them both quickly and followed Selenia into the Rift.

When she landed in the Lunar Court, the air was charged with an acid she could taste, but not name.

A storm was going to break.

Selenia brought her to the Celestial Hall where Leona held court, her eyes sunken. The pain of being away from Solan never left her, never dulled. Her emerald eyes sparkled just a bit when they found her sister's face.

"Out," she commanded everyone in the room.

The room emptied around Oestera, her nerves tangling into orange ribbons.

"This has to stop, Leona."

Whatever light had returned at the sight of her sister extinguished at the words of their mother.

"The Court Above has been informed of your rebellion. I've convinced them to look the other way and forgive you, but only if you sever the tie with Solan."

Oestera gasped, "She cannot!"

Selenia pulled a dagger from her robes, a smoky blade that made Oestera's insides curl.

"If Solan uses a shadow blade, it can be done. If you sever the tie, the gods will not exterminate everyone who assembled in this very court last week. But if you won't..."

Her choice was clear.

"Leona." Oestera's fingers twisted around one another.

"Perhaps it would be better," Leona said, her eyes darkening. "To be free from this."

"You must go. Now," Selenia barked.

"I'll go with you," Oestera offered, extending her hand. They walked together to the garden, a heavy maroon settling between them.

Leona paused on the platform, cradling her sister's face in her hands. "If something goes wrong—"

"Leona," Oestera glared.

"Just make sure he's safe, Os."

An understanding passed between them, Oestera's eyes closed against the tears that formed.

And then they were consumed by pastel mist.

Ehlaria reached out and rested her hand on Oestera's arm,

her eyes glistening with tears. Oestera took a breath but it didn't quite make it to her lungs.

"When we lost Leona, when I lost her—" Her voice shattered, unable to keep up with the flood of emotions.

"Take a second," Luxuros nodded solemnly, understanding her frayed nerves in a way so few could.

Oestera's lips shook, a sight that set Astra's heart on fire.

"You lost so much, too," Oestera whispered, her eyes fixed on the commander's face. She took a deeper breath and released it. "When we lost Leona, Solan never recovered. He became consumed by the grief. A severed Tether can kill a normal man! After The Flare, he became convinced we'd plotted it with the gods, that we'd tricked him. He's been shut off from us since—no attempts at communication have worked. And besides that, we were in such a precarious position. Lunelle was a child, you were an infant. I couldn't risk the gods turning their eyes onto our court and digging deeper. The other Nova chapters faded away, crushed under the weight of courtiers and monarchs unwilling to relinquish their power. So we fell back. We waited. And then you."

Oestera reached her other hand to Astra's cheek, the touch so foreign.

"You were born wide awake, Astra. We'd never seen anything like it. We were sure that you were Leona sent back to take her revenge."

Maeve and Oestera glanced at each other, soft laughter passing between them.

"From the moment you could sit up and crawl, you could read us. You had *Light*. We thought maybe it was a side effect from The Flare, but now I realize, all along, you'd found one another."

Oestera reached past Astra and tapped Lux's forearm

gently, her eyes holding a thousand different emotions—regrets, hopes, fears.

"As you grew, your power was alarming, and Selenia noticed it immediately. Her desperation to stomp out any hint of Light from you was clear. Even after her Ascent to the Court Above, she spent more and more time around us, watching. Watching you. She'd visit constantly, even when the gates were closed. When she threatened to tell the gods about you, I broke. Selenia made us a deal."

She pulled them through space and time and they landed in Lunaria, twenty-five years prior.

"I don't trust you." Oestera waved her arm toward her mother. "There is nothing you could say to convince me to put her life in your hands."

They stood in the Celestial Hall, Ehlaria behind one shoulder, Nayson behind the other. Selenia stood before her daughter, lips twisted.

"If you want to protect her, you have to do this, Oestera. If they catch a whiff of Light within her, they'll extinguish it. But if she never learns to wield it, they won't have a reason to look."

"Perhaps something more significant," Ehlaria mumbled. "A blood oath."

Selenia rolled her eyes. "I suppose my word is meaningless to you?"

"Less than," Oestera replied.

"Fine. A blood oath. Neither of us will reveal Astra's powers or the Nova Rebellion to anyone. God or man alike."

Oestera's lips twisted into a knot. But then, a little red-haired princess squealed across the hall, running from her sister, and the decision was made.

She'd do whatever it took to protect her.

Ehlaria, Maeve, and Nayson would, too.

Selenia produced that same sickly shadow blade and it was

done, her gilded blood spilled into Oestera's scarlet, dripping onto the palace floor.

Oestera rolled back her sleeve, a faint line running across her wrist, the scar already fading now that Selenia had no blood to bind her. It would be gone soon.

She shook her head. "I couldn't let her get to you. So we locked you down. I distanced myself so you'd never be able to see the truth, you were too powerful, so I had to shut you out —I hated every moment. But I did what I had to, and I let your dad become your safe place. Ehlaria became your confidant. I knew someday we'd be here, we'd be able to tell one another the truth, but until then I had to sacrifice myself for your safety. The blood between mother and daughter is powerful. I knew that one question would be all it took to break me, and the blood oath would have cut me down.

"Every minute of your life has been crafted to enrage you, to keep the fire within you alive until the time was right. I have been training you from day one to hate everything about the gods by becoming just like them. I was selfish and closed off, hoping you'd grow to crave more for our people.

"I sent you to Celene because I knew if you saw what was possible... if you saw the beauty in community, in working together, it would be the final nail in the coffin. I knew you'd never be able to look away, and with the power we'd seen from you without even trying, it would come together.

"We missed you desperately, Astra. I spent every night terrified I'd wake up to find that a god had taken you, or that Solan had finally mounted a return. But I had to let you go. I knew it would work in my bones.

"A few years ago, the High Priestess in Ellume heard rumors of Rebels building again. I had to act like the queen I never wanted to be and stamp out their efforts. Lumas and his crew were warned beforehand. I heard a rumor that there were similar rebellions building in the Inner Courts, like Mercury.

"I knew if I could just get Mirquios here... Antares followed a similar plan, raising his son to rebel against him the moment he was gone. The young king couldn't tell you about the rebels outright, but I hoped he would involve you eventually. This new generation, they're better about security than we were. Luxuros can confirm, I'm sure, that the price of entry is a similar blood oath. Not only can you never reveal another Rebel to someone outside of the bond, but you can't even reveal them within the bond. They have to reveal themselves."

"You tried to tell me," Astra turned to Lux. "So many times. You tried to tell me that I was wrong about my mother."

"No easy feat." He smirked. "I wasn't certain. We had our suspicions, but the original Nova Rebels members were mere rumors. No proof, and I couldn't outright accuse your mother because of the oath."

"So... my entire life has been a lie," Astra murmured, her mother's eyes watching her carefully.

"A good deal of it, yes. And I imagine that will be difficult for all of us to navigate, but especially you. I love you. I always have. You are the great hope of our family, and if there had been another way..."

Astra shoved the bubbling violet overwhelm in her gut back down in a desperate attempt to process. She twisted in her seat to Lunelle.

"How much did you know?"

"Very little."

Oestera chimed in, "We only told her what we could, when we could. I cherished my sister so much, we hoped to keep things between you girls as pure as possible."

Astra's nose scrunched. "Why don't you have the same abilities? Or Lunelle?"

"We Tethered to mere men." Oestera's lips pressed into a smile. "The alchemy has to be between a Light and a Shadow God. Otherwise, we all have our little tricks, but nothing quite at the scale of you two."

"Mother," Lunelle whispered, leaning over the table. "How long did you know about Mirquios?"

"Please," Oestera laughed. "I was with you in Pluto for months. It was hard to watch. Though, from what your father tells me, not nearly as hard to watch as you two. How did you manage it, Luxuros?"

"Not well," he replied. "Ehlaria helped."

Oestera snapped her attention toward her friend, Astra realized, not just a tolerant ally. She suppressed a giggle.

"I gave him an enchanted moonstone to suppress his light and ground his feelings. I had nothing to do with the Tether in all actuality. They weren't quite ready for it when he came to me, and I knew that. Tethers aren't always instant. The Fire Queen needed to come into herself a little more. And you needed to loosen up, Commander."

Astra shook her head. "Why did it happen when I broke it, then?"

Ehlaria shrugged. "He fell in love with you the second you saw what he considered to be the worst part of himself, what you should have *hated* about him, and accepted it with no hesitation—"

"There was a healthy amount of hesitation," Lux quipped.

"And *you* fell in love with him the moment he challenged you. Forced you to slow down, stop, and think about what you were doing. You've been Tethered in some ways your entire lives, but until you gave up your stubborn denial, it wasn't able to break through. When you broke the amulet, I think seeing the commander's inner world was the final wall that needed to come down between you two. The amulet certainly numbs the pain and probably saved it tonight when Selenia attacked you, but you cannot fight Fate, Astra."

Lux leaned forward and pressed a quick kiss to the back of Astra's hand.

"Perhaps you can fill us in on the rest of the story, then," Ehlaria gestured toward them. "You figured out the Shadow Bargaining? And took on the Court Below... we need to know what happened down there."

Astra took a long sip of tea, her head spinning as she tried to reframe thirty years of personal grudges in this new light. She took a deep breath.

"My turn for some confessions, then."

FORTY-EIGHT

"Ameera and I realized that if Luxuros could get into the Lunar Gate, the Rift was no longer warded against Solarians."

Astra sipped her tea one more time and rounded her shoulders, every eye in the room hanging on her words.

"We started poking around and that led us to Ellume. We broke into Ivonne's office and learned she was researching Shadow Bargaining—she had that same manual you got from Ehlaria. She knew something wasn't right with Selenia—with the Rift—but she wouldn't admit it to me. Her notes all but accused you, Mother, of covering her tracks. We thought perhaps you were in on whatever deal she made with Luciela."

"Always hated Ivonne," Ehlaria scoffed beside Astra.

"I held a council meeting and distracted them long enough for Ameera to seduce a clerk—you know what, maybe not so much detail," Astra added as Ameera's eyes widened. "Anyway, she borrowed Ivonne's notes and Lux found the passage about Shadow Bargaining. That tipped us off that Ivonne was on the hunt for dirt on Selenia."

Astra was on a roll now, her mother's eyes widening with every word she dropped before her.

"On our way home, a Solarian soldier attacked us. He almost killed Lux, and something inside me snapped. I immolated him without even touching him. We both know my fire has been an issue when emotions run high, but I'd never purposefully tried to do anything with it before. So we started training. Lux helped me find my limits when he wasn't busy flirting with Father," Astra laughed.

"I needed you not to hate me, Nayson," Lux sighed. "I knew from the second we touched in Celene it was over for us. It was just a matter of time. I needed Nayson on my side so your mother wouldn't have me beheaded when she returned."

Astra grinned. "Fair enough. We visited Ehlaria during the Equinox. I realize now that she was oath-bound not to tell me anything, but she hinted that my fire was actually sunlight, which set us down a whole other path. And then one of us got a little pissy—I won't name names—and fired a spark at the other, knocking the moonstone amulet off. And that's when all Nether broke loose."

"You both needed a push. I knew the looking glass would set you off."

A warm smile melted over Ehlaria's lavender complexion, reflected by her own, she was sure.

Astra chuckled. Passion was predictable when you'd seen it boil over for centuries, she supposed.

"When you came back from Pluto with Arcas, I was floored that you would throw Lunelle to our enemies. I see now that you were feeding a fire you'd been tending for decades. You needed me to make a final stand, and my sister's happiness was one thing I'd never risk. Mirquios and Lux took me to Mercury to see the Sun, and I met Maeve and then Lunelle waltzed in. In *pants*!"

Oestera released a laugh, a melodic sound she'd been starved of for too long.

"They broke their news to me and that's when I knew I had to do something drastic. I couldn't let my sister live her whole life shackled to some pouty prince when she had real, true love on the table. I tried to ask you about The Flare, but you shut me down so quickly."

Oestera held her wrist up again, the dull scar pale in the morning moonlight. "I knew what you were asking, but I couldn't get into it. I hoped if I showed you the fear, the genuine anguish, it might motivate you to seek the truth in other avenues."

Astra nodded, remembering the pain in her words.

"I went within that night and watched Leona and Solan's last few moments together, which was *awful*. But it did reveal how little we actually knew of our own history."

Astra turned toward her mother, reaching for her hands again.

"And I watched you save a little Solarian boy before The Flare could kill you both, but it didn't register at the time who that might have been."

Lux's hand grazed her shoulder, a soft calm from his touch soothing the heavy feelings weighing on her.

"On my way to the Rift, I saw Selenia in Solaris, our eyes locked. I wasn't sure what was real or just a dream when I was in the Astral. I didn't expect her to come looking for me."

Oestera smiled, holding up her hand. "Do you remember that I asked you about that dress you were wearing?"

Astra nodded.

"I thought all these years that Leona's ghost had screamed at me to run. You just look so much like her. But you were there, you yelled at me."

"Yes," Astra gasped. "That was me!"

"A Light Goddess, a Shadow Goddess, an astral traveler... what can't you do?" Oestera's eyes warmed as she laughed.

"Wait patiently for anything," Lux snorted.

Ameera piped up, "She's not very good at math."

Astra rolled her eyes, but she laughed despite herself.

"When I jumped into the Rift, I got stuck. I couldn't find my way up, but Lux pulled me out. The Tether disappeared when I went within, so he came looking for me. We were enjoying a pleasant dream in the Earthen Court when I was kidnapped by—"

"Me." Nine sets of eyes snapped toward the end of the room, where a pale figure in all black leaned against the wall, silently watching.

"Alastair," Oestera cooed, holding her hands out to him. He embraced her warmly, her lips brushing against his cheek as he sat beside her. Lux tensed against Astra, his guard immediately up.

Alastair sighed. "Don't be so sour, Luxuros. We're just getting to the *really* fun part."

"I don't know if we can take any more fun," Ameera sighed.

"Anyway, Alastair here took me to the Court Above—"

"Oh gods," Oestera cried. "We had a deal!"

"I promised not to take Astra into the Rift. And I didn't. I took her from the dream, but the prince here took her into the Rift. Many, *many* times might I add."

Astra pushed forward, ignoring the tension building in both their chests.

"He took me to the Court Above and Selenia paraded me around. She knew I'd seen her at The Flare and she had to control the narrative. We struck a deal. I'd go down and get Leona's soul for her and she'd nominate Mirquios as a champion. We knew with the lie we'd told about the Tether and our tenuous relations with Pluto that we'd be endangering our courts if we weren't careful. A goddess declaring it would give us the out we all needed."

"I am the queen of broken engagements. You could have come to me."

She stared at her mother. She'd wanted Astra to trust her.

"I was afraid of fucking up your plans yet again. I don't enjoy disappointing you."

"You've never once disappointed me, Astra Leona," she said. "Not once in your life."

"Thank you." Astra tried to suppress the wave of emotions that crashed over her. "When I spoke with Leona, she told me that Selenia was trying to get her soul to destroy it, so I couldn't get access to her. Knowing that I could go within spooked her and put a few puzzle pieces together about Lux, as well. So I went into the forest and I called to her. I used the locket she'd given me and I captured her. I didn't know if we'd need it or not, but I figured if things went left, the leverage would be crucial. Luciela... she told me that Selenia had actually been Tethered to Lucian and traded her shadow for that dagger.

"She severed her Tether to Lucian and then he convinced her to do the same with Leona and Solan. There's an empty throne in the Court Above. Only one ruler can sit on it, and they have to have both Light and Shadow, but no Solar and Lunar gods have been willing to give up their own power to the other. Leona and Solan got too close."

Oestera took this in, her lips twisting as she tried to understand her own mother's plight.

"We've all waited a long, long time to be rid of Selenia. I watched my sister die and my court fall under the tight reins of the Court Above. I've been forced to live a life separated from you, from Lunelle. You had to end it. I knew you were ready. Alastair will reshape what the courtiers saw tonight as they sleep, we'll ensure that everyone is on the same page about Selenia's attack on you to prevent the truth from spreading. We can't stop the Court Above from investigating, but make no mistake, they will come looking into things. We'll have a plan in place.

"We need to be careful with how we navigate the next few months. We don't have to decide it all tonight, of course, but I think we need to put some distance between you two until we can formulate a plan for Solan." Oestera gestured between Luxuros and Astra.

"At the very least, we can't crown a Solar heir the Lunar King," Ehlaria said. "It would be declaring war on both Solan and the Court Above."

A notion rippled in Astra's gut. Subtle, but hard to deny once she heard it.

"What if we didn't crown either one of us?"

Oestera shook her head. "I know you never asked for this, but I promise you, it gets better. With your sister on the Mercurian throne—"

"No, I don't mean keeping Lunelle here. I mean we crown no one."

Every ear leaned over the table, waves of muddied reds and oranges blooming across their chests. Oestera pressed again.

"Someone has to lead the court, and I can only stay so much longer. The Lunar Throne Above is now vacant and if I can Ascend to it, Alastair and I can work together to get the Nova chapter in the Court Above whipped into shape. A peaceful transition of power is so important."

"The gods aren't going to be satisfied with our secret for long," Astra said, rising from her seat. "Selenia's blood oath may have kept her from ratting the rebellion out to Lucian, but who knows what she told him about Luxuros? Even with Alastair's help, how long can we really keep the courtiers at bay?"

"Not long," Maeve said, folding her arms across her chest. "I'm more concerned about the Court Above than Solan at this point. With Luxuros here, there's a chance we can actually get him on our side. But the gods? They've been trying to prevent this for centuries."

Astra pushed. "If everything we've learned about the Divine Throne is true, and the Tethers between us... how many other Solar and Lunar demigods are just going about their daily lives, with no idea of the power running in their veins? If we could get Solan to understand the truth, to see what we're really up against..."

"We can't rely on him," Oestera muttered. "We don't know how bad it is. His madness was intolerable thirty years ago and it's only had decades to fester, Astra."

"But it's not impossible," she insisted. "In theory?'

Nayson cut through them. "It's not impossible, but it's not probable."

She glanced at Lux, who sat quietly, his hands tucked in his lap. Astra paced behind him, touching his shoulder as she spoke again.

"None of this was up to probability. It was predestined. I don't think there's anyone in this room that believes all of this was accidental."

"What are you suggesting?" Lunelle asked.

Astra set her face, mimicking her mother's queenly mask she'd studied her whole life.

"I'm suggesting that we do what none of you could for thirty years. We tell people the truth. And we do it quickly. We make a bold declaration and topple the Lunar Court. Rebuild it from the ground up. Show the other courts what's possible, and tell them exactly what's preventing them from all living much better lives... maybe we wouldn't need Solan's buy-in at all. If enough Solarians knew the truth, maybe that's all it takes. You said yourself, we're the stewards of the Living Courts' sentiments... if we rebelled... wouldn't that spread like wildfire amongst the human realms?"

Oestera's gaze held hers from across the table, a tangle of complex colors weaving into a tapestry she'd have to learn to read.

"We bear a responsibility to the Living Courts to be thoughtful, but revolutions do not come without bloodshed. You're the queen now," she said, her tone strong despite a nervous current rising over her shoulders. "For however long you decide to hold the title. You tell us what to do, and we'll do it."

A thrill rose in Astra's chest, alluring—not at all the fear she expected to feel.

"I want all the Nova chapter leaders assembled immediately," she said, looking to Maeve and Alastair.

Alastair's lips twisted into a satisfied smirk. "Right away, Your Highness."

As he exited the room, Maeve hot on his trail, Astra fell back into a chair near her mother, crossing her ankles and stretching her arms.

"Mother?"

"Yes, dear?"

"Who in the Nether is Alastair?"

Oestera's eyes closed softly, a choked laugh escaping from her chest as she turned to Lux. A lapis sadness pooled in her eyes.

"I am so sorry, Luxuros. I feel we've handed you an endless parade of life-altering news over the last day and I'm sure you're reeling, but you should know this, too. When your father was younger—before he met your mother, before he met Leona—he was attached to a Jovian dignitary, a young woman named Naomi. She presided over one of Jupiter's moons and, though she was not a demigoddess, she practiced very similar Lunar customs. Humans rarely realize how powerful they actually are, and Lucian would not hear of it. He felt she polluted the Solar Court with her intuitive abilities. So he sent her away.

"None of us knew about Alastair until The Flare. He was one of the Jovian courtiers lost in the Rift. He didn't know the truth about his lineage until his Ascension, and I believe my mother used his powers to her advantage after severing her tie to Lucian. He had been a young recruit of the original Nova rebellion, and when he arrived in the Court Above, he immediately contacted us. We've been working together since."

Astra shook her head. "So Alastair is... he's—"

"He's my half-brother." Lux nodded as if this made the most sense in the world.

"Yes," Oestera murmured, patting his hand. "We don't believe Solan knows of his birth, but we've never been able to confirm it. His abilities with dreams have been extremely useful to us as we've bided our time."

Astra felt a blush creep over her, her eyes flickering over Lux's face.

"Is that what caused all the dreams? His meddling?"

"What dreams?" Nayson asked, his interest piqued.

Luxuros shook his head, eyes still glued to the table.

"No dreams," he muttered, his throat closing around yet another secret.

Lunelle's quiet giggle beside her was all the answer Astra needed, but she clarified anyway.

"I think every Tethered couple has those dreams, As." She cast a longing stare toward Mirquios who looked about as mortified as Lux did.

"Ah, of course," Astra cleared her throat. "Ameera? Should

we prepare for the Nova Captains' arrivals? I think... you're in charge of that sort of thing now?"

Her eyes slipped toward her mother, who nodded subtly.

"Right away," Ameera grinned, unable to hide her excitement as she bounded from the room.

"If I could have the room, I think the commander and I have a few things to discuss," Astra said.

They wasted no time clearing the space.

"I KNOW we've both taken in a *lot* of new information," Astra started, sitting beside him and resting her hand on his knee. "I have no expectations of you to forge ahead with my plans, Luxuros. You went from Mercurian Commander to Solar Prince with a whole-ass family and history in twenty-four hours. A complex one."

"Yes," he said quietly, nodding his head, his eyes unfocused. "All of that is true."

Astra snorted, dropping her carefully curated tone and finding her own voice—the one that softened at the sight of his lips twisting into a frown.

"Are you fucking *okay*, Lux?"

"I don't know," he laughed, turning his amber eyes to hers. "I will be. But Astra, I'm a bigger threat to you than we ever feared. Just being in your court is an act of war at this point! I can't be selfish about this."

"It's not my court."

"It *is* your court, Astra. *You* are the leader they need right now."

"It's my court for the next few hours, Luxuros. After that, it's the people's court, and we *need* you here. *I* need you here."

He leaned forward, resting his head against the table, weighing his question.

"You'd really give it up? The throne, the power? All of it? You'd be opening everyone up to total destruction from the Court Above. Do you realize that?"

Astra flinched. "Of *course*, I realize that. I'm not making the decision for my own benefit! I'm making the decision to stop the madness, Luxuros. If we don't do it, who will? How many more generations have to suffer before we finally take them on?"

Lux's eyes closed, his chest locking up in a thousand warring emotions. She stood, anger bubbling up under her skin that needed movement to think clearly. She circled the table as he stretched his massive frame over the back of his chair, the wear from the last day showing in the lines of his face.

"We know too much to just go back now. You wanted to be a rebel, Commander. Don't lose sight of that now because you're scared of losing me. *That* is the selfish decision."

Lux let this sink in, a familiar misery washing over him.

"Your Highness?" A maiden knocked at the door. "The Nova Captains are assembling in the Celestial Hall."

"Thank you." Astra turned to leave.

He caught her hand as she brushed by his chair. "I will not take the Lunar Throne," Lux murmured, hardly audible. His voice dropped so low it sent a shiver over her spine. Astra's heart sank, the words shredding the muscles between her ribs. She didn't want the throne, but she especially didn't want it without him by her side. "But I think you should. You cannot overthrow your own monarchy in one night. We need to buy some time."

"Perhaps you're right," she said, trying to concentrate as an intriguing red wave within him crackled to life.

The silence settled between them as she ran a hand through his hair, letting the silver streak slip between her fingertips.

"Make me the Solar Captain."

Her hand froze against his temple. "What?"

"The Solar Nova Captain. *That* I know how to do."

Astra stared at his face, resolute in his decision.

"Done."

He tangled his fingers between hers, bringing her hand to his lips. She searched his eyes, swirling with shock and confusion and pain. Trailing her fingers over his cheek, she placed a soft kiss against his worn expression. His fingers snaked over her back, breath stilted as she moved her mouth over his.

"I need you to try something," she whispered. "When Solar and Lunar demigods Tether, they inherit each other's abilities... the light between us in Celene—what else are you capable of?"

Lux leaned back, his lips twisted together as he concentrated.

"I can see the slightest hint of color when I think of you."

"Yes," she nodded. "That's how it was when I was a kid. Just barely there. But the more I tried to identify the colors, the easier it got."

"What's the rosy pink? In your chest?"

She pressed into him, closing as much space between their bodies as possible, letting the delicate hue rise within her as she tangled her fingers into his hair. The soft pink glow consumed her, a glittering silver thread dancing through the middle.

She swallowed as she felt it glowing within him, too.

"*That*, Commander, is the kind of love gods tear rifts through time and space for."

FORTY-NINE

"Anyone else?"

They'd been at it for nearly nine hours, debating the plan that seemed to rise from Astra's bones. She'd heard just about every concern in the universe at this point and they'd sorted through every one of them.

Lux slipped a plate of fruit on the table next to her, patting her shoulder as Pluto's Captain, Kwan, stood to speak again.

"I believe we have enough outlined to move your plan into action, Astra. The details can come together as we go."

"We'll put it to a vote," Astra stood, her legs sore from yesterday's hike through the Court Below. "Mercury?"

Maeve smirked, lifting a glass of wine. "Aye."

Astra went around the room, each Nova Captain raising a glass and confirming their support. Venus, Earth, Mars, Jupiter, Saturn, Neptune, and Pluto all followed.

"And the Court Above?"

Alastair tilted his head to the side. "Aye, even if I think it's a bit dramatic."

Astra grinned. "If we want word to spread quickly, a little excitement is a must."

He held his hands up in surrender.

"That leaves the Courts Between. Lumas?" The Lunar Captain nodded, Daria hovering behind him, a strange mix of pride and resentment in her chest.

Astra took a deep breath and glanced over to Luxuros, his smirk permission enough.

"And what says the Solar Captain?"

The air left the room as dozens of eyes followed hers to the Mercurian Commander, arms folded across his chest. The collective swell of chartreuse confusion ringed the room.

"Aye," he said, a stark confidence in his answer.

"Then we're decided. This evening at my coronation ball, I will make the announcement. Lumas, Cam, Daria, I'll need to speak with you. There will be some tumult for our court after and we'll need to have a plan."

"Everyone else," Oestera added. "Make yourselves at home."

"ARE YOU READY?"

Ameera stood beside her outside the Celestial Hall doors, the buzz from the crowd inside a manageable hum, as long as she focused on quieting her mind.

Astra took one last second to adjust the robes that fell over her hips, their glistening metallics capturing the moonlight in perfect bubbles of gold and silver. The cape behind her flowed like a dream, slipping over the onyx floor and casting a warm hue around her. Originally designed for Lunelle, the maidens worked all night to embroider gilded Suns between the Moons, a touch she was grateful for.

Her mother pinned her hair into a soft cascade of curls down her back. A starry crown balanced at the back of her head like a halo—the gilded stars bounced light all around her, the soft glow nearly letting her pass as a Light Goddess.

Nearly.

She tossed one last look at Luxuros, who faded back behind the doors as they swept open.

Let your light burn, Fire Queen. He beamed to her.

"I'm *very* ready," Astra said.

Tula's eyes sparkled with pride as she introduced Astra to the courtiers below, a hush falling over the crowd as the music stopped.

"Queen Astra Leona Aurellis, may she reign with the love of the Mother, Within and Without."

Astra let a smile rest on her face, despite knowing what she was about to do.

What they were all about to do.

She stopped at the balcony's edge instead of turning toward the steps. The first face she saw as she looked down into the crowd was Oestera's, her lips set in a reverent smile as Nayson whispered something to her.

The second face she saw was Lunelle's, braced for what was to come.

And the third?

Ivonne Bloodmoon, her dull eyes searing into Astra. She judged everyone in the room, but especially the young queen —the rebellious princess who was never good enough for the court, let alone the throne.

She shoved the midnight fear rising aside and found her center; found who she was in the chaos, the way Lux had patiently shown her time and time again.

"Thank you all for attending this joyous occasion," she started. Hundreds of eyes cast over her as the room dripped in golden candlelight and silver moonlight. Moonshine and champagne floated around on trays as greedy fingers plucked the crystal glasses and drained them.

"For too long, we've thrown elaborate celebrations at this palace while our cities and villages fall into disrepair."

The room shifted from metallics and rosy pastels to a confused murky gray, eyes slipping from her face to their neighbors.

"For too long, we've reveled in our wealth while entire villages wonder where their next meals will come from."

The room plunged deeper into the shadowy grays, each rotted conscience sinking below the mire.

"For too long, we've been convinced by the gods that the Courts Between *were chosen*. Better than the Living Courts, but not good enough to stand up to the Court Above."

The charcoal and dust swirled to a bruised maroon as skepticism gave way to outrage at her blasphemy.

"But that was merely an illusion, carefully crafted to keep us appeased and sow distrust amongst us. If they could make us feel like we held power over those below us, we'd never have a reason to look up."

Astra stepped forward, the weight of the robes dragging behind her. She ran a finger along the banister before her, watching the faces below flush in shades of pink.

"There was a time when those same gods *feared* us. Feared what we might do if we knew who we really were. They kept us divided so that we might not come together against them. They made us hate each other so that we might not realize the strength that comes from embracing one another's ways of life. They pitted Sun against Moon, and we never batted an eye."

Chests swirled in shades of orange, red, and yellow. Some, though few, bloomed in excited greens and blues.

"The Court Above decided our Fates and made sure to

never let us know how much control we had all along. But because the bravest among us were willing to turn away from their rules—to love without fear—our eyes were opened, and now we cannot close them. For too long, the Courts Between and the Living Courts have been home to corruption and greed at the hands of gods who feed off our fear. But that fear ends tonight."

Astra brushed her hands along the carved banister one more time, resting them gently against the smooth stone. Ivonne's lips twitched, the irritation rolling in red waves along her spine.

"Thank you, all of you, for bearing witness to the first and only night of the last Lunar Queen's reign."

Chests erupted in brilliant shades of burgundy fury. But something else rose with them, along the edges—a pale blue, like the rushing waves of the Somnia. *Hope.*

"Tomorrow, you will wake up in a new court, a new era. A world built on the strength of our community, and not on the fears of the gods who only interfere when they might lose something. A court that honors the least of us as the greatest. A court built for her people, not on their backs. Tomorrow, you wake up in the first of many realms to stand against the Court Above. And if that does not appeal to you, if you do not think you can stomach a world in which wealth is shared and greed is no longer a choice... if you do not wish to be amongst the workers and the builders, then I advise you to begin your exodus."

She smiled at the crowd below, whispers already rising on a tide of crimson outrage as she plucked the golden crown off her head and set it on the banister. Steps echoed off the edges of the hall as black-clad Rebels poured into the seams, ready for whatever came next.

She held the crown in her mind, sending a righteous heat

through the star-barbed twists. Two thousand years of anger slipped from her veins, melting the crown into liquid gold that dripped over the balcony like the blood of the gods who'd be next.

She set her face again, her amber irises flaring.

"If you cannot contribute meaningfully to this new world, consider this your formal invitation to get the fuck out of the Nova Court." Their eyes flickered across the ballroom, unsure what to do, or what to think, betrayal pitching up from their chests in scarlet plumes.

"She's a traitor!" Ivonne stammered. Deep dragon's blood fury clutched at her throat, launching her forward as hushed murmurs agreed with her. But as she looked around she found herself quite alone in her willingness to stand against the ring of armed Rebels that blocked the exits.

Her eyes locked on Oestera's and she was met with only a chilled glare. Ivonne lifted a hand and Astra reached for the shadows beneath her, whipping them up and around her wrist. Ivonne struggled against the hold.

"You—"

"Careful now," Oestera chided. "I wouldn't provoke a Shadow Goddess, Ivonne."

"Arcas," Astra called, gesturing toward the icy figure leaning against the wall. "I believe Ivonne will be the first volunteer to relocate to your court."

Ivonne's wicked glare snapped toward the prince moving toward her, his tall frame consuming hers easily as he wrapped a twist of silver threads around her wrists.

"Anyone else who feels utterly betrayed by their queen is welcome to gather their things and proceed to the Plutonian gates. We are not monsters, you can have your city. But we're done funding your greed. May the gods be with you—you're all they have left."

A wine-red river flowed from the Celestial Hall as dozens of bodies ribboned from the arches, off to pilfer whatever they could from their living quarters before disappearing into the Rift. When Astra turned her eyes back to the half-empty hall below, she found a gentle blue sea lapping at the ribs of the remaining courtiers.

"If you stay and join the Nova Court, your needs will not go unmet. There will be changes, but they will be worth it, I promise. Enjoy the rest of the evening—tomorrow, the work begins."

She stayed for a moment, watching as the reality sank in. Then she waved a hand to the orchestra, striking the music back into a sweeping crescendo.

She backed through the doors, searching for Lux.

"Where'd he go?"

Ameera reached for her cape, fiddling with the clasp.

"He said the council could have you tomorrow, but tonight is his."

Ameera wiggled her eyebrows, bursting into laughter as a scarlet wave ran over her cheeks.

"But I don't know—"

"I believe I'm to escort the Nova Queen somewhere," Mirquios's smooth baritone bounced off the hallway. He was still in his Mercurian blues, an aventurine circlet wrapped around his head. "Astra."

"I assume I'm dressed completely inappropriately?" Astra glanced down at the elaborate robes falling behind her in a dramatic train.

"I actually think you've never looked more like yourself," Mirquios said, grinning as he held his elbow out for her.

"I'll let your mother know who has you," Ameera said.

"No need," she laughed. "I can do it." She tapped her temple and Ameera's eyes widened.

I'll meet with the Nova Council in the morning. Can you hold them off for tonight if I take a quick trip with the Mercurians? It didn't take much to find her mother's mind in the crowd down the hall. It was so sharp and calculated, but a warmth lingered.

A fire.

Of course, dear. Just be safe. Well done this evening.

Astra looped her arm through Mirquios's.

"Where to, my king?"

FIFTY

"Follow the hall to the aventurine doors, and then straight through. You'll know where to go. It's the middle of the night here. No one will bother you."

Mirquios left her at the Mercurian gate, pointing to a hall across from where Lux had taken her when they visited The Dune. The Sun was long gone, leaving everything in a cool, dull haze.

Astra followed the hallway in silent steps, wondering where, exactly, the aventurine doors led. Lux's room, perhaps. Or maybe a courtyard. Her hands rested on the smooth, pale green doors before she shoved them open.

A sprawling open-air market unfolded in front of her, dead silent at the late hour. Stalls were boarded up, lamps extinguished. She strolled through tents and carts, patchwork covers tossed over artists' precious work and shelves of rare artifacts. A swirl of foreign spices lingered in the air, dancing with delicate perfumes. It looked like it went on for a mile. She was tempted to stop at a cluster of shelves housing books from the Outer Courts, but a throat clearing caught her attention.

She spun, hyper-aware that anyone could be here in the dimmed lights.

"Miss?" A woman stepped out of her tent, maybe a few years older than her mother. "I have a gift for you."

Her wide, green eyes were just like her king's.

"For me?"

"Yes," she whispered, the same lilting accent as Mirquios and Luxuros entrancing her as she dipped behind a clothing rack. "Here."

She pulled Astra into her tent, incense burning in the corner drifting a soft, herbal scent across her collarbones. She ran her fingers over the racks, the fabrics rich in color and delicate to the touch.

"This one." The woman handed her a deep green pile of fabric.

"What—"

"Put it on. He was right, green is your color." She made a show of busying herself behind her makeshift counter, so Astra wasted no time. She slipped the ornate coronation robes off her shoulders and let them fall into a heap of silk on the floor, replacing them happily with a simple, unremarkable dress that fell in a dark wave over her hips, stretching over her curves.

She'd seen women wearing similar dresses when she was here last time in the street. Sturdy, comfortable, *normal*.

"I'll put this one in a bag." The woman reached for her coronation robes but Astra waved her off.

"Could you sell them?"

Her eyes widened. "Miss—"

"Could you?"

She nodded.

"Then they're yours. Where did he want me to go next?"

Her lips pressed into a smile. "End of the stalls, two rows over."

Astra ducked out of the tent and jogged lightly toward the end of the market stalls, much more mobile in her new dress. She rounded the corner and saw it—one singular lantern lit, dangling over a wooden sign with an Earthen court insignia carved into the grain.

However much he paid the poor teenager waiting behind the counter was not enough. His eyes sparked when he saw the queen and he lurched to life. He reminded her of Nayson, the same kind, warm eyes, and olive complexion.

"Evening, miss," he called. "Coffee?"

Astra glanced around, expecting to see Lux waiting, but she was alone. Her heart raced as she approached, a kettle already singing over the fireplace behind him.

"Coffee would be great," she smiled. He crushed dark beans against each other in a metal burr, collecting the grounds in a cloth before resting it over a clay mug. He poured slowly, letting it bloom before running the rest of the water through.

Astra felt the pull of him in her chest but held her gaze on the cup as she reached for it, lest she ruin his entrance. A bronze hand jutted out beside her, landing on the cup first.

"Oh," Lux murmured. "My mistake."

Astra turned, letting her eyes linger on his hand before sliding over his arm, clad in Earthen armor she hadn't seen before. She couldn't stop the grin from breaking over her face at his earnest expression, committing to his bit.

As their eyes locked, he reached to the back of his neck and pulled at the leather cord, letting the amulet fall to the ground. He dropped any last inner defense he might have clung to all at once, the rush of it crashing down on them not quite as intense as the first Tether, but so much more beautiful. Lush greens, dreamy blues, sweet violets—they all tangled with passionate reds and pinks, vibrant sunshine yellows and oranges.

They swept around her, catching her breath between her ribs.

"Am I crazy," Lux whispered, leaning closer to her. "Or did you just Tether with a complete stranger?"

She didn't break his eye contact, mesmerized by the heat of him once again. "Can I get a coffee for the gentleman here? He's clearly exhausted and imagining things."

"Oof," Lux huffed, rubbing his hand over his chest. "You wound me."

Her eyes narrowed, taking him in. "You look like the kind of guy who might be into that."

Lux grabbed her mug of coffee, taking a sip from it. "Look. I'm just a simple Mercurian warrior on his tour of the Earthen Court, basking in the glow of a newly discovered Tether to...?"

She twisted her lips as she thought. If Leona was still on the throne, and she'd been raised in the Earthen Court as her parents intended... who *would* she have been?

"An Earthen bog witch."

Lux closed his eyes, fighting ripples of shimmering gold begging him to laugh. "Does one just become a bog witch? Or is there some sort of curse required?"

She shrugged. "It's the family business."

"Ah, of course. And do bog witches enjoy coffee?"

She nodded. "Oh yes. Very much so. My father was a coffee farmer, in fact."

He leaned against the counter, moving closer to her. "Your father sounds like he'd like me."

"Hmm," she mused. "Don't be so sure. He's very protective of me."

"I think I could charm him."

Astra glared at him. "I'm afraid you'd have to charm *me* before you get to *him*."

Lux glanced at their hands, tangled together against the

wooden counter. He leaned in to whisper, "I believe I may have already won that battle, hmm?"

She held his stare. "When do you think we lost the kid?"

"I only paid for the one coffee. He was gone before you even ordered the second." Lux grinned, pulling her close and wrapping her in his arms as he brushed his lips against hers.

The kid was smart to leave when he did.

Everything within her relaxed at once—if only for tonight —releasing months of tension, inhaling the colors around them, and finding new places to store their vivid hues.

"I know we're fucked when the Court Above hears about the Nova Court," she sighed, pulling away from him reluctantly. "But I don't care how hard they come at us. I know we made the right choice."

Lux stroked his finger along her jaw. "We're in a lot of danger. The Nova Court is one thing, but when they find out about us... if Solan—"

"We don't have to have all the answers today."

Luxuros nodded. "The good news is the Court Above does nothing hastily. And they can't afford to lose the monarchs of the Outer Courts to the rebellion by being excessively violent, either. They'll take their time and find a way to make it look like the Solar and Lunar Courts attacked each other again."

She pressed her hand to his chest, running her fingertips over that aching space between sternum and soul. "We'll be ready."

"We'll *get* ready," he laughed, stroking her hair. "Tomorrow."

"Tomorrow," she agreed.

EPILOGUE
SPRING EQUINOX

"I used to wear my hair just like this."

Oestera sprinkled golden dust over the white moonblossoms she'd pinned in Astra's curls.

"Did you?"

"She did," Nayson confirmed, leaning against the door frame, watching as Oestera rearranged the pins. Astra wondered if she looked like an adult woman to him in this moment, or if he was staring at a five-year-old version of her.

"I used to love flicking the petals and watching the dust swirl into the air."

Astra's heart swelled, she'd never been able to appreciate their love for one another up close.

"I think you're just about ready, my darling," Oestera brushed the excess shimmer off her hands, placing a soft kiss on her forehead.

"Thank you." She watched her reflection in the mirror, her face transformed in the last few weeks. Stronger. Bolder.

"He's waiting on you outside the temple," Nayson said, a thrilled smile spreading across his face. "Looks good, too."

"You two need to get over your weird love affair," Astra laughed.

"We'll see you in there, darling. We're going to go get your sister ready," Oestera hummed, guiding her father out of the room.

Ameera's presence waited outside the door. Even her neatly organized spirit was on fire with anticipation today.

"You can come in."

"I didn't know if you wanted a moment alone. I know today is intense for you."

"You're basically an extension of me at this point. You're always allowed in."

She smiled as she took in her best friend's glowing face. "You look beautiful, As."

"Mother did a fine job, but don't tell her I prefer your braiding skills."

"I knew it," she grinned.

"Why didn't you tell me you could see Tethers?" Astra spun on her vanity stool, securing the backs to her moonblossom earrings as she watched Ameera's face drain.

"Who—"

"Arcas is half Venusian."

"Damn him!" She wrapped her arms around herself. "I knew you'd tell me when you were ready. There was so much out of your control. I wanted you to have one thing to yourself."

"You're a much better friend than I am," she snorted. "I would have been up your ass immediately."

"Trust me," she giggled. "I know. Are you ready?"

"No," she frowned.

"It's a lot of change, Astra. But this is a beautiful one."

She rose from her stool, pulling the skirt of the golden gown she borrowed from her mother to straighten it. She stole one more glance in the mirror, admiring the way it showed off her soft curves and held onto the full Moon's shine.

Ameera threaded her arm through Astra's, humming quietly to herself as they walked through the palace gardens. The early evening breeze tinted with the slightest hint of sweet Spring. They passed the faces of women she'd missed so dearly from Celene going about their daily roles. The transition from palace to community was well underway thanks to Cam and Ameera's leadership.

"Today's the day, huh?" Sephone called out as Astra passed her, a group of girls at her feet watching with wide eyes.

"Come watch!" She waved the girls toward them, their giggles tickling her ears in shimmering waves. They followed Astra to the temple where Sephone shushed them as they found their seats.

Ameera placed a brief kiss on Astra's cheek as she reached for Cam's hand outside of the temple, their matching orange gowns like bright rays of sunlight as they slipped in through the intricately carved archway.

"Unreal."

A low thunder rolled through her chest, Lux's warmth pouring over her. She spun in his arms, weaving her hands into his hair, neatly braided away from his face for such a celebratory occasion.

"Not so bad yourself." She ran her fingers across his matching gold tunic, gleaming under the moonlight.

"Save it for later," Mirquios chuckled behind them. He glowed in pale green, his deep skin alive with the magic of the same moondust she'd loaned to Lunelle that morning.

Lux glanced around, curving his dark brow. "Where is Lunelle?"

"I'll handle her. You two get going."

"I'll see you in there, *Sol'ah*," Lux whispered just for her, kissing the patch of golden freckles that hadn't faded after their first appearance.

Astra beamed to her sister. *Where are you?*

I'm coming, I'm coming, I'm so sorry I'm late!

No sooner did she beam it back did Astra hear her footsteps jogging down the path.

"Sorry!"

Lunelle was an absolute vision in silver, radiating under the full Moon, her cheeks glowing from her short run from her chambers. She reached for Astra's hand and squeezed it, her heart pounding with nerves.

"What are you apologizing for? The bride can't be late to her own wedding."

"Was he nervous?" Her eyes slid toward the temple, trying to peer inside.

Astra shook her head. "Not even a little bit."

"Are you ready?"

Astra laughed. "I'm ready! Are *you* ready, Your Highness?"

She adjusted Lunelle's neckline one more time, admiring the face of the future Queen of Mercury, flushed with love and excitement for what was to come.

"Of course. I was born to be a queen, you know," Lunelle giggled.

Astra cupped her sister's face, tapping her glowing skin one final time before she gave her up to another court.

"Let's put another Rebel on the Mercurian throne, then."

READ MORE BY CB WOODS

Lux and Astra's story continues in *The Courts Between Book Two: Rebel*, coming March 20th, 2026. If you simply cannot wait, get four bonus chapters, including a steamy bonus epilogue, at cbwoods.net/bonus

Curious what you missed out on while Lunelle, Mirquios, and Arcas were in the Plutonian Court? *Courting Death & Desire* follows Lunelle on her own adventure. Visit reademrae.com/cbwoods to read now.

Follow CB on Instagram and TikTok for character art, behind-the-scenes content, and more: @cbwoodsbooks

Join fans of CB Woods on her discord at cbwoods.net/discord

ACKNOWLEDGMENTS

I started telling this story to myself more than a decade ago, and if it wasn't for the encouragement of a very long list of people, *Rift* never would have made it to paper (or screens, or... soon, headphones)!

To my husband and children: I'm sorry mommy was so busy, but someday it will have been worth it.

To my sisters and aunt: Thank you for feeding my delusions.

To my mom: Pretty rude of you to Ascend before I finally got up the nerve to write the book. Sorry it took me too long, I hope your welcome party to the Court Above had Arbor Mist on tap.

To my editor, Erin: Thank you for tolerating fast timelines, high word counts, long text chains, and *so* very many Canva boards. This story would be a mess without you! Let's do it all again for book two.

To my beta readers: Authors KL Andersen and Haven Price and readers Raleigh, Anandi, Amber, Kaitlin, Cassie, Meghan, Sarah, Tonya, and anyone I missed—thank you so much for coping with the earlier drafts of this story. It went through so many transformations and you are a *huge* part of that journey.

To my book club: Thank you for creating a monster within me, I hope the payoff was worth listening to me ramble for months as I worked out the plot with your invaluable insights.

To all my ARC readers and those who engage with my

social media: As a debut author, I can't tell you how surreal it is and how much it means seeing you care about my book and characters. Truly, truly thank you for the time you've invested in my world.

And to you, reader, for hanging in until the end—you are my dream come true.

PS: Special shout out to the book ending that pissed me off so much I had to write my own romantasy out of spite to fill the void. You know who you are and what you did.

EMRAE PUBLISHING

Emrae Publishing challenges traditional and hybrid publishing models with a profit-share system that keeps money in the hands of authors and creatives. With direct distribution and partnerships with indie bookstores, Emrae gives authors the flexibility of self-publishing with the support of a dedicated team.

Our mission is simple: keep money in the pockets of storytellers—and billionaires out of their business.

Learn more at www.reademrae.com

529